PRAISE FOR *DEEP DOWN DEAD*

'This is a good one – fast, confident, and suspenseful. My kind of book' **Lee Child**

'With a Stephanie Plum-style protagonist in bounty hunter Lori, *Deep Down Dead* has a *Midnight Run* feel to it, but much darker. Really, really good' **Ian Rankin**

'Read some great debuts this year but *Deep Down Dead* is a real cracker. Steph Broadribb kicks ass, as does her ace protagonist Lori Anderson!' **Mark Billingham**

'Crazy good ... full-tilt action and a brilliant cast of characters. This is a series and an author to watch' **Yrsa Sigurðardóttir, author of *I Remember You***

'*Deep Down Dead* is a blast of a book – fast-paced, engaging and hugely entertaining' **Simon Toyne, author of *Solomon Creed***

'Steph Broadribb has written a brilliant, pacey, bounty-hunter tale that marks the beginning of what will undoubtedly become a sparkling career' **Steve Cavanagh, author of *The Defence***

'An action-packed crime thriller dripping with intrigue from the Deep South, and with a feisty no-nonsense heroine to boot. It's a debut that demands to be read, with excitement and exhilaration flying off every page. In Lori Anderson, Broadribb has created a memorable and authentic female lead – and readers will be left wanting the next instalment of her adventures as soon as possible' **David Young, author of *Stasi Child***

'Tough as a pair of rhino-hide cowboy boots and unremittingly energetic. An explosive, exciting debut' **David Mark, author of *Dead Pretty***

'An action-packed Southern road noir that pulls no punches. Single mom/bounty hunter Lori Anderson is an engaging new heroine, and *Deep Down Dead* is quite simply a hell of a thriller' **Mason Cross, author of *The Killing Season***

'A fresh and compelling debut with an intriguing plot, a great new heroine, and a setting that zings with authenticity' **Anya Lipska, author of *A Devil Under the Skin***

'If anything, Broadribb and her protagonist, tough Florida bounty hunter Lori Anderson, have more than a hint of Lee Child and Jack Reacher about them, with (literally) no punches pulled. The other parallel with Lee Child is, of course, the fact that this is an English writer making a sterling job of finding an American voice for both the narrative and the characters, and Broadribb proves to be just as adroit in this area as her male counterpart ... a promising debut delivered with both energy and colour' **Barry Forshaw, *Crime Time***

'Fast, furious and thrilling' **Graeme Cameron, author of *Normal***

'*Deep Down Dead* grabs you like a whirlwind – once you're in, there's no getting away till it's through with you. Pacey, emotive and captivating, this is kick-ass thriller writing of the highest order' **Rod Reynolds, author of *The Dark Inside***

'A relentless page-turner with twists and turns that left me breathless' **J.S. Law, author of *Tenacity***

'*Deep Down Dead* oozes authenticity. This is an engaging, original thriller with the type of characters you wish you knew in real life. Fresh, compelling and beautifully written, with a real cinematic quality. Read it. Now' **S.J.I. Holliday, author of *Black Wood***

'Lori Anderson is a bounty hunter like none you've ever encountered before. This is a series that will run and run. You'll need to clear some time in your diary to read Steph Broadribb's *Deep Down Dead* because you won't want to set this one aside till the end. A genuine page-turner' **Howard Linskey, author of *No Name Lane***

'Fast, furious and utterly addictive, *Deep Down Dead* is a blistering debut and marks Broadribb as a rising talent to watch' **Neil Broadfoot, author of *Falling Fast***

'Non-stop adrenaline rushes in this romantic action-adventure, introducing a gritty, earthy, unstoppable heroine in bounty hunter Lori Anderson – and a bad boy opponent/partner who is actually worthy of her. If you love romantic suspense, you'll love this ride' **Alexandra Sokoloff, author of The Huntress/FBI thrillers and co-author of The Keepers series**

'The story moves at a frantic pace, and the plotting, along with the writing, is so deft and assured that it's really quite staggering that this is a debut. But what really sets this book apart is the characterisation of Lori and JT; it's kind of like reading early Reacher, where you know you're at the beginning of something very special, characters that will stay with you, books that you'll wait patiently for each year' **Chris Whitaker, author of *Tall Oaks***

'A stunning debut from a major new talent' **Zoë Sharp, author of the Charlie Fox crime series**

'This is perfect for fans of Lee Child and Janet Evanovich, with the same American charm you find in Charlaine Harris, but it also has a sensibility that is completely unique and totally Broadribb. Lori Anderson is a fascinating heroine, with plenty of secrets and depth, but also totally kick-ass and relevant. *Deep Down Dead* is just so assured for a debut, and there wasn't a single false step. It's fun, thrilling, edge of your seat but also dealing with some seriously dark issues, and introduces a cast of characters I want to meet again! A great start to what is already one of my favourite series. Can't wait for the next one' **Alex Caan, author of *Cut to the Bone***

'Powerful, passionate, and packs a real punch' **Fergus McNeill, author of *Knife Edge***

'A gem of a read that delivers thrills at breakneck pace ... Lori is a feisty heroine we all wish had our backs' **Marnie Riches, author of *The Girl Who Wouldn't Die***

'There are a couple of different ways to think about this debut. One is an entertaining bounty-hunter adventure, and on that level it's quite a ride. But another take is as a character study, with depth – the relationship between protagonist Lori, daughter Dakota and male lead JT. It's assured and emotionally moving. Will be keeping an eye on this author and what she does next' **Daniel Pembrey, author of *The Harbour Master***

'A kick-ass American thriller and a great read ... crying out to be a Hollywood movie. I couldn't put it down' **Louise Voss, author of *The Venus Trap***

'I ripped through this high-octane, breathlessly paced thriller in almost one sitting. Loved kick-ass Lori and her sexy-as-hell love interest JT – a combo to get your heart racing, and then some' **Ava Marsh, author of *Untouchable***

'Steph Broadribb's debut novel has been a long time coming, but it was definitely worth the wait. Dripping with authenticity, filled with unforgettable characters, and with a plot to die for. The writing is fantastic, making it one of my favourite debut novels for a long, long time. *Deep Down Dead* is just the first novel in what will be an incredible career for Broadribb. I can't wait to read the next Lori Anderson book!' **Luca Veste, author of *The Dying Place***

'We all need a fast-talking, gun-toting heroine with a heart of gold in our life, and Lori Anderson is a most compelling creation. If you don't read *Deep Down Dead*, you'll really be missing out!' **Claire Seeber, author of *The Stepmother***

'This writer! This book! I haven't witnessed such a buzz about a new author for quite some time, and that buzz is entirely deserved. Breathtakingly pacey and authentic. You have to read it' **Michael J. Malone, author of *A Suitable Lie***

‘This thrilling debut is a masterwork of suspense, as bounty hunter, Lori Anderson, takes us on a road trip fraught with danger, passion and high-octane jeopardy. Steph Broadribb is top crime talent! Unputdownable’ **Helen Cadbury, author of *To Catch a Rabbit***

‘Finished this at a gallop! Great action scenes and great atmosphere in a top romantic thriller’ **C.J. Carver, author of *Spare Me the Truth***

‘Relentless, breathtaking and emotionally charged. A roller coaster of a read!’ **Jane Isaac, author of *Beneath the Ashes***

‘Steph Broadribb’s gritty debut will appeal to fans of the Sue Grafton alphabet series. I can’t wait to see what bounty hunter Lori Anderson gets up to next!’ **Caroline Green, author of *Hold Your Breath***

‘*Deep Down Dead* might be a fast-paced, adrenaline-fuelled read but Steph Broadribb does not sacrifice character development to achieve that. Instead we are treated to three characters who will live on in my memory ... easily one of the best books I’ve read this year’ **Book Addict Shaun**

‘*Deep Down Dead* is an ass-kicking thriller of the highest order. I can’t recommend it highly enough!’ **Bibliophile Book Club**

‘*Deep Down Dead* is an all American thriller. A real page-turner, full of pulsating action. It sucks the reader in from the very start through to the nail-biting conclusion’ **Trip Fiction**

‘*Deep Down Dead* has an authentic American feel with a fantastic plot, vivid setting and amazing writing that puts you right into the heart of the action – a clear winning formula. *Deep Down Dead* heralds the start of a new series. It’s contains everything you want in an action thriller – a strong female lead, sexy potential partner, thrilling plot and a lot of heart. This book is going to fly its way up the charts! Bring on the next Lori Anderson book!’ **Vicki Goldman, Off-the-Shelf Books**

'This book is set to be one of the debut hits of 2016. Steph's writing is tight, flowing and the book rockets along at a pace that entertains the reader. Steph has a beautiful way with language and you feel right there with the main characters as they set off on their journey. I haven't read anything like this and the setting and style is wonderful. If you love the work of Cormac McCarthy then this book is for you' **Ian Patrick**

'An action-packed thriller that grips you from page one and never lets go, characters you can't help rooting for, and fantastic cinematic writing that puts you right in the thick of the action. This book is smart, sexy and one hell of a read. If I'd been reading the paperback version rather than the ebook, I'd probably have ended up with paper cuts from turning the pages so fast' **Lisa Gray**

'Broadribb has combined accurate research with compelling characters, a fast moving plot and an authentic American voice. Add fantastic writing and you have one amazing debut. Best of all, we're left with a bit of a cliffhanger. Book 2 is on its way! **Joy Kluver**

'A fast-paced, nail-biting, hard-hitting novel that not only takes you on an all-guns-blazing action adventure but also through the emotional ringer' **Chillers, Killers and Thrillers**

'The writing is superb, the language crackles and the character voices are spot-on perfect – descriptively this is an utter joy, a truly immersive experience where the world around you fades and you are thrown into Lori's world. A stripper turned bounty hunter, whose skeletons are about to come rattling out of the closet in the form of JT, a blast from her past, Lori will capture your heart and your attention in utterly memorable fashion. I loved, loved, loved it' **Liz Loves Books**

Deep Down Dead

ABOUT THE AUTHOR

Steph Broadribb was born in Birmingham and grew up in Buckinghamshire. Most of her working life has been divided between the UK and USA. As her alter ego – Crime Thriller Girl – she indulges her love of all things crime fiction by blogging at www.crimethrillergirl.com, where she interviews authors and reviews the latest releases. Steph is an alumnus of the MA in Creative Writing (Crime Fiction) at City University London, and she trained as a bounty hunter in California. She lives in Buckinghamshire surrounded by horses, cows and chickens. *Deep Down Dead* is her debut novel, and the first in the Lori Anderson series.

You can follow her on Twitter *@CrimeThrillGirl* and on Facebook at *Facebook.com/steph.broadribb*, or visit her website: *www.crimethrillergirl.com*.

Deep Down Dead

Steph Broadribb

Orenda Books
16 Carson Road
West Dulwich
London SE21 8HU
www.orendabooks.co.uk

First published in the UK in 2017 by Orenda Books

A catalogue record for this book is available from the British Library.

ISBN 978-1-910633-55-7

Typeset in Garamond by MacGuru Ltd
Printed and bound by CPI Group (UK) Ltd, Croydon CR0 4YY

SALES & DISTRIBUTION

In the UK and elsewhere in Europe:
Turnaround Publisher Services
Unit 3, Olympia Trading Estate
Coburg Road,
Wood Green
London
N22 6TZ
www.turnaround-uk.com

In the USA and Canada:
Trafalgar Square Publishing
Independent Publishers Group
814 North Franklin Street
Chicago, IL 60610
USA
www.ipgbook.com

In Australia and New Zealand:
Affirm Press
28 Thistlethwaite Street
South Melbourne VIC 3205
Australia
www.affirmpress.com.au

For details of other territories, please contact *info@orendabooks.co.uk*

For Pod

Prologue

Today

I open my eyes and the first thing I see are the cuffs. Flexing my wrists, I test their weight and try to ignore the dull ache in my right hand where the gash across my skin has dried crusty brown. The bruising on my forearms has turned a deep purple. From the way my ribs feel, I figure they must look the same. I keep my breathing shallow; seems it hurts a little less that way. I look up.

He's sitting opposite me, arms folded, legs stretched out beneath the table. Waiting. In this windowless box it's impossible to tell how much time has passed. Still, I can't look at him, not yet, so I focus just below his eyes, where the dark shadows lie. My heart's racing, a voice in my head screams, *run, just run*. I want to, I surely do, but I can't. For all that's gone down, someone has to pay. It's time for me to pony up.

'You lookin' at me now? Good. So answer the question.'

Same Kentucky accent, but he's not at all how I'd imagined. Guess that's the way it goes when your only contact has been by cell. I force myself to meet his gaze, swallow down the nausea, try not to let fear distort my voice. 'Can't believe all you hear.'

'Tell me why.'

Now the moment's come, I don't know if I can. Was he in on it? Should I trust him? Sure, he looks the part. He's wearing the uniform black suit, smart and efficient, shades hooked inside the breast pocket. He's a little older than I'd imagined, nearer fifty than forty, and wears his hair on the long side, slicked back to keep it tamed. He runs his hand through it, smoothing the strands into place. I wonder if he's nervous. I sure as hell am.

His cold stare says he figures that I'll talk eventually. All he need do is wait, because time's almost up for me. Every second I baulk, the people I love get dragged further from me. So we both know I have to give it up on his promise, tell him enough to end this, to stop all the talk of death row. But there's an order to these things, and we both know that too.

He puts a plastic beaker on the desk, pushes it from his side to mine. Inside there's a red liquid, two shades paler than blood. 'Drink. Medical said you're dehydrated.'

They're right. My mouth's drier than gator hide in August. Can't remember the last time I drank or ate properly. Shit like that hasn't figured much these past few days. The drink looks real tempting, but I need something from him first. This situation, it's all about power. If I do something for him, the balance swings over to his side, but if he does something for me, I get it a little more on mine.

I glance down at the cuffs. Look back at him. Wait.

He takes the hint. Leans across the table with the keys in his left hand, ready. As he moves, I catch the scent of his cologne – lemon, clean and sharp. Hope he's that way too. I have to trust him; we're all out of time to do anything else.

I push my hands over the wooden veneer towards him, palms up. The torn muscle in my shoulder feels like it's on fire. I don't let it show; bite back the pain. He uncuffs me, slips the bracelets and key into his jacket pocket. Eases back in his chair. Watching, again.

That's first base, right there.

So I drink. Show willing. Know I need the fluids, can't risk the dehydration muddling my mind, confusing the story. Have to tell it right. The liquid's raspberry-flavoured water. It's sweet, too sweet, and stings the corner of my mouth where I've taken one too many punches. I grimace at the taste. 'So how does this work?'

He stares right back at me. 'Tell me everything.'

I jerk back, spooked. Try not to wince at the spur-sharp pain in my side. He's moving way too fast. You can't jump from first base to fourth, it ain't polite and I can't allow it.

The pain doesn't fade. Nausea rises real fast and bile hits the back of my throat. I cough. Makes my bruised ribs hurt like a bitch. I bite my lip and press my arm against my side. Show no weakness. 'I have to get out of here, take my daughter home.'

He shakes his head. Leans forward, elbows on the table, face level with mine. 'Not going to happen. This situation? It's real serious. You're in no kind of position to be making demands.'

He's testing me. Wants to know how desperate I am. The answer? Real desperate, but I know way better than to let that show. This game here is all about timing. What I say, and whether he believes me, that'll be the difference between life and death. 'So what then?'

He stares at me, unblinking. Leans closer. 'Tell *me* the real story. Multiple homicide an' the rest that's gone down? There's no one else can help you. *I'm* the guy you've got to convince. Right now, and right here.'

The room seems to shrink. The space feels airless, more claustrophobic. What he's just said, I hate it. I want to howl at the unfairness of it all, punch him until he feels the pain too. But I don't, because I know that he's right. I've got no other choice but to trust him. So I put down the beaker. Watch the liquid ripple once, twice, before lying still. Count in my head, all the way up to ten, then look up and meet his gaze. I can't delay any longer, need to move us on to second, defuse the situation. 'Honey, I can give you answers, just as soon as I know we've got a deal.'

He sits back in his chair, and crosses his legs, real relaxed. Keeps eye contact. 'Depends.'

There's a certainty about him, a determination that's somehow quite attractive. He plays hard to get real well; oftentimes I like that. Not today, though. Not now. Hard to get is hard to read, and one wrong move, one wrong word, will only end one way: everyone I love gone. 'I'm listening.'

'You tell me what happened. No bullshit, just the absolute truth from start to finish. Do that, then I'll tell you if we've got a deal.'

No guarantee, but I figure it's my best shot. So I nod, and let him take third. Act like it's my idea, though. Force a smile as I swallow down the fear. 'You best get comfortable, sweetie. This'll take a little while.'

He nods, and I know that it's time. Now I have to get us to fourth, tell the story right, secure a deal.

There's a click as he switches on the audio recorder. He leans forward and places it on the table, dead centre. Looks me right in the eyes. 'You're up.'

And so I tell him.

1

Three days earlier

CF Bonds sits two minutes from the main drag of West Colonial Drive. It's nothing special, just a squat one-storey on Franklin, a few hundred yards from some fancy dog-grooming parlour and a take-out chicken joint. Not that Quinn, their top bondsman, would let fried anything past his lips. He's a health nut, into protein shakes, moisturiser and eighty-dollar haircuts. Looks good on it though, if having a man all waxed and buffed is your kind of deal. All that gym work does build a guy's stamina real nice. I found that out when I took him for a little test ride a couple of years back.

So I parked up outside, and me and my baby girl, Dakota, loped across the sidewalk to the entrance. The silver bell above the door jangled as we walked on through. Sounded real quaint, unlike a lot of the folks requiring the services of Quinn and the crew, but anyways, the noise had him jumping from his chair and striding out front to greet us.

I was glad of it. The small waiting area, divided off from the main office by a bulletproof glass screen, could get you to thinking that you were some kind of human goldfish if you stood there long enough. I never did like the feeling of being confined.

Quinn grasped my hand, pumping it up and down in that steady rhythm of his. 'Lori, good to see you.'

'You too,' I said, extracting my hand. Overfriendliness most likely meant he'd got a job that needed doing. Good. What with the rent due and being three months behind with the payments for Dakota's medical treatment, I needed cash, and fast. 'Can we talk?'

He nodded. Turning to Dakota, he smiled and ruffled her strawberry-blonde hair. 'Hey, kitten. Ain't *you* growing like a weed. Why, you must be at least ten years old by now?'

Rolling her eyes, she put her hands on her hips and thrust out her chin; a stance that never fails to remind me of her daddy. 'I'm nine, and I'm not a kitten or a weed, I'm a tiger.'

Quinn laughed. 'Well, alrighty then. Can I get the tiger a glass of milk?'

Dakota nodded, grinning.

Quinn glanced at me. 'You want coffee?'

I shook my head. Quinn makes weak-assed coffee. 'Tea.'

While he fetched the drinks, I led Dakota through the glass door and across the office. It wasn't a large space, just two desks with a couple of visitor chairs in front of each. On the wall behind Quinn's workspace a map of Florida was pinned to a bulletin board. The desk itself looked as neat as a showroom display: paper in trays, pens in their tidy, mouse on its mat. From experience I knew that the red tray closest to me was the spot where he stacked the jobs to assign. I took a peek. There wasn't much, two or three files at best. Damn.

Quinn returned. He sat behind his desk and gestured for me to take the seat opposite. I sat down and turned to Dakota, who'd gotten on to the other chair, her bare legs squeaking against the faux-leather seat. 'How about you go see what Mrs Valdez is working on?'

She frowned. 'Can't I stay here?'

'No, sweetie. This is a business meeting.'

Quinn leant across the desk. 'Mrs Valdez is out back in the filing room. I hear she keeps a jar of cookies there.' He took a blank bond application form from his drawer, wrote something in the box in the top corner and handed it to Dakota. 'If you deliver this to her for me, maybe she'll give you a cookie as a reward.'

Dakota's eyes lit up. She leapt from the chair, picked up her milk and took the paper. 'Cool. I'll find her.'

We watched her skip over to the back office.

'She's looking well.'

'For now.' I stirred honey into my tea, slow and steady. Didn't look at Quinn.

I nodded towards the files in the red tray. 'So what have you got for me?'

Quinn shook his head. 'Not much.'

'Shit. I've got rent to pay, Quinn. And the hospital instalments, they're real high, y'know?'

He shrugged. 'I've only got what I've got.'

Problem was, as a bail runner, I was associated to CF Bonds but not directly employed by them like their in-house investigator, Walt Bailey. For them, it was cheaper to have Bailey to do the work. In truth, Quinn owed me nothing.

'Like I told you last month, and the month before that, things have been running smoother.'

'Is that right?' I stared at him hard. His cheeks flushed a little. I kept on staring. 'You know what happens if I don't make a payment this month? They cancel her follow-ups. You know what that means? If the cancer comes back they won't be watching, they won't catch it in time.'

'Yeah. Look, I get it, but I just—'

'Quinn, you gotta give me something.' I pictured the letter sitting on my kitchen counter, the big red words stamped across the top: *FINAL DEMAND*. I had to find a way to pay. Couldn't think on the alternative. My baby couldn't get sick, not again.

'Look, maybe I can shift one or two of Bailey's cases your way. A couple of skip traces, few hundred bucks a shot.'

Shook my head. 'Thanks, but that won't cut it. I need something big.'

He glanced at the files in the red tray. 'Well, there is this one job, but it's not local, and you've always said—'

'What's the money?'

'Five figures.'

That sounded more like it. 'How "not local"?'

'West Virginia.'

Not local, for sure, but at that money could I really refuse? I smiled my most charming smile. 'I'm listening.'

If Quinn was surprised, he didn't let it show. 'There's only three days left until the summary judgement, so you'd need to get it done fast. You interested?'

'Depends.' I pulled the spoon from my tea. There was still a dab of honey on the tip. I put it in my mouth and sucked while I let Quinn sweat a little.

You see, a bond gone that far along means just one thing: no one else has managed to catch the guy. Since they'd skipped out on their original court date, you could bet Quinn had been trying his damnedest to find them. In Florida there's a thirty-day statutory surrender period between non-appearance in court and the bond being forfeited. If this guy wasn't brought in by the summary-judgement date, CF Bonds stood to lose a whole bunch of dollars, and they really hated that. So, if this fugitive was still out there, they had to be real smart or real fast or, most likely, both. 'How much you offering?'

'Ten thousand.'

Damn. Ten grand. I worked at keeping my expression Texas-Hold-'em neutral. As a bail runner, I was entitled to ten percent of the bond value if I brought in the fugitive in time for the summary judgement. Most of the cases I'd worked had been worth a whole lot less – three or four figures rather than five. 'He's on a hundred-thousand-dollar bond?' I asked. 'What he do?'

Quinn flicked through the short stack of files and found one with a sticky note on it marked *JULY*. He plucked it from the pile, opened it and scanned the document inside. 'Caused some aggravation in that amusement park down near Fernandina Beach – Winter Wonderland. Seems our guy had a problem with the owner, a Randall B. Emerson. Security stepped in and called the cops.'

'Much violence?'

Quinn flicked through the pages of the thin file, shook his head. 'Some posturing, perhaps.'

'Guns?'

'Not that it says.'

I frowned. Was I being paranoid or was Quinn acting a little evasive?

He needed this fugitive back fast, so was he skimming over the truth to be sure I'd take the job? 'Why the high bond, then?'

'Well, you know what the amusement parks are like. We need those tourists, and places like Winter Wonderland pull them in from all over. I'm guessing it was about making an example of the man rather than him being a danger.'

Made sense. Part of the whole amusement-park experience was that you were entering a world where bad things never happened. Any kind of disturbance in that sugar-coated ecosystem would be bad for business across the whole state. 'So why isn't Bailey getting him?'

Quinn sighed. 'He was. Trouble is, Bailey had an accident a couple of days back. He was chasing down this young guy and tried to vault over a wall.'

I tried not to smile. Bailey is built more for the couch than the chase. 'Bailey did? Now that I wish I'd seen. Hell, I'd have paid for the privilege.'

'Yeah, it didn't go so well. He landed bad, got himself a busted wrist.'

Fractures are never fun, but Bailey had been riding my ass ever since I'd signed up with CF Bonds. The jokes at my expense never grew old for him. Perhaps this was him reaping a little of what he'd sown. I hoped so. 'How come this bond's gotten so far along, anyways?'

Quinn's expression turned serious. 'Yeah. About that. Look, the guy isn't local. We only did his bail as a favour for an old business associate of the boss. The fugitive lives out in Georgia, but when Bailey made a visit, he was already in the wind. We've been tracking him these past few weeks. Bailey found a location for him yesterday, over in West Virginia, so I called Bucky Dalton, thinking he could go collect him. Turns out Bucky got himself all shot up by some drug dealer he was tailing and he's in the hospital peeing into a bag. So Bucky's older brother, Merv, agreed to pick our fugitive up and hold him until we can collect.'

I raised an eyebrow. 'Last I knew, Merv wasn't licensed for work here in Florida. Any pick-up he'd make for you would be unlawful.'

'Yeah, well...' Quinn stared at the weak-assed coffee in his cup like it was real interesting. 'So, as I said, the job's yours if you want.'

But did I want it? I needed the money, that was for sure, but with school being out, and Krista – my neighbour and regular sitter for Dakota when I was on a job – about to set off visiting her folks in Tennessee, chances were I'd have to take Dakota along on any work I did out of state.

Through the door to the back office I spotted Dakota sitting beside Mrs Valdez, helping her fold letters and stuff them into envelopes. She was chattering away all happy, her pigtails bobbing up and down as she nodded at something the older woman had said. As if sensing my gaze, Dakota looked up and met my eyes. She grinned.

I looked back at Quinn. Shook my head. 'The thing is, I've got no sitter for Dakota right now. She'd have to come along, and I'm not real keen on some fugitive being around my kid.'

Quinn shrugged. 'I get that, Lori. But if you're looking for a high-money job, this is all I got. Should be easy, no complications, just a taxi-driver gig. The man you'd be collecting is a professional who got mixed up in a bit of trouble when tempers ran high. Bailey's done the tracking. Merv's picked him up.'

It did sound easy. And a taxi ride – well, that sounded safe enough. But would it be safe enough for my daughter to ride shotgun? I wasn't real convinced of that.

'All I need,' Quinn continued, 'is for you to collect the man and bring him back for the summary judgement in three days. Your Silverado's fitted out with restraints and a full transport kit, isn't it?'

I nodded. 'Yeah.'

He smiled, revealing thousands of dollars' worth of dental work. 'So there's no chance of this man getting close to your little girl, is there? The way I see it, this is easy money, and fast. Hell, I'd go do it myself if I wasn't needed here.'

I snorted with laughter, couldn't help myself. The most physical Quinn had ever gotten was a Boxercise class at the gym. 'Is that right?'

His smile sagged. 'Sure is.'

Guess I'd deflated his ego a little. I studied his expression for a beat, considering his offer. He was right, it sounded easy and the money was good. My Silverado had a proper travel cell, real secure, so there'd be no need for Dakota to be in contact with the fugitive. But I'd had another idea. Krista wasn't due to leave for her folks' place until that afternoon. I could offer her a thousand bucks to delay her trip by three days and watch Dakota for me. What with three kids and her husband out of work she always needed cash, so I was sure I could convince her.

'So, will you do it?' Quinn was looking hopeful again. He needed this man back fast, and he knew I had the skills to get it done. Seemed like I was near on his last shot.

That got me to thinking. CF Bonds might be prepared to pay a little more than usual for this job, and any extra sure would help. 'West Virginia is an awful long way from Florida. Perhaps if you upped my percentage I could work something out.'

'Well, maybe,' Quinn said, trying to cling on to his smile. 'I could go to eleven percent.'

I shook my head. 'It's gonna cost me more than one percent in gas money. I was thinking closer to twenty.'

'Jesus, Lori. You're trying to bleed me to nothing here.' He opened the top drawer of his desk, pulled out a calculator and tapped in a few numbers. 'I guess I could scrape by at fifteen. Final offer. What do you say?'

Fifteen percent on a hundred-thousand-dollar bond would give me fifteen thousand bucks. That sure was a decent stack of money. It'd pay the arrears I'd gotten into on the medical bills and allow for me to pay a few months' rent in advance. But it all hinged on Krista sticking around, and on me feeling able to leave Dakota with her. It'd be the longest I'd have been apart from her since before she'd gotten sick. This past year I'd never stayed away overnight; was always watching for the slightest sign of the cancer returning, so I'd be sure to catch it early and get her help. Three days. Could I bring myself to leave her that long? I sure hoped so. Her treatment had to continue.

I was still thinking on it when I heard the flush of the john followed by heavy footsteps trudging from the backroom to the office. Bailey.

'Oh look, it's *Barbie the Bounty Hunter*,' Bailey said, his tone loaded with sarcasm.

He waddled over to me and offered the hand that wasn't in plaster for a flaccid handshake. His palm felt clammy as he gripped mine. He stepped closer; too close. I could feel the press of his generous belly against my hip and smell the chilli dog on his breath.

I removed my hand and resisted the urge to wipe it on my pants. 'So you tracked this guy for a few weeks. What can you tell me?'

Bailey ignored the question. He walked to his paper-scattered desk and plonked himself down in his chair. The wooden frame creaked under the strain. He glared at Quinn and shook his head. 'You're sending *her* after *my* fugitive?'

I smiled real sweet as I imagined punching Bailey in his doughy, three-chinned face. 'Don't look so troubled, sweetie. This ain't my first rodeo.'

'So you'll do it?' Quinn said.

I winked at Bailey, whose cheeks had turned an ugly shade of puce, then looked back at Quinn. 'Sure.'

Quinn smiled, looked relieved. He nodded towards the file. 'The warrant and auth-to-arrest are inside. You—'

'Did he tell you that your fugitive is one of us?' Bailey interrupted. 'The leads I followed, they're all in the file, but from what folks said he's quite the superstar bounty hunter out in Georgia. Shit, some even called him a legend.'

I frowned. 'Yeah, and now he's a fugitive.'

'A smart one.' Bailey sucked in his gut, pushed his chest out. 'Been in the wind over a month, but I found him.'

Poor Bailey. So competitive. He just hated that my clearance rate was higher than his. 'Good for you, sweetie.'

I'd forgotten that Bailey never got anyplace fast. He either wanted to impress me, or show his superiority, or maybe both. Whichever it was, he launched into a description of all the web searches he'd done, the papers he'd pulled, the folks he'd talked with. All that information would be in the case file, I didn't need it verbal too. From Bailey's yammering it sounded like he'd interviewed everyone but the neighbours' pet dog's cousin before he'd gotten lucky with an address.

'... works for a Victor Accorsi, known as Pops, he's a bondsman based in Savannah...'

Pops I knew. He'd given me my first job when I'd gotten into this game. My mentor had made the introduction almost ten years ago. I felt my heart rate quicken. 'You got a name, a mugshot?'

Quinn thumbed through the papers in the file until he found the booking photo. 'That's him,' he said, passing it to me.

'Son-of-a-bitch.' I dropped the picture like it was the business end of a branding iron. It landed face up on the desk.

I stared at the photo. Heart racing, mouth dry.

It was him.

The man I'd seen in my nightmares for near on the past decade. The only other living person who knew the truth of what happened all those years ago.

2

Robert Tate. Robert *James* Tate. The man I'd known as JT.

I glanced again at the mugshot. I knew every inch of him, or at least I did ten years back, when he'd taught me the first rule of my trade: *Never trust no one*. The booking picture wasn't great, but it told me JT still had his rugged good looks; the same remarkable blue eyes, which looked azure or cobalt depending on the light and which, in this photo, squinted a little into the camera; and the same foppish, dirty-blond hair.

Quinn was watching me real close. He raised an eyebrow. 'Friend of yours?'

I nodded. 'Something like that.'

Bailey gave a long whistle. 'Well, shit, girl. You do get around.'

I glared at Bailey. 'He was my mentor. Taught me the business. Trained me. Helped me get my licence, before I came to Florida.'

Bailey leered at me, his yellow-toothed grin mocking. 'Is that right? How come you didn't stick around in Georgia?'

A simple question with a complicated answer, which I wasn't going to spill to Bailey. 'He always worked alone. Said it was safer that way – with no one to worry about he could think clearer. I respected that. Training me was only ever a short-term thing.'

Quinn shook his head. 'Sounds like a real charmer.'

Sarcasm. Nice. But Quinn was righter than he knew. JT had been charming, but he was tough too. I still remembered his lecture on clarity of focus. We'd been heading back to the truck after a job that had very nearly gone bad. I'd delayed cuffing a woman who'd been holding a Moses basket. She'd clung to the basket, crying that she couldn't leave her baby. I'd stepped far closer to her than I should have done, tried to assure her it would be okay, that we'd not be leaving her baby behind. JT had told me that my sympathy was a weakness, drilled into me that emotion would get me injured, or worse. And he'd been right. There was no baby. The woman had fired at me with a long-barrelled revolver she'd hidden under the blanket in the basket. If her aim had been better, or JT hadn't pulled me to safety, it would have been game over. Stay objective, he'd said in our debrief. Focus on the job. Don't form close bonds. Never let anyone get under your skin.

That wasn't the only one of his rules that I'd broken.

Quinn looked at me real funny. 'You still up for this job?'

I nodded. Didn't hesitate. I wasn't going to throw away the opportunity of a fifteen-thousand-dollar pay-out because of the way things had ended with JT. All I'd lost back then had cost me dear. I wasn't going to add my daughter's health to the list.

'Good.' Quinn tapped the details into his computer and printed out a job docket – the agreement that made my pick-up on CF Bonds' behalf legal – and handed it to me. As I took it our fingers touched. The contact did nothing for me, but from the way Quinn's expression had gotten a whole lot more intense I figured he was about to say something deep. That, I could well do without.

Looking away fast, I picked the photo from the desk and slipped it and the docket into the back of the file. 'Three days then.'

Quinn sighed. 'Yeah.'

I waved through the doorway at Dakota. 'Come on, honey.'

She said her goodbyes to Mrs Valdez and skipped over to me. Taking her hand, I led her to the door. Before opening it, I turned back to Quinn. 'I'll text you when I have him.'

⥥

The drive to Yellow Spring, West Virginia, would take me the best part of fourteen hours, getting me to the location where Merv was keeping JT a little before midnight. Even with a smooth run, the round trip would have me on the road for near on two days. First, I needed food, a change of clothes and to persuade Krista to delay her trip and watch Dakota.

Home is a two-bed apartment at the Clearwater Village complex. Residential, not holiday lets, and a reasonable kind of neighbourhood for the price. Still, as we climbed the concrete stairs to the second floor I noted a fresh pile of cigarette butts heaped in the corner of the twist. I guessed Jamie-Lynn's teenage son and his buddies had been hanging out here again, and made a mental note to speak with them on my return.

Our apartment is second along from the stairs. Krista's place is right next door. Her blinds were down, not a good sign, but I pressed the buzzer and waited anyways, willing her to be home.

Didn't do no good. Maybe she'd just gone to the store for groceries, but seeing as she was about to take a long trip I knew that was real unlikely. Still I waited. Had to hope.

Nothing. As Dakota pressed the buzzer again, I unlocked our door – first the Yale and then the upper and lower deadbolts. Pushed it open and paused, just for a moment, to listen.

A sheet of paper caught my eye. It must have been pushed under the door while we were out. I scooped it up, unfolded it and read the note. Shit. I turned to Dakota. 'It's no good, honey. She's gone.'

Dakota looked up at me, disappointed. 'So I won't get to have a sleepover?'

'I guess not.' In the note Krista said she'd be visiting with her folks for the next three weeks. She asked me to water her plants when I got the chance.

'What about your job, Momma?'

Damn good question. There was no one else I trusted to watch Dakota – no friends and certainly no family – but I'd already agreed to do the pick-up. Going back on the deal would have me look a fool, and make Bailey's taunts even less bearable. Worse still, I'd lose out on the fifteen thousand bucks that would guarantee Dakota's treatment continued.

I remembered what Quinn had said: Take her along – you've got a full transport kit. True, I did, but if I took her along she'd meet JT, the man who knew my worst and darkest secret, who could threaten the life I'd built for us here in Florida, and who I'd promised myself right back at the very beginning would never know about Dakota. I couldn't stand for him to learn the truth, but what choice did I have? I'd be damned if I did, or damned if I didn't. Either way, I'd put her at risk. Forcing a smile, I held out my hand. 'I'm not sure, baby.'

Dakota stepped away from Krista's front door and joined me. Slipping her hand into mine, she looked up at me with those big blue eyes of hers and said, 'I could help.'

I thought back to how things had been when she'd first gotten sick. The sleepless nights I'd spent sitting beside her hospital bed; all the drugs they'd pumped into her fragile body; her pain, which I'd been powerless to erase. It never got easier to live with the fear. Even when she'd gotten better, the doctors had said she was in remission and the cancer could come back at any time. So far it hadn't, but that didn't stop me from worrying, watching for the slightest sign.

I knew the choice I had to make. Whatever else he was capable of doing, JT would never hurt a child. 'You know, sweetie. Maybe this one time you could come on a ride-along.'

'Really?' Dakota beamed. She hugged me, then rushed through the gap between me and the door. 'It'll be so fun. I'll make us a picnic.'

'Stop.' My tone sounded harsher than I'd intended. Not her fault, but mine. The fear was back, churning in my stomach. Fear about the decision I was making, about seeing JT again after all these years, about having to remember what I'd done, what he'd done. About facing up to the horror of what had happened to Sal.

I tried to smile, almost pulled it off. Forced a lighter tone. 'Sneakers, sweetie.'

She scuttled back to the door. Slipping off her sneakers, she placed them in a neat pair on the mat beneath where our coats hung from two metal hooks. Glanced up at me, all bashful. 'Sorry, Momma.'

I smiled, genuine this time. 'Go make us that picnic.'

Our little apartment might not be much, but clean is one thing that doesn't cost. I'd gotten the place a little cheaper than the going rate due to the water damage caused by a hurricane the previous year. The roof had been mended, but the box room had looked pretty nasty, with the walls discoloured where rainwater had flowed through the gap in the roof and been left to dry. Didn't matter. I'd fixed it up real nice. With a few pots of paint and a bit of effort I'd converted it into Dakota's bedroom. I hung bright pictures to cover the more stubborn stains and used two pretty bead lampshades and some purple drapes I'd found at the thrift store to cosy up the place. After living there ten months, it was someplace we could finally call home, and it sure as hell beat the last place. I hoped I could afford for us to stay.

In the kitchenette, I put my purse and the CF Bonds file on the counter and dropped my keys into the teal bowl we'd picked up at the weekly street market in Celebration. Next to the bowl sat Dakota's end-of-term science project: a papier-mâché volcano that glowed red as it erupted and, so long as the water reservoir was filled, produced an impressive cloud of steam. Dakota had spent weeks perfecting the wiring of the electronic circuit board and remote control. She'd sure deserved her first prize.

I stared at the dormant model, trying to resist the lure of the file beside it, and more specifically, the mugshot. Didn't want to think about JT. There's no sense in being sentimental about a person you haven't seen in years. Sentimental doesn't pay the rent, and it sure as shit couldn't keep up the repayments on my baby's medical bills. I had to be practical, to focus. Make the pick-up, bring him back to Clermont, get him booked in at the precinct. Done.

Dakota was busy choosing food from the refrigerator, narrating her choices as she put them in the cooler: '... and some peanut butter cups, and this cherry yogurt, and a pack of cheese strings—'

'And these peaches, and a pack of salad,' I said, pulling them from the upper shelf and stashing them on top of the yogurt.

She pulled a face, and fished the plastic bag of salad out again. 'Lettuce, Momma. Really?'

I took the salad and dropped it back inside. 'Yes, really. It's good for you.'

Dakota gave an exaggerated sigh. She opened the icebox, took out four ice packs, and pushed them against each side of the cooler. 'I think we need some ice cream.'

'Honey, it'll melt.'

She took four snack-size tubs from the icebox. 'They'll be okay. I'll put them right up against the ice.'

I nodded. 'All right. Now go pack your overnight bag.'

When she'd scampered off to her room I opened the cupboard below the sink and removed my metal footlocker. I opened the combination lock and checked my tools. I wasn't expecting trouble. JT knew how things worked, and if Bailey had located him and had Merv pick him up, then my money was on JT wanting to be found. Still, there was no sense in going underprepared.

My brown leather carryall, the 'go-bag' I'd used ever since I'd started in the business, was stowed at one end of the box, battered but serviceable. I pulled it out, unzipped the front section and inventoried the equipment: my leather rig, two canisters of extra strength pepper spray, three sets of plasticuffs, a roll of twenties totalling two hundred bucks – my emergency cash, which, if I hadn't gotten this job, I'd have offered as a token gesture towards Dakota's outstanding medical repayments – and my X2 Taser. Almost everything I needed.

In the bottom of the footlocker lay my Wesson Commander Classic Bobtail. I stared at it for a long moment. I remembered how my mentor had lectured me on the foolhardiness of doing what we did without a gun. Remembered what had happened when we did.

I reached into the locker, my fingers stretching towards the weapon. They started shaking, first a slight quiver then, as my fingertips grew closer to the wooden grip, more violently. I couldn't do it. Still couldn't. After almost ten years, the memory of that night, as vivid as ever, began to replay again in the dark place behind my eyes. I shuddered. Squeezing my eyes tight shut, I tried to force the images away. It didn't work, though. Suddenly, it was as if I was right back there, and it was happening all over again.

I see the blood. Watch it gush from her chest, crimson spreading across the pink fabric of her shirt, pooling on the ground beneath. There's so much, too much, it's impossible to stop the flow. I have to try though, and I try real hard. Press my fists against the wound. She's lying on her back, pale face turned skywards, eyes unfocused. I think that I'm crying, but all I can hear is that sound, the wheezing, gurgling. She's trying to talk, and failing. Trying to breathe. Failing.

I opened my eyes, yanked my hand away from the gun. Standing, I gripped the edge of the worktop, breathing hard. I needed to get control, knew I had to get past this, because things were different this time. Dakota would be there. I had to be able to protect her.

I took the dishtowel from the hook beside the sink and folded it in half. Leaning down, I lifted my carryall from the footlocker and unzipped the front pocket. I took a breath, and before I could think on it any longer, scooped the gun and a box of ammo into the dishtowel, bound them real tight and stuffed them into the pocket before zipping it closed. I told myself it was a precaution; I'd never have to use them. But it sounded hollow, like a throwaway line I'd bullshit someone else with. Didn't help.

I turned towards Dakota's bedroom. 'Honey, you ready yet?'

'Nearly, Momma.'

I took the carryall to my bedroom and set it down on the patchwork quilt of my bed. The bag was always packed for a last-minute job, with changes of clothes and underwear: practical, non-sexy underwear. All I needed. So why, this time, was I wondering about more? I took two steps towards the closet and stopped. Shit. It was a job, not a date. I hesitated a moment longer, then opened the door and yanked a matching set of black lace panties and bra from the underwear tray and threw them into the carryall. Be prepared, always. Another of my mentor's rules.

I went into Dakota's room to see if she was done. I found her sitting on the fuchsia-pink rug beside her bed, selecting bottles of nail polish from her dress-up box.

'Hey, sweetie. How many you got there?'

'Five.'

'You think it's enough?'

She tilted her head to one side. 'I guess. Maybe we could do each other's nails?'

I smiled. 'That's sweet, honey, but I'm gonna be real busy these next three days, and there's going to be a lot of riding in the truck. It could get dull.'

Dakota smiled. 'I don't care. I wanna go with you, Momma. I always have to stay home, and you *promised* we'd spend more time together this holiday.'

She was right, I had promised. But that had been before the final demand arrived. 'Okay, sweetie, but I need for *you* to promise me something.'

'Like what?'

'That you'll do exactly what I say, no question. I have to know I can count on you.'

'Like in the look-out game?'

I smiled. The look-out game was one I'd invented to teach her about being vigilant, staying safe. I never wanted her to get into trouble the way I had when I was a kid, but if she did, I sure as hell wanted her to be able to get herself out of it. 'Just like in the look-out game.'

Dakota grinned. 'I promise, Momma.'

I nodded. 'Okay, good. So you got your toothbrush?'

Dakota rummaged in her rucksack and pulled out her purple toothbrush. 'Right here.'

'Good job.' I picked up her sleeping bag from the frilly purple duvet. Nodded towards her rucksack. 'You ready then?'

She zipped the bottles of nail polish into the side pocket of her pack, hoisted it over her shoulder and grinned. 'Ready.'

⇓

I triple-locked the apartment and we started down the stairs to the parking lot. Dakota was humming a tune to herself, jumping down the steps two at a time, acting like we were heading out on holiday rather than a bounty-hunting gig.

I couldn't share her joy. Taking the job had been all about the money. And it was good money, for sure. But since I'd first realised the fugitive was JT, a doubt had nagged at me. And the more I thought on the case, the more I felt a real uneasiness about the thing. See, back when I'd known him, JT had been all about justice. Sure, justice by any means – rough or legal – but the mentor I'd known had stood by his actions, every time. So him turning fugitive didn't sit right. If he'd committed a crime and skipped out on the consequences, I figured the facts of the matter must be a whole lot more complicated than Quinn, Bailey and the thin file in my purse were telling. I needed to figure out the real truth, had to know what'd changed him.

Hoped to hell that it wasn't my fault.

Course, I should have guessed just where my curiosity would get me, but right then I had no idea that the new life I'd built for myself and my daughter would be shot to shit inside of twenty-four hours.

3

Yellow Spring, West Virginia. A place deep in Hicksville country, and much further from my Florida territory than I'm usually inclined to travel. We'd covered the nine hundred miles in thirteen hours – quick work even by my standards. Still, all that driving had sure made me ache. Good job we'd almost reached our destination.

With all that had happened to his brother, I knew Merv would be twitchy and trigger happy, so it was important for anyone keeping lookout to believe I'd come alone. I gave no mind to Dakota's protesting about it. The safest place for her when we entered the location would be behind the blacked-out windows in the fully kitted out fugitive transport section of the truck. There, ducked down in one of the moulded plastic seats, she'd be hidden from outside view, but visible to me through the Plexiglas screen.

When the navigator's display showed we were three miles from our target, I pulled off the road. It was near on midnight, and it'd been a long half-hour since we'd passed any indication of human life. As we'd swept around a sharp bend, the headlamps had picked out a gap in the trees and given me a glimpse of an old gas station with two pumps and a rusty sign out front, all shuttered up for the night.

With the Silverado's engine idling, I took my cell from its cradle on the dashboard and dialled the number for local law enforcement. I usually work alone, but this place was real remote and I reckoned that the assistance of a lawman or two could help ease the situation should things get ugly.

The call didn't connect. No signal. Damn.

I'd have to get things done the old-fashioned way. I sure hoped that wouldn't be a problem. I reminded myself this was a straight pick-up, a transfer from Merv to me. Told myself the only reason I was worried was because Dakota was here. Didn't quite convince myself, though. I was uneasy. I'd not managed to connect with Merv even though I'd tried to call several times these past few hours. There'd been no answer on his cell, although maybe the signal was patchy this high up in the mountains. But there was no answer on the home phone either. Seemed unusual behaviour if he was waiting for my call, as he should have been. I do not like unusual. Unusual has a bad habit of causing me grief.

I glanced at Dakota. 'In the back now, honey.'

She rolled her eyes. 'But I hate it in the cage, the seats are too hard. Why can't I just stay up front with—'

'No. You promised you'd do whatever I said.' I knew she'd hardly slept on the journey, and tiredness made her cranky. 'I need you to do this for me. Please.'

'Can I play Goldrush Galaxy on your cell then?'

I didn't want her to be bored. An unhappy child was in no way helpful for my focus, and without a signal the cell was of little use to me. I unplugged my smartphone from the charger and handed it to her. 'Sure. But volume off, okay?'

As she climbed into the back, I reached into the stowaway box beneath the passenger seat for my carryall. Taking my rig from the bag, I removed my jacket and fastened the straps in place. I made the usual checks: plasticuffs, taser, pepper spray. Left the gun in the bag. Satisfied, I pulled my jacket back on and turned to secure the Plexiglas screen between Dakota and me.

With the divider in place it felt like I drove the final miles in solitary. Me and the radio was all. Mountainside FM: Classic Country. Those whiney lyrics, guitars and shit seemed fitting companionship. Besides, I couldn't get a clear signal for any other station, not smothered under the heavy blanket of the trees. So I drove those miles listening to the sounds of *The Grand Ole Opry*, winding my way up the crumbling blacktop, the temperature falling the higher I went. Whether it was the gloom, or the lonesomeness of the tune on the radio, or the melancholy that came over me when I allowed myself to dwell on the fact that I was about to pick up the man who'd been my mentor, I don't rightly know. Still, in that moment I'd gotten the strongest feeling that this job was going to be trouble.

The road had hugged tight to the route of a broad mountain stream for a good while before the navigator told me I'd reached my destination. To my left the ground fell sharp away from the raggedy edge of the asphalt, a clear twenty-foot drop to the water below. The stream, wide and shallow, had more power than a casual glance might give it credit. But I knew from the way that white foam kicked high over the stones in the riverbed that it took no prisoners. I shuddered. No doubt that feral beauty had lured many folks to their death.

On my right, the ranch looked like your average mountain homestead, but then appearances don't always tell the whole story. The feeling was stronger, sitting at the base of my throat, an invisible hold tightening its grip notch by notch to somewhere between fear and excitement. It should be easy, I told myself, a straight collection and return. It should be, yet part of me was wondering why JT had come out here, so far from his native Georgia, and if he'd meant for himself to be found.

I braked to a halt and grabbed the file from the dashboard. Inside the cover lay a ripped-off sheet of yellow legal paper with the address scrawled across it: Yellow Rock Ranch, Yellow Spring. The handwriting was Quinn's, not mine, the letters neat, tight, economical. Merv's aunt's place, he'd said. This was where Merv had JT held. After a long moment I turned the truck on to the driveway. It was time to get this done.

The wooden gate had once been painted white but in the glare of my headlamps I could see it was past its best. It stood rotten on its hinges, propped forever open by a boulder. I continued on, bumping along the dirt road flanked by more of the same ageing, whitewashed railings. I reckoned the road would at one time have been stone, but after years of dirt and weather it was now camouflaged by earth. As I drove, I noted the land, the way the hillside swelled up to the front and the left of the driveway, and fell away a few hundred yards to my right.

I came to a ranch house.

Two vehicles stood parked outside: a Ford with the licence plate MERV and a black SUV. Could mean up to eight people inside, could mean jack. I'd seen wooden horse barns as I'd come up the hill. There'd be plenty of room there to hide a vehicle, or as many as you pleased.

The energy of the place felt ambiguous, hard to read. Unusual.

I parked a little ways from the house, killed the lights and climbed out of the truck.

Silence.

I heard no bug chorus like back home, no sounds from cattle or ponies or whatever animals this ranch was supposed to work, and nothing from the house. Didn't seem natural. The tension in the base of my throat tightened yet another notch.

Tucking my purse under the driver's seat, I kept my eyes down and whispered to Dakota, 'Stay out of sight.'

I locked the Silverado and put the key in my pocket. Reaching inside my jacket, I double-checked the paperwork from Quinn was secure; I needed to have it on me to make my entry into this property and JT's surrender to me lawful. It was where it was supposed to be.

On my reckoning, twenty-three paces would get me to the front porch. I set out towards it. By my sixth stride it seemed like the slap of my heel on the baked earth could raise a giant from slumber; by the eleventh I'd grown real aware of the inches between my right hand and the place where my X2 lay snug against my ribs under cover of my beat-up leather jacket. At stride seventeen I heard them.

I'm no rookie, but having Dakota so close added a whole other layer of tension to the situation.

I slowed my pace. Listened harder. I counted three voices, all male. None was JT. By stride twenty I saw that the glass had been slid back from the high window in the front room, leaving the mesh screen the only thing separating the inside from the out. I could hear enough to know that the men were playing cards, and that the one called Gunner was winning and oftentimes was inclined to cheat. From the clinking of glass, I reckoned they were drinking too and that this wasn't their first of the night.

A twig snapped beneath my boot. I froze on instinct, although rationally I knew that made no kind of sense. With the window open those inside would have heard me drive up. Yet they didn't appear to be interested. That meant they were either stupid for paying no mind to me, cocky in believing that they didn't need to, or secure in the knowledge that there was someone else on guard duty.

My dollars were on options one or two. Sure, if there was a lookout somewhere up in the trees then they'd have had eyes on me from the moment I left the highway, but, seeing as Merv knew I was coming, there would've been little point. What I didn't understand is why these men hadn't reacted to my arrival. Unusual. Again. The best thing to do now was to get inside and find JT.

The wooden boarding of the porch creaked as I stepped up on to it. The planks felt spongy, bending beneath my steps. I flinched at the tuneless clank of the wind chimes that hung from the canopy above an old wooden swing. A three-person bench was positioned over to my right. Beside it were two ceramic dog bowls. In one the dregs of water were green with algae. It was hard to know what the meat had once been in the other, for now it was putrid and festering. A good sign, for me at least. I guessed whatever dogs they'd had here had been gone a while.

I opened the screen door, and rapped my knuckles against the more solid inner door three times. Inside, the voices fell quiet. The familiar surge of adrenaline fizzed inside me. I started to count, slow and steady in time with my breath; holding my focus.

I'd reached fourteen by the time the inner door opened. A youngish man, mid-twenties I guessed, stood in the doorway. He wore faded denims, a plaid work shirt and an unwelcoming scowl. He looked me down and up again, then spat tobacco on to the wooden board an inch to the right of my boot. 'What?'

I stood a little taller. Weight balanced evenly on the balls of my feet. Ready. 'I'm Lori Anderson, Bail Runner for CF Bonds. Here to collect Robert James Tate.'

He frowned. Whether he knew JT had skipped bail or not, I guessed he hadn't reckoned on meeting a bail runner who was a woman. In my business, I had that a lot.

I put my boot against the doorframe. 'I'm here at Merv's invitation.'

He sniggered. 'Is that right? Well, seems y'all are out of luck. Merv's gone for takeout.'

This seemed real unlikely seeing as his truck was parked out front. Still, if it were true, I guessed Merv could be gone a while; I'd passed no food joints of any description on my way in.

Pulling the papers from my pocket, I waved them at the guy. 'I have reason to believe Tate is at this address. He's a fugitive, skipped bail back in Florida. You need to stand aside.'

He didn't move or speak. I took his silence as an invitation and stepped past him into the house. He kept his back to the wall, allowing me along the hallway to the front room with him following behind like a faithful pup. But, despite this attempt to keep it hidden, I'd clocked the semi-automatic stuffed in the back of his pants.

Half a step into the room, I knew my earlier instincts had been correct. This was no place for a child. Quinn might have thought this would be an easy job, but I was standing in a nest of Copperheads that were a whole other level of wrong. Two heavy-built men stood before me. Not our kind of people. They had knives tucked in their belts and the recklessness of liquor shining in their eyes. If you counted the pup with the semi-automatic blocking my exit, there were three. There was no sign of bounty hunter Merv Dalton, or of the elderly aunt who owned this place. I was the only girl at the dance.

Not a great situation, but there I was with a job to be done. Stay or leave, I had a feeling these boys weren't going to make either option easy. 'I'm looking for a fugitive. Robert James Tate. I'm here to take him into custody.'

The biggest guy, a bloody dagger tattooed on his left forearm and a red bandana tied over the crown of his lank brown hair, took a step towards me. He didn't look none too friendly. 'Is that right?'

I recognised his voice as the guy winning at cards, Gunner. I nodded. 'Give me Tate and I'll be on my way.'

Behind me, the pup sniggered. The weasel-faced man next to Gunner stared at me with dark eyes, a lusty smirk spreading across his lips. 'Why you want to leave so fast?'

I knew what he was thinking: I was a woman for the taking. But he couldn't have been more wrong. I held my ground. 'I don't want any trouble. Just Tate.'

Weasel-face ran a hand over the black stubble covering his skull. 'Hell, woman. Don't you like a little fun?'

The men slid closer, like a bunch of coyotes circling their prey. I scanned their faces, but not one of those boys made eye contact. They were having themselves a good old look-see, checking out what they thought I had to offer. The tension tightened another notch at the base of my neck. I did not like where this was heading.

The way those men stared made me feel real naked. Straight-up predators they were. Bailey must have gotten his information wrong. There was no way this house was inhabited by an elderly widow; it was a loveless place with bare-bulb lighting and cracked plaster walls, and Merv's boys didn't seem inclined to give JT up that easy. I figured there were two ways things could go. With Dakota waiting in the car out front I had to make sure both ended in my favour.

Gunner looked past me, towards the pup, and nodded.

What happened next flowed real fast. Overeager to obey his master and get started on me, the pup closed his grimy fingers tight around my shoulders and pulled me back towards him. Well, manhandling a girl from behind without invitation is just plain rude.

I thrust my weight rearwards, accelerating fast, using the momentum to throw him off balance. He staggered back. Advantage: me. Whipping round, I slammed the side of my clenched left fist into his temple and followed it real quick with a right-handed punch to the throat.

One-two, the pup hit the floor before he'd barely registered the blows. The semi-automatic fell from his grip. I guessed he was weaker than he'd acted. From his wide-eyed expression and the wheezy gasps he was making at my feet, I reckoned he'd just realised that too.

I kicked his weapon out of reach and spun to face the others.

Gunner looked at the pup, real disappointed. 'Beat by a damn girl, that's plain embarrassing.' He glanced at the weasel-faced man. 'Show the boy how it's done.'

Weasel-face threw himself at me. I deflected his first blow with my left forearm and punched him in the stomach. He groaned, but kept on coming, grabbing for my hair. The skull thumb ring on his left hand glinted in the artificial light. I feigned left and moved right, but he was too fast. He yanked me to him, twisting me around, so his forearm was across my throat and the bulk of his body was pressed up against my back. He smelt of stale sweat and tequila. I had to get out of this. These men couldn't get near Dakota.

'Feisty, ain't you?' Weasel-face growled in my ear. 'I like a woman with a bit of spirit.'

Gunner laughed. 'Seems this one ain't broken to saddle.'

Weasel-face ran his free hand up from my waist, across my stomach to my breast and pinched my nipple hard. 'Best get her taught.'

No way was that going to happen. Focus. I took a breath, then kicked back hard as I could. The heel of my cowboy boot struck Weasel-face's kneecap. I heard the pop as cartilage and muscle gave in to the pressure. Weasel-face howled. His grip around my throat loosened, but didn't yield.

I pivoted left, pushing my chin into the crook of his elbow and my hips sideways. His arm tensed across my throat. I jabbed my elbow fast up under his ribs. As he doubled over, my second blow caught him hard in the groin. He stepped back on to his busted leg. Wrong move. I heard his knee crack and watched him drop like a felled maple.

The game had tipped in my favour: two out of three down, one to finish.

Gunner, by my reckoning the leader of this band of lowlifes, grinned a yellow-toothed smile. He beckoned me forward. 'Seems like you need to learn some manners.'

'Seems you should learn them yourself.'

I reached for my X2 Taser. Too slow. I was still releasing it from the holster when Gunner lunged at me, his shoulder slamming me hard to the ground. I gasped, winded, and then he was on top of me, grabbing for my wrists.

I struggled against his bulk, beating on any bit of him I could reach. I couldn't let him get a hold of my hands. If he did I'd be powerless and he knew it.

His fist slammed into my face. I felt my lip split and the metallic taste of blood in my mouth. I thrashed wilder, twisting on to my side. He punched: my ribs, my shoulders, my head. But he had less power at this angle. As he yanked me round to face him I planted a decent right hook to the side of his jaw. That surprised him. Grabbing his right ear, I dug my nails into his flesh and used the momentum and his moment of recoil to yank him sideways, propelling him on to his back, me on top. I dug my knees in tight to his ribs like I was a champion bull rider playing for the title.

'Bitch,' he spat. I felt a whoosh of air near my left ear and ducked. The knife in his hand glinted silver.

I slammed the side of my clenched fist hard into the bridge of his nose. Heard it break. He wheezed, coughing blood, and loosened his grip on the knife. I prised it from his fingers.

He tried to punch me, but his aim was off. I dodged it. He grabbed one of my wrists instead. Out the corner of my eye I saw the pup moving towards me. Not good. I had to finish this.

I plunged the knife hard into Gunner's shoulder, twisting it, cutting into muscle and sinews, maximising the damage.

As he yowled I leapt to my feet, aimed a kick at the pup's head and brought him down. Gunner was still moving. I rolled him on to his front and pulled his arms behind his back. Hard as it was, I fought to keep him still enough to get a pair of plasticuffs around his wrists. He floundered around like a landed fish. Damn redneck didn't know when he was beat. I stamped the heel of my boot hard into his back and tugged his arms higher, twisting them in their sockets. Must have hurt like a bitch with that shoulder wound. He roared in fury.

The plasticuffs slotted into place. I strode around to face him. 'Attacking a woman? Weren't you boys raised right?'

Gunner spat at me.

'Your momma must be real proud,' I said, shaking my head.

I glanced at the other two. The pup was out cold. Weasel-face was down and whimpering. His leg was twisted out at the knee at the strangest angle.

The game was mine: three out of three, a perfect score. Now I had to find JT.

As I moved across the room to the hallway, I noticed the semi-automatic was wedged snug against the dresser. I couldn't leave it. I nudged it free with the toe of my boot, and kicked it along the floor in front of me as I stepped into the hallway.

The heels of my boots knocked a cautious beat across the wooden floor. Pressing my back against the wall, I peered around the doorframe into the next room. A kitchen. Dark and empty. Ahead there was one final room before the stairway. The door was shut.

Standing to one side, I gently turned the doorknob. It moved a small way, then stuck. Locked.

Interesting. It seemed these boys had been holding JT prisoner. I'd gotten the sense from Quinn that this deal was civilised, that JT was willing to come in. Maybe Merv's crew were local boys looking to cash in on the bond by helping him out. But even with what I knew of Merv's reputation, it didn't make sense for them to attack me. We were meant to be on the same side.

Whatever the reason, I needed to get JT and get gone. That left me with a few choices: pick the lock – but I only had the knife to hand; shoot the lock off, but that would mean me using the semi-automatic, which I couldn't handle; or kick the door in. The first would take time, the second two would announce to whoever was inside I was coming.

I heard shuffling noises from the front room. Had the pup come to? I needed to move fast. There was no time for finesse.

I kicked the door a few inches shy of the doorknob. The wood was old and brittle; a split appeared, but it didn't give. I heard a muffled shout from the other side; a man's voice, JT's perhaps. I kicked again, harder. The wood splintered apart, the middle panel collapsed into the room.

I peered through the gap. A single chair was bolted to the floor in the centre of the room, a man tied to it. He smiled, and I felt my breath catch in my throat.

'It's good to see you, Lori.'

4

His smile had me ruined from the first time we'd met. Of course, ten years ago I was younger, more naïve and a whole lot less wilful than I am now. Still, I had known he'd been drinking bourbon – I'd smelt it on his breath as he'd said good evening. Right then my head had told me, girl, you go sit someplace else. But my heart, or perhaps somewhere a little further south, knew the barstool right alongside his was the place I had to be.

So I broke my rule of never socialising with a customer and I smiled at him, not with my red-lips-empty-promises work smile, which made men kid themselves that I might give them a ride, but with something a little more genuine. Somehow, I knew he was different.

Not a cop. Plenty came through here, most of them off the clock. But this guy's energy was all wrong for that. He was something else. Kinda mysterious. I liked that.

Anyways, that scent of aged bourbon with a base-note aroma of tobacco worked real well on him. What with the dark-blond hair that fell over his eyes and the two-day-old stubble lingering across his jaw, he looked a dirty kind of perfect: big and dangerous and sexy as hell.

He turned. Met my gaze. 'Drink?'

I nodded. The thumping music and drunken crowd around us seemed to fade out to nothing. And sure, I knew that I shouldn't have been sitting with him, that I should have been checking my make-up, using my ten-minute break to get ready for my next dance. But I stayed right there. Just plain did not want to move. Instead I held his gaze, worked my lashes and asked, 'How are you liking the show?'

He said nothing. Paid the barkeep to leave the bottle and sloshed three fingers of bourbon into two glasses.

For two of my ten minutes we drank in silence. I noticed his fingers were long, ringless and real elegant, aside from the purple bruising across the knuckles of his left hand.

He caught me looking. Shrugged. 'Occupational hazard.'

'What occupation?'

'A measure of last resort. Finding them that don't want to get found.'

Not a cop, for sure. But what? 'So why'd you ask for me?'

He ignored my question. Picked up the bourbon and splashed another triple into his glass.

I sipped at my whiskey, watched him gulp his. His Adam's apple moved as he drank it down. I wanted to lean in closer, run my tongue across his throat, over that stubble, to his lips. Find out if he tasted as good as he looked.

In the fourth minute he got around to the why.

'I need your help,' he said, all earnest in that deep-gravel voice of his that made every word sound both serious and smutty all at once. Then he smiled. Not a big, false, you-can-trust-me smile, like every lying cheater had given me since my curves filled out nice. But a small, almost bashful smile that tweaked up one corner of his mouth a fraction higher than the other.

I pouted just a little more and asked, 'How so?'

'We've a mutual Person of Interest.'

I couldn't think who. 'Person got a name?'

'Thomas Ford.'

My stomach lurched, and not from the whiskey. 'Is that right?'

The big guy nodded. 'You tell me where he's at, things could work out nice for the both of us.'

He held my gaze. His face looked honest, and his expression seemed to tell me that everything *would* work out just fine. I wanted to believe him, really I did. But life had taught me otherwise. And what could he really know about me, my problems? I never wore my wedding band when I was working.

So I didn't answer, couldn't find the words. Looked away.

Over by the stage, Old Hank was jumping about like a rodeo clown, gesturing at me: two minutes.

I slid off the barstool. Took a moment to steady myself then thrust into the crowd and went back to work. Tried not to show that my hands were shaking.

Sal was entertaining a table of young moneyed types. She was sitting astride one, grinding against his lap, letting him and his three friends touch far more than they ought. As I passed she raised an eyebrow.

I paid her no mind. Strode backstage to get ready. Tried real hard not to think on the big guy's words: *Person of Interest. Thomas Ford. Work out nice.* Because no matter who he was – cop, PI or whatever else – I knew that he was wrong.

No good would *ever* come from something involving my husband. Fact. But still, in that moment, I sure wished I could believe otherwise.

I was still thinking on it as the stage lights dimmed. Old Hank, with his greased-back hair and nineties throwback suit, stood out front and shouted into the mic, 'And here she is, the gal y'all have been waiting for, tonight's feature attraction, Miss Whiskey Bang-Bang.'

And, by Whiskey Bang-Bang, he, of course, meant me.

The beat started. The velvet curtain opened. The spotlights lit the stage, blinding my view of the audience. I strutted through the dry ice to start my act as I had done so many times before. But that night, as the sultry tones of Peggy Lee sang 'Fever', I couldn't shake the memory of the big guy at the bar. Of the chance he'd offered me. Of his smile. So bashful. So honest. So hot.

I performed for that smile. Imagined it was his touch on my skin, his hands unhooking my bra, his fingers peeling down my panties. When my dance ended I'd gotten more dollars for that one performance than I ever had in a whole night. The stage was covered with bills: tens, twenties, fifties and more.

The spotlights dimmed and the houselights came up. I peered out towards the bar. The stool he'd been sitting on was empty. In that crowded, smoke-filled room, as the barflies whooped and clapped, I felt his absence like a punch to the chest.

He'd gone is all, and I was just as I always would be.

Alone.

5

The night I first met JT, my husband had been gone eighteen days. Tommy had never liked my line of work, although that didn't stop him using my wages to fund his gambling habit. After seven years together I hardly remembered things hadn't always played that way. See, grief can change a person; harden them into granite until no amount of loving can soften their heart. For the past three years of our married life we'd gotten ourselves into a familiar pattern: I'd work, he'd bitch, we'd fight.

What happened then oftentimes depended on his state of mind. If he was sober he'd take off for a day or two, do some gambling and most likely some whoring, then come back and there'd be a truce for a short while. But if he'd been on the tequila things tended to turn ugly. He'd throw stuff: my china, his fist. Eighteen days ago he'd taken things to a whole other level. He'd grabbed a fistful of my blonde hair, right up by my brunette roots, and smacked my head against the nice china cabinet my grand-mammy left me when she passed.

The impact broke one of the glass panes. I'd yelled out, on account of the pain in my head and the destruction of the furniture. Wild-cat fury altered the tone of my voice. Made it raw, more animal. I'd never seen Tommy look so shocked.

Still, I'd expected him to come home once he'd cooled off some, tail between his legs and acting all sorry, as was his way. But he didn't. At that moment I didn't understand why. And I wouldn't until later.

Neither did I realise that the seemingly chance meeting with a stranger would set me on course for a real open-your-legs (or your eyes) moment, although as time played out I chose to do both. On stage I might have played the part of Whiskey Bang-Bang, but in real life I was still plain old Jennifer Lorelli Ford.

That night, as I came off stage, my hands full of sweaty dollars and the crumpled lace of my panties, the big stranger's words repeated in my mind: *I need your help.*

Needed help, my ass. He hadn't even stuck around to find out my answer. And what kind of a man leaves a titty bar when he's still got a half-bottle of bourbon with his name on it and a quality act giving her all on stage?

Stomping into the little space out back that served as a dressing room for us dancers, I ignored Sal, who was sat at her mirror, kicked off my glitter, fuck-me pumps, chucked the dollars on to the table and plonked down in my chair naked. I yelped as I felt a sharp pain. Twisted in the chair. Cursed as I picked a splinter the size of a toothpick from the right cheek of my butt. Madison Square Garden that shithole certainly wasn't.

I glared at the girl in the mirror. She didn't look so hot: too much make-up, too little sleep. I pulled off the long black 'Cher in Vegas' wig that turned me into Whiskey and shook out my hair from the braid beneath. It felt greasy to my touch. A yellowing bruise was just visible where my foundation faded into the hairline around my right temple. Damaged goods. No wonder the big guy didn't stay.

On the other side of the room Sal swivelled her chair round to face me. 'Temper, temper. So who was he?'

I glared at her in the mirror. Shook my head.

Unfazed, she continued wiping off her candy shimmer eye make-up. 'Oh, come on. Spill.'

Shivering, I pulled the tattered red silk robe from the back of the chair and wrapped it around me. 'Just some guy.'

'Nah-ah. You were having something intense.'

I grabbed the cleanser from the assorted potions on my dressing table, tipped some on to a cotton pad and scrubbed at my face. 'It was just business.'

A goofy smile spread across her face. 'He was dreamy. You could—'

I shoved my wedding band back on to my ring finger and held it up. 'I'm married, Sal.'

'I wasn't saying you—'

'He was just a mark. You know the rules. Leave it, okay?' An instruction, not a request. I used to be a romantic, way back when my fifteen-year-old self met Tommy. Punch by punch he'd knocked the fairy tales clean out of me.

Sal sighed and turned back to her mirror.

I'd been mean, and I knew it. At seventeen, she was a sweet kid, but even more delusional than I had been at that age – still waiting for her knight to pitch up on some mighty steed and rescue her. She didn't get that the guys who'd visit with us were about as far from knights as we were from ballerinas.

At almost twenty-two I'd seen what this business could do. When Sal arrived fresh off the bus from Nebraska, looking for a new life in the sunshine state, away from her Momma's overfriendly boyfriend, she'd gotten a job at the Bang-Bang Bar to help pay her way through school. I was real determined not to let her get chewed up and spat out like so many of the other girls had been. So far, she'd been doing pretty well.

Scraping my hair into a low pony, I watched her in the mirror as she pulled on jeans and a pink sweater with silver sequins along the seams. Damn, that girl never wore anything dull. Even the ends of her dark-brown hair were dip-dyed bright pink.

She caught my eye and smiled. Guilt had me smile back at her.

Grabbing her purse, she came across and hugged me. 'Maybe Tommy's not coming back this time.'

If only. I tried to stay relaxed, knew that this was Sal's way of comforting me, but her closeness made me feel trapped. I wriggled to loosen her hold.

She released me. 'See you tomorrow.'

I forced another smile. 'Sure thing, sweetie.'

I didn't feel much like going home. It never felt good sticking my key in the lock, not knowing if Tommy would be there, waiting in the darkness. But I couldn't very well stay at the Bang-Bang, not without getting roped into doing a double shift, anyways. So I stood, hauled on my jeans and a black tee, zipped up my jacket and slipped my bare feet into my boots.

It wasn't until I lifted my purse from the dressing table that I saw it. A calling card, stuck into the corner of the chipped frame of the mirror.

I plucked it free. For a fancy cream card with black embossed lettering it didn't say much; no name, just a single cell number and fifteen words, handwritten: *Call me if you change your mind. I know the truth. I can help you.*

Holding the card between my thumb and forefinger, I re-read the number over and again. It had to be his, the big guy at the bar. The sickness returned, swirling in my belly.

I didn't stop to wonder how he'd known that seat at the dressing table was my spot, or even how he'd come to get backstage to this room when Bobby and Zack, the bar's security guys, had a tally going for how many eager admirers they could sling out on their asses. All I thought was, what truth? Was it something about Tommy? Something bad? And, if the answer was yes, why did the big guy believe I could help?

I wanted to call him, really I did, but as I opened my purse, I remembered how I reacted to Sal, how I'd made a big deal of my being married. I'd taken vows; misguided, not thought-out vows, for sure, but binding nonetheless. I was married to Tommy, Thomas Ford, and whatever the big guy wanted him for, I doubted that it was good.

I stared at the card in my hand. It didn't seem right to call this guy, to betray my husband, especially when I knew how it might go. If Tommy found that card I'd get more than a bruise in my hairline for sure. And hell, I didn't even know the big guy's name.

So I tore his calling card clean in half and tossed it into the trash. Truth or no truth, things were what they were. I'd made my vows, chosen my path. No good could come of pipe-dreaming about more.

6

The torn-up card was still lying in the trash the following evening. By rights I shouldn't have seen it, because I shouldn't have been working at all. But I'd swapped nights with Callie on account of one of her military friends being unexpectedly in town. I guess some might say it was fate, or some business about the planets being lined up or whatnot. Personally that kind of hokum doesn't hold any with me. The truth is the cleaner fell sick, so the trash didn't get taken out.

I was still staring at the card when Sal arrived. She banged open the door and I jumped, half from the noise and half from guilt, knocking my purse over on to the dressing table. My make up pots and brushes scattered, some of them plunged to the floor. Cussing under my breath, I lunged for them. Missed.

Sal rushed over, knelt beside me and helped collect up the brushes. Handing them to me she asked, 'You okay?'

I nodded, forcing a smile. 'Sure, honey. Just a little tired.'

'Me too,' Sal grinned.

Plonking the brushes and a handful of pots back on to the dressing table, I turned to get a better look at Sal. Something about her seemed real different. Her skin was flushed and she was grinning wide, like a Cheshire cat on crystal.

I raised an eyebrow.

She snorted, and pulled back the collar of her pink gingham shirt to reveal a hickey.

I shook my head. 'Jesus! Girl what *have* you been doing?'

'Nothing,' she giggled.

'Looks like all kinds of nothing to me.'

She fluttered her lashes, acting all coy. 'It was just a little fun.'

A little fun? Why, that's how it starts out. But later there's always blame and guilt and fighting – at least in my experience. Still, Sal had a plan. She'd dance to pay her way through school, or at least for as long as it took to find a husband with a bit of money. Then she'd live happy ever after.

No matter how many times I told her things just don't work out that way, she wouldn't listen. I knew marriage couldn't get rid of the fear she'd carried ever since her momma's boyfriend did what he did to her. But she was fixed real stubborn on her plan. And who the hell was I to be giving out advice, anyway? I'd lost my cherry on my fifteenth birthday in the back of Thomas Ford's pickup, and then gone and married him. Neither choice did me any favours.

'So tell me,' I said.

She perched on the edge of my dressing table. 'Well, it's this guy, Daryl. He's a real gentleman. Took me to dinner at the Olive Garden, three courses, all proper.'

I nodded. 'And then he tucked in all gentlemanly to your neck?'

She blushed a little deeper. 'Well, I invited him in for coffee, but he declined. He wanted to be respectful an' all. So we had ourselves a goodnight kiss.'

From the state of her neck I'd say a bunch of vampires gave her a goodnight kiss. This Daryl must have been real enthusiastic. 'Sweet. So you're seeing him again?'

Sal's grin widened. 'Yep. Tomorrow night. Dinner and a movie, he said.'

Most guys only got one date with Sal. They'd be keen enough, she was a pretty girl after all, but if she didn't figure they were marriage material, after one date she'd call it quits. Most of them never even made it to first base. 'That's great, honey. I'm real happy for you.'

She giggled in that cutesy-girl way that seems false on most, but on Sal was genuine, and sashayed over to her dressing table, humming a tune. I couldn't guess the song, Sal was tone deaf and sounded like a strangled coyote if she ever tried to sing. Still, she sounded real happy.

I sat back on my chair and fought the urge to pick the card out of the trash. Instead I got to rearranging my pots. I'd always gotten a real sense of satisfaction from the order of my dressing space, but on that night it couldn't distract me. All I could think about were the two halves of the big guy's calling card sitting in the trash, and the fifteen words written on the back: *Call me if you change your mind. I know the truth. I can help you.*

I'd no clue what truth he was meaning, but he'd said he needed my help. Maybe I should call him.

I heard a double knock on the door and Bobby's deep voice said, 'Five minutes for Miss Sally and fifteen for Whiskey.'

Sal was fully made up in her baby-doll get-up: kohl eyes and pink shimmer lipstick, her dark-brown hair in bunches tied with pink ribbons, her bangs hanging low over her eyes. She glanced across at me as she fastened her white satin corset. 'Cutting it close, Lori.'

I stared at her a moment, my mind still thinking on the card and the message.

She waved at me. 'Hey, Earth to Lori, did you hear? Hank said fifteen minutes till your curtain. You can't go out there looking like that.'

That was for sure. Old Hank would never allow me to step on stage in my cut-off jeans, faded Bon Jovi tee, and zero make-up. 'Shit. Guess I'd better move.'

'Finally you listen to me about something,' Sal laughed, and blew me a kiss as she strode to the door.

'Own it,' I said. 'Tits and ass.'

'Like you taught me.'

I smiled and she gave me a little wave as she headed out the door to show her assets to a room of drunken men looking for a flesh fantasy. I'd been playing that part near on three years. I'd learnt every move, every role. Maybe this guy, and the help he needed, would lead to something different.

I leant down and reached into the trash can. With my forefinger I traced the outline of the card, first one half and then the other.

What truth could he tell me, and why did he think we could help each other? My gut told me it was worth knowing, or at least I let myself think that was the reason I decided to call. In hindsight I reckon I had myself fooled. It was plain lust that made me want to see the big guy; lust for the truth and, perhaps, for him. Whatever the real reason, I snatched the two pieces of his calling card from the trash, and thrust them into my purse.

I should've known better.

⥥

Every day Tommy stayed away I felt stronger. Still, I knew it would be foolish to call the number on the card from home. Even if Tommy wasn't there, he was always real suspicious of any numbers that he didn't recognise on the bill, and when he got suspicious things never ended well. So that night, after our shift, when Sal asked if I wanted to get pie over at the all-night diner that'd opened up across the street, I said yes.

She squealed in delight, hooked her arm through mine, and led me out of the dressing room to the back door. 'You're gonna love it, Lori,' she said in that breathless voice of hers. 'They have all kinds of amazing flavours. There's cherry, of course, and candy apple and blueberry, and lemon curd, like they have in England, y'know?'

I nodded. Sal had a thing about accents; her latest crush was the English variety, ever since a group of men in town for a work conference had visited the club and declared her charming. Now everything from England was exciting to her. I smiled. 'So I hear.'

As it was we both ordered cherry pie and black coffee. It was served by a middle-aged waitress wearing a plastic name badge that told us her name was Lindy. Even though it was near on four in the morning she looked fresh and neat in her black slacks and white cotton shirt.

Of the fourteen booths in the diner, only three were occupied. The plastic-coated tables were clean and pre-set, and the music, Elvis and others from that era, helped give the place a retro feel. I couldn't help but wonder if clients of the Bang-Bang Bar ever stopped by on their way home. The two places might be only yards apart, but in taste they were in whole other worlds.

Anyways, once the waitress had delivered our order, Sal leant across the table and said, 'So did that guy visit with you again tonight?'

'Guy?' I said, acting real dumb and taking a bite of pie to give myself an excuse for not saying more.

'Come on, Lori. *That* guy, the one you sat with on your break last night, who you were staring at all soulful.'

I chewed my pie slow. Shook my head.

She sighed. 'Shame. You looked real cute together.'

Cute? I couldn't help but laugh. The stripper and the ... what – PI, cowboy, or something else? Sounded ridiculous. Still, no matter how I'd tried, and truly I had, to put the memory of the big guy and what he'd said away in a box labelled 'fantasy', it wouldn't stick. In my gut I knew I was dumb to attempt it. I was done fighting. 'He gave me his card.'

'Did you call him?' she said between mouthfuls.

I shook my head. 'Not sure I'm gonna—'

'You must.' She stared at the yellowish bruise on my temple. 'Maybe *he's* not coming back this time.'

'We're doing just fine,' I said, my tone way harsher than I'd intended.

She looked away, her cheeks colouring pink.

Damn, I'd upset her. All she'd done was say what I'd been thinking. What maybe I'd been hoping. I glanced down at the table. Sal's plate was empty; all I'd eaten was one mouthful. I pushed my pie across to her as a peace offering. 'I didn't get his name.'

'How could you not?'

'It wasn't that kind of conversation.'

Sal nodded to the payphone over in the corner of the diner. 'So call him and ask.'

I tried not to look fussed. Made out like I'd not clocked the phone as we arrived and been thinking about calling the big guy every minute since. 'I guess I could.'

Sal took a big forkful of my pie, then stared me straight in the eye and said, with her mouth still full, 'What's stopping you?'

I looked away. My gaze fell on the cop over in the far booth, hunched over a newspaper, reading as he shovelled eggs into his mouth. I thought of Tommy, and of that one last almighty fight I'd had with my Pappy. I thought of my empty apartment with the leaky faucet and the smashed pane of glass in my grand-mammy's cabinet. I thought of the life I'd *imagined* I'd be living by the time I'd reached twenty-two, and wondered why I'd let myself settle for so much less. Finally, I thought of my little Ethan, lying in his cot for those few short weeks.

Reaching into my purse, I pulled out the two halves of the card and re-read the message. Figured, what the hell.

I looked back at Sal. 'Nothing.'

She squealed, clapping her hands together like a little kid. 'Oh, Lori.'

'Jesus, girl,' I said, sliding out from the booth. 'You think this is exciting, you should really get out a whole lot more with that Daryl of yours.'

Nine steps across the tiled black-and-white floor of the diner and I reached the payphone. I read the number on the card, then glanced at Sal. She grinned and made a goofy thumbs-up gesture. I turned away, feeling like a fool.

Lifting the receiver, I cradled it in the crook of my neck and punched the numbers on the dial pad. The call clicked through the exchange, there was a pause, then the ringtone began: one ring, two, a third, then a fourth.

It cut off halfway through the fifth repetition. The call answered. I gripped the handset a little tighter. Waited. Heard no breathing, no words. Nothing.

'Hello?' I said.

Silence.

It seemed real odd. Should I hang up, or wait some more? I didn't know. Held my breath and began to count.

I'd gotten to six before he spoke. That gravel-deep voice, both new and familiar, said, 'You know the Little Sugar Diner on the corner of Sixth and Clayton?'

I'd heard of it. 'Sure.'

'Be there in thirty.'

The line went dead. I stared at the phone, my heart thumping against my ribs as I worked out the fastest route. Wrong move. I should have stayed right there, or gone straight home.

But I didn't.

7

Sal went real giddy with excitement when I told her, and didn't mind at all me running out and leaving her. So we said our goodbyes and I went to meet the big guy.

Twenty-seven minutes later, I was sitting on an uncomfortable plastic bench in a four-person booth towards the back of the Little Sugar All-Night Diner, watched by a sour-faced waitress with bad skin and caked-on foundation. I ordered another black coffee, but this time no pie. I was the only customer there.

At four fifty-six, dead on thirty minutes from when he'd put the phone down, the big guy from the bar showed up. He stepped inside, strolled casual as you like towards me, and slid on to the bench seat opposite.

The waitress brought coffee. She smiled at the big guy. I waited until she'd poured his and refilled mine before I spoke.

'So you said you needed my help, and that you could help me too?'

He took a mouthful of coffee, then set the cup back in the saucer and looked straight at me, all intense with those blue eyes of his. 'Your husband skipped bail.'

That I had not expected. Tommy had promised no more trouble. The last DUI had wrecked our car, and our cash flow. I'd worked double shifts to pay the fine. He hated that, and the hate had made him act out real bad. After the bruises faded, and he came over all remorseful, he'd promised it'd never happen again. Like a fool, I'd almost believed him.

I took a gulp of coffee. It scalded my tongue, but it still didn't rid me of the bitter taste in my mouth. Damn son-of-a-bitch. 'What'd he do?'

The big guy said nothing. Watched me for a long moment.

I looked down. Noticed a patch of spilt sugar lying to the right of his elbow. Wanted to brush it away. Couldn't.

The waitress hovered closer, coffee pot in hand. I glared at her. She retreated back to the counter.

The big guy leant forward. 'You do know who he works for, right?'

I shrugged. 'He doesn't have a steady job. Never did. We get by on my wages and his occasional winnings at the tables.'

'Seems your husband hasn't been at all honest about how he gets his cash.'

I snorted. 'Cash? He doesn't have any. The man is always flat broke.'

The big guy frowned. Reaching into the inside pocket of his leather jacket, he pulled out a stack of photos. He flicked the spilt sugar off the table, and spread the pictures out in front of me. 'Do you recognise these people?'

I stared at the images. They were all a bit blurred. Clearly snapped covertly. The first showed Tommy entering a casino; no surprise there. The next couple had him sat at a poker table with a bunch of other men. I guessed from the volume of cards and chips in play that they were mid-game. The last one was different. Tommy and another guy – a man with a dagger-dripping-blood tattoo on his arm, were dragging a grey-haired man, bloodied and helpless, along an alleyway.

I shook my head, pushed the photos away. 'He's a gambler, not a—'

'Isn't he?' The big guy's stare fixed on the bruise in my hairline.

He put another photograph on the table. The grey-haired man cowered beside a heap of garbage bags, his arms raised in a feeble attempt to shield himself. The tattooed man had his foot raised, poised to kick the fallen man in the stomach.

Then the big guy laid down his final picture. My husband was face-on to the camera, his mouth twisted in rage, eyes fixed on his victim. The shot captured the exact moment Tommy's baseball bat had connected with the old man's skull, the fine mist of blood arching from his head captured in the blink of the shutter.

I looked away. The diner seemed to spin around me. I gripped the table, tried not to vomit. 'Who is he?'

'Drayton Millard. He's a small-time salesman and gambler. Had himself a bit of a habit, which was just fine until he stopped settling his account with your husband's employer.'

What the hell was Tommy mixed up in? I swallowed hard, looked at the big guy. 'What happened?'

He tapped the last photo. 'This CCTV picture was taken by a new surveillance camera outside the casino. The local police department had put it there the night before. It got your husband good. He was arrested, bailed, and was due to appear eighteen days ago to answer assault charges.'

'*Was* due?'

The big guy nodded. 'Drayton Millard died in hospital the night before the court date. Your husband must have heard and figured he'd be up for worse than assault. Could have been manslaughter, or maybe the prosecutor would've pushed for homicide. Guess he decided not to find out. He never showed. That made his bondsman real pissed. He called me, asked me to find Thomas Ford and bring him in.'

I frowned. 'What the hell are you, some kind of bounty hunter?'

The big guy nodded.

Well shit. It didn't seem real. My husband worked as a hired thug, and was now a fugitive, with a bounty hunter on his tail? 'You're shitting me, right?'

'I need you to tell me where your husband would have run.'

I shook my head. 'I don't know.'

'You sure about that?'

I stared at my coffee. Didn't speak. Tommy was a slacker for sure. He gambled and drank more than most, and no doubt cheated on me, though he'd always denied it. But homicide? I struggled to process what I'd learned.

'He killed a man. You think he should walk free?'

I glanced at the photos. Shuddered. 'Oftentimes he drinks at the Twisted Wheel, or you could try the poker room over at the Redwood Lounge.'

The big guy shook his head. 'I've been to both, no one's seen him.'

'I can't help you then.' I'd known for a long while that Tommy wasn't a good man, but I'd never have believed he was truly this bad. I touched the bruise on my forehead, reminded myself of his temper. 'Who does he work for?'

'No one you would want to know.' He held my gaze for a beat, then picked the photographs off the table and put them back into his pocket, all apart from the picture of Tommy and the baseball bat. 'I've been tracking your husband for two weeks. He's acted smart, not left much of a trail, kept me a half-step behind him. The thing is, from the pattern he's taken across state, I believe he's coming home.'

My heartbeat accelerated. 'He hasn't been home in weeks.'

'I think he will soon, and when that happens, I need for you to call me.'

'What makes you think I'd do that?'

He held my gaze. 'The way your expression changed when you looked at these pictures. You know what's right, and you know that it isn't your husband.'

I stared at the photo, at the rage on Tommy's face, the bat in his hand smashing into the old guy's head. How could he have changed so much, and how had I not even known? *Till death do us part*, I'd promised in my vows, but how could I live with him, cover for him, knowing what he'd done, and what he might do again?

The big guy looked at me all soulful. 'You can see the kind of man he is now. And that,' he pointed at my bruise, 'is all part of it. Why would you stay with a man like that? What's holding you?'

Good question, one that Sal had asked many times, and my answer had always been the same: I'm married. But there was more to it than that. See, things weren't always this way. The first few years we were together my Tommy didn't drink all that much, and he didn't ever gamble. But when our Ethan was taken from us, he changed. Numb with grief, I guess I'd stayed with him out of habit and, perhaps, in the hope that one day Tommy would stop blaming me for Ethan's death and things would go back to how they'd been before. They never did.

I shook my head. 'I'm not sure anymore.'

He pushed the photo a little closer to me, tapped it with his finger. 'This gives you the chance to do the right thing.'

⥥

I don't know how long we sat there; me staring at the photo, the big guy watching me. I was vaguely aware that the waitress came over to offer us refills, and that the first time the big guy, this bounty hunter, took one, and the second time he said no.

The more I looked at the photo and thought about what Tommy had done, the more convinced I became that I should help. Now I'd learnt the truth of what Tommy had been doing, what he'd become, I could not unlearn it, no matter how much I wanted to. But could I act on this knowledge? Of that I wasn't rightly sure.

Finally, I looked up at the big guy. 'What's your name?'

He smiled. It made him look younger, less world-weary. 'Folks call me JT.'

I nodded. I knew staying with Tommy would never bring back Ethan. I'd known it a long time, really. My baby son was gone, dead in his crib before he was a month old. He'd been buried in the cemetery deep down beneath the white tombstone with the carved teddy bear and the inscription: *Ethan Ford. Blessed this world for twenty-seven days. Taken too soon.*

There was nothing anyone could have done, they'd said. Crib death was like that. But it didn't stop Tommy blaming me, hating me because of it. The anger had twisted the man I'd once loved into someone different. The things Tommy had done – to me, to others, like the man in the photo – meant he'd travelled a long road away from the man, the boy, I'd married back when we were still kids fooling around at life.

I met the big guy, JT's, gaze and said, 'Okay.'

'Appreciate it. All you need do is call me if he comes back home. It's a long shot, but, given the direction he's heading, it's likely he'll visit with you, especially if he thinks you don't know about the charges. If he does show, don't be doing anything yourself. Don't challenge him or provoke him. Just call me.'

I nodded. Glanced at the photo once more. Shivered.

JT reached out, took the photo, and put it into his pocket, his expression all serious. 'Who your husband works for, they're bad people. Things could turn real nasty. You need to be ready to protect yourself.'

I held his gaze. Wondered precisely what it was that he meant by 'turn nasty'. Hoped I would not have to find out. 'Sure.'

That's when he gave me the gun.

8

A week had gone by since my meeting in the diner with JT, and there'd been no sight or sound of my husband. I'd stored that wooden-handled gun in the top-left drawer of my dresser, and tried to forget it was even there. But, no matter how hard I tried, I never could get it out of my mind, just like I couldn't rid myself of the image in the last photo, the one of Tommy dragging a beaten old man into the street like he was a piece of garbage. That image gave me nightmares. The sort that wake you in the dead of night, have you burning hot yet feeling cold, screaming.

So Sal came to stay. She'd said I looked like crap, and she was right. Even my thick stage make-up couldn't hide the dark circles beneath my eyes. Sal told me she'd take care of me, and although I protested a little at first, in the end I agreed. My one condition was that she took the bed. I'd not slept in it since the big guy had shown me the photographs, and, besides, the couch was a better lookout spot.

The night it happened, we made dinner, drank wine and talked about the club. Then, with a laugh and a grin, Sal told me her news. Daryl had proposed. He'd taken her to dinner at a fancy seafood place and ordered the most expensive champagne. She said she'd gone to the bathroom, and when she'd come back and finished her drink, there, in the bottom, was a gorgeous diamond ring. It might have been only a few dates, but she was getting married.

We hugged, and I told her I was happy for her. Still, deep down I couldn't shake off the irony that she was so excited about starting a life with a husband, just as I was helping get mine locked away.

She asked me to be her maid of honour.

⥥

It was almost midnight when I heard him. I hadn't been sleeping, so when I heard the key easing into the front door lock and turning real slow I knew that it was Tommy. It had to be. No one else had a key.

Heart thumping against my chest, I fought the instinct to sink lower into the couch, pull the blankets higher and pretend I wasn't home. It wouldn't help none. I had to make good my promise, call the bounty hunter, have Tommy face his crime.

I heard the lock click, and knew I had to be quick. Sliding off the couch, I padded barefoot across the rug towards the kitchen.

Not fast enough. The door closed, and I heard footsteps in the hallway; work-boots on tile.

I kept going, hurried into the kitchen.

The footsteps stopped. 'Lori, what the hell you doing creeping 'bout in the dark?'

I froze, my butt pressed up against the old oak dresser, my bare legs cold beneath the flimsy cotton of my nightdress. Less than three yards away, I could see the telephone sat on the countertop; JT's cell number was written on the pad beside it.

If I hurried maybe I could reach it before Tommy. My heart rate accelerated, my legs felt weak, unstable. Still, I forced myself to step forward. Had to get to the phone.

Fingers closed around my wrist, yanking me to a halt. 'Damn you, woman, what you up to?'

The light switched on. Tommy pulled me closer to him. He was unshaven. His crumpled shirt was torn across the right shoulder; a dark-red stain spread over one knee of his cargo pants. He looked terrifying. Not because of his unkempt appearance, but because of the expression on his face. I'd seen that look far too many times before. I knew what happened next.

I felt sick. Knew I had to get to the phone. I forced a laugh. 'You had me scared, Tommy. I thought you were someone coming to rob me.'

He looked at me real suspicious, kept a tight hold on my wrist. 'This is *my* home.'

I ignored the sour taste in my mouth, tried to act like I was pissed he'd been gone, that I'd missed him. 'That right? So how come you've not been here for near on a month then?'

'Jesus, woman.' He shook his head, but his tone was softer, his expression less angry. 'Here now aren't I?'

I forced a smile. 'I guess so.'

'Good.' He relaxed his grip on my wrist. I turned to the phone. Knew I had to make my move. Do it fast, before he saw the number.

That's when I heard the creak of the top stair, the one with the busted plank. The one I'd not warned Sal about. Shit.

Tommy wrenched me back to face him. 'What the hell's going on?'

I didn't speak, didn't move.

He took a step towards me. 'You cheating fucking bitch. You got a man here?'

'No. It's—'

The first punch knocked me sideways. The second shoved me back against the wall. I tasted blood in my mouth, swallowed, tried to speak, to tell him it was Sal.

He didn't let me. His hand was around my throat, squeezing. I couldn't breathe.

Tommy didn't care. He forced my legs apart with his knee, his free hand tearing at my panties, yelling, '... bitch. Always knew you were a goddamn whore ... you best remember how a real man feels...'

I tried to shake my head, to tell him he was wrong, but I couldn't. I heard him unbuckle his belt, smelt stale sweat as he pressed himself against me. Felt the pain as he forced himself inside.

He rammed me harder into the wall. I tried to push him away, but my arms felt heavy, my strength gone. I was stuck, unable to fight back, unable to tell the truth. Helpless.

He hit me again.

My vision blurred, my breath sounded tornado-loud in my ears. I could hardly hear Tommy's shouting, but I heard the scream. Could just make out Sal, make-upless, her pink nightshirt swamping her skinny body, standing in the doorway. I felt Tommy's fingers loosen a fraction around my throat. Took a rapid breath.

Heard Sal say, 'Let her go.'

The room was still hazy. I blinked, trying to re-focus.

Tommy didn't move. He smiled, looked amused. 'What, you whores been getting busy? How's about you give me a show. A nice bit of girl-on-girl to—'

'Let her go, or I'm calling the cops.' Sal had her cell phone in her hand. 'I mean it.'

Tommy's expression changed. Not amused any longer, furious. 'Don't you fucking—'

'I'm dialling now,' she said, pressing three numbers – 911. 'It's on speaker.'

'You little bitch.' Tommy let me go.

I collapsed against the wall, gasping for air. And saw Tommy reach beneath his jacket.

He pulled out a gun.

Sal's eyes widened.

I froze, slid halfway down to the floor, still breathless.

Tommy pointed the gun at Sal. 'Hang up.'

She shook her head. Bravest thing I ever saw.

'Don't do this Tommy,' I said, my voice croaky, weak. I took a wobbly step towards him, reached out.

He shrugged me away. Kept staring at Sal. 'Fucking bitch.'

I grabbed his arm, trying to pull his gun hand down. 'Please, don't.'

For a brief moment he glanced at me. Anger had contorted his features into the exact same expression he'd had in the photo the big guy had shown me. Tommy raised the gun, smacked me on the side of the head. I felt myself falling.

On Sal's cell phone speaker, the ringing stopped. A nasal voice bounced off the kitchen walls. 'Nine one one, can you tell me the nature of your emergency?'

The gun fired. My eyes closed. Everything faded to black.

9

Blood. Sticky, hot, blood. That's the thing I remember most.

As I blinked back into consciousness I saw Sal. She lay on her back, arms outstretched, broken cell phone beside her, her eyes staring at me, unfocused.

'Sal?' My voice rasped in my throat. 'Oh Jesus.'

My head throbbed. My vision was blurred, still hazy. I remember crawling over to her. Those few yards felt like a hundred miles.

The blood pooled on the tiled floor, slippery beneath my hands and knees. I watched it gush from her chest, the crimson stain spreading across the pink fabric of her nightshirt. There was so much, too much, impossible to stop or replace. I had to try though, and I tried real hard. Pressed my fists against the wound. 'Sal? Say something. Please, honey...'

She looked real pale, eyes darting side to side.

I kept the pressure on her wound, watched the blood oozing through my fingers. I think I was crying, but all I can remember hearing was that sound, the wheezing, gurgling.

She tried to talk but failed. Tried to breathe. Failed.

I stared at her. She was so still, unnaturally so. I knew that she was gone. Felt the panic building in my chest, like I was suffocating.

'Sal? You can't—'

'Lori, get up.' Not Sal's voice, but a man. Tommy.

I turned. Saw the gun in his hand. That's when I remembered. 'You did this.'

He pointed the gun at my head. 'Get up, and fetch me those savings you got stashed.'

I looked away. Stared at Sal, her beautiful face lifeless. At my hands, pressed into the hole in her chest, her blood staining my fingers red. 'Tommy? I … Sal's…'

'Leave that whore, and get me the cash.' Cussing, he stepped around the pool of blood, grabbed my hair with one hand and pressed the muzzle of the gun against my cheek. 'Don't make me shoot you too.'

I didn't move. Couldn't. Kept staring at Sal, willing her to breathe again, for her eyelids to flutter, for any sign that she wasn't dead.

'Fucking bitch.' Tommy yanked my hair, pulling me to my feet. 'Get the fucking money.'

I shoved him away with my bloodied hands.

He stepped back, surprised. Hadn't reckoned on me standing up to him. His free hand curled into a fist.

I didn't cower this time, I held my ground, even though my legs were like jello, and my head felt as if it were splitting in two. My whole body was shaking, so was my voice. 'She's just gotten engaged, and you…' I looked back at Sal. 'You, killed her. For what?'

'Yeah, yeah.' He lunged forward, grabbed me. 'The money. Now.'

I heard sirens. Guessed that the neighbours had heard the gunshot, called 911.

'Fuck.' Tommy glanced at the window. Blue-and-white lights danced across the glass. He flung me away from him, moved towards the kitchen door.

I tried to stop him. Lost my balance, fell, landed heavy on my knees. Pain vibrated through my bones. Glared up at him. 'You'll *never* get away with this.'

He kept the gun pointed at me. Opened the door. 'You stupid, disobedient bitch, this isn't over.'

I watched him disappear out into the night. 'No,' I whispered. 'It ain't.'

10

Tommy killing Sal hadn't been the end. The cops might not have found him, but it wasn't over. It couldn't be. I made damn sure of that.

After the crying and the burying I knew what had to get done. I'd spent every moment of the funeral replaying Sal's death in my mind: the gunshot, the blood, Tommy. It was curse-to-hell wrong. Sickeningly, agonisingly wrong. I had to get her some justice.

I left the service as dirt started falling on her coffin. Couldn't look at her Daryl's grief-stricken face, or listen to her momma's wailing for a moment longer. I'd taken all that I could of the hymns and prayers and bullshit about Sal being at peace. How could she be, with Tommy still free? I needed to move, to act, to *do* something. So I left them at the graveside and hurried towards the exit.

JT stood smoking under the stone archway that framed the gates to the cemetery.

I wanted to say something, but the still intensity of his expression stopped me. He was concentrating – on what I wasn't sure. Perhaps a memory, a puzzle, a plan? Whatever it was, it made him look real unreachable. He might have been standing just ten yards away, but the distance felt more like ten hundred miles.

Then he looked my way, and smiled. 'You doing okay?'

I stared into those vivid blue eyes of his. 'What do you think? She's dead.'

'I'm sorry.' He took another drag on his cigarette, then threw it on the ground, crushing it beneath his heel. 'She seemed like a good kid.'

I looked away, pissed at his understatement, furious at the tears in my eyes. Across the cemetery I could see the mourners moving away from Sal's grave, heading towards the parking lot. I turned back to JT.

'She was my *friend*. Now she's dead and that bastard's still out there. It's my fault. She had a life, y'know? She could've—'

'Don't.' He stepped towards me, pulled me close, his arms tight around me as if shielding me from the world, just for a moment. That was the first time he held me. 'You didn't cause it. He did. You and her are both victims here.'

A victim? Shit. I'd played that role for long enough. I felt the anger, the grief building inside me until it felt as if I could hardly breathe. Shoving my fists against his chest, I pushed him away. I wouldn't be this broken, beaten girl for one minute longer. 'I'm done being a victim.'

He looked at me for a long moment.

I held his gaze. 'Teach me.'

He frowned. 'Teach you about what?'

'Bounty hunting. I don't want that fucker going free. I want to find him and take him to the cops. Get Sal some kind of justice.'

JT was silent. Looked like he was considering it real hard.

I put my hand on his arm. 'Please. I need this.'

He exhaled hard. 'I can't, Lori. You have to know that.'

I shook my head. Couldn't believe he was refusing me. 'Can't or won't?'

'I work alone.'

I blinked back the tears. Wouldn't let him see me cry. Hardened my tone as I said, 'That's too bad. I thought you were a better man than that.'

I turned and walked away.

⇓

Four days later I found him sitting on my stoop.

I'd just gotten home from work. It was late; well, early – almost four in the morning – and I was dog-tired. Still, when he raised a bottle of bourbon in greeting, and gave me that lopsided smile of his, I nodded and invited him inside.

JT sat down at my kitchen table as I fetched the glasses. The room felt smaller with him in it. Intimate. I put the glasses on the table and watched him pour the bourbon. Waited for him to speak first.

He pushed one of the glasses towards me. 'So how've you been?'

How could I answer that? My husband had killed my best friend. It felt as if my world had imploded. 'Angry. Tired. Wanting justice.'

JT nodded. 'That's natural enough.'

'I wasn't looking for your reassurance.'

'Well, I'm giving it anyways.'

I looked at my glass. Took a gulp of the bourbon. Savoured the burn.

'You're back at work then?' he asked.

'Yeah.'

'That's good.'

'Is it?'

'I'm guessing so.'

Small talk didn't suit JT. It wasn't his style; it made him seem awkward, his manner forced. I was tired. Couldn't be doing with it. So I drained my glass and looked at him straight. 'What are you doing here?'

'I wanted to check in on you. Be sure you were okay.'

Not to help me find Tommy and get some justice for Sal, then. 'Is that all?'

'Lori, look—'

'No, don't.' I pushed back my chair. Stood up and handed him the bottle of bourbon. 'If you're not going to train me, why bother coming back?'

'You know I can't train you.'

I sighed. 'Then leave.'

He got to his feet. Stepped real close to me. The look on his face was real earnest.

I felt my breath catch in my throat.

That was the second time he held me. It felt different, and ended up differently too. I can't remember which one of us kissed the other first, but I do know that it was me who took his hand and led him up the stairs.

I should've known better.

⇓

By the fifth time he showed up on my front porch, I knew I'd got feelings for him. I hadn't meant to. Knew it would have been simpler if it was just about the sex, but it didn't work out that way. Our history might have been short, but it was charged with pain and desire; a mixture as volatile as dynamite, and one doomed to blow up sometime, that was for sure.

We were lying in bed when I asked him. My back pressed up against the warmth of his chest; his arms tight around me. 'What's going on here?' I murmured.

'How'd you mean?'

I turned to face him. 'With us.'

He stayed silent a moment. His expression gave away nothing about what he was thinking. I wanted to know what was going on in his mind. Felt anxiety flutter in my chest.

'I've been thinking,' he said to the ceiling, 'I should train you.'

I hadn't expected that. The fluttering in my chest became a fight. 'Why?'

'Because that's what you want.'

He was right; I did want that. But it wasn't an answer to the question I'd just asked him. 'What changed your mind?'

He smiled. Kissed me on the tip of my nose. 'You, Lori. You did.'

I felt uneasy. Back-footed. 'How do you figure on it working?'

'Come stay with me. I'll train you, and we'll find Tommy. Then afterwards, I'll go back to working alone.'

I'd been talking about the thing between us, the sex and the feelings, and where the hell was it leading, if it was leading to any place at all. But now he was offering me the chance to find Tommy, to get Sal justice. I couldn't ignore it. And him asking me to go stay with him, that had to be a good thing, a step forward. So I said, 'Deal.'

And tried not to think on what would happen afterwards.

⇓

I was a quick study. I did all that JT instructed, and followed his teaching exactly. I learnt how to investigate a person; how to profile them, finding their behaviour patterns and their weaknesses, and using that knowledge to gain the advantage. I read up on the law, discovered what I had to do to bring someone in legally, and watched how JT applied those rules in the field. But most challenging of all, I had to toughen up. Get match fit. Make myself so familiar with the tools – cuffs, taser, gun – they felt like they were part of me. I learnt how to defend myself, how to stand my ground, and when to close in on the target.

I moved into JT's cabin. Kept practising hard, pushing myself until I thought I might die from exhaustion. And, in a way, I kind of did. In fact, Jennifer Lorelli Ford died right then. I changed my name by deed poll, created a new identity all of my own; not Thomas Ford's wife, not my parents' daughter, just me. I dropped the Jennifer, legally shortened my middle name to the one I'd always preferred using, and picked one of the most common family names in America. From then on I was Lori Anderson, Bounty Hunter.

I memorised JT's rules, and all that he taught me about the business, the law, and the tracking techniques he used. But, although I had my new name, and with his help was quickly building myself a new life, there was something else I needed before I could properly move on.

We kept hunting for Tommy. The bail bond forfeiture period might have long since expired, but this had gotten personal for the both of us. Tommy couldn't be allowed to get away with what he'd done to Sal, he just couldn't. Still, finding him proved far harder than I'd hoped. So I went out on other jobs with JT, kept training until my target shooting was near perfect; and when I felt the burn on those long runs JT was so fond of, instead of wanting to give up I'd grit my teeth and push on through the pain.

Somewhere along the line, things changed.

Me and JT, us working together, was only ever meant to be a temporary deal. He'd told me that right from the get-go, and I listened, surely I did. I told myself not to get comfortable. Knew that what we had

– the work, the sex – was just for now and there were no guarantees for the future. But that didn't save me from falling real hard.

It wasn't smart, not at all, and I knew it. As the weeks blurred into months, and JT said nothing more about our arrangement being time limited, I started to believe, to hope, that we *could* have a future.

Like I said, not smart.

It took us near on five months to get a firm lead. One of the dirt-bags Tommy oftentimes partnered with was spotted by a contact of JT's visiting some lodge out in a real remote area of country. JT felt certain he'd have something on Tommy. We just needed to make him talk.

We geared up for a fast pick-up: double-checking our go-bags, keeping our rigs stowed in the trucks instead of hanging on their nails in the kit room, and then we waited. JT's contact would call us just as soon as the douche returned to the lodge.

Two days later, we got the call. It was late, near on midnight, and I'd just told JT that I didn't want what we had, whatever you might call it, to end; I wanted our temporary deal to become more permanent.

When the cell phone rang, I could tell JT was relieved. Not that he'd said as much, but I saw it in his expression. He didn't respond to what I'd told him, instead he nodded towards the cell and said, 'It's time. Saddle up, kiddo.'

⥥

We took both trucks. I followed JT from the cabin, along the winding forest road and out on to the freeway. I tried not to feel mad at him for not responding to my honesty. Hated how insecure not knowing what he thought made me feel. I knew I had to focus on the job, on this douche who might have information on Tommy's whereabouts, and that I had to put my personal feelings aside. JT had told me how dangerous it was to let feelings cloud your judgement, that when emotions took over things oftentimes turned bad. I'd listened, and nodded in the right places, but I'd never really understood. Right then, though,

I got it; JT stayed unattached and remote so he'd never be unfocused. I thought back to him not answering me, and wondered at what little hope I had.

The journey took a while. We'd been travelling a couple of hours, maybe a little longer, when JT took a sharp turn off the freeway. I followed. After a few miles, I saw JT's brake lights flare, and watched him turn across the road and on to a gravel track. I stopped on the road, pulling in tight against the trees, and killing my lights. Stared through the gloom at the sign beside the track: Big Mo's Fishing Shack.

In the distance, I spotted a line of wooden lodges, evenly spaced around a large lake. I knew the type of place Mo's would likely be: a hunting getaway, the type city folk use when they need a weekend of shooting up shit, catching fish and drinking beer. What with it being out of season, all the lodges looked empty, aside from the one sitting furthest from the highway. That one had a light on inside.

I watched the lights on JT's truck go dark as he crawled it closer towards the lodge. My heart thumped in my chest, and I felt almost dizzy from the adrenaline. I was JT's back-up, I had to be sure the douche didn't get away. I got out of my car and sprinted along the gravel track.

The moon was full and high that night, and for that I was thankful. By its light, I watched JT park up by the occupied lodge, get out, and approach it on foot, fast.

I ran quicker, counting down the seconds since JT had disappeared inside: five, ten, fifteen. It felt like a lifetime. Given what he knew of the douche's previous form, he'd have taken a covert approach, searching each room by stealth. JT always told me that surprise could beat firepower eight times out of ten.

After twenty-five seconds, I reached the lodge. I stopped, listening hard.

Silence.

I crept around back. Stayed alert, knew the drill. JT always said there was a whole lot more chance of capturing a target if you had someone guarding the exit.

So I stood in the bushes bordering the lodge's yard. Waiting. Behind me, I could hear the water from the lake lapping against the bank. The highway, a way off to my right, was empty. On the other side of the lodge, trees stretched out into the distance. I wondered if there were bears.

That's when I heard him.

A couple of thuds against the frame of the small window on the far left of the lodge, and the douche had gotten it wide enough to crawl through. He eased himself out, feet first, and slid down on to the dirt. He hadn't seen me waiting in the scrub.

As I watched him scramble to his feet, I reached into my holster and drew my Wesson Commander Classic Bobtail. I didn't want to think on how he'd gotten clear of JT. Heart pounding, I stepped out of the scrub, into the moonlit yard. 'Stop, you're surrounded.'

He froze.

I felt crazy sick. Knew all the bad things this douche had been into, all the evil he was capable of. I couldn't let him escape. 'Now raise your hands and turn around real slow.'

The douche turned. He squinted at me, all confused.

'I said raise your hands where I can see them.'

He didn't raise his hands; he laughed. 'What the hell you doing?'

I exhaled hard, as if I'd taken a roundhouse kick to the chest. Felt dizzy. Told myself to hold it together. I had to; the douche was Tommy.

I pointed my gun square at his chest and forced myself to meet his gaze. 'I'm taking you to jail.'

He shook his head. Started walking towards me. 'Don't point that thing at me, you ain't gonna use it.'

'I will,' I said, hating the way my voice trembled, fighting the urge to run. 'You gotta pay for what you did to Sal.'

He stopped, but kept grinning, as if me holding a gun on him was no big deal. Shook his head. 'Jesus. You still bleating over that two-bit prick tease? Shit, woman, you—'

'Don't call her that.' I kept the gun pointed at him, tried to ignore that it was shaking. Told myself I could do this, it was what I'd been training for. I had to bring Tommy in, for Sal, and for me. I dug my heels into the dirt. Held my ground.

He laughed again. 'You won't shoot me. I'm your husband.'

I glanced toward the lodge, wondered where the hell JT had gotten to. 'We're getting a divorce.'

Tommy's grin faded. 'We ain't. You're mine, and you gonna stay that way, y'hear? Some little whore bleeding out on our floor ain't doing nothing to change that.'

I felt the rage building inside me. He didn't give a damn about what he'd done. 'She was a sweet kid who didn't—'

Tommy stepped towards me. 'Shit, woman. You saying I'm a liar?'

I glanced again towards the lodge; still no sign of JT. I felt the panic rising in my chest. I didn't have long; if Tommy reached me I'd be in real trouble, unless I could get him cuffed. I had to think fast, plan my next move as I was talking. 'Yes, I am. You've been lying to me almost our whole marriage. I've seen the photos, I know what you really did at the casinos.'

He frowned. Looked deflated, suddenly less threatening. It reminded me of how he'd looked after Ethan's death, as if the life had been sucked clear out of him. 'Well, shit. I didn't want to believe it, but it's true.' His tone was softer, sadder. 'You're the one helping that goddamn bounty hunter?'

'Yes I am.' There was too much pride in my voice, and you know what folks say about that. I reached back to unclip my cuffs from my rig. Lowered my gun a fraction. 'And now I'm taking you to—'

'Dumb fucking bitch.' He reached behind him, pulled a gun from the waistband of his pants, swung it towards me. 'You're going to—'

I didn't think, just pure reacted. Dropping the cuffs, I raised my gun and pulled the trigger. Kept pulling it until every bullet was spent.

Tommy dropped to the ground, his body jerking as each bullet hit. I knew he was dead, he had to be, but I still expected him to put a hand out to break his fall. He didn't. Just lay there, blood seeping out on to the dirt.

I kept the gun pointed right at him, shaking.

'Put the gun down, Lori.'

I heard what JT said, but I couldn't move, felt frozen.

Footsteps. Then his voice again. Closer. 'Lori?'

I felt JT's hand on my arm. Flinched.

'It's okay. Give me the gun.'

I let him take it. Noticed he'd gotten his own weapon, a Glock, in his other hand, along with a pair of cuffs. A voice in my head, which sounded nothing like my own, told me that he may as well put the cuffs away. Dead men don't struggle.

I stared at Tommy, lying all crumbled like a bloodied rag in the dirt, his fingers still curled around his gun. The same gun he'd killed Sal with, the one he'd have shot me with too.

I started to shake, couldn't help it. I'd killed a man. Not any man, my husband. And yet, although my body was reacting, inside I felt nothing. I was numb, like it wasn't real.

JT took hold of my shoulders, turned me towards him. 'You're in shock. It'll pass.'

But I wasn't. Tommy dying, that wasn't the kind of justice I'd been looking for. Death had been too easy for him. I'd wanted to follow JT's rules, to take Tommy to the cops, and for him to do his time.

'Lori, you hear me?'

I looked into JT's eyes. Couldn't find the words to explain. Nodded.

After that, JT didn't say anything. He took command of the situation – damage control I guess you'd call it. I didn't argue. It was my fault he'd been put in this situation, the least I could do was not bitch about it.

After we'd removed any traces of our being at the lodge, he carried Tommy's body through the trees. I followed with the shovel. I don't know how long we walked, but when JT put Tommy down I started to dig.

He took the shovel from me. 'Let me.'

I watched JT dig the hole, deep down in the earth, a place to bury my husband's body. I wanted to feel something: fear, relief, regret, anything. But I didn't. Sal was still gone. Tommy being dead hadn't made a damn difference.

I helped JT roll Tommy into the hole. He fell awkwardly on to the damp soil, his arm twisted behind him, his neck bent back. I felt glad. He didn't deserve comfort, not even in his final resting place. He'd gunned down Sal as she tried to help me, like she was nothing, an inconvenience. I kicked at the mound of dirt, pushing it into the hole. Then I turned away, shivered, cold to my bones despite the mugginess of the night.

JT shovelled the earth over Tommy's body.

When he'd finished, the soil packed down beneath our feet and a scattering of leaves pushed over the spot, JT turned to me. 'I shouldn't have let him get away from me. He got in a lucky punch as I got my cuffs out, dazed me a while.'

I shook my head. 'Don't you do that. This wasn't your fault. When Sal died, you told me I wasn't to blame and you were right. But this tonight, it's on me.'

'You didn't need to kill him.'

'He went for his gun, he was going to—'

'And I taught you better than that. You could have disabled him – taken out his gun hand, if you'd wanted to.'

I thought about Sal, about the hateful things Tommy had said about her, and how he wasn't at all sorry for what he'd done. In that moment I'd hated him, despised him; felt white-hot fury pump through my veins.

I stared back at JT. Knew there was no point me trying to explain my actions. My mentor was real strict on his eighth rule: *Force only as necessity, never for punishment.* So I nodded and said, 'I could have.'

'But you didn't.'

I'd let him down. I heard the disappointment in his voice. Saw the sadness in his eyes. I felt like a wayward child being scolded. 'No, I didn't.'

He touched my face, gently raising my chin so I had to look him in the eyes. 'Then your training's finished. As of right now, we just need to be done.'

I saw it then. The way he looked at me, it was stone cold. Whatever he might have felt for me before was now gone. I knew the problem wasn't that I'd shot Tommy, or even that I'd taken away JT's chance to collect on the bond percentage. It was because I'd broken his rules, every damn one of them. And it seemed he couldn't forgive me for that.

I pulled away from him, blinking away tears. Whispered, 'Okay, sure.'

His sigh was barely audible.

I'd never felt more alone.

11

I had walked out of JT's life that night. Hadn't allowed myself as much as a glance in the rear-view mirror. We were done, that much had been clear; no sense in kidding myself things would change. And the more I thought on it, the more I believed he'd never had any real feelings for me; that's why he'd always dodged the subject. All he ever cared for was his job.

For a long while I'd been angry. Angry at him, but angrier at myself. I vowed I'd never let myself fall hard that way again. I'd have no contact. Move on. And for ten years I'd held firm on that vow. Right up to the moment I kicked in the door at that godforsaken ranch house in West Virginia and saw him tied to a chair in the centre of the room.

He kept on staring right at me.

My heart pounded against my ribs. I couldn't look away.

I heard a crash from the front of the house. A reminder. Focus. This was a job. Nothing more. It was all about the here and now – about collecting JT from Merv and taking him back to Florida. About getting the bond percentage so I could pay those final demands on Dakota's medical bills. I'd no time for any trips down memory lane.

Pushing aside the remains of the door panel, I climbed through the gap and into the room. As I approached the chair and JT, the splintered wood crunched beneath my boots.

I looked JT straight in the eye and said, 'Robert James Tate, I'm authorised to take you into custody and deliver you back to the State of Florida for your summary judgement.'

He chuckled, like what I'd said was real funny, and glanced down at the rope securing him. 'You gonna liberate me then?'

I didn't reply. Instead I used the knife I'd taken from Gunner to slice the top coil of rope binding JT to the chair. Reaching around him, I tugged the rope free.

'Get up,' I said, taking hold of his elbows and pulling him to his feet.

Damn he was big: six foot three and a whole lot of muscle. He towered over me, standing so close, I could feel the heat of his body. Too close. I stepped back.

He smiled. 'Just like old times.'

Personally, I preferred to leave the old times right where they were buried: back with ancient history and a good six feet of dirt. Unfortunately, it seemed the present had developed a nasty way of digging up the part of my life I wanted to keep hidden. 'We need to get out of here.'

He held out his hands, still bound by a thick weave of rope. 'Would you mind?'

Yes. I would. 'You're a fugitive. That rope stays.'

He shrugged. Even in the dim light I could see that the years had been kind. He still had that shaggy cut, dirty-blond hair, now with a touch of grey at the temples. Aside from that he looked as fit as he ever had.

I picked up the rope now lying slack across the chair. If Gunner and his boys were getting restless I'd need to rope and tie them. I glanced back at JT, my expression serious, professional. 'Follow me. Don't try to run.'

We climbed through the busted door and into the hallway. I could hear movement in the front room, like something heavy was being dragged across the floor. Could be they were moving furniture, blocking our exit, setting up for a fight.

I trod light as I could along the hall. JT kept close and quiet, just as I'd asked. We reached the doorway to the front room. Keeping my back pressed against the wall, I peered inside.

The shabby furniture hadn't moved; there was no barricade. The pup was still out cold. Gunner was cussing, secured by the plasticuffs. It was Weasel-face who had moved. He was leaning against the wall now, a few yards away from me, and was using his left hand to help his balance while the right hung lose behind his back. The scuffing sound must have been him dragging his beat up leg across the floor. It would have been agony with that busted knee. I wondered why he'd done it.

As I stepped into the room, Weasel-face grinned. His mistake: that's a warning sure as a poker player's tell. I saw the muscles in his right arm tense, noticed the knife from his belt was missing. I didn't hesitate, didn't think. It was him or me, and I was going to make damn sure which. I threw my knife, hard and straight. It buried itself up to the hilt in his right bicep. Yowling, Weasel-face dropped the hunting knife.

If these guys were friends of Merv's looking for a fast buck, they were gonna be real disappointed. I'd be telling Quinn how they had been more Wild West than modern-day professionals. Holing up in a house with their fugitive, refusing me access when I'd been invited to collect, now that just wasn't how business got done. Yet, still the thought nagged me – whatever kind of hicks they were, the way they'd attacked me made no kind of sense.

I looked at JT. 'Who the hell are these people?'

He shook his head. Looked away.

Gunner was safe, the plasticuffs and the shoulder wound saw to that. The pup was no threat right now, but soon as he woke, the others might send him after us. Weasel-face was bleeding and looked real pale. He'd gotten my knife out of his arm, but he wouldn't be going anyplace in a hurry. Still, I needed to be sure.

I strode across the room and kicked both knives out of Weasel-face's reach. 'Go join your friend,' I said, nodding to the pup.

Weasel-face glared at me. Said nothing.

I heard footsteps behind me. JT. He towered over Weasel-face. 'Do as the lady asks.'

Cursing and puffing, Weasel-face dragged himself across to the pup. I tried not to take too much offence that he'd obeyed the command of a shackled man rather than the woman who'd just whipped his sorry ass. I bound him and the pup together nice and tight with the rope they'd used to hold JT. Kind of poetic justice, I thought.

I glanced at JT. 'Let's go.'

He nodded, but instead of following me to the door he walked over to where Gunner sat. Gunner's lips curled back in a snarl. Crouching down, JT reached into Gunner's shirt pocket and removed a pack of cigarettes and a silver Zippo. 'Mine, I think.'

I recognised that lighter.

'We'll find you. And that bitch,' Gunner spat.

JT leant closer to him. 'Like I said before: you tell your boss I've got information. I'll trade, if he gives his word this can end more civilised.'

Gunner laughed. 'You can go to—'

JT slammed both his fists into the side of Gunner's head. Surprise flitted across the man's face, then he dropped, unconscious, to the floor.

⇓

Outside, we ran across the hard-baked earth to the truck. I unlocked the doors as we approached. Opening the driver door, I called to Dakota. 'You okay, sweetie?'

She sat up, grinning. 'I killed the boss monster and saved the Platinum Planet. I'm on level thirty-nine now.'

'Good job. Now can you jump out real fast and scoot around to the front seat?'

Her gaze shifted, focusing on the figure just behind me. Her eyes widened. 'Is that—'

'Honey, into the front.'

This time she did as I asked, but I was uncomfortably aware of the glances she kept taking at JT.

I opened the door to the travel cage behind the driver's seat, and nodded to JT. 'Get in.'

He frowned. 'Why's the kid here?'

'It's no business of yours,' I said, nodding towards the open door. 'Don't make me gag you.'

JT stared at Dakota. Then, shrugging, he met my gaze. 'Whatever you reckon you gotta do, Lori.'

He climbed into the security cage with its tight-woven wire mesh and Plexiglas divider between the cab and his seat. I'd invested in this particular truck because it was the best for fugitive transport. I'd heard the horror stories of prisoners getting free during transit and strangling the driver, and the less violent but disgusting experiences of fugitives peeing on or spitting at the bounty hunter riding in the front. The Plexiglas screen prevented both kinds of problem, and with Dakota along for the trip, I was even more thankful for it. Not that I thought JT would do any of those things. But the fact was, I wasn't prepared to take the risk.

Sat inside the security cage, JT held his roped hands out to me. 'You going to remove this now?'

'Sure.' I took the back-up set of plasticuffs from my belt and snapped them around his wrists. Not so tight as to chafe, not so loose he could slip out of them. Once they were secure, I undid the rope and smiled. 'Better?'

He nodded. 'Played real nice.'

Pretending to ignore the compliment, I reached across and belted him in, adhering to passenger safety and all that. Last thing you need in this game is a civil action against you for putting your fugitive in danger during transport, and we had a hell of a lot of miles to cover. 'What's that you said to the guy inside – about information you've got for Merv?'

He shook his head. 'Don't matter.'

It mattered to me, but right then my priority was to get us out of there. I slammed the door and climbed into the driver's seat. Dakota was still playing on my cell, her thumbs hammering the touchscreen as she shot up alien spaceships and the like.

'Belt up, honey.'

She glanced up at me and frowned. 'What happened, Momma? Your lip's bleeding.'

I touched my mouth, felt the dried blood against my fingers. 'Nothing, sweetie.'

Dakota turned and looked at JT, her eyes narrowed. She leant closer to me and whispered, 'Did *he* do it?'

I forced a laugh. 'No. A little trouble with a naughty dog is all.'

Her eyes widened. 'Does it hurt?'

'I'm fine, really.'

She nodded. So trusting. I felt like shit for lying to her.

As Dakota fastened her belt I took the cell. The battery was almost out, the icon flashing red on the screen. Damn. Less than five percent left. At least, finally, I'd gotten a signal. One bar. I texted Quinn: *01:08 Tate acquired. On way back.*

Firing up the engine, I smiled at Dakota and shifted the gear into drive. The next thirteen hours could not pass quickly enough.

12

I sped away from Yellow Rock Ranch, bumping down that dirt drive and out on to the highway with my foot flat on the gas pedal and the speedometer needle fixed at bat-shit crazy. I wanted miles between us and that place, and plenty of them.

The highway was pitch-dark, the only light coming from the truck's headlamps. Still I pressed the gas as hard as I dared, clinging tight to the wheel and trying to stay focused on the road. It was tough. Dakota wouldn't stop staring at JT.

'Eyes to the front, sweetie,' I said. 'Don't look at him. And plug the cell into the charger, okay? It's nearly out of juice.'

She rolled her eyes. 'But, Momma—'

'Plug it in. It's not good to keep staring at that little screen for hours, anyway. It'll make you sick.'

Dakota looked back at JT. 'Hello, Mister. I'm Dakota.'

Glancing in the rear-view mirror, I watched for his reaction.

JT smiled. He raised his bound hands to his forehead in a strange kind of salute. 'Well, hello yourself, kiddo. It's real nice to meet you. But I'm thinking you look a little young to be a bounty hunter like your momma here.'

She thrust out her chin a little ways. 'I'm nine. That's plenty old enough.'

He looked at the mirror, met my gaze. 'Nine years old, huh? Is that right...?'

I stared at the road ahead. Pushed the Silverado harder; the engine roared. I knew he was watching me. Could feel his eyes on the back of my neck.

I turned the volume of the radio higher. An old Tammy Wynette tune played. As she sang about standing by your man I glanced at JT again. Sometimes standing by is the opposite of what should be done. Some things can't be fixed; they're just too broken.

Dakota sighed. Twisting further round in her seat she smiled at JT. 'So, how old are you?'

'Honey,' I said, my tone serious. 'Stop.'

She leant closer to me. 'He doesn't look so bad. What did he do?'

I gripped the wheel as I swung the truck around a hairpin bend. The highway was a little wider here, but I was mindful that to the right of us the ground fell steep away for a good eighteen feet. 'That's no concern of yours.'

JT cleared his throat. 'I tried to take a bad man to jail.'

I glanced at him in the rear-view mirror, caught his eye. 'Be quiet.'

Dakota frowned. 'But you said he was a bad man, Momma. How can *he* be a bad man if he tried to take a bad man to jail, isn't that what you do?'

'What I do is different, honey.'

She tilted her head to one side. 'How so?'

Shit. 'Enough with the questions.'

JT smiled. 'Your Momma was always like this when she was younger. Never answered a question straight. Always firing back a question of her own or using that smart mouth of hers to out-talk you.'

I stepped harder on the gas, jerked the truck around the next bend. Felt a touch of satisfaction as the movement lurched JT off balance, his shoulder banging against the side of the Plexiglas cage. Glared at him in the rear-view mirror. 'I said for *you* to be quiet, too.'

Dakota ignored me. 'How do you know what my Momma was like when she was young?'

JT chuckled. 'You're real curious aren't you kiddo?'

'Enough,' I said. Keeping one hand on the wheel I used the other to take hold of Dakota's shoulder and push her back to face the front.

She wriggled out of reach, turning back to JT. 'So tell me more about—'

'I said no more talking.' I looked sternly at Dakota, tried again to catch hold of her shoulder.

JT banged on the Plexiglas. 'Lori! The road.'

I turned. Saw the bobcat as it leapt out from the trees on the higher ground to our left, its eyes illuminated by the beams of our headlamps as it darted across the highway.

'Shit.' I yanked the wheel hard right, missing the animal by inches. The truck lurched across the blacktop, wheels screeching as the vehicle swung right-left-right. I wrestled the wheel, trying to get back control.

We were going too fast. The hill was too steep. The bend too tight.

I tugged the wheel. The truck's front end turned, but the back swung wide. Ahead the road continued on, but our momentum carried us sideways. The back tyres dropped off the blacktop, first one then the other. The wheel bucked beneath my hands. I couldn't hold it. The front of the truck slid off the highway. The tyres hit dirt, rocks, whatever was between the road and the riverbank and for a moment time seemed to slow. Then gravity took us, plunging us backwards until we hit a tree.

The truck pitched on to its side. The force flung us right, twisting us round until we were facing down the mountainside again. Five milliseconds of flight before the seatbelt ripped at my neck.

'Momma!' Dakota shrieked.

I heard the crack as my baby's head hit the side window.

In the light from the headlamps I glimpsed the river below us, the water flowing black in the moonlight, white foam dancing along the surface. Then the truck flipped on to its back. The roof hit the bank. The windscreen shattered. The belt bit into my stomach. My knees hit the steering column and I cried out in pain. I heard JT groan behind me. Dakota stayed silent.

The truck kept moving, sliding like an upturned beetle down the bank with rocks and tree roots pummelling the roof. We hit something solid. The impact stalled us, and for a moment I thought it was over. Then we flipped again.

My life didn't flash before me, and I didn't see a bright light. Only one thought repeated in my mind as I waited for the ground to hit.

Please. Don't let her die.

13

His voice woke me. So distant at first I thought I was dreaming. Remembering. My neck ached, my pulse thumped at my temples. I heard his voice again, closer this time, more urgent.

'JT?' My voice sounded strange, my breath loud and rasping in my ears.

'Lori. Are you hurt? Can you move?'

The air tasted of burnt rubber and gasoline, acrid on my tongue. I coughed. 'You can't be here. You're not real.'

'Open your eyes, Lori. We have to get out. The kid's hurt.'

Dakota? I opened my eyes.

First darkness. Then spots of light ahead of me: headlights illuminating branches. I blinked, my vision clearing. Shit. I remembered: the argument, the bobcat, losing control, the shattered windshield. Falling.

I reached out, pressed the interior light on. The truck was lying on its side, passenger side down. Dakota was slumped against the door, an airbag lying flaccid around her. 'Oh, shit. Baby?'

No response.

Behind me, JT thumped on the Plexiglas. 'Let me help.'

Ignoring him, I twisted right, and reached out to Dakota. At full stretch I could just touch her. The truck creaked as I moved. I hoped to hell it wasn't going to slide further.

I needed to get closer. I moved my legs, got my left foot against the side of the footwell and used it to push myself further towards Dakota. As I did, a sharp pain spasmed through my right leg. Shit. I couldn't see what was causing it; the now-lifeless airbags limited my view. I clenched my teeth. Tried to block out the pain.

Behind me, JT thumped on the Plexiglas again. 'We need to get out of here, Lori. We're leaking gas.'

I inched closer to my angel. Stroked her face. 'Can you hear me, sweetie?'

Nothing.

Her skin felt cold, clammy. A dark bruise had already begun to form from her left eyebrow across her forehead. But she was so still. I couldn't tell if she was breathing. I grabbed for her wrist, couldn't find a pulse.

Without turning, I called to JT. 'How long was I out?'

'A few minutes.'

Shit. Dakota needed oxygen. Didn't the brain start to die after four minutes without? My heart raced. Why the hell couldn't I remember? I had to do something. 'How many?'

'Maybe three.'

Double shit. Should I give her mouth-to-mouth? I'd learnt first aid as part of my licence, but this situation was nothing like how we'd practised it in class.

CPR: two breaths, fifteen chest compressions. Was that right? I couldn't be sure. What if I did it too hard or too shallow? It'd seemed so easy on the plastic mannequin. They'd said to only do compressions if there was no pulse, get that wrong and you could do real damage. Shit. I had to be certain.

Check airway: with trembling fingers, I released her seatbelt and rested her on her back against the door. Thankfully the window was still intact. I pushed the airbag out of the way as best I could, tilted her head and looked inside her mouth. Empty.

I heard water flowing fast somewhere below us. In the transport cage behind me I could hear JT shifting his weight, trying to get free. The trunk groaned. I half turned my head. 'Quit moving.'

JT was still. I focused back on Dakota.

Check breathing: they'd said to put your cheek to the person's mouth to feel. I pushed my left foot harder against the footwell, trying to get closer. Couldn't. Pain spiked in the front of my right shin.

This wasn't going to work. We needed to get out of the truck. 'It's okay, baby. Just hold on. I'll have you out of here real fast.'

Turning, I grabbed the steering wheel and heaved myself up to the driver's door. The truck moaned as the wheels turned, hitting tree branches, rocks, dirt and whatever else was out there. The smell of gas grew stronger.

I pulled the door release. Didn't work. I yanked at it with my left hand, shoving my right palm hard against the door. It held firm, stuck.

'Let me help.'

JT. I'd forgotten he was there. I swivelled round. 'How?'

He raised his hands, nodded at the plasticuffs. 'Without these I can pull the pair of you free.'

I pressed the door release to the transport cage. 'Your door?'

He pulled the handle. His door opened just fine.

Could I trust him? I hoped so. Taking my keys from the ignition, I flicked through the bunch until I found the smallest one. Twisting back around I unclipped my belt and reached towards the top corner of the Plexiglas screen. The muscles of my right leg felt like they were on fire. I ignored the pain. Concentrated on the first of the six locks that held the Plexiglas divider in place. At full stretch I could just reach the lock in the left-hand corner. I inserted the key and turned it. One down, five to go.

I repeated the process until the screen was free, then shoved it to the right, out of our way. My right ankle throbbed, the shin above it numb. I glanced at Dakota, thought I saw the slight rise and fall of her chest as she took a breath, but I couldn't be sure. I didn't like how pale she'd gotten, or the thin film of sweat that'd formed across her skin. We needed to get out of the truck. Now.

But, shit. The only way to get JT out of the plasticuffs was to cut them off. Problem was, my cutters were stowed with the rest of my tools in the lockbox in the pickup bed. I'd have to improvise. 'Where's the lighter?'

JT frowned, then understood. 'Left pants pocket.'

He moved forward, slow and steady, putting his hip near the back of my head-rest. Not slow enough. I heard a screech, like a cat under torture, and the truck slid an inch or two along the ground, nose-end first. Branches scratched against the paintwork. The sound of running water grew louder. Time was running out.

Gripping the seat with one hand to steady myself, I reached into the transport cage and shoved my hand into JT's pocket. I felt the cold metal of the Zippo, and pulled it clear.

JT eased his weight back, held out his hands. Nodded.

I flicked up the hood, sparked the flame, and held it against the centre of the cuffs. The plastic started to melt, drips of liquid plastic fell on to his skin. He didn't flinch. I noticed his wrists were cut, bloodied. I swallowed down the guilt. Focused on the flame, the cuffs.

A few seconds later JT pulled his hands apart, snapping the weakened plastic. Turning, he put his feet on the door of the passenger side and released the other door. He thrust it open, heaved himself out on to the side of the truck. Disappeared.

The vehicle slid again. We travelled a foot or so down the bank.

I didn't have long. Had to be ready to get Dakota out of here. I reached down for her, scooping her into my arms. 'It's okay, baby. Momma's got you. It's gonna be okay.'

She was limp, like a rag doll. Holding her close, I put my cheek close to her mouth and waited. I felt it. A slight breath, I was sure of it. I waited, one more, to be certain. There it was again. I shifted back in the seat, watched her chest, saw the slightest movement. She *was* breathing.

Relief flooded through me. I put my fingers to her neck, checked for a pulse. Faint, but there. 'Dakota? Sweetie, can you hear me?'

Her eyelids flickered open. 'Momma? Where are we?'

'It's okay, baby. We're in the truck. We'll be out soon.'

We waited.

Where the hell was JT? Had I been wrong to free him? He was a fugitive, and I'd let him go. He could run, abandon us. I swallowed down the fear. Tried to stay calm. Surely he'd not leave with us trapped in here.

The door remained shut. Son-of-a-bitch.

Dakota clung to me like a limpet. 'I'm scared, Momma.'

I wanted to tell her it'd be all right. But what if he *had* left us?

Something banged against the side of the truck. The vehicle began to tilt, turning on to its roof. I heard the creak of metal buckling. We needed to get out of here, fast.

My door opened. JT reached into the cab. 'Pass her to me.'

I lifted Dakota as high as I could, my arms shaking from the strain. 'Be careful.'

JT pulled her from me, held her tight. 'It's okay, kiddo. I've got you.'

They moved out of view. The door closed. The truck lights died. Alone in the dark the water sounded closer, faster.

Focus. Think. Don't get distracted. We'd need to get help. I saw my cell phone lying against the passenger door. The screen was cracked, but maybe it'd work. I grabbed it, and the charger that was still plugged into the lighter socket. Pulling open the glovebox, I seized the flashlight and extra bottle of water stashed there.

The driver's door opened again. JT held out his hand. 'Lori, let's go.'

Gripping my stash with one hand, I heaved myself up to JT. I felt his hands on me, heard him grunt with the effort as he pulled me free. The truck was moving, falling. I kicked my feet away from the steering column, used my good leg to boost myself higher.

We fell from the truck, slammed into the ground hard. JT landed on his back, me on my front beside him. A rock dug into my hip. Dirt tasted peaty in my mouth.

Behind us the truck flipped slowly on to its roof.

Ignoring the pain shooting through my right leg, I scrambled up the bank a little ways to where Dakota was sitting. 'You okay, honey?'

She nodded, wide-eyed. One of her braids had come loose. 'I'm cold.'

JT took off his shirt. The black singlet beneath looked moulded against his chest.

Before he could get to Dakota I pulled off my jacket and put it around her shoulders. 'Put this on.'

'Any idea where we're at?' JT asked, scrunching his shirt into a ball between his fists.

I shook my head. The movement was a mistake. The world seemed to swirl and warp around me. I put my hands on the ground to steady myself. 'I'd say we're twenty minutes from the ranch in Yellow Spring, maybe thirty. The nearest town will be a good hour away.'

JT gazed at me, his expression all tender and concerned. 'You okay?'

I stood, moved closer to him. Looked deep into his eyes. We were out of the truck because of him. If he'd not woken me, Dakota could be dead. I put my lips to his ear. 'Thank you.'

He turned his head, his mouth inches from mine. 'For? ... shit.'

I'd snapped my last set of plasticuffs on to his wrists. I learnt a long time ago that you can't ever trust a man. JT had saved us, and for that I was real grateful, but I'd be a fool to trust him. 'I'm sorry. It's just business.'

I'd expected anger. Instead he looked hurt, disappointed. I turned away, didn't want to see that look on his face. 'We can't do anything until dawn. We need to find some place to sleep.'

'We should get your weapons. You got them stored in the lockbox?'

I shook my head. Decided not to tell him about the Wesson in my go-bag. 'I don't do guns anymore.'

JT frowned. 'That right? You know, sometimes, you should listen to me.'

I glared at him. Felt the rush of fury. Remembered what had happened all those years ago; all that blood.

Didn't he realise? I'd listened real careful, hung on to every word he'd said. That had been the problem.

14

Pitch-dark mountainside, unknown terrain, no shelter. Not the ideal situation. I pulled my cell from my pocket. The cracked screen showed no sign of life. I pressed the button, hoping it might activate. No luck. Either the force of the crash had killed it, or it was out of juice. Either way, right now it had little value.

Shoving the cell back into my pocket, I switched on the flashlight I'd taken from the truck and used its narrow beam to get my bearings. The forest was dense, the thick tree branches above blocked out most of the light from the half-moon, making the night seem darker. I looked up the mountainside, shone the flashlight's beam past the broken branches and into the distant blackness. Somewhere up there was the road.

'We should get moving,' JT said.

'No.' Dakota needed rest, and my ankle was too sore to get far over this terrain in the dark. Besides, if Gunner and his boys had managed to get themselves free and had decided on coming after us, we'd be sitting ducks out there on the highway. Better to hold hard a short while. At first light we could assess the damage to the truck and figure out our next move. 'I'm pretty sure we passed a gas station on our way up – in the valley maybe forty-five minutes before Yellow Spring. In the morning we can hike there, get some help.'

JT nodded, but his expression, illuminated by the flashlight, showed that he was pissed. I could understand that.

'Right now we need to get what we can from the truck and make camp,' I said.

Dakota was still clinging to me. I could feel her shivering, and she looked real sleepy. Not good. I couldn't let her sleep so quickly after a bang on the head, I needed to keep her awake. 'Dakota should eat.'

JT nodded. 'Where's the food?'

'A cooler in the lockbox.'

'Key?'

I removed it from my keychain and handed it to him. He looked pointedly at his cuffed hands. I shook my head.

I kept the flashlight beam aimed a step ahead of him as he pushed through the undergrowth around the truck, his forearms held high, shielding his face from the thorns. The truck had butted up close against the trunk of a large sugar maple. As he studied it, I checked our surroundings as best I could. There was just a whole bunch of trees. No sign of Gunner and his boys. At least that was something.

Dakota stared up at me. 'Will he be okay?'

I hoped so. Without JT we'd have nothing, no money for the medical bills. 'Sure. He'll be just fine.'

JT stepped up on to the belly of the truck, then dropped down the other side. Bending low, he scooted beneath the truck bed. I couldn't see what he did, but I heard the familiar squeak of the hinge on the lockbox as it opened, and a thud as the contents that had been stowed inside dropped to the ground. Moments later JT reappeared carrying our orange cooler. 'There's a purple rucksack. You want it?'

Dakota stepped closer. 'The Miranda Lambert one? That's mine. Yes please.'

JT set the cooler down and slid back under the truck. I kept my hand on Dakota's shoulder. She strained, like an overeager puppy on a leash, watching what he was doing. 'Let him, honey. The truck's not stable enough for you to go in there.'

He emerged with the rucksack. Taking hold of the cooler – not an easy task with his hands cuffed and Dakota's bag to carry too – he returned slower than he'd gone in, following the same path through the thorns.

He dropped the cooler at my feet. 'Here you go.'

Dakota took her rucksack, hugged it close, and looked up at JT. 'Thank you, thank you, thank you.'

'You're very welcome.' He smiled, and nodded at the picture of the sequin-covered singer on the front of the rucksack. 'Matches your shirt. Guess you're a big country music fan, then.'

I caught his gaze. 'There's a leather carryall. I can't leave it.'

JT nodded. He understood, or remembered, that it was my go-bag. He pushed his way back through the thicket to the Silverado. 'Whereabouts?'

The carryall was in the passenger footwell the last time I'd seen it, but that had been before the impact and the fall. It could be anywhere. 'The front, somewhere.'

He opened the driver's door, his only access due to the passenger door having been shoved tight against the tree. In the beam of the flashlight I could see that, despite the beating it'd taken, the cab had retained its basic structural shape. The roof, however, now resting on the ground, looked pretty caved.

JT peered into the truck. 'I see it.'

Before I could reply, he crawled inside. A tight squeeze for a big guy, I reckoned, and tough to manoeuvre, especially with his wrists bound. Still, perhaps he should feel proud. Me keeping him in cuffs meant I was still following his rules, his code. Rule number three: *Limit your risks.*

The Silverado creaked as JT moved through the cab.

Dakota gripped my hand, squeezed it tight. 'Is he okay?'

I hoped so, and not just because he was our bargaining chip with Quinn.

'Momma?'

Before I had the chance to answer my brown carryall appeared, shoved through the open driver's door. JT followed.

I exhaled, and gave Dakota's hand a light squeeze. 'There. He got it.'

JT made his way back through the undergrowth and handed me the carryall. Taking it from him, I tried not to let my gaze linger on the scratches and bleeding tears that zigzagged across his forearms. I felt guilty. Knew I should at least have let him put his shirt on before sending him into the wreck. I guess that was the way things always went with us: a fistful of should and a butt-load of guilt.

'We should find a spot to make camp.'

We moved a short distance from the truck, to a small clearing with flatter ground. I looked up the mountainside. The tree canopy was dense, shielding us from view of the road above. If Gunner and his boys were coming after us I reckoned on this being as safe a place as any to hide out a while. 'This'll do.'

'Yep.' The way he said it made it sound more like a grunt than a word. Still pissed at me and letting me know it.

Well, too bad. I wasn't asking for permission. 'Can you find us some wood?'

'Yep.'

I turned to Dakota. 'We'll get a campfire going, sweetie, just like last holiday when we went to Krista's cookout.'

She nodded, but didn't speak. Not normal, not for her. She was way too quiet. That worried me. Physically she seemed fine, but I guessed that the shock of the crash had kicked in. I needed to keep her alert, stop her worrying. I knelt down beside her. 'Now how about you check what we've got for dinner?'

Dakota opened the cooler. There wasn't much left: two bottles of water, half a packet of peanut butter cups, a yogurt and two tubs of ice cream.

She gazed into the darkness in the direction JT had gone. 'Should we wait for him?'

I shook my head. 'You go ahead, honey.'

Dakota reached in and took an ice cream. 'It's still good, Momma. I told you the ice would work.'

'Is that your dinner?'

She grinned. 'Yeah.'

I figured after the events of the last few hours she deserved a treat. I smiled. 'Okay.'

She fished in the bottom of the cooler for a plastic spoon, and got to work on her ice cream.

'You stay here, sweetie. I'm going to check things out.'

With an eye still on JT and Dakota, I hobbled a few steps away from camp and used the flashlight to sweep the hillside. The river lay eight yards away. The bank back to the road was steep and littered with tree roots and boulders. A lot of the undergrowth had been scraped clear by the truck, which would make climbing up easier. Still, I had been right – what with the near-vertical slope and the darkness, we couldn't safely navigate out until morning.

I limped back to our makeshift camp. My leg hurt like a bitch, but there was nothing to be done about that. There was no medical help nearby and no way to call for it. For now, we were on our own.

⥥

Using the moon to light him, JT had brushed a small patch of earth clear of leaves. He and Dakota were now crouching in the middle of the space, a small pile of twigs and branches beside them. I watched as JT selected two sticks from the pile.

He showed them to Dakota. 'These two right here, they're perfect for making fire. One flat, one round, and they're good an' dry.'

She looked up at him, eyes wide. 'Could you show me?'

I clenched my fist tighter around the flashlight. Maybe it was the eager tone to her voice, or the way she looked at him like he was the most interesting person in the whole damn world, but whatever it was I hated it. I didn't want her looking at JT that way, and I sure as shit didn't want him encouraging her. Not when I knew he'd soon be gone.

He smiled at Dakota. 'Well, the first thing we need get ourselves is a little bed for the end of the round stick in the belly of the flat one, like this.' He used his thumbnail to gouge a hollow in the middle of the flat stick. 'Then we lie the flat one on the ground and press the end of the round one snug into the hollow. Next thing we need is a little of that tinder.'

'Can I do it?'

'Sure you can. Nice and close to where the sticks join.'

Dakota sprinkled a handful of ripped up leaves and small twigs over the flat stick. 'And now?'

With the free end of the round stick between his palms, JT rolled it back and forth, pushing down as the other end rotated in the hollow of the flat stick. It looked awkward, the plasticuffs limiting his movement, but he still managed. I guess I could have fastened the cuffs tighter. I wished that I had.

Dakota peered closer. 'Is it working?'

He kept rolling the stick. 'We just need ourselves a little more friction.'

I hobbled over to them, cussing my hurt ankle beneath my breath.

Dakota grinned up at me. 'JT's showing me how to make fire.'

'There are easier ways.' I pulled the Zippo from my pocket, leant down and lit the tinder. Flames sparked into life. 'There you go.'

JT didn't speak. Instead he got to heaping the twigs and branches around the flames. But Dakota stared at me. I pretended to ignore her disappointed expression, and after a short while she turned away and looked into the fire.

I moved back a few paces. Guilt gnawed at my conscience.

JT stood. He came over to me, leant close. 'I figured it'd take her mind off—'

I held up my hands. Fought to keep my voice to a whisper. 'Well don't think. Don't speak. Hell, don't even look at her.'

Shaking his head, JT walked around to the other side of the fire. He picked up his shirt and without a word or a glance at me, lay down and arranged the material over himself as best he could. He closed his eyes.

I put my hand on Dakota's shoulder. 'Come on, honey. It's time to rest.'

We lay down; Dakota next to the fire, me real close beside her. I wondered how much time had passed since the crash – one hour, two? Debated whether I should keep her awake longer. Decided against it. She'd need her rest for whatever the dawn brought. Switching off the flashlight, I put my arm around her. 'Sleep tight.'

I heard a mosquito buzzing close to my face. Somewhere in the distance an owl hooted. I felt Dakota's body go rigid.

'It's too dark, Momma.'

'It's just for tonight, sweetie.'

She wriggled closer to me, gripped my arm, her fingernails digging into my bare skin like claws. 'I'm scared.'

'You see those stars up above us?' JT said.

Shit. Couldn't he just stay quiet?

'Yes,' Dakota said.

'They're nature's nightlights. While we're sleeping they'll be watching over us. Keeping us safe.'

Dakota was quiet a moment. Then she said in a small voice, 'I'm still scared.'

JT exhaled. 'How about I keep watch then? You and your momma get some rest, and I'll promise to stay awake. Could you sleep then?'

I felt her hair moving against the crook of my arm. A nod. 'I guess.'

In the gloom, I watched him sit up and reposition his shirt around his shoulders. 'Good. That's what I'll do. Ya'll sleep well.'

I lay still in the darkness, staring up at the stars and listening to Dakota's breathing as she relaxed into sleep. She barely knew JT, yet she trusted he'd keep her safe, just as I had all those years before. If I'd never sat next to him at the bar, never asked him what he wanted, and never agreed to help him, then things would have been different, better. At least that was what I'd always told myself.

15

With the dawn came a pale sunlight. It reached through the gaps in the tree canopy, burning holes in the ground mist surrounding us. JT was awake, sitting on a fallen tree a couple of yards from where I lay.

I sat up. As I did, JT's blue shirt fell from my shoulders. I frowned, wondered how it had gotten there.

'You were shivering in your sleep,' he said, nodding towards his shirt. 'Thought you needed it more than me.'

'Did you stay awake all night?'

'Promised didn't I?'

He held my gaze longer than was comfortable. Didn't do him no good. I looked away. I didn't want to think about promises. A promise is just a disappointment bought on credit.

The fire had burnt itself out. Black cinders and a few charred sticks were all that remained. It'd been dead a while. The dew had formed over the ashes, over us. My jeans and singlet felt damp against my skin. I shivered. Beside me, Dakota sighed in her sleep. I watched her for a long moment, checked the rhythmical rise and fall of her breathing, wondered how her head would be feeling when she woke.

'You got a plan?' He was testing if I still worked the way he taught me. Interesting.

'Always.'

'So you gonna tell me?'

I met his stare. Despite my determination not to get drawn into whatever drama he'd gotten involved in, I had to ask. 'Why'd you let Merv pick you up?'

Silence. From the look on JT's face I guessed that there was a whole lot more juice for the squeeze than he was willing to let on. I wondered again what more he knew about the three rednecks who'd been holding him captive. Something about that set-up still felt out of whack: them not expecting me, Merv not being present, those boys attacking me. I just couldn't figure out the why.

I tried to keep my tone light, teasing. It didn't quite work out. 'Come on, spill. You could have kept free if that's what you'd wanted. Hell, you could have run out of here while I was sleeping, but you didn't. Why?'

He held my gaze, but still said nothing. Stubborn – just as I remembered him.

I raised an eyebrow. 'I read in the file that you didn't speak when they arrested you either.'

JT shook his head. 'This isn't about what I did, or what they charged me with. You've got to ask the right questions, Lori. Didn't I teach you that?'

He'd taught me a lot of things, some I wished I could forget.

I gazed down at Dakota snuggled close to me. The mentor I'd known hadn't been shy of physical contact, but he'd never have launched an unprovoked attack in a public place like an amusement park. 'What did they do to make you take the law into your own hands?'

A smile twitched the corners of his lips real brief before disappearing. 'Now *that's* a better kind of question.'

I waited, but he didn't give me an answer. Beside me Dakota mumbled something in her sleep. She always did that as she woke. We'd need to continue the conversation later.

I stood. My muscles felt board-stiff, my limbs ached deep into the bone – the aftershock of my run-in with Merv's three rednecks, rolling the Silverado, and a night sleeping under the stars I guessed. 'We need to get moving.'

JT glanced at the cooler. 'Got any food left?'

I stepped over the remains of the fire and handed him his shirt. 'Some.'

'We should eat first.' He nodded to Dakota. 'Or at least she should.'

'Don't tell me how to raise my child.'

He put up his hands in a clumsy surrender, waved his shirt in front of him like a flag.

I didn't smile. Turning away, I knelt beside Dakota, put my hand on her shoulder and woke her with a gentle shake. 'Wake up, honey.'

She blinked awake then frowned, obviously confused by her outdoor surroundings.

'It's okay. You're safe.'

She focused on my face. 'Momma?'

'Right here, sweetie. It's time for breakfast.' I opened the cooler, looked at the food inside – one yogurt, a tub of ice cream and some peanut butter cups. I handed her the ice cream. She smiled.

I looked over at JT. 'Yogurt or peanut butter cups?'

He shook his head. 'You have it. I'm good.'

'You should eat.'

He shrugged, took a few peanut butter cups, and strode the short ways over to the battered path the Silverado had cleared as it plunged off the road. He squinted up the mountainside. I knew he'd be analysing the best route. Figured I could use his help on that.

We ate quickly in uneasy silence, no talking. The only noise came from the stream below and the birds above us in the trees. Under different circumstances the tranquil surroundings would have been perfect. Right now they were anything but. We needed to get help and get home. Fast.

Once we were done, I packed the peanut butter cups and water into my carryall. Standing, I turned to Dakota and held out my hand. 'Time to go.'

She gripped my hand, her fingers cold against mine. I rubbed them warm, and helped her to her feet.

JT strode back to us. He gestured to the right of the path cleared by the Silverado, where the undergrowth was less dense. 'That looks to be our best way up to the road.'

Dakota let go of my hand and stepped towards him. 'Thank you for keeping watch.'

He nodded. 'No problem, kiddo. You sleep okay?'

Dakota smiled. 'I did.'

'Glad to hear it.'

Enough. We had forty-eight hours to get JT back to Florida, it was time to get gone. I nodded at JT, took Dakota's hand again and set off in the direction of the Silverado.

We walked through the trees, closer to the injured truck. If Gunner and his boys had decided to come after us I hoped to hell that they'd driven on past. Dakota was still woozy with sleep, I felt unsteady on my sore ankle, and, with his hands cuffed in front of him, JT moved all awkward. If it came to another showdown I did not fancy our chances. The smart money would be on them.

The damage was worse than I'd feared. I doubted the vehicle would recover. If it did, the surgery wouldn't come cheap: busted wheels, dented bodywork, fender ripped off, windshield shattered. As I totted up the problems the dollar signs kept on rising. Damn. I hoped the insurance would cover it.

It also gave us an immediate transport problem. Even if the vehicle had been operational, it was stranded on its roof near the bottom of a steep bank a couple of yards from the riverbed. We'd need a tow truck, and perhaps a crane, to pull it free. For that we'd need help. As I'd figured last night, our best option would be to hike down the hill to the gas station and for me to call Quinn.

I could organise a rental car to get us back to Florida, and leave Quinn to fix up the recovery of the Silverado. He'd have to take the cost from my percentage of JT's bond. Shit.

⇓

We climbed the steep bank to the highway. JT up front, his blue shirt tied across his waist. Dakota next, holding the tail of JT's shirt real tight, like a baby elephant following its parent, and me behind her, with the carryall and her rucksack.

As we started our hike along the mountain road I thought about the events of the previous night: JT being held by those three rednecks, but with no sign of Merv; my having to fight them off; the crash. Most of all I thought about the uneasy feeling I'd had at the ranch. It still hadn't left; was lurking at the bottom of my belly.

I blew out hard, and tried to forget about it. I'd caught my fugitive and time was counting down to the summary judgement. We'd got five states to cross, less than forty-eight hours to do it, and no vehicle. Surely my luck had to change soon.

It did. Just not in the direction that I'd been hoping.

16

The gas station seemed a lot further on foot. We moved as best we could down the mountainside, following the crumbling blacktop. As the temperature rose, moisture formed a shiny film across our skin. The sweat ran down my spine, under the waistband of my jeans, and into my panties. Damn humidity. I slapped my forearm, killing yet another mosquito trying its luck.

'How much further, Momma?'

Honestly, I had no idea, but that wasn't what Dakota needed to hear. She'd fallen behind again and with every passing minute her grumbling was getting more persistent. I stopped, waiting for her to catch up. 'Not too long now, sweetie.'

She looked at her watch, then up at me. 'But you said that thirty minutes ago and we're still not there yet.'

I forced a smile and starting walking again. 'Then we're a lot closer than we were.'

JT fell in step beside me. He pulled a pack of cigarettes from his pants' pocket, took one and put it between his lips. Holding out his hands he said, 'How about you give me the lighter?'

Taking the Zippo from my pocket, I ignored his outstretched hands, and lit the cigarette instead. 'How about you quit talking?'

JT glanced at Dakota and raised an eyebrow. 'Gets riled easy, huh?'

Dakota giggled.

I stared at JT, held his gaze. Him skipping bail, it just didn't fit right. 'You wanna know something?'

He shrugged. 'Hardly matters if I do or I don't, I reckon you're gonna tell me anyways.'

I ignored the jibe. 'I don't get it. The mentor I had, he never would've turned fugitive.'

JT shook his head. 'Things change. Ten years is a long while.'

'You expect me to believe you broke bad? I don't buy it.'

He frowned. 'Well, y'see, Lori. Good. Bad. They're relative terms.'

'Justice ain't.'

He paused for a long moment, then nodded. 'True. But it has its price. You know that.'

Sure, I knew it. We both did. I gave JT a shove, pushing him ahead of us. 'Shut up. Keep walking.'

Dakota gasped. 'Momma. That's rude.'

Well, shit. My daughter was taking JT's side? That I did not need. I looked at her real serious. 'If you'd done as you were told last night then we wouldn't be walking now would we? I've had quite enough of your smart mouth, Dakota Anderson. Now be quiet.'

Dakota's cheeks flushed crimson. Immediately I regretted my outburst. The heat and the situation were getting to me. I reached out to her. 'Sweetie, I—'

She shrugged me away and trotted a few yards ahead. From the rise and fall of her shoulders I knew she was crying.

JT stepped closer. He nodded towards Dakota. 'You want to be thinking about the lessons the kid is learning from all this. Why'd you bring her with you?'

I refused to look at him. 'Quit worrying. We're none of your concern. If you wanna be thinking on something, think about how I ended up doing this in the beginning.'

'I wasn't the one who left.'

True. But he was the one who said we were done. And him letting me walk away like that, it told me he never really cared for me anyways. So I didn't speak, knew there was nothing I could say that'd make things right. Broken bones hurt for damn sure, but even that kind of pain had nothing on the damage JT did to my heart.

'You sure seem to have done—'

'Momma, look!' Dakota called. 'We found it.'

She was right. Around the corner, a couple of hundred yards down the hill, was a two-pump gas station. It wasn't fancy. The pumps out front looked like they came from the last century, and the forecourt had weeds growing up through cracks in the asphalt. But the hand-painted sign outside the squat wooden one-storey told me they stocked beer, cigarettes and household essentials. I was pretty sure that they'd have a phone too. I smiled. 'Good job, sweetie.'

We hustled down the hill with renewed energy. It wouldn't be long now. One call to Quinn and in less than an hour we should have ourselves a new ride and be on our way back to Florida.

Before we stepped on to the forecourt I beckoned JT and Dakota to stop. Looking JT straight in the eye, I untied the blue shirt from around his waist and hung it over his wrists, covering the cuffs. 'Don't try anything funny.'

'Yes, ma'am.'

It was hard to tell from his expression whether he was mocking me, but I reckoned he was. I raised one side of my jacket, showed him the holster. 'I've got my taser, and I will use it on you. Don't make me do that.'

He raised his chin: a defiant pose. 'Sure.'

I took hold of Dakota's hand. 'Keep close, honey.'

She nodded.

We stepped off the blacktop and crossed the forecourt. Through the grimy window on the far right of the store building I thought I glimpsed a face peering out at us. Next moment it was gone.

I pushed open the door and we entered the store. It wasn't a big space. Long and narrow with shelving around the outside, and a couple of displays along the centre creating a middle aisle and one either side. There didn't seem much order to the arrangement: candy bars were stored alongside motor oil, magazines beside bread, and a large display of Furre Babies – the latest kids' fad: talking toy owls, mice and rabbits – stood directly across from the doorway. I nodded to the candy and smiled at Dakota. 'You wanna pick us something nice?'

She grinned. 'Cool.'

'You stay right here and do that.' I turned to JT. 'You come with me to the counter.'

The counter was at the far end of the store. Sitting behind it was a pimply-faced teen with a shoulder-length mullet sticking out from under a grubby Miami Dolphins cap. He was hunched forward, his elbows resting on the register as he muttered into his cell phone. Ending the call, he turned to the left and stared at the screen of a portable TV. He didn't look up as we approached, just kept on watching and chewing gum.

I knocked on the wooden counter. 'You got a payphone?'

The teen nodded. Still chewing, and without looking at us, he pointed towards the restroom on the other side of the store.

'Thanks.'

As I stepped away from the counter, the teen whistled. 'You gotta be shitting me.'

I turned, then realised he wasn't talking to us, he was watching some kind of news bulletin. I peered at the screen. A neatly made-up news reporter was standing outside a shabby weatherboard ranch house. It looked real familiar. On the banner at the bottom of the screen I read: *Multiple Homicide Fugitive At Large.*

The teen shook his head. 'Found them folks up there in Yellow Spring. Shot 'em right in the head. Ain't right doing that when they were tied. Couldn't defend themselves. No honour in that.'

True. No honour at all. Despite the humidity I shivered. Something was very wrong. I glanced at JT. His expression stayed neutral, hard to read.

The teen turned up the volume.

The reporter was in full flow: '*... and so, with three dead and a fourth in a critical condition, if you see the fugitive Robert James Tate, call 911 and do not approach him. He is armed and highly dangerous.*'

Shit. We needed to get away from here, and fast. I took a step back.

Too late.

The teen turned and took his first look at us. 'So where you folks heading?' He stared right at JT. Then, for the briefest moment, glanced back to the TV, where JT's mugshot was displayed with the *'Call 911, do not approach'* message written below. He tightened his grip on the cell phone. 'Don't do anything—'

JT flung himself across the counter, slamming both his fists into the teen's face in a double-handed punch. The teen fell backwards, hit his head on the wall, and fell to the ground.

I rushed around to the other side of the counter. Dropped to my knees beside the boy, checking for a pulse. Relief. He was out cold but breathing. Looked like his nose was broken, maybe his left cheekbone too. He'd be needing some ice when he came round.

I glared at JT. 'What the hell?'

'He was calling the cops ... or worse.'

Dakota called, 'Momma, are you okay?'

I tried to keep my voice calm. She couldn't know what had happened. 'Stay over there, sweetie.' I looked back at JT. 'What the hell are you mixed up in?'

He met my gaze. 'Better you don't know.'

Shit. 'That news report was from Yellow Rock Ranch. Did you hear what they said? Three people dead, one critical. And you're in the frame for it. Tell me how.'

JT shrugged. 'I was with you the whole time, you know that.'

'Someone murdered those men. Why?' I clasped my hands together, tried to stop them shaking. 'I tied them up. They couldn't defend themselves. Now they're dead.'

'You didn't pull the trigger.'

I shook my head. Even before yesterday I'd had enough blood on my hands for them never to feel clean. 'What is it with you and trouble? For ten years I've avoided this kind of shit. A few hours with you and I'm right back in it up to my waist.'

JT stepped towards me. His hands closed around mine, fingers stroking my skin, his palms warm, comforting. 'They weren't good people. Nothing's changed. You still need to get me back to Florida.'

Wrong. Those dead men changed everything. My easy pick-up had been a little tougher than it should have been at the ranch. But I'd put it down to unprofessional rednecks looking to make money by piggybacking on my percentage. The crash had been a setback, but those things happened, especially on unlit mountain roads at night. But now three men lay dead, and a fourth was fighting for his life. Sure, I knew JT hadn't done it. But whoever did shoot them was free and clear. Was maybe chasing us, maybe high-tailing it with loot from the ranch. Whatever the truth, I saw two options, neither of which would get me the bond money: I could call local law enforcement and let them take JT to jail, or I could cut him loose.

I knew I wouldn't cut him loose, but that wasn't to say I wasn't tempted. He'd saved Dakota's life, and mine, less than twelve hours earlier. But he'd committed a crime, and he had to face the consequences. It was for a judge and jury, not him, to decide whether his actions were justified. So even with the gratitude I felt for his pulling us free from the car wreck, I could not allow the devil he had chasing him near my daughter.

Shoving him away I said, 'I'm calling this in.'

'Lori, I—'

I raised my hand, signalling for him to stop. My mind was made up; talking wouldn't help none. Stepping to the counter, I reached for the pimply teen's cell. 'I'll tell them you had nothing to do with the homicides, I'll make sure they...'

I heard the squeal of tyres. Through the grimy window I saw a black car hurtling on to the forecourt. 'What the—?'

JT flung himself at me, knocking me away from the counter and on to the dusty concrete floor. The air rushed from my lungs. A dull pain vibrated through my left hip. I cussed under my breath. Tried to push JT away. But he was using his bodyweight to trap me. His breath was hot against my face. 'Stay down,' he growled.

I heard the gunshot, close and loud. Held my breath. The store's plate-glass window shattered. Behind me, Dakota screamed.

17

Fragments of glass rained down on us. I glanced towards the window, a large hole, maybe a foot from where we'd been standing, gaped open like a wound. Bullets thwacked into the wall, the roof, the floor. More glass shattered.

'Jesus, fuck, get off me.'

'Lori, don't. These men, they're real serious. They killed those boys at the ranch. Must've gotten the kid here to tip them off about us.'

Shit, he was right. I remembered the face watching us from the window as we approached, the teen muttering into his cell phone as we entered the store. 'Let me go.'

JT released his grip and I wrestled out from under him. One thing on my mind: Dakota.

She wasn't by the candy. Keeping low, I ran along the middle aisle. I tried to keep the panic from my voice. 'Dakota, you okay?'

'Momma?'

Her reply came from the other side of the display, I ducked through the gap between the toilet tissue and the breakfast cereals. Dakota sat a few feet ahead, her knees pulled tight to her chest, rocking back and forth.

Tears ran rivers down her dirty cheeks. 'What's happening?'

I said the first thing that popped into my head. 'Bad men are trying to rob the store.'

'Why?'

'I don't know, honey.' A lie, of course. I knew what they wanted, I'd guessed it the minute I heard the first shot, but I couldn't tell Dakota. The truth would only scare her more. They wanted JT, and if they'd tracked him to the ranch and killed those men, they were going to be a serious problem.

'Lori?' JT yelled. 'I could do with some help.'

I stroked the tears from Dakota's face. 'Stay here, baby. Don't move.'

She nodded. I forced a smile, then turned and hurried back to JT.

A bullet hit the upper door hinge, ripping it away from the wood. The door swung drunkenly inwards, listing at an angle. Through the gap I caught a glimpse of them: a bunch of men, guns in hand, climbing out of the black car.

JT was behind the counter, searching for weapons. Stores in remote country like this always had a gun.

'They're coming.'

He put a baseball bat on the counter. 'How many?'

I glanced back to the doorway. 'Four. Maybe five.'

He nodded. Knelt beside the store attendant and searched him. Found a set of keys in his pants' pocket. The guy murmured but didn't wake. JT unlocked the cupboard beneath the till. 'Jackpot.'

He took out a sawn-off shotgun and three cartridges. I hoped it would be enough.

JT held out the shotgun. 'Take it.'

I shook my head, grabbed the bat instead.

He frowned, from confusion or frustration I couldn't be sure. 'It'll be—'

A bullet ricocheted off the metal sign above the store window, the next one hit the window again, tearing through the glass and ripping through the magazine display in the first aisle.

Through the busted window I glimpsed two of the men: they were halfway across the forecourt.

JT grabbed the shotgun. Not the easiest weapon to fire wearing cuffs, but a whole lot better than something you needed to aim real careful. He adapted fast, pressed up against what little of the cinderblock window surround was left intact, and braced the shotgun's handle against his left hip. He held it steady, and fired one cartridge. If the kick of the gun hurt, he didn't show it.

The man closest to us dropped to the ground.

A volley of bullets smacked into the window and the surrounding wall. JT hit the floor, and slid the store attendant's keys to me. One of the keys had a Chevy logo stamped on the fob. 'Get the kid and find some transport.'

It was an order, like we'd gone back into the past and he was in charge. I nodded. No time to argue.

Keeping low, I took the bat, and moved fast along the second aisle to Dakota. She was still rocking, her face tight against her knees, eyes shut.

I put my hand on her shoulder. She flinched. 'Come on, sweetie. Let's get out of here.'

She looked up. Nodded.

I grabbed my carryall and hurried towards the back door. I hoped it wouldn't be locked. It wasn't, but a pile of boxes had it blocked. I yanked them away, ignoring the cans of tuna spilling out of them, and shoved the boxes up against a crate of bottled beer. Dakota stood beside me, statue still, looking back towards JT.

I heard more gunfire at the front of the store. Glanced round. Saw JT fire another cartridge. I heard a shout, not JT's. Another man down.

'Quick, sweetie.' I grabbed Dakota's hand. Opened the door.

A bearded man was rushing at me, gun raised, firing. I leapt back into the store, pulling Dakota with me, using the door as a shield. The shots went wide. To my left I heard the bottles of beer shatter, felt liquid spray across the back of my legs, saw broken glass and cans of tuna scatter across the floor.

Stepping out from behind the door, I swung the bat and brought it down hard on the bearded man's gun hand. He dropped the weapon, staggered, recoiling from the blow, slipped on the loose cans and fell sideways on to the concrete. Seeing my chance, I let go of Dakota's hand and rushed forward, kicking the gun out of his reach just as he regained his balance.

Shit.

I tried to get back to Dakota. Not fast enough. I gasped as he hit me in the chest, ramming me hard against the wall, knocking the breath clean out of me.

Dakota screamed.

He lunged for my throat, squeezed hard. I struggled, kicked at his legs. I could hear Dakota crying, guessed that if he overpowered me, he'd be after her next. Knew I could not let that happen.

I thrust the handle of the bat forward and up into the soft tissue beneath his ribs. He groaned, let go of my neck, doubled over. I hit him again, and then again: his shoulders, his head. He went down, didn't move. Bleeding but not dead.

I had to get Dakota out of here.

She stood just inside the door, staring at the bloodied man. Her whole body was trembling.

'Don't look at him, sweetie.'

She kept staring at the man.

I took her hand. Glanced through the doorway, checking our exit – all clear. Glanced back at Dakota. 'Listen, honey. He was a bad man. If I didn't stop him he'd have hurt us. Now we have to go.'

She looked up at me. Nodded. 'Okay, Momma.'

'Good girl.' I heaved my carryall over one shoulder, and with Dakota's hand tight in mine we crept out back and around the side of the store.

Parked over on the far side of the forecourt was a blue Chevy. An older model, but updated with alloys and a spoiler. I reckoned it had to be the teen's ride. We made our way over to it.

The two men JT had shot lay on the ground ten and fifteen yards away, not moving. With them and the guy I'd taken care of we'd accounted for three. But I'd seen at least four get out of the car, maybe five. We weren't clear yet.

I kept Dakota behind me as we passed the fallen men, shielding her view with my body. We reached the car okay. I unlocked it with the store attendant's key and opened the passenger door. 'In you get, sweetie.'

Dakota climbed in. I closed the door behind her, moved around to the driver's side, opened the door and dropped the carryall on to the back seat.

A shotgun fired inside the store. I flinched. Dakota cried out.

Four men confirmed.

Dakota peered through the windshield. 'Who's that with JT?'

I heard a crash. Turned. The store window was completely blown out. Inside two men were fighting.

Shit. Three shots. Three cartridges. JT was out of ammo.

I couldn't leave him. He was still cuffed, disabled in any fight. If he died it would be my fault. Another life ended because of me. I looked at Dakota. 'I'll get him. Stay in the car, okay? Promise me.'

She nodded. 'Promise.'

I hurried back across the forecourt. Through the shot-out window I glimpsed an athletic figure dressed in combat pants and a white tee, standing beside the candy display. I moved a little closer. Spotted JT. Inhaled sharply. He was on his knees in front of the man, a handgun pressed against his forehead.

I crept closer. Hoped the man stayed looking at JT.

JT glared at his captor. 'We know what your boss did, and we've got the proof. He can't buy himself out of trouble this time.'

The guy with the gun laughed. 'Big talk for a man all out of options.'

I glanced back at the Chevy. Dakota was still inside. Still safe.

Looking back at JT, I knew I had to get closer, much closer. I crept along the outside wall to the gap where the door had been. Eleven steps. The sound of my breathing hissed loud in my ears.

Inside the store, the man with his back to me said, 'Last chance. Where is he?'

JT stayed silent.

I hoped that he'd seen me. That he was ready to react. Leaning down, I picked up one of the Furre Baby toys, which had rolled from the collapsed display into the doorway. I pressed its belly, and as the electronic squeaky voice said, 'You're cute!' I threw it into the store in the direction of the counter.

The gunman spun around, fired two shots into the toy.

JT leapt forward, planting his shoulder into the gunman's legs. As they sprawled on to the floor, I sprinted along the aisle.

I reached them in ten strides. Shoved my taser into the side of the gunman's neck and pressed the trigger. The fight went from him instantly, his arms and legs flailing. It wouldn't last long, but it would be enough time for us to get away.

JT was already on his feet. 'You came—'

A scream.

Outside.

Dakota.

I whipped round, sprinted for the doorway. 'Baby?'

Only one man lay on the ground. The second wasn't dead; he was bundling Dakota into the black sedan. I could hear her screaming, crying, calling my name. Another man was in the driver's seat. The engine was running.

'No!' I hurtled across the forecourt.

They'd had us fooled.

Not four men, not five. Six.

JT was beside me. He grabbed the handgun from the dead man's body.

The car pulled away. I ran behind it, yelled for them to stop. Watched Dakota's hands clawing at the window. Saw the tears streaming down her pale face, her blue eyes wide with terror.

As they swung towards the exit, they were picking up speed.

JT raised the gun, fired at the car. Missed.

The black sedan accelerated away. Disappeared from view.

'Dakota?' I was frozen to the spot. My lungs felt about to explode. My legs felt like jello. I'd failed to remember JT's fourth rule: *Don't make assumptions*. I'd assumed the driver had gotten out of the car. That the two men JT had shot were dead. One wasn't. He had taken my baby.

'Lori. Come on,' JT yelled.

I didn't move. Couldn't. 'She promised to stay in the car.'

He grabbed my arm, tugged me towards the store attendant's car, half threw me into the passenger seat. Fired up the Chevy's engine and floored the gas pedal. 'We've got to catch them.'

18

I don't know how long we chased them, half a day, an hour, a minute; time had lost its beat for me. Dakota was gone. Taken. And I had let it happen.

The mountainside flashed by, JT jerking the car around the twists as best as his cuffed wrists would allow. Didn't do no good. However fast or long we drove it wasn't enough. We didn't catch them.

I sat. Numb. Slumped in the passenger seat. Staring out of the windshield, past the dream-catcher hanging on a frayed blue thread from the rear-view mirror, scanning the highway ahead. Still empty.

We reached a crossroads. Saw no sign of the black sedan in any direction.

JT took a right. Glanced at me. 'You should put on your belt.'

I heard him, but didn't respond. Put my belt on, he'd said. How the hell did *that* matter? Then I realised the beeping noise I'd been listening to since we'd started the chase must be the car's seatbelt warning. I didn't care.

I glared at JT. He looked calm, his gaze focused on the highway. He held the bottom of the steering wheel, his movements minimal, controlled. But that hadn't stopped the plasticuffs biting into his flesh. His wrists were bleeding, blood dripped from them on to the denim of his jeans. I didn't feel bad about that; couldn't. If I'd not gone back for him, if I hadn't left Dakota in the car, then she'd still be with me. 'We've lost them, haven't we?'

'Yeah.'

'So why the fuck are you still driving?'

He frowned, said nothing. Accelerated.

Bastard.

Adrenaline fired through my body; fight or flight, attack or chase. I wanted to run, to scream, but I was stuck in this car, with him. Damn son-of-a-bitch. Whenever he was near, the people I loved got hurt: first Sal, now Dakota. His silent act wasn't mysterious; it was plain infuriating. I raised my voice. 'Where the hell are we going?'

Silence. His face was immobile, showed no emotion.

I hated him for it. Needed him to react, to say something. 'Tell me!'

Nothing.

Fight. I grabbed the wheel.

'Jesus! Lori, what the hell?'

He braked hard. The vehicle skidded on gravel at the side of the highway. Halted.

Shoving the gear into park, JT turned to face me. His expression wasn't neutral anymore. 'You need to get a—'

I punched his arm, his chest, his thigh; any bit of him that I could reach, the clinical rules of hand-to-hand forgotten in my fury. Tried anything, everything, to make him care, or at least act as if he did.

JT didn't defend himself, didn't even try to block me. That only made me madder. I lashed out harder. Still he didn't react. I slapped his face, watched his cheek flush red from the impact of my palm. Raised my hand again.

Finally he put his hands up to block me. 'Lori, stop.'

I stopped. Knew that I'd lost it. Control. Focus. All gone. Turning away from him, I stared at the dream-catcher. In my mind's eye I saw Dakota, those last moments: *The car pulling away. Her hands clawing at the window. Tears down her face. Blue eyes wide. Gone.*

My fault. I stifled a sob.

'You done?' JT's voice sounded husky, gentle.

I didn't look at him. Couldn't. Kept staring at the dream-catcher. Wondered if it caught broken ones.

'They'll contact us. They want me, not her.'

I turned to face him. Said quietly, 'Why?'

'Because I've got something their boss wants.'

'So why take my daughter?'

JT shook his head.

Son-of-a-bitch. He knew damn well, just as I did. They'd taken Dakota as a bargaining chip, a threat, or both. They took her because there was a game in play and they wanted to win. Well, it wasn't a game that I wanted any part of.

I pulled my cell phone and its charger from my pocket, stuck the charger into the cigarette lighter and plugged in the cell. 'I'm calling the police. They—'

JT yanked the charger out of the socket. 'No cops.'

'What the hell?' I slapped his hands away, shoved the charger back into place and kept one hand on the cord, blocking JT. The cell beeped. I was thankful it still worked. I glanced at the cracked screen: four text messages, nine voicemails. All the same number: Quinn.

'Lori, listen. You do not want the cops involved. These people...' He shook his head. 'They've already manipulated the police and the media into thinking I've committed multiple homicide. My fingerprints and DNA, yours too, will be all over that crime scene. They want to flush me out and shut me up – you as well if you're in their way, and from what just went down at the gas station they'll assume that you are. We can't know if they've got the cops round here in their pockets. And anyway, after the ranch and the gas station, the cops will shoot first and ask questions later.'

He sounded so calm, so clinical. I felt my cheeks flush. 'So I *let* them take her? That's your big idea on how I keep her safe? Jesus. I'm *so* glad you're not a parent.'

'I don't like it any more than—'

'Really? Because from where I'm sitting it seems you don't give a rat's ass.'

He shook his head. 'That's not—'

'So tell me who has my daughter and why the hell they're after you.'

He was silent for a long moment, then nodded. 'They work for a man called Randall Emerson.'

I'd heard that name before, from Quinn. Emerson was the name of the guy JT had threatened at the amusement park he'd been arrested in. 'The owner of Winter Wonderland?'

'Yeah. That and a bunch of other parks.'

I frowned. 'So what does he want with you? *I'm* taking you back for the summary judgement. I don't need any damn help. And why the hell would they take my daughter?'

'The parks are a front. Emerson isn't the model citizen everyone thinks he is.' JT turned to look at me. 'He has a thing for kids.'

My throat tightened. I tasted a bitter tang against my tongue. Spat out the words. 'A thing?'

JT nodded. 'And he's not the only one. He has a sideline, using the parks as a base. Beneath all the glitter there's some sick shit going on. I've dug into it. I'm close to blowing the whole thing wide open, exposing Emerson and the stuff he's been—'

'And this man has my daughter?'

'His men do.'

Enough. Whatever JT had going on, I could not get any deeper into it. I had to get Dakota back. Nothing else mattered. 'We're done here. I'm calling the cops.'

I pretended not to notice the hurt flicker across JT's face. Reaching for my cell, I began to dial.

'Please, Lori. Don't.' He leant closer, his cuffed hands resting on the edge of my seat. 'I'm so close, I need to finish this.'

I shook my head. 'I just can't.'

The cell phone beeped. A text. Not from Quinn. A different number, one I didn't know. I opened the message.

It felt like the breath had been knocked clean out of me. 'Oh Jesus. Shit.'

JT moved closer, trying to get a look at the screen. 'Lori? What is it? Talk to me.'

Dakota must have given them my number. The photo was blurred, but it was definitely my daughter: a child with strawberry-blonde braids, one half unravelled, wearing a purple *Miranda Lambert* tee. She was sitting on the back seat of a car. There was duct tape around her arms, her body, her mouth. Terror in her eyes.

I forced myself to read the words: *TELL TATE TO GIVE US THE DEVICE. NO COPS OR THE GIRL DIES. WAIT FOR INSTRUCTIONS.*

19

I stared at the screen. Couldn't breathe. Couldn't speak.

'Lori, what the—'

'They've ... they've...' I couldn't finish the sentence. Held the cell phone out to JT. Knew my hands were shaking.

Gently, he prised the phone from my fingers. Exhaled real sharp, cussing under his breath.

I clung on to the seat, dug my nails into the fabric. Tried to breathe. Tried not to cry. Just about managed both. I had to act. Snatching the cell from JT, I selected the unfamiliar number. Pressed call.

JT grabbed for the handset. 'Lori, don't. We should talk about this.'

'There's no time.' I pushed his hands away. Heard the number dial. Waited for the call to connect.

It took too long. There was no ringtone. I held my breath, listened harder. My pulse, punching at my temples, seemed loud as thunder. Then I heard it; a flat, continuous drone.

I flung the cell back at JT. 'How the hell can it be unobtainable? They only just sent the text.'

He frowned. 'They'll have ditched it. It's a pre-pay, no doubt. These people are smart.'

And they had Dakota.

I stared through the grubby windshield at the highway. It was empty. Just us. I thought about the message. No cops, they'd said. Wait for instructions. Tell Tate to give us the device. The photo of my baby bound in duct tape. I felt the fury burning in my chest. 'This doesn't change anything, I'm calling the cops.'

He put his hands on mine. 'Lori, you read the message. We have to keep this away from the cops. It's the only way to keep Dakota safe.'

I shook my head. 'Kidnappers always say that, but there's a better chance of catching them if—'

'Not true this time. Emerson is too well connected. You need to believe me. I've been digging into what's been going on in those parks. The people involved, they're powerful. You can't trust the cops, but you can trust me. I'll get her back.'

I didn't answer. Didn't know if I could believe him. 'If you want me to pin my child's life to your word, tell me what the hell is going on. Everything.'

I let the silence hang between us. Waiting.

He sighed. 'Okay. A few days after I'd been arrested at Winter Wonderland a man called Scott Palmer contacted me. He told me he managed the surveillance at the park, watched the CCTV, and analysed what went on. He'd seen what happened between me and Emerson, and he knew the charges were bullshit. He said he could help me.'

'How?'

'He could get me proof of what Emerson was doing. Scott's one of those conspiracy nuts. He's a smart guy – book-smart, not practical. And in that job, bored. He discovered the pattern.'

'What pattern?'

'Kids go missing all the time in amusement parks. They get over-excited, run about, get lost in the crowd and separated from their families. The parks have teams of people whose sole job is to find lost kids and reunite them with their folks.'

'And this is relevant to getting my daughter back, how?'

'Because the pattern showed that each time a specific set of CCTV cameras went offline at Winter Wonderland, a child went missing.'

'But you said that happened all the time.'

'It does. But these occasions were different. These kids weren't found fast. They were missing for near on ninety minutes, every time.'

I frowned. 'How the hell could he—'

'Scott went through all the missing-child reports filed with park security around the times that the cameras had been turned off. The dates and times matched. A child – usually a girl aged between eight and ten, always visiting the park as part of a large family group or organised trip – went missing. It wasn't usually spotted right away. It wasn't an accident either.'

I tasted bile at the back of my throat. Fought the urge to gag. 'They'd been taken?'

JT nodded. 'That's what Scott thought he could prove.'

They took children. Girls like Dakota. I tried to process the information, struggled to keep focused. 'So why weren't the cops called?'

'Scott figured it was due to the timing. As soon as park security had been called the search team would go into operation. The kid's family would be taken someplace calming, be told about all the measures in place to find their child, that the gates had been notified, that there was no way the kid would stay lost. They'd be told no kid stayed missing, ever. They'd tell them that it'd take a little over ninety minutes to search the park, and if that failed, the cops would come. But it never got to that. The park team always found the missing kids. So the families waited, or they joined the search. Either way, the cops never got involved.'

'And on the occasions the cameras went offline the kids were found too?'

'Always. Just before ninety minutes was up, they turned up someplace inside the park. And although the reports said they seemed dazed and unable to remember what they'd been doing – aside from how they'd been playing hide and seek or whatever, and had gotten lost – there were no other problems reported.'

Despite the heat of the day, I shivered. 'Shit, no memory, how the hell did they do that, drugs?'

JT twisted around in his seat, reaching for a bottle of water in the carryall on the back seat. With the cuffs on he couldn't stretch far enough. I didn't comment, just turned and pulled the bottle from the bag, opened it and passed it to him. He took a swig. Grimaced as he swallowed, like it left a bad taste in his mouth.

'That's what I figured. Something short term and fast acting, with little or no residue. Most likely Rohypnol or Midazolam. Both cause memory loss and make the person highly suggestible.'

I thought of Dakota, held captive by these people. Felt my chest tighten. 'But, shit, weren't the parents suspicious?'

JT shook his head. 'Seems not, or if they were, then the park persuaded them otherwise. They were so relieved, so grateful that they'd gotten their kid back safe and seemingly unharmed, no complaints were ever filed.'

I guess I could understand that – the relief they'd have felt. 'But, still, wouldn't they ask some questions?'

'Not the ones they should've, and if they did, their concerns were explained away. Emerson's people are very plausible, they come across as real caring. They're smart too, varying the pattern, changing up regularly, making it near on impossible for an outsider to spot what's really going on. Plus they're super careful: these things didn't happen close together, and never on the same day of the week or time of day. Scott believed they're working across all five parks, the infrequency in any one location keeping them undetected.'

'Until now.'

'Yep.'

I knew the question I had to ask. Didn't want to know the answer. 'These kids, were they molested?'

JT's jaw clenched. He closed his eyes a moment, then nodded. 'That was Scott's assumption. It made him angry, which made him get stupid. He started taking bigger risks, determined to get hard proof. He'd figured out where they were taking the kids – some empty rooms in a storage facility away from the public section of the park. They kept all sorts of gear there: old parade floats, character props and the like. Well, Scott set up some secret cameras there, tiny things that were motion activated. The next time he got an instruction to take the cameras offline he kept them running. He got his proof.'

I felt sick. Dizzy. I tried to ignore it. Stay focused. 'Tell me.'

JT shook his head. 'Trust me, you don't want to know.'

From the look of anguish in his eyes I knew it must be bad.

Whatever it was, he didn't like thinking on it, and he sure didn't want to tell me. I got that, but I had to push him anyways. I had to know who these people were who had my daughter, and what they were capable of doing. 'Trust me, I do.'

He took the pack of cigarettes from his pocket and tapped one out. I passed him the lighter. He lit up, inhaled deeply, closed his eyes a moment, and exhaled. Didn't look at me, kept staring right ahead. 'The kids were being taken to order. Emerson was caught on the secret cameras talking to his clients, asking them what type of child they wanted. Seemed they'd find a child that matched the client's wish-list, abduct them, and then the client would get a photo session with the kid, stripped naked ... touched ... but nothing that would leave any physical evidence.' JT's voice cracked. He took a long drag on the cigarette, like he needed it to help him keep talking. 'Scott recorded all of it.'

My heartbeat raced. I felt sick, faint. 'And they've got my daughter? Fuck. What the hell will they do to her? Dakota's *nine*. She can't...'

JT clenched his jaw. His expression tough, like barbed wire and rawhide. 'We'll get her back.'

But, shit, after what? Having been cold, I was now hot, panicky, I couldn't breathe. 'How? We don't know where she is, and if the cops are in Emerson's pocket, then how the hell can we—'

'Lori, listen to me. They need her. As long as she's bait for us, they won't do her any harm.'

I stared at JT. He looked real earnest. I hoped to hell and back that he was right, wanted so much to believe him. Tried not to think on the alternative. Couldn't.

'The device they're talking about holds all the evidence Scott had gotten: the secret camera feeds, the CCTV footage, the security reports, and the list of people he thought were involved.'

No wonder Emerson wanted it so bad. 'Where is it?'

JT sighed. 'Scott figured the same set-up was happening in the other parks Emerson owns – GatorWorld in Florida, Mountain Mystery Frontier in Virginia, and a couple more in the Carolinas. He was right, found that the same camera maintenance shutdowns happened in all the parks. He persuaded the CCTV guy at Mountain Mystery Frontier to leave the cameras running and record the footage. He did, but Scott didn't want him to email the files, said it wasn't secure. That's why I went to Virginia, I was meant to collect them.'

'Meant to?'

JT took a last drag on his cigarette, flicked the butt out of the window. 'The guy was gone, but there was a bunch of thugs waiting for me. We'd been played, or they'd beat the guy until he talked. Either way, Emerson was on to us and he knew Scott had saved evidence on to a portable hard drive. I had to fight my way out. As soon as I was clear I called Scott. He panicked. Said he'd stashed the device in a safe place but he couldn't go back for it now. He was crying, terrified. I told him to go to my cabin and wait. That he'd be safe there. That I'd help him.'

'So where's the device?'

JT shook his head. 'I don't know, but Scott does. We need to go to the cabin.'

'Then what?'

'We'll get the device, and we'll find Dakota.'

Not sitting here we wouldn't. We had to move, drive to JT's cabin in Georgia, get Scott and fetch the device. I looked at JT. 'Get out. I'm driving.'

He frowned. 'You think you're—?'

I didn't listen to the rest. Pushing open my door, I leapt out and ran around to the driver's side. Yanked his door open. 'I said get out.'

This time he didn't argue.

20

I put the car into drive and pulled back on to the highway. Out the corner of my eye I could see JT watching me, staring. I ignored him. Kept my eyes on the road.

Back when I'd taken on this job, Quinn had told me JT had been arrested disturbing the peace at the Winter Wonderland amusement park. That it was nothing serious, just a minor disagreement. I'd had my doubts, and now I knew they were justified. The JT I'd known had always done things for a reason. 'You never told me what took you to Emerson and Winter Wonderland in the first place?'

'Something personal.' JT's expression didn't change, but his tone told me to back off.

I stared straight ahead, my gaze fixed on the highway. Kept my fingers tight on the wheel, trying to disguise the fact that they were trembling. The road snaked into a series of razor-sharp bends. I didn't ease off the gas. Coaxed the Chevy through the twists, the tyres squealing in protest.

I knew JT was waiting for me to change the topic, to let it go. I wanted to, surely I did. But even though I'd decided not to call the cops, the one question repeating in my mind, over and over, would not go away: *Can I trust him with Dakota's life?*

The thing is, trust only works to a point. It has to go both ways, otherwise it's not trust, it's just blind faith or stupidity. Both can get you killed. So I knew I had to push, had to know every angle on the situation, including what had gotten JT into this nest of vipers right back at the start. Couldn't risk missing something that'd come back to bite us in the ass.

I glanced over at JT. 'Like what?'

He frowned. Disappointed. 'As I said, it's personal.'

Not good enough. 'And my *daughter* was taken. Tell me why you got involved?'

JT looked out of the side window. 'Scott asked, I agreed.' His tone was low, angry.

I ignored it, had to keep pushing. 'No, before that. Scott was a witness to criminal activity. Even without the proof you should have made him go to the cops. You uphold the law, that's your job. You've never let nothing, nobody, get in the way, and certainly nothing *personal*.'

He clenched his fists, his tanned knuckles turned white. 'You have no idea.'

'Then tell me.'

His scowl was intense, furious.

I ignored his anger. Swung the Chevy out around a big log wagon, matched it, pace for pace for fifty yards, then gunned the engine and lurched us past and back on to our side of the highway.

'Well?'

When he spoke, his words were slow and measured. 'Something happened to a person I care about. Winter Wonderland took no responsibility, shrugged the whole thing off. The cops did shit. I needed answers, proof.'

Something about the tone of his voice made me feel suddenly cold. His expression was unreadable. I wondered who this person was that he cared so much about: a woman, a child? There'd been no mention of a family in the file. I'd never figured he'd change, let anyone get that close. Maybe I'd been wrong.

'Needed?'

'Scott has what I need.'

I eased off the gas a little. 'But you're not done?'

A muscle in his cheek began to pulse. 'Not until I've gotten her justice.'

I flicked an imaginary strand of hair from my face. The way he said that one word, *her*, told me how much he'd changed. If he was emotionally involved perhaps working together would give me the best chance of getting Dakota back. Still, from his tone, I doubted he was talking about taking the evidence to the cops. There was something else. Something primal.

'A wise man once told me revenge never does taste like the sugar you expect.'

He stared right at me. 'And did you listen to him?'

I didn't look at him. Couldn't. Concentrated on the road, trying real hard not to remember the feel of the Wesson Commander Classic Bobtail recoiling in my hand, the bright crimson of the blood leaking into the dirt, that rasping sound a person makes as they try to breathe through perforated lungs. Didn't work. 'You know how that story ended.'

'So we understand each other.'

I nodded. We always had.

Whatever he was planning, the situation remained. I needed the device Scott had to get Dakota back, and I needed JT to get to Scott. For now, we were hogtied together, like it or no.

Stepping harder on the gas, I forced the old Chevy faster. Gunned it down the blacktop. Ignored the rattle of the muffler getting louder. I cussed under my breath. JT's cabin was hours away in Georgia. I wanted to be there now.

'This isn't on you,' JT said after a while.

I kept my eyes on the highway. 'How so?'

'You getting this pick-up job, it wasn't luck.'

Wasn't luck? What the hell did he mean? 'What are you—'

'As soon as I discovered Emerson was on to us, I knew I had to protect Scott. I couldn't get taken down. I'd known CF Bonds were tracking me before, but it was Bailey and, well, I looked him up and...' He shrugged.

'Yeah, I know. Bailey's got as much gumption as a beet in a pickle factory.'

JT nodded. 'But after the run-in with Emerson's boys in Virginia I knew things were gonna get serious. When I heard Bailey had gotten injured on another case I hit on an idea. I knew if I could get back to

Scott, get the device and get it to the cops then they'd have to listen. So I figured on a way to swing the odds in my favour, to get help.'

I frowned. Couldn't take in what JT was saying. He wanted to protect Scott, and get the device to the cops. But I couldn't let them do that. I needed the device. I kept thinking about Dakota. Seeing her face, her terror, as they bundled her into the black sedan. I shook my head. 'But you always work—'

'Alone. Yep. But this was different. If I failed, I needed someone who could help Scott get things done.'

Failed? JT didn't do failure. He had the top clearance rate across the Southern states, specialising in taking down the most hardened and vicious fugitives. My hands began to tremble. I gripped the wheel tighter. 'Why me?'

He smiled. It looked more like a grimace. 'Well, you always were my best student.'

'Don't shit me. I was your *only* student. So how do I fit with this?'

'When I heard Bailey was out of action, I figured they'd put someone else on me, given how close my bond's getting to the summary judgement. I knew you worked for CF Bonds, and after a bit of digging I found out their other bail runners already had cases, so I guessed they'd assign me to you.'

It made sense. 'So you took a risk.'

'Odds were good. They had to send someone. I hadn't reckoned on them having Merv pick me up, but then even he wouldn't haul me back to Florida without a licence.'

'How'd Merv know where to find you?'

'I called up Bailey. Tipped him off.'

Shit. The whole damn thing had been a fix. JT had outmanoeuvred Bailey. Quinn. Me. 'All this to have me help you? You could have just called.'

He glanced at me. 'Could I? You'd have taken my call?'

Yeah. He had a point. Unlikely. I said nothing.

'So, as I said, what's happened, at the ranch, the gas station. Dakota. It's not on you, it's on me.'

I was silent. Tried to process what he'd said. I thought I'd been free from him all these years. But he'd known exactly where I was the whole time. 'So you manipulated me, my work. Got me sucked right into the middle of this shit-storm. How could you do—'

'Didn't know about the kid.' He shook his head. 'I'd never have got you in on this if I'd known about Dakota.'

The anger tightened around the base of my throat like a noose. This was just like the first time: he'd gotten me involved in his shit and the people *I* loved had been hurt. I'd trusted him. Loved him. And then he'd hurt me too. Less than twelve hours after seeing him again it seemed history was already starting to repeat. 'You're right. It *is* on you.'

I stepped hard on the gas, and forced the Chevy to its limit. The cabin was near on three hundred miles' drive. For me, the time could not pass quick enough.

21

Miles passed. West Virginia became Virginia. We followed the forest route. By the time we hit I-77 the mountain terrain was well behind us. The landscape flattened into wide-open spaces. Green. Pretty. Made no difference to me. What JT had said about him being to blame hadn't been any kind of comfort. All I felt was guilt. It gnawed at my stomach lining, making me sicker with every passing moment.

My fault.

I shuddered. Tried not to think about what they could be doing to Dakota now.

It'd been my mistake, going back for JT. I should have left him, shouldn't have abandoned my child. Should have gotten into the car and driven as far away from him, and the devil hunting him, as I could. But I hadn't.

So I fought the nausea. Kept my foot on the gas. Hoped to hell we'd get Dakota back safe.

⥥

We crossed the state line and entered North Carolina just before noon. I figured I couldn't leave it much longer to call Quinn. He'd already left thirteen messages on my voicemail.

JT wasn't happy about me calling. He said the last thing we needed was a bondsman with a deadline. Reckoned Quinn would have the cops on our tail just as soon as he'd worked out our location. I disagreed. I knew the way Quinn worked. The way I saw it, I should follow my usual pattern, and that meant checking in with the office.

I picked up my cell. Held the wheel steady with my right hand, dialled with my left.

From the way JT clenched his jaw a little tighter I knew nothing I'd said had stopped his fretting. 'I know what's at risk,' I said. 'I won't tell Quinn about Dakota.'

He nodded, said nothing.

So be it. This was my job. I was expected to bring JT in and I'd do my damnedest to make that happen. But Dakota came first; always had, always would. I needed to buy us some time, convince Quinn we'd had no part in the trail of bodies at the ranch and the gas station, and reassure him that I was on my way back. Even supposing we made it in time for JT's summary judgement, the way things were heading there would still be a bunch of awkward questions coming my way. I needed Quinn onside.

I called the number. Put the cell to my ear.

JT glanced across at me. 'Be vague.'

'I got this.'

The phone rang once before Quinn picked up. 'Lori?

'Hey.'

'You okay? Jesus. I've left you like a million messages. I saw the news. The shooting ... those men dead, and I thought—'

'I'm fine.'

'Are you sure? Is he making you say that? It's just that I saw the—'

'Quinn, hold up a minute. I'm good, okay. I've got Tate. He's in cuffs. We're on our way back to Florida.'

Silence.

In the traffic up ahead a small Toyota's brake lights lit up. The cars around it braked too. I noticed a state trooper sitting in his ride just off the blacktop on the opposite side of the highway, watching. Judging by JT's frown, he'd seen him too.

I went easy on the gas, held back a little ways away from the car in front. Tried not to cause any drama. 'You still there, Quinn?'

'What the hell have you been doing?' His voice sounded louder, angrier. 'Did you kill those men?'

I kept my tone light. 'They were breathing when we left.'

We passed the state trooper. I felt my shoulders tense, held my breath. Watched in the rear-view mirror for him to pull a u-turn and pursue us. He didn't.

I exhaled.

Quinn was still sounding pissed, 'Well, they aren't anymore. And why shoot Merv, what'd he done?'

So Merv had been the fourth man mentioned on the news bulletin. 'I don't carry. You *know* that. And we didn't shoot Merv. We didn't kill anyone.'

'What's with the *we*?'

I sighed. 'Look, when I got to the ranch I saw Merv's car but there was no sign of him. Those three guys had Tate all tied up. I walked right in, thinking they were redneck friends of Merv's, and they tried to take me down. I still don't understand what the hell they were doing there. Was Merv able to give a statement? He needs to tell the cops it wasn't Tate.'

'Merv's in the ICU. Whoever shot him didn't do the job right. But he's in a critical condition, still hasn't regained consciousness.'

'Shit.' Until Merv told the cops what had really happened at the ranch, we'd remain their primary suspects.

'The cops from West Virginia called. They'd seen Tate's warrant, guessed that I'd have sent someone after him.'

Double shit. JT made a winding motion with his finger.

I ignored him. 'What did you say?'

'Well, given Merv wasn't licensed to act for me, I couldn't say a whole lot about it, now could I? Most I said was that you'd been on Tate's trail.'

'Thanks, Quinn. Appreciate it.'

'There's this other guy, a Fed, whose been asking too. Minute they caught wind you could be heading out of State they got in on this. Their man in charge, Alex Monroe, out of the Richmond field office, has already been in contact. Seems a real serious type – you know how those guys are. Anyways, now we've spoken I'm going to have to call him right back and tell him you've got Tate.'

'A Fed?' I glanced at JT.

He cussed under his breath.

Quinn sighed. 'Hell, Lori. This whole business with Tate, it's too dangerous for you and Dakota. If I'd have known what was going to happen I'd never have given you the job. Drop Tate off at the first police precinct you pass. Get yourself safe.'

If only I could, but if I gave up JT I'd lose my only bargaining chip with the people who had Dakota. I needed to keep him out of jail, for now at least, so I could get to Scott and the device. But I couldn't tell Quinn that. If I did, he'd pass it right along to the cops, and that could not happen – the people who took Dakota had been real clear on that. 'No, this is my job. I'm bringing him back to Florida. I'll let you know when I'm close.'

'Don't be so stubborn—'

Quinn was still talking as I ended the call, his voice rising in pitch and volume.

I turned to JT. 'He's going to tell the cops I've got you. If they've figured out we stole this car, which I'm betting that they have, we need to change vehicles, fast. Failing that, we need new plates for this one.'

JT smiled. 'Yes, ma'am.'

'What?'

'Seems you did pay some mind to what I taught you.'

⥥

Fourteen miles later we pulled into a rest stop. It was the second we'd passed. The first had been small, its surroundings too open. This one had a large convenience store, a fast-food taco place and a parking lot enclosed by a high timber fence. It was the convenience store I needed.

I'd reckoned that it would be easier to change the plate than the car. Modern cars are damn-near impossible to hotwire. I couldn't risk it. Better to unscrew the plate, swap with another, and get on our way. I needed this done, fast. Every minute lost delayed me from getting to Scott, and finding Dakota.

So the plan was clear. Get in, find a screwdriver, and get out. No messing.

I parked the Chevy in the far corner of the parking lot, nose-in. Best chance of JT not getting noticed that way. With his mugshot all over the news channels we couldn't risk him getting spotted. For now, he needed to stay free.

He stretched, his arms reaching up above his head. Placed his hands back in his lap. 'You going in, then?'

Killing the engine, I unbuckled my belt and turned to JT. 'Stay here. Don't move.'

He nodded. 'Go ahead. You've got my word.'

I guess I trusted him, to a point. But leaving him alone in the car was a risk. I needed the car to get to Scott, and I needed JT to help me get him. I couldn't chance losing either of them. Besides, my mentor had always been real clear on risk-taking: *limit it or eliminate it*. I pulled the keys from the ignition. Limited the risk.

JT didn't look pleased.

I didn't let it rile me. Him being pissed at me meant nothing. I'd do anything to get Dakota back. Whatever it took. JT had to understand that.

I climbed out of the car. In the parking lot, without the Chevy's rattling old air-con, the temperature was a whole lot higher. The humidity clung to me like a damp blanket, my skin was sweaty in moments.

By contrast, the store was air-conditioned to the max. I scanned the aisles, searching for the stuff I needed. Grabbed bottles of water, snacks. Tried to be fast, without drawing attention. Needed to find the tool section.

I headed towards the far end of the store. Dodged an old couple, and scooted around a young girl picking out ice creams with her momma. I remembered how Dakota had packed her ice cream in the cooler for our trip. Wondered how that could have been barely twenty-four hours ago; it felt like another lifetime. Everything was different now. My lower lip began to quiver. Stop, I told myself, crying wouldn't help none. I kept moving, hurried around the corner to the next aisle.

There I found what I needed. A screwdriver. I grabbed it, and a pair of wire-cutters. Turned on my heel and hustled to the front of the store.

The line at the counter was three-deep and slow-moving – one server getting coffee and operating the register. Looking over the rack of candy beside me, I peered out of the window. The Chevy was still in the parking lot. JT was sitting inside. So far things were working out just fine.

On the wall beside the checkout a flat-screen television was showing the news. A suited male newsreader reeled off the top stories: a drive-by shooting in Charlotte; a missing teenager in Fayetteville. The third story was the shooting in West Virginia.

Damn. I hoped no one spotted JT. Willed the line to move quicker.

The newsreader looked earnestly into the camera. *'The investigation continues into the multiple homicide in Yellow Spring, West Virginia, where three men died and a fourth remains in a critical condition...'*

The line moved along; now I was one from the front. I turned around to watch the screen. They were showing film of the ranch house, a body bag being wheeled across the porch on a gurney. Any moment I felt sure that JT's mugshot would flash on to the screen. And, given that, by now, Quinn would most likely have spoken to the Fed, Alex Monroe, I wondered if I'd be seeing my own face up there too.

My heart beat faster. I felt cornered. I had to stay in the line, needed the screwdriver to change the plates, just couldn't risk the Chevy getting pulled over on the drive to the cabin. But I couldn't be spotted here either. If my face appeared on the screen, one of these people would make the connection. I'd never get out of here, and even if I did, the cops would know where to look for us. That could not happen.

Stepping to my left, I pulled a newspaper from a rack in front of the counter. Opened it, held it up as if I was reading it. Hoped that it covered most of my face.

'... the identities of the murdered men have been confirmed as Richie Royston, Johnny Matthews and Gunner Zamb of Broward County, Florida. All three men have previously been connected to a Florida drugs cartel. The purpose of their visit to Yellow Spring is as yet unknown, but,

given the recent increase in drug-related homicide as turf battles grow ever more violent...'

I peered over the top of the paper, stared at the screen. My heart banged double-time against my ribs. Drugs. Was that what JT had gotten himself mixed up in? There was only one Florida cartel with that kind of power: the Bonchese crime family, otherwise known as the Miami Mob. I'd never dealt with any of their players, but everyone in my line of work knew exactly who they were. Their fingers were stuck deep into many pies. Drugs, trafficking, gambling and prostitution formed the mainstay of their business.

What I couldn't figure out was how JT was connected to them. I thought back to the ranch house, remembered how JT had leant close to Gunner as we'd turned to leave, how he'd given him a message for his boss, something about having information and working out a deal. Sure it'd been a long while since I'd last seen him, and people changed, I knew that. But JT being a willing player in the Miami Mob's business just didn't sit right. Maybe that was why they'd gotten him restrained.

On the television, the news report continued on to the next story, '*... also in West Virginia, an attempted robbery at a gas station earlier today has left one man dead and another with serious concussion, as yet...'*

The Miami Mob were vicious and smart. If the people who'd taken Dakota, Emerson's men, had killed three mob guys, then they were at least as dangerous, possibly more so.

I felt sick.

The certainty descended on me: no matter what we did we'd be dead, all three of us. We'd seen their faces. Once they'd gotten what they wanted, we'd be done. Ended.

No. I could not let that happen.

The elderly guy in line behind me tapped me on the arm. 'Lady, you're up.'

I lowered my newspaper. A peroxide blonde sporting heavy make-up and an artificial smile was looking at me real expectant. A spot of crimson lipstick had rubbed on to her top teeth – a red smear, like blood. I couldn't help but stare at it.

I put my items on the counter. Forced a smile.

'... this man is wanted for questioning in connection with both incidents...'

I glanced at the television screen. There it was, JT's mugshot. Not mine, not right at that moment anyways. That was some relief, but only a little. I handed lipstick-woman a twenty.

'He's believed to be travelling in a blue Chevrolet with the plate number...'

Shit. I grabbed my stuff. Didn't wait for the change. Had to get away, and fast. I ran from the store.

The Chevy was still parked where I'd left it. JT was slumped low in the driver's seat, good as his word.

I was ten yards out when a large SUV with blacked-out rear windows pulled up beside the Chevy and reversed into the adjoining parking spot. I slowed my pace. Didn't want to get too close. Wanted to avoid them getting a good look at my face. Limiting my risk, just in case my mugshot joined JT's on the news report next time around. I didn't want these people to remember me.

They tumbled out of the vehicle. A father, momma, and three little kids. The kids were hyped up, the parents looked exhausted. They were talking about getting food at the taco place. The smallest boy wanted the bathroom. They locked the SUV and headed towards the buildings. Didn't even glance my way.

Perfect.

The SUV was parked butt-in, tight against the fence. I slipped along the gap between it and the Chevy, glanced at JT through the windshield. He nodded like he knew just what I was thinking, stayed low. I flicked my gaze across the parking lot, made one final check. No one was close by.

Dropping to a crouch, I eased myself between the rear of the SUV and the wooden fence. There wasn't much room. I slid my legs beneath the SUV, and sat my ass down on the blacktop. The fender pressed tight against my chest, and the rough wood fence scraped my back where my shirt and leather jacket had risen up.

The SUV's plate was from West Virginia. Good. They only required a rear plate. With just this one we'd be good to go. I reckoned the family would be a while having their meal. And I was counting on them being too preoccupied with getting back on the road to notice their missing plate. With the SUV parked back against the fence, there was little chance they'd spot right away that it was gone. And we only needed a few more hours to get to the cabin.

I took the screwdriver from the plastic bag, lined it up with the first screw and began to undo it. Working it was real awkward. I was too close, couldn't get enough purchase. Leaning to my left, I angled my elbow higher and drew back until it was pushing against the fence. Better. The screw came out. I repeated the process for the second. The plate came away real easy.

Putting it and the screwdriver into the plastic bag, I swung my legs left and crawled around the SUV into the gap between it and the Chevy. I was sweating, my singlet felt damp against my skin. But I'd gotten the plate. Things were halfway done.

The next part would be trickier.

I walked between the SUV and our Chevy, scanned the parking lot for trouble. It was pretty quiet. I spotted a few people around the storefront but none of them seemed to be coming our way. Good enough.

I popped the trunk. Eased the spare wheel out, and propped it against the fender. From the direction of the store it'd look like I was fixing some car trouble.

The Chevy's plate was old and mud-crusted. I crouched beside it, pulled the screwdriver from the plastic bag, and got to work. The left-side screw came out easy enough, but the right one was altogether tougher. It had rusted tight. The screwdriver slipped out of position. I pitched forward. 'Son-of-a-bitch.'

I regained my balance. Lined up the screwdriver. Pressed hard, tried again.

It twisted in my hand. My palm felt like it was on fire. I cussed under my breath. It wasn't no damn good. The plate had to come off, and fast. I was going to have to ask JT to help. But him being out of the car made him easier to spot, plus just the thought of asking grated real bad. I'd lived alone a long while. I didn't want to start relying on a man just because he was around. But time was passing, and we needed to be out of there. I had to suck it up and ask for help.

I stepped around the spare tyre to the passenger door, opened it.

JT straightened up a little. 'You done?'

I shook my head. 'One of the screws is rusted solid.'

He got out, followed me round back. Handing him the screwdriver, I positioned myself in direct line of sight from the store to JT. 'Be fast.'

The screw was real stubborn. JT gripped the screwdriver double handed – the only option with the cuffs binding his wrists together – and put some effort into it. Didn't work, he needed more leverage.

He shifted to the right a few inches, angled the screwdriver. Tried again. The screwdriver slipped off the screw. No dice.

I glanced back towards the store and the taco place. More people had parked up, families unloading from their vehicles and heading inside. We'd not attracted attention so far. No way of telling how long our luck would hold.

I looked back at JT. He was still struggling to get a better grip on the screwdriver's plastic handle. Shit. If he was going to get this done, I needed to remove the cuffs.

'Hold up,' I said, reaching into the plastic bag for the wire-cutters.

He raised an eyebrow at me.

Kneeling beside him, I slipped the mouth of the wire-cutters around one of the plasticuffs' straps. Hesitated. If I did this, I left myself vulnerable, at risk. JT could overpower me and run. I'd lose the lead on Scott, on the device, leaving me nothing to trade for Dakota. But if I didn't do it, we'd be stuck driving a stolen car with a plate known by every law enforcer in the state. Get stopped and the game would be over. Dakota would be as good as dead.

Rule number three: *Limit your risks*. I thought on it a short moment more, weighing up the choices. Picked the option that gave me the best chance of getting my daughter back safe. Hoped to hell I wouldn't regret it.

Snipping the plastic from around JT's left wrist, then his right, I pulled the plasticuffs away and shoved them into the plastic bag with the pliers. I tried to ignore the raw, bleeding cuts around his wrists.

He tried again. This time the screw gave way and the plate came off. I took it from him, handed him the plate from the SUV. 'Hurry.'

As he got to work, I heard voices behind me. My breath caught in my throat. Were the owners of the SUV back already?

Turning, I saw a couple of teens sauntering our way. Not the owners of the SUV. These dudes weren't paying us any attention; instead they were looking at something on the lankier guy's cell phone, laughing. But, damn, just a few yards closer and they'd get a good look-see at JT and what he was doing.

I glanced back at him. He was still kneeling by the plate, had gotten one screw done, and was finishing up on the other. The teens were getting closer. They'd stopped looking at whatever had been on their cell. Damn. How long before they noticed JT? How long before they figured they'd seen his face someplace?

The lights flashed on a red Honda parked opposite. The teens were three yards away and closing. Shit. I had to do something.

My options were limited. The taser in my holster was spent, the spare cartridges sat in my carryall on the back seat of the Chevy. And anyways, I couldn't fire on these kids, it'd only bring more attention; the precise thing I was looking to avoid.

No, this situation called for a little more finesse.

JT stood up. 'We're all set.'

I leant towards him, whispered, 'Stay facing the trunk.'

When I turned back, the teens were looking at us, curious. I willed them to keep on walking.

They didn't.

The shorter one stepped closer. He glanced at the spare wheel, then at me, his eyes stopping at my boobs. 'You need a hand?'

I forced a smile. Bent down as if about to pick up the spare. 'No thanks, we're about done.'

Now both the teens were looking. Good. Hopefully that's what they'd remember. Not my face. Not JT.

I lifted the wheel into the trunk. Let JT push it back into position. When I turned back around the teens were getting into their Honda. Moments later they pulled away, stereo thumping.

Closing the trunk. I looked at JT, nodded to the Chevy. 'Let's get the hell out of here.'

⇓

Back on the highway, I pushed the Chevy to the max. The muffler was blowing, almost shot by my reckoning. Loud and unrelenting, it joined the constant rattle of the passenger-door window in a duet.

'I appreciate your helping me,' JT said after a spell.

'Isn't like I had a choice.'

He was silent a moment. I could feel his stare on me, but I kept driving, didn't look.

'We'll get her back, Lori. I'll make damn sure of it.'

His words were nice an' all, but they didn't do a thing to fetch my daughter home safe. I swung out around a slow-moving truck. Accelerated hard. 'Those men at the ranch, they were Miami Mob. Did you know that?'

He looked out of the rattling window. 'I did not.'

A lie, it had to be. So much for his appreciation. 'You sure? They had a television playing in that store. The news report made out it was some drugs deal gone bad, so quit holding out and tell me the truth. Are you working for the mob?'

'If I was, do you think they'd have tied me up?'

If he'd double-crossed them on a deal, sure they would. I met his gaze now. Wasn't done yet. 'They must have had a reason.'

'It's not about drugs.'

I swerved back into the slow lane. 'So what *is* it about?'

'It's complicated.'

'Meaning you won't tell me.'

'Meaning there are some things it'd be safer for you *not* to know.'

I gritted my teeth. Felt the anger rising inside me. 'Is that right?'

Silence.

There was a large rig ahead of us. I reckoned we were travelling a good twenty miles an hour faster. I held the car steady, didn't move to overtake, kept accelerating.

'Lori? The truck.'

I ignored him. Held my line.

JT cussed under his breath. 'Look, the Miami Mob have a grudge against me due to a skip trace I did on one of their boys. It's got nothing to do with Scott.'

'So, what, Merv's working with the mob?'

He shook his head. 'Nope. Gunner and his boys finding me at Merv's ranch was bad timing is all. They were foot soldiers, a search team, under order to hold me until one of the main guys from Miami arrived.'

'Lucky for you I showed when I did.'

JT nodded. 'Yep.'

I eased off the gas a little. 'So them finding you was what, coincidence?'

He shook his head. 'I doubt it, but that isn't important. The mob aren't working with Emerson. They don't have Dakota. Like I said, they're trying to get payback for a skip trace I did.'

Shit. If he'd kept this from me, what else was he hiding? The cuffs were off, and I didn't have another pair.

I glared over at him. 'So we've got *two* sets of murderous bastards on our trail. Thanks *so* much for the heads-up. You got any other secrets I should know?'

'We'll get her back, Lori,' he said, his expression all intense.

I pulled out around the rig, rattled the Chevy past, and swung us back into the off-side lane. 'So you keep saying.'

'Let's get to the cabin, get Scott and the evidence. Then we'll have what Emerson wants and we can trade it for Dakota.'

I shook my head. 'They'll kill us anyways.'

'I'm sure as hell not letting that happen. *We* won't let it happen.'

'And why should I trust you?'

He looked at me a long moment. 'You know why.'

And I did. The memory of that night all those years ago flashed into my mind. I heard the gunshot echo, saw Sal fall, smelt the blood, felt the horror. Watched her bleed out. Remembered what JT had done to help me fix things. What I had let him do when I had fixed them. Knew that should be reason enough.

The rage ebbed out of me. In its place I felt an ache, deep and raw, like a festering wound that would never heal right. Sal had been taken from me all those years back, just as Dakota had now. My fault, both times. I should have protected her, protected them.

I suppressed a sob as the memory of Dakota being taken replayed in my mind. Nausea ripped through me. I clung to the wheel. Focused on the horizon. Told myself that losing control now would solve nothing. I had to believe we could get her safe. Knew I'd go crazy if I didn't.

I glanced at JT. He was still watching me. The man I'd known before would never have gotten mixed up in the Miami Mob. He was a loner, sure, but he was all about justice. Thing was, whenever he was around me bad things happened. So I promised myself I would hold true to the vow I'd made ten years previously: however this thing played out, I would not allow myself to get close to him again.

I exhaled softly. Stared at the highway through the grubby windshield and shook my head. 'Why? I don't know you anymore.'

22

We reached JT's cabin at six o'clock that evening. Nestled deep in the forest, the building stood alone, shielded by the trees surrounding it. The nearest civilisation was the town of Martinez, a few miles away. The only passers-by found here were the occasional hiker or hunter, and mostly they stuck to the trails.

The place looked pretty much as I remembered. Of course, the wooden cladding had been a shade or two lighter then, but aside from that, it felt like I'd stepped back in time. If only the circumstances were different. But they weren't. This was about getting Scott, and saving Dakota.

It was almost nine hours since Emerson's men had snatched her. I'd kept my cell close all the while I'd been driving, coaxing the old Chevy through to Georgia, even when we'd stopped for gas, and refuelled on sandwiches and water. I'd checked the display every few minutes. Willed for them to call.

They hadn't.

Still, I knew that my cell was working just fine. Quinn had called again, twice. He'd left a voicemail, both times. I'd listened to them as we crossed the state line into Georgia. He hadn't anything new to tell me, just kept yakking on about how he wanted me to take JT to the nearest police precinct. When he'd rung a third time I aborted the call. If I'd have answered he'd have given me grief. There was nothing of value to be had from us speaking.

Taking us a little ways past the cabin, I parked beside the wooden barn JT had always used as a garage. Turning off the engine, I checked my cell once again. No messages and, now we were in the forest, no signal either. I didn't like that. What if Dakota's captors tried to make contact? We needed to get Scott and get out of here. Fast.

JT eased open his door. 'You ready?'

I nodded. Climbed out of the Chevy and stretched, trying to ease my aching muscles and the throbbing pain in my injured ankle. Paused. JT was already in the yard. He had an intense stillness about him, like a mountain lion measuring up a deer, calculating its next move. He watched the cabin; I watched him.

Mirroring his stillness, I listened hard. High above us, a bird twittered in the tree canopy, the leaves rustling as it moved from branch to branch. Aside from that, I heard nothing. This place had always felt secluded, sheltered. Safe. The silence was a part of that.

'Something's not right.' JT pulled the handgun he'd taken from the dead guy at the gas station and stepped slowly towards the cabin, beckoning for me to follow.

I eased the taser from my holster, glad that I'd gotten JT to swap out the spent cartridges on the drive over, and followed a couple of paces behind. I couldn't spot any sign of activity – no tyre tracks or disturbed ground – but that meant nothing. High summer never brought much rain. The dirt was packed solid. A ten-ton rig could have passed through and we still would've been none the wiser.

Ahead of us, the cabin stood on wooden stilts, the only access via six steps up to the porch. In the crawl space beneath, I noticed a neatly stacked pile of logs. The handle of the axe that'd been used to chop them stood tall, its blade half buried in a medium-sized stump. I sped up, closing the gap between me and JT, and whispered, 'Did Scott drive here?'

JT shook his head. 'Told him to take the bus or hitch. His car would've been too easy for Emerson to track.'

Keeping his focus on the cabin, he took the right side of the stairs, using the stone chimneystack for cover. I followed him up the steps and on to the porch. Seven strides and he reached the door. Eight and I was beside him again, my back pressed against the wooden cladding of the outside wall. He turned, nodded. I tightened my grip on the taser.

He eased down the door handle until it made a soft click. Unlocked, the door opened. JT stepped inside, moving fast. Strode through the living space, his gun raised. I followed, scanned the area.

Empty.

The place was ordered and tidy. No signs of disturbance. No clutter or gee-gaws. The furnishings basic and functional: a pair of brown leather couches, a small table between them, and a large open fireplace. The green rug that had covered the centre of the floor space had gone, replaced by a smaller blue one. That rug was the only thing that had changed.

I turned right, crossed the room to the bathroom. Fourteen strides from the front door to the bathroom door, just as I remembered. As I'd practised, been drilled to practise, way back when, before all this started. *Create your own blueprint*, my mentor had said. Rule number five: *Know your surroundings*. That way, when the lights go out, you can find your fugitive and get out safe. That one rule had saved my ass more times than I cared to remember. Counting distances, assessing height and sizing up obstacles had become second nature. I guess that had been the point.

I opened the door. Scanned the taupe bathroom suite. Clean, no clutter, just a brown hand towel hanging from the rail and a lone toothbrush in the holder. Aside from that, empty. I reversed out, closed the door. Turning, I caught JT's eye, mouthed the word, 'Clear.'

He nodded, eased open the door on the far left of the room. From previous experience, I knew it led to the bedroom. I stayed right where I was. Waited.

Four seconds later he reappeared. Shook his head.

'Shit.' The knot of fear I'd had in my belly ever since the gas station pulled tighter. We needed Scott. Needed whatever Emerson's men wanted. Without him we had nothing.

JT strode over to the breakfast bar. 'I told him to damn well wait.'

If he'd had no vehicle how the hell had he gotten out of here alone? It was miles to the nearest town; leaving on foot made no kind of sense. 'What if Emerson's men took him?'

'They didn't.' JT nodded to the larger of the two couches. Beside it a pile of linens had been neatly stacked: pillow, duvet, sheet. 'It's too neat, everything's in order.'

I felt dizzy, sick. How could Scott not be here? The past nine hours had been all about getting here, getting him, and getting back Dakota. I put my hand out, gripped the back of the nearest couch to steady myself. Tried to process the situation. 'So if he's gone, now what?'

JT leant against the breakfast bar, put the gun down on the countertop; metal against granite. I tried not to flinch at the sound. Didn't quite manage it.

He noticed, but didn't comment. Watched my expression for a long moment before saying, 'We need to find him.'

Sure we did, but how? JT had been so certain that Scott would be at the cabin. My vision clouded. In my mind's eye I'm back at the gas station. I hear Dakota screaming, watch her fighting as the man holding her shoves her into the black car. Stand powerless as it pulls away. Watch her hands clawing at the window. Tears down her face. Blue eyes wide. Gone.

I blinked hard. Stared at JT's gun. Felt my hands begin to shake. It was a nightmare. I should have known something bad would happen. JT always had attracted the worst kind of drama. I should never have taken the job. It was *all my fault*.

'You okay?'

I nodded, but didn't look at him, couldn't. How could I ever be okay? But *I* didn't matter. Not now. Not with Dakota gone. I could feel JT staring at me, all concerned. Thing was, I didn't want his concern. I just wanted my daughter. 'We should search the woods.'

Turning, I walked to the back door. Four paces. Drew level with the archway to the kitchenette. Halted.

Two baseball caps hung from the pegs to the right of the doorframe. I took a step towards them, then a second. Both caps were thick with dust. On the peg closest to the door hung a 1916 Cooperstown Yankees replica: red and navy stripes on white, with a navy peak. Hanging next to it, almost touching, was a smaller, faded navy cap. I reached out, touched the image on the smaller one, a crimson *B* with white piping around the edge. Brushed off the dust, near on ten years' worth. I traced the outline of the *B* with my finger. Couldn't believe he'd kept the caps all these years.

I heard footsteps behind me, turned.

JT was staring at the cap in my hand, frowning.

I didn't say anything. Couldn't meet his eye. Looked away.

That's when I spotted the note. Part hidden, pinned beneath a mug to the left of the sink. Stepping into the kitchenette, I put the cap down on the granite worktop and reached for the folded sheet of paper.

'What's that?'

I read the single word written at the top: *Tate*. Turning, I held the note out to JT. 'It's for you.'

He took the paper, unfolded it and scanned the writing. 'Son-of-a-bitch.'

'What?'

'Damn idiot's gone to get himself killed.' JT thrust the paper at me, stormed away across the living space and out of the door.

I rushed after him on to the porch. JT was out in the yard already. Pacing. Smoking. Not his usual calm self. Shit. It took a whole lot of trouble to get JT's fur all backwards. 'What's—'

'Just read it.'

I opened the note, and read the spiderlike scrawl:

Tate. You said wait, and I did. But you're not back, and it's way past when you said you would be. Have they got you? I hope not. Either way, I can't leave the device there any longer. If they get it, I'm screwed. I guess we both are. So I've gone to get it. Don't worry, I know what I'm doing. Meet me at the place we agreed, at ten o'clock on the night of the thirtieth. If you don't show I'll know you've been compromised. I'll take the device to the cops myself. SP.

So I guessed that SP was Scott Palmer. Today was the thirtieth. Shit. We had to get to him before he took the device to the cops. 'What place?'

'Thelma's Bar, downtown Savannah.'

It was a little after six o'clock; Savannah was a good two hours' drive. I re-read the note, glanced back at JT. 'Why didn't he wait?'

'Because he's a damn fool.' JT took a final drag on his cigarette, threw it on to the baked dirt and crushed it out with his heel. 'This is exactly what Emerson wants.'

'Meaning?'

Saying nothing, he turned and strode across the yard to the barn.

'Don't you damn well walk away from me.'

I jumped down the steps, and ran after him, catching him by the arm just as he reached the barn. He froze at my touch.

'You said Scott would be here,' I said, my voice louder now, angrier. 'But he's gone, and we're gonna have to chase further across state to find him.'

JT shrugged my hand away. 'I know what I said. I thought Scott *would* wait.'

'Seems you were wrong.'

'Yep.' He turned towards the barn, yanked back the bolt and flung open the door with a raw anger I'd not seen in him before.

I watched him disappear inside, heard something metal clatter. JT cussed loudly.

Opening the door wider, I peered into the gloom. JT was standing a little ways ahead. Lying on the ground beside him was a rusted oil drum with a deep dent in the middle. I looked from it to him. 'What?'

'Well, shit. Scott took the bike.'

No wonder he was pissed. JT's Harley Super-Glide was a thing of beauty. Right then though, I didn't give a damn. 'Get over it.'

'Look, I told him to stay put. He's smart, and he's into his conspiracy theories and spy shit, but he's not built for stealth.' He shook his head. 'You can be damn sure Emerson's boys will be watching out for him. He needs help.'

'So what'd we do?'

'I'm thinking.'

'Look, we need to haul ass. You said Scott's smart, so we have to work on the assumption he's dodged Emerson's boys.'

JT frowned.

I knew he didn't like assumptions, but shit, right then that was all we had to work with. 'I say we go to Savannah and the meet-up with Scott. There's no time for sitting around and—'

'Hold up. Let me use your cell, I'll call him.'

I shook my head. 'There's no signal here. I checked already.'

'Then we need to consider—'

'There is *no* time. They've got my daughter. My *child*. We need to find Scott.'

'We can't charge at this all guns blazing. Emerson has too many men, and we've no back-up. We need to have ourselves a plan. Be thorough.'

Of course, I'd forgotten rule number six: *Always have a plan*. Well, yeah, I could work with that. 'What are you suggesting?'

He stepped towards me. 'I'll go meet Scott tonight. You stay here and—'

'I'm coming with, no discussion. You're still in my custody.'

JT shook his head. 'It's too dangerous. It could be a trap.'

'In which case they'll most likely take us to the same place they're holding my daughter. We've still heard nothing from them: no time to meet, no location. Maybe we should be looking for Emerson.'

'We know what they want. They're giving us time to get it.'

I glared at him. 'You think?'

JT held my gaze. He looked beat, like his years had started to catch up with him. 'I hope so.'

So did I. The alternative was too horrendous to consider.

'Look, there ain't no telling where Emerson might be. He travels a lot, never stays in the same place more than a week or so, always moving between his amusement parks. Going after him would be like searching out a quarter in a mineshaft. We focus on finding Scott, and getting the device. It's our best chance.'

I thought on this. True, it made no kind of sense chasing after Emerson without the proper back-up, but I *had* to do something. I couldn't stand by while my child's safety was on the line. I'd work with JT's plan, sure. But I'd add an embellishment or two of my own.

'I'm coming with you.'

He thrust his chin out at me in that stubborn way of his. I held his eye, showing no weakness. Wouldn't back down.

A long moment passed, then he nodded. 'So be it.'

'Good.'

'We'll need a base, some motel on the edge of town, a room round back, real anonymous. Once we've gotten Scott we'll take him back there. Wait for Emerson's men to give us instructions about the exchange. Savannah is as good a place as any for that. It's bang in the middle of Emerson's territory.'

'Deal.'

'We should get on the road. I'll get some things together.'

I watched him stride across the yard and disappear inside the cabin. I was seething over our lack of progress. The frustration made me want to yell and scream. Instead I paced the yard outside the barn. Watched the sun's orange glow cast dappled shadows beneath the trees. I would have thought it beautiful in another circumstance; right then it just reminded me that in a couple more hours the sun would go down, and Dakota would have been gone for a whole day. The guilt gnawed harder in the pit of my stomach. She'd be spending a night as Emerson's captive. Afraid. Alone. I shuddered. Forced myself to focus on the plan, on finding Scott. Told myself that was the first step towards getting my baby home.

Three minutes later JT was back. He'd changed into a fresh shirt and jeans, and carried my carryall and his own black canvas go-bag. 'All set?'

'Yep. Where's your truck?'

He shook his head. 'Ditched when Merv picked me up. Someplace out in Covington, Virginia. No help to us now.'

Shit. 'The Chevy's dying. It's been running on fumes these past few miles, and the plate change will get called in at some point. I doubt it'll hold good for much longer. We need another ride.'

'Well, that I do have.' He carried on past me, pacing further into the barn. 'You remember how to drive a stick shift, right?'

I followed. 'Sure.'

'Good.' He stopped in front of two large wood panels that were screening off the back end of the barn. Dropping our bags on to the floor, he grabbed the closest panel and heaved it out of the way. Seemed it hadn't been moved in a long time – it creaked and groaned, dust flying up all around. He repeated the process with the second panel, dragging it to the side wall and propping it up there.

That's when I saw her. Sitting alone in the gloom, all tucked up in a cream dustsheet. The familiar shape of a 1968 Ford Mustang.

'You kept her.'

JT smiled. He peeled back the cover with the precision of a burlesque dancer removing her stockings, unveiling the car's cornflower-blue paint and chrome trim. 'Why wouldn't I?'

Fair point. He'd had the car far longer than I'd known him. She'd been rotting in a garage when he found her. He'd bought her and restored her, but never driven her. Kept her in the barn as a homage to his father, who'd raced, won and died on the track. He'd let me take her out just once, way back at the beginning. As we'd sped along the highway, windows down and the stereo blasting out classic rock, JT had told me her nickname: *The Dakota Daredevil.*

He came back for the bags, slung my carryall and his go-bag on to the jump seat, then took the keys from under the rear wheel arch and threw them to me. 'We'd best move if we're going to make Thelma's Bar for ten.'

He didn't need to tell me twice. I opened the driver's door and slipped inside. The cream leather seat cradled me like a child in a bassinet. I put the key in the ignition and fired up the engine. Heard it thunder like the hooves of a hundred-head herd of mustangs were stampeding under the bonnet. I glanced across at JT and grinned.

He nodded, smiled that crooked smile. His lips looked real tempting.

Just for a moment it felt like old times. Then I remembered the hurting at the end, and the horror of the now – Dakota, Scott and Emerson; the whole cruel mess. Felt the guilt, like barbed wire, twisting around my chest.

There was no time for old times. No time for sentiment.

I stepped hard on the gas.

23

The drive to Savannah would take us a little over two hours. If all went to plan we'd arrive around eight and have a couple of hours to check into a motel and get to Thelma's Bar. I hated the waiting. Adrenaline spiked my blood, making me restless, the confines of the car seemed like a straightjacket. Still, I couldn't do anything but drive. The delay before we could meet Scott felt like a slow, brutal torture.

As we left the forest behind us, my cell vibrated in my pocket. It'd found a signal. I checked the screen: two missed calls from Quinn. No messages. Good.

I held the phone out to JT. 'I've got cell coverage now. You gonna call Scott?'

He took the cell, dialled and waited.

I squinted into the low-slung sun, at the freeway stretching arrow-straight ahead, watched the burning air shimmer above the blacktop. Near hot enough to melt anything. I fancied I could taste the bitterness of the tar against my tongue, almost. I hoped that Scott would answer.

He didn't. JT ended the call, and handed back the cell.

I couldn't read his expression. 'Not answering?'

JT shook his head. 'Straight to voicemail, which makes no sense. He never switches off his cell.'

'He might. If he's a spy buff, into his conspiracy theories, like you said, then maybe he took out the battery so he couldn't be traced. It'd be a good move if he's worried about getting caught by Emerson.'

JT frowned. Didn't look convinced. 'Could be.'

I tried not to think further on why Scott's cell would be switched off. Needed to believe that in a few hours we'd be meeting with him in downtown Savannah. Couldn't consider failure, not when it came to getting Dakota safe. It just wasn't an option. I felt my bottom lip start to quiver and said, almost in a whisper, 'She must be so very afraid.'

'For what it's worth, I'm real sorry,' said JT, all earnest.

I ignored him. Kept staring straight ahead through the windshield, at the spot where the highway merged with the sky, far off on the horizon.

This was my fault. Regret prodded me, sharp like a cattleman's spur. Why hadn't I stayed with Dakota, why had I gone back to help JT? Why had I taken the damn job in the first place? I felt the guilt taking hold, ready to consume me, just as it had ten years back.

Two more hours and we'd be in Savannah. As I drove, I kept replaying what had happened at the gas station in my mind. Wished I could change the past. Knew it wasn't possible. If only I'd acted different, none of this would have happened. I exhaled hard. It wasn't my only regret.

'Lori?'

I shook my head. 'Just leave me be a moment, please.'

JT frowned, but said nothing.

I switched on the radio to fill the silence. Wondered how different things might have turned out if I'd never agreed to help him when he first came into my life all those years ago.

24

By eight o'clock we'd almost reached Savannah. I'd followed the highway, kept my foot on the gas, left behind small towns, farms and grand mansions, heading towards the city.

I felt another vibration in my pocket: my cell. Like the other times, my heart raced, hoping it would be Dakota's captors ready to set up a meet. I pulled it out, and checked the screen. Quinn, again. I didn't answer. Felt crushed.

To our right a church stood just off the highway. As I drove past, I peered up at the huge white cross towering high above the blacktop. We'd passed several roadside churches and more than once I'd spotted an adult store standing alongside, sharing the same parking lot. This one was no exception. I wondered if the preachers gave those stores their custom. Wondered what was available under the counter, if they traded in sick filth like the films being made at Winter Wonderland. Whether the men who used Emerson's VIP service had started off by buying illegal material from places like that.

Sons-of-bitches.

A kaleidoscope of nightmare images flooded my mind, Dakota in every one of them. I shuddered. On the radio Dustin Lynch was singing 'Cowboys and Angels'. I loved that song, used the music as a distraction, anything to stop me from thinking about what they could be doing to my baby. Had to stay focused on getting her back.

JT had long since fallen asleep, cramped in the passenger seat. I couldn't understand how. Sure, he'd been dog tired, we both had, but the very thought of sleeping seemed impossible to me. I swung the Mustang a little faster around the bends, just to see if I could wake him. Couldn't.

We'd agreed to stay away from downtown, to find a motel less popular with tourists to use as a base. Someplace where management wouldn't ask questions and the guests would mind their own business. In short, a rent-by-the-hour or the-night kind of place.

I chose the industrial quarter, an area near the Savannah Paper Company on the outskirts of town. From there it should be real easy to slip away from the motel and get back on the road in whichever direction we'd need to go to find Dakota.

As we descended the final hill, through the gaps in the trees, I caught brief glimpses of the sprawl of the city below. The sun was almost down and the streetlights were already lit, illuminating neat rows of boulevards and avenues. From the west, the paper mill's towering stacks spewed smoke like sinister breath across the houses.

My cell buzzed again in my pocket. My heartbeat quickened even though I was pretty sure that it would be Quinn once more. Still, I pulled it out, checked the caller ID: a blocked number. My heart thumped harder. I fumbled with the handset, pressed *Answer*, held the cell to my ear. 'Hello?'

Nothing. The caller had hung up.

Two blasts of a horn made me jump, dropping the cell into my lap. I jerked my head up. Realised I'd let the Mustang drift over the centre line. A large truck was bearing down on us. The driver was pointing, his face contorted with anger, yelling things that I couldn't hear, but could imagine real easy.

I turned the wheel, took us back into our lane. Cussed under my breath, banged the steering wheel with my fists. I'd been too slow, again. Just like at the gas station. I'd failed Dakota, nearly got me and JT killed. That call had to have been Emerson's men, and I'd missed them. I stared at the road ahead. Numb.

In the passenger seat, JT straightened up. 'What's going on?'

'Oh you're awake now? Great.'

He frowned. 'What'd I miss?'

In my lap, the cell vibrated twice. A voicemail. Hope. I pulled on to the dirt at the side of the highway, dialling the answer service before the Mustang had come to a stop. 'I missed a call, a blocked number.'

JT said nothing. Knew what I was thinking. Watched me real close as I waited for the answer service to pick up.

I listened. I'd gotten three new messages since I'd last checked. The first was from Quinn, left earlier that afternoon, asking where I was and telling me to call him back. The second was him too, an hour later, again asking where I'd gotten to and saying to call him real urgent.

The third message wasn't Quinn, but it wasn't Dakota's kidnappers either. It was Special Agent Alex Monroe. The Fed that Quinn had been getting a hair up his ass about. He said he hoped I was safe, and left a cell number, asking me to call him. I pressed two to save the message, and hung up. Wasn't concerned with anything he wanted right then, only with what was happening to my baby. The Fed would just have to wait.

Still, I couldn't help but wonder what this man who was chasing us was like. From his accent I'd have bet on him being Kentucky-born. I wondered if his conformation matched his breeding and the smooth richness of his voice.

The cell was still in my hand when it started buzzing again. I answered without thinking. 'Hello?'

'Lori? What the hell? Do you know how many times I've called?'

Quinn. Not calm, not happy. His voice was an octave or two higher than usual, and certainly a few notches louder in volume. I took a breath, tried to sound normal. 'Hey, yourself.'

'Jesus, Lori. What the hell's going on?'

Damn. He was freaking out. 'I've been a little busy.'

'The cops have been here crawling all over the office. And that Fed has called again. Twice. They all want to speak to you.'

'I know.'

'Tell me you've called them.'

JT moved in the seat beside me, looked at the cell, raised an eyebrow.

'Quinn,' I mouthed silently at him. JT nodded.

I spoke into the cell. 'Not yet.'

'Jeez, Lori, they're saying that Tate's right in the shit and that there's a mob connection. He's in with some bad people. The Feds are all over it. You need to take him in right now. Go to the closest precinct and hand him over.'

Shit. No way could I do that. 'He's my pick-up. I'm bringing him back to Florida as agreed. Quit worrying.'

'It's too dangerous. You can't—'

I ended the call, shoved my cell phone into my pocket, and swung the Mustang back on to the highway.

JT glanced at me. 'Trouble?'

I shook my head. 'I can handle Quinn.'

JT gave a half-smile. 'That I do not doubt.'

I piloted the Mustang along the highway as it twisted through the outskirts of the city. Log wagons hugged close on either side of us, making their way to the mill. Here the air tasted smoky, the texture chewier on my tongue than at the cabin, the atmosphere more claustrophobic.

I went with the flow of the traffic, letting it pull us, like a canoe on the rapids in the fall, past the entrance to the mill and on around its boxy, grey buildings and smoking chimney stacks. Just as the highway began to straighten, stretching away from the industrial quarter and inviting us to escape to the more attractive downtown, I took a left into the parking lot for Motel 68.

Most spaces were large enough for an eighteen-wheeler. Few were for cars. Good. That meant this place was perfect for what we needed. I swung the Mustang into a spot between a pick-up truck and a Toyota, and killed the engine. Glanced at JT.

'You set?'

He nodded.

I pulled my carryall from the back seat and climbed out. It was good to stand straight after all the driving we'd done. My back felt all bent out of shape, like it might have gotten permanently curved into the shape of the Mustang's seat. We walked towards the motel.

It took twelve minutes and five rings of the bell to get service.

Judging from the scabby paint in the lobby and the stains on the grey carpet tiles, Motel 68 sure wasn't fancy. When the skinny guy in an oversized grey shirt and black pants came out from the back room, the scowl on his face and the red creases along his left cheek told me we'd woken him.

He made a show of tucking his shirt tails into his pants, huffing and puffing like it was a physical effort, and then, with no better grace, signed me and JT into room forty-three. Low-rent joint or no, I didn't care for his attitude, but in that situation his lack of interest was a real advantage.

I asked for a twin room and paid fifty-two dollars cash. Still making no eye contact the skinny guy wrote me a receipt. I tucked it into the small billfold I kept in my purse for expenses. Habit, I guess.

'There's no twins left, only doubles,' the motel guy said, handing JT the key and not raising so much as an eyebrow when JT's shirt cuff rode up, revealing the red-raw cuff marks scored around his wrists. 'Forty-three's on the second floor, all the way around back, last one on the end. Check-out by two.'

I clenched the handle of my carryall tighter, pissed that we'd gotten a double room, and at the motel guy for giving JT the key when I'd done the paying. Then I spotted the object on the end of the keychain: a chunky wooden block, like the type Dakota had loved playing with when she was little. She'd spent hours sat on the purple rag-rug, building up towers and knocking them down. I pushed away the memory. That JT had gotten the key seemed of no importance anymore.

JT nodded thanks and we left the lobby in search of our room. Outside, in the hall, I bought a couple of sausage-biscuits from the hot-food vending machine. I passed one to JT, and we ate them as we walked. Despite my hunger, every swallow felt like an effort.

It'll be okay, I told myself. It had to be. We'd made it this far, and in less than two hours we'd have Scott and the device. From there it'd be a short step to Dakota. Problem was, no matter how much I repeated it like a mantra, I couldn't quite believe it was true.

The motel was laid out in a traditional horseshoe pattern: three lines of cream, two-storey buildings with blue doors to each room, all arranged around a small rectangular pool. The pool was flood-lit, and looked clean enough, with a white picket fence around the outside to stop kids or drunken adults falling in. It was doing its job well enough: the water lay dead calm; not a ripple broke the surface.

Our room was plain and functional: double bed, a desk and chair, and a small bathroom with a shower and no tub. The walls had been painted a dark-red hue, a colour no doubt chosen for its ability not to show the dirt. And, if regular patrons went against the dog-eared notice pinned to the back of the door, thanking folks for not smoking, then at least the telltale stains of tobacco would be lost in the shadows. I put my carryall on the bed. One bed, and two of us, gave more than a few possibilities.

I checked my watch and glanced at JT. 'I'll take first turn in the shower.'

He had his back to me. He'd liberated the coffee-maker from where it had been stashed on the top shelf of the wardrobe, and was filling the water reservoir from the basin tap. He caught my eye in the mirror, nodded.

He seemed to dominate the small space, like a giant in a dollhouse. What was to say that as soon as I stepped into the shower he'd not be gone? He hadn't wanted me to go with him to meet Scott, and I was all out of cuffs, so had no way to restrain him. If I wanted a shower I'd either have to trust him or have him in there with me. Neither was perfect, but only one option would give me eyes on him the whole time; and I needed that, couldn't let him bolt. Had to do whatever it took to get Dakota back.

I took my washbag from the carryall. Paused a moment, watching as JT tipped double the recommended sachets of coffee into the filter paper. Knew what I was planning didn't feel right, but that I had to do it anyway.

Trying to ignore the nerves fluttering in my chest, I stepped across to him and slid my hands up his back, over his shirt, to his shoulders. I felt the muscle, firm and toned beneath my fingers. Felt him tense beneath my touch. 'Why don't you come join me?'

He turned to face me, his expression real serious. His eyes searched mine with that intense gaze of his. 'You don't need to be doing this.'

'I want to.' I held his stare, my heart thumping, my mouth dry. Told myself I had to do this to keep him close, even though it felt real wrong. Knew I should kiss him, touch him, do *something* to make him believe I was sincere. I felt paralysed, didn't move.

JT shook his head, said softly, 'No, you don't. You want me to stick around, and I'm gonna do that anyways.'

I frowned. He'd always been able to read me real well. I should have known that he'd see right through my play. I definitely felt relief, but it was tainted with the bite of disappointment. Wondered briefly what was driving it – regret I'd offered myself so easily as bait, or regret that he'd not taken it?

He put his arms around me, pulled me close. The firmness of his hold felt like comfort, the warmth of his body like safety. I wanted to relax into him, to pretend just for a moment everything was okay.

I couldn't. I just couldn't.

JT must have felt me go rigid beneath his grasp. He sighed and released me. Looked real sad. 'Like I said, you don't want to.'

I stepped back, my heart pounding against my chest, put a little more distance between us. 'Tonight, you take the chair.'

He held my gaze a long moment. 'Sure.'

'Okay then.'

He nodded towards the bathroom. 'Go ahead and take your shower, kiddo. I'm not going anyplace.'

I believed him, and that had to be good enough. I forced a smile and made my tone sound a whole lot lighter than I felt. 'Just make sure that you don't.'

He smiled, and for just a moment my pulse quickened for a whole other reason than the fear that had been hounding me since Dakota was taken. Two steps, and I could have gotten close to him again. Instead I snatched up my washbag and hurried through to the shower, slamming the door behind me.

Turning the dial to the max, I stood beneath the jets of water for as long as I could bear it. The air-conditioning unit whirred and rattled, trying to keep up with the steam filling the compact space. I let the water pummel my aching muscles. Pushed away the memories of how things had been before. Refused to let myself think on how he'd felt, how he'd tasted, how I'd wanted him. How, maybe, despite my vow, I still wanted him. Even though I knew it could only end in hurt.

Goose-bumped and shivering, I stepped out of the shower and pulled a towel around my shoulders. There was no wisdom in allowing those kind of feelings back, confusing the situation, pulling my focus from Dakota.

Me and JT together were like gasoline and fire. Intensely hot, but impossible to control. And when we did partner up, the people I cared for died. This time, I knew for damn sure, I could not let that happen.

25

We arrived downtown fifteen minutes before the meet. Leaving the Mustang a couple of blocks away, we hustled towards the river. Thelma's Bar occupied a prime bit of real estate overlooking the water – a part of town popular with both tourists and locals, and traffic-free, give or take the occasional cab.

We scaled the stone steps down from street level to the harbour and followed the crowd heading for the bars on the waterfront. The atmosphere felt fun and hopeful; laughing people strolled to their evening's destinations. To me, their smiling faces seemed alien, impossible, their fun somehow ugly and distorted as if warped by a fairground hall of mirrors. How could the world just carry on as normal when my daughter had been stolen? It seemed twisted, a sick joke, like I'd been stabbed through the heart and they were laughing at me as I bled out.

JT strode fast. Fresh from the shower, he wore clean jeans and a long-sleeved shirt to hide the cuff marks scored into his wrists. I did my best to keep pace with him and disguise the limp still dogging me from the crash. I tried to focus, but damn if the cobbles weren't a bitch to walk on in my thin-soled sandals. I'd worn the only dress I ever carry in my go-bag – a plain black number, short and stretchy enough to chase down a fugitive. And I'd used a thick layer of foundation to conceal the dark bruising that'd developed along my shin. I didn't want to risk Scott getting spooked by any signs of violence.

The sound of smooth jazz filtered out from a bar a few doors down. I ignored the chilled rhythm, and concentrated on tailing JT, a little to his left and seven paces behind. A loved-up couple and a family of three filled the space between us: camouflage.

As we got closer to Thelma's the atmosphere changed from chilled to party. It felt like carnival. People laughed, kissed and danced to the music that flooded out from the bars. I tried to act as if that was how I felt too, put some wiggle in my walk and swung my purse a little, pretending like it was full of night-out nonsense – lipstick, rubbers and the like – not a weapons-grade taser.

Moving through the crowd, we passed the Cotton Exchange, and drew level with the sports bar alongside Thelma's. I checked my watch: five to ten. Felt nervous, hyper-alert. I heard a wolf-whistle from the balcony above. Looking up I saw a bunch of guys smiling. A real cutie raised his beer in salute. I stared up at him. Felt numb. For just a moment my usual savvy deserted me.

Then autopilot took over. Blend in, I told myself. Get your head back in the game. There was no choice, Dakota was depending on me, I had to make things right.

So I smiled at the cutie. If I'd been there on a social visit I would have gotten myself a piece of that. It would've made for a good distraction; a safe, no-history, no-future kind of distraction. The only kind of fun I allow myself these days. But I hadn't the time or inclination. Scott Palmer was the only man I needed in my crosshairs. He was the key to getting my daughter safe.

JT paused in the doorway to Thelma's Bar and nodded me through. As I stepped over the threshold, I felt his hand press against the small of my back, guiding me through the door. I glanced up at him as I passed.

He nodded again. Time to get this done.

They were still serving dinner. I smelt it before I saw it. Sizzling shrimp gumbo, just like my grandma used to make. I figured it must taste as good as it looked as all the tables were taken.

JT scanned the room, then looked back at me and shook his head. No sign of Scott. I guessed that, until he showed, we'd have to cool our heels at the bar.

Ignoring the grumpy expression of the waitress when I waved away her offer to put us on the list for a table, I followed JT to the bar. I was relieved Thelma's didn't have a television. No chance of JT's mugshot appearing on-screen for all the folks to see. I hoped our luck continued to hold good.

I ordered a soda. JT asked for a coffee, black, and two bourbons, no ice. The bartender, a final-year college kid with an easy smile and blond-frosted tips to his dark hair, fixed our drinks. JT handed him a twenty.

I raised an eyebrow, guessed that he'd picked up some cash at the cabin. Wondered what else he'd gotten there that he'd not run past me.

He ignored my gaze. Shook his head as the bartender put his change on a small silver tray and pushed it across the bar to him. 'Have one yourself.'

I glanced around the room. 'So what does this Scott look like?'

JT took a sip of his coffee. He slid one of the whiskeys along the polished oak to sit alongside my soda. 'Five-eight, about one hundred forty-five pounds, black hair, nerdy-looking. But he's so into his spy shit he'll probably have fixed himself some kind of disguise.'

Oh great. That really helped. 'Tell me as soon as you see him.'

'Relax, will you. And stop scanning the room so obviously. If he thinks someone's watching he'll bolt.' JT nodded to the bourbon. 'And have a drink, for old time's sake.'

'The old times weren't that great,' I lied.

JT shrugged. 'Well just be cool, then. I've been doing this a long while. I reckon I know a thing or two about pulling off a bar bust.'

He downed his whiskey in a single gulp. I left mine sitting on the bar and took a sip of my soda.

JT stared at me from under the flop of his dirty-blond hair. The years hadn't dimmed the vivid colour of his eyes; their blueness remained unnaturally bright. 'So Florida, then, how's that working out?'

'Just fine.' I answered the question he'd asked, not the one hidden beneath it. He wanted to know why I'd gone back there when I'd sworn that I never would. Tough.

He nodded, put another five dollars on the bar. The bartender refilled his bourbon.

'And you're doing okay there?'

'Sure.' I'd done plenty of skip traces, catch and deliver, but that wasn't really the question. He wanted to know how I had coped. If I'd ever forgotten that night. If I'd been able to forgive him, if I'd forgiven myself. Questions that I'd spent ten long years avoiding. Questions I did not want to have to think about. Not now, not ever.

So I turned away, glanced around the room, searching for new faces. The bar area had filled up, standing-room only. Still, I saw no one fitting Scott's description.

JT was examining me. He raised an eyebrow. 'You happy?'

'I work for CF Bonds. I've got an eighty-nine percent clear rate, highest in Lake County. What'd you think?'

He stared real pointed at my bourbon sitting on the counter. 'Sounds like a fact.'

'It is,' I snapped. Didn't like the judgement, the disapproval in his tone. He asked a question, I answered. On no account did I want to talk about how things had been, how I'd felt about him, and how he hadn't felt about me. This was not the time for that conversation. In fact, I was pretty sure that there was no time for that conversation. Ever. It was history, done. 'Didn't you always tell me to focus on the facts?'

JT nodded. 'I guess I did.'

The atmosphere between us had changed. Sure, he was pissed that I'd not drunk the bourbon, but it was way more than that. A single unclaimed measure of whiskey didn't explain the vibes of anger I felt coming from him. He might have been sitting still, but his energy was bronking like an out-of-control horse. And out of control wasn't an emotion I had ever associated with JT.

What I wanted to do was ask him what it was that he *really* wanted to know. But I didn't. Right now wasn't about me or JT, or the history between us. It was about Dakota. I tried to act calm. Reminded myself again of rule number seven: *Focus on the facts*.

I glanced at my watch: two minutes after ten. Scott was late; fact. I wondered what that meant. I looked back at JT, caught him off guard, gazing at his empty glass with unseeing eyes. The expression on his face looked like ... what? Anger. Concern. Regret. Perhaps a combination of all three.

He turned to face me, his expression neutral again. Damn. Who knew what was going on in that man's head? Maybe it was nothing, or perhaps I was just projecting my own feelings on to him. I shook my head. I needed to stop that kind of thinking and focus on the task at hand.

JT was a fugitive, just business. Scott was necessary to free Dakota. And I had a little rule of my own: *Use whatever you've got to get the job done.*

Forcing a smile, I acted like the obedient pupil I'd once been and picked up my bourbon. I raised the glass, gave a little nod to JT, and downed the whiskey. Held his eye the whole time.

He inhaled sharply.

I licked my lips, set the glass back on the bar. 'Is Scott usually tardy?'

'Not in my—'

I didn't hear the rest. Because at that moment I felt the barrel of a gun press hard into my ribs.

26

I stayed real still. The guy with the gun was on the other side of me from JT, and was standing in my blind spot, just behind my left shoulder. My first thought was that it was Scott, but that didn't fit right. There was no reason for him to threaten me. This guy was something else.

He pressed himself closer to me, whispered in my ear, 'Don't scream, darlin".'

I didn't recognise his voice, but I knew the tone; real serious with the menace to make good the threat. So I nodded, once. Glanced across at JT.

He looked from me to the guy. Frowned, and, guessing something wasn't right, stood up. 'Hey, you want to step away from—'

The dark-haired man sitting on a stool on JT's other side reached out and put a hand on his shoulder. 'You need to sit back down, buddy.'

JT swung around to face him. Fists clenched, ready to act.

The guy shook his head, his expression hard to read behind his shades. He gestured towards JT's barstool. 'Please, sit. Don't make a scene. My friend has a gun at your girlfriend's ribs; she's dead unless you come quiet.'

JT looked back at me. Now his face did betray his thoughts. He'd gotten this wrong. It was an extraction, if not an execution. Question was, who'd sent them: the mob? Emerson? And how fast could we get away? If Scott saw us with these men he'd bolt. I couldn't let that happen.

The man leaning close against me jabbed the gun harder into my ribs. I gasped. JT sat back down.

'Good choice,' said the man in the shades. 'Now, put your hands on the bar where I can see them, nice and slow.'

He waited until we'd both complied, then called over the bartender and ordered two Bud Lights. As the bartender fetched the beer, Shades leant closer to JT, nodded towards his empty glass. 'Anything for you?'

JT said nothing.

Shades laughed. 'No? Not thirsty, buddy? Suit yourself.' He took a gulp of his beer, acted real relaxed, like we were all friends catching up on a night out. The guy with the gun didn't touch his drink, kept the barrel against my ribs, stayed silent.

JT looked at Shades. 'So what's the deal?'

Shades grinned, raised his beer in a mock salute. 'Just having a friendly drink.'

I knew that wouldn't last long. Using my peripheral vision, I checked out our options. Didn't see many. The bar was crowded, the restaurant tables still full. Shades and his gunman friend acted serious enough. Chances were, they'd react real bad if we attempted to get loose. I noted the exits, seemed there were three: the main door where we'd come in; a glass door on the opposite side of the room, marked as an emergency exit but blocked by a table of four; and a swing door to the kitchen, which most likely had an exit out back.

Shades set his beer down on the bar. 'So let me tell you what happens next. Unless you want my friend here to put a nice big hole in your girlfriend, you're going to come with us, Mr Tate. We're going to finish up our drinks, and walk out of here all nice and civilised.'

'And if I don't?'

Shades laughed again. Glanced at me, gave a rueful smile. 'Well, if that happens, I guess it means he don't love you, sweetheart.'

No guessing was required – I was real sure JT never loved me – but I wasn't going to be telling Shades that. Still, his threat told me this *was* an extraction, not a kill order, not yet anyways, but they wanted JT bad enough to be comfortable with a little collateral damage. That they'd picked a public place like Thelma's showed they had balls and confidence. Scooping us off the street where we'd parked up would have been a smarter, lower-risk move.

That meant they more than likely hadn't been following us; they hadn't had to – they'd known we were coming here to meet Scott. Shit, if that were true, it meant these were Emerson's men, and there was only one way they'd gotten the details of the meet: from Scott himself.

'So I go quiet.' JT nodded to me. 'What about the girl?'

Shades looked at me a moment, then said, 'Comes with us, as insurance.' He drained the last of his beer. Glanced at the gunman. 'Let's go.'

The guy behind me prodded the gun into my side. 'Stand up, slowly.'

I did as he said, kept thinking. If they'd gotten to Scott, we'd never get the device, and if we didn't get it, then I'd never get Dakota back.

As my feet touched the ground, I half turned to the guy with the gun. He was younger than I'd expected – early twenties, bad skin, lean muscle rather than bulk. 'Where's my daughter?'

He shrugged. 'Ain't seen no kid.'

A lie, it had to be. 'I know you've—'

'Walk.' Keeping the gun barrel pressed against my ribs, he gripped my elbow with his other hand and steered me out of the bar behind Shades and JT.

Around us, folks just carried on as if nothing was wrong: a family to our left were laughing at something their youngest kid had said; an older couple to our right held hands over the table, gazing into each other's eyes. Johnny Cash played through the speakers: 'Walk the Line'. Felt like that was what we were doing.

Up ahead, through the street-side windows, I glimpsed a large SUV parked right outside the main door. It shouldn't have been there, the area was closed to traffic, letting only cop cars and taxis along the waterfront. The man in the driver's seat was staring into Thelma's. Shit. He was waiting for us.

We had to break free, and it had to be soon. Once they'd gotten us outside and into that vehicle we'd be screwed. We'd already thwarted their plans back at the gas station in West Virginia; they'd not let it happen a second time. So our problem wasn't just getting free, it was how these two gunmen might react. They opened fire in this bar and there'd be one hell of a lot of collateral damage. But I doubted that there was a thing I could do to prevent that.

We were fifteen paces from the main door. Three more steps and JT would be directly level with the kitchen entrance on the far right of the room. I watched him real close, waiting for my cue.

He kept walking beside Shades, and I kept watching. Nothing changed, not his speed or his body language. The guy with the gun was holding my elbow, the gun still pressed firm against my ribs. Still, I knew I had to be ready. So I kept walking, and with my free hand, the one carrying my purse, I felt for the fastener, and eased it open. Inside was my taser. I knew I'd need to get a hold of it fast.

Another step and JT would be level with the kitchen door. I felt the gunman tense beside me, realised he'd clocked the exits too, that he was ready to react if we made a move. That narrowed our odds of success a whole lot.

JT had passed the sweet-spot for the exit; he didn't even look.

The gunman relaxed his grip on my elbow a fraction. The gun didn't seem so tight against my skin. Big mistake.

Ten paces from the main door, JT made his move. It happened real quick. In one fluid movement, he stepped wide to his right, and swung his fist into Shades' face, connecting hard. Shades dropped to his knees, but wasn't out. Leaping up, he came back at JT with a punch to the stomach, then grappled beneath his jacket, going for his gun.

I couldn't help. I'd gotten problems of my own. A beat longer behind JT's move than I'd intended, I twisted away from the gunman's grasp, shoving him off balance as I grabbed for my taser.

He lunged for my arm with his free hand. 'Bitch, stop, or I'll shoot.'

'Me first.' I raised the taser and fired. The electrodes hit his chest before he'd a chance to deflect. His eyes widened as the volts jolted through his body. He crumpled forward.

I shoved him away. Dropping the gun, he fell back, sprawling on to the nearest table. Glasses and plates shattered on the floor, and diners leapt from their seats, shouting. He was flapping about like a landed fish. Worst five seconds of his life, I'd bet.

That's when the screaming started.

27

People screamed. Children cried. Glass and china shattered.

I swung round, looking for JT. Spotted him six paces away, still fighting Shades. JT looked to be winning, but there was a bigger threat: the driver from the SUV was out of his vehicle and heading towards the main door, weapon in hand.

'JT,' I shouted. 'We gotta go.'

He planted a swift uppercut to Shades' jaw, followed by a head-butt to send him down. Broken nose, concussion, and the man's lights were out for the near future.

People were on their feet, grabbing their things, rushing for the exits. There wasn't much time, someone would've called 911. We had to get out.

JT crouched beside Shades, pulled a Glock from the holster beneath the man's jacket then headed my way. Behind JT, the SUV driver was coming through the main door, blocking our closest exit.

'This way,' I said, and sprinted towards the kitchen.

We pushed through the mishmash of chairs, dodging round people: teenage girls with black mascara tears running down their faces; an elderly man with his glasses crooked across his face; parents carrying their children, whispering reassurances.

We'd just made it to the other side of the room when I heard the gunshot.

Bullets thudded into the polished oak behind us. I dived for cover behind the hostess station. JT followed, returning fire. Two shots.

A little ways to my right I saw a middle-aged lady with a frizzy perm crouching beneath a table. Her shoulders were shaking, dark patches of sweat spreading beneath the armpits of her 'I ♥ Savannah' t-shirt.

She stared at me, her eyes wide and terrified. I motioned for her to stay down.

More shots fired. Two wall lights shattered above us. SUV guy's aim was either real poor or real good. My thinking was his orders were to take us intact. The lady with the frizzy perm fainted.

SUV guy shouted, his words slow and deliberate: 'Robert Tate. You come nice, and no more of these good people need get hurt.'

Son-of-a-bitch.

Above the screams and cries of the people still trapped in the bar, I heard the wail of sirens in the distance, getting louder, closer. Turned to JT. 'We've got to get out of here.'

He nodded. Ejected the magazine from Shades' Glock and checked the ammo. Almost out. 'They've gotten to Scott. He gave me up.'

More gunfire. The black-and-white pictures on the wall to our right shattered. The SUV guy spoke again, 'There ain't no place to run, Tate.'

By my reckoning it'd take six paces to reach the kitchen door. We'd be exposed the whole time, no cover. Not good odds. 'What about Dakota?'

'They want me alive. Means they're still looking for the device.'

I peeped around the edge of the hostess station towards the front door. No way out that way, SUV guy was blocking our path. He raised his weapon, fired again. I ducked back out of sight. 'I have to find her.'

'We will, I promise.'

Great. Another promise. The sirens were real loud. Blue-and-white lights strobed across the ceiling. 'We gotta—'

Glock raised, JT scooted to the edge of the hostess station. 'Get out through the kitchen. I'll be right behind you.'

I shifted forward into a crouch, ready to run.

As JT fired at SUV guy, I leapt to my feet, shoved my way through the swing door to the kitchen and sprinted to the exit.

Didn't look back.

⇓

It was chaos on the river front. People milled around in all directions, the carnival atmosphere of earlier was gone, replaced with fear. Head down, I stepped out of the narrow alley between Thelma's and the sports bar, and tried to blend in with the crowd.

Up ahead, cops were entering the bar, firearms drawn. I glanced back towards the alley, scanning the faces around me. No sign of JT. Shit. I couldn't risk waiting much longer, but I didn't know if he'd gotten out, or whether any of our would-be abductors had either.

I moved with the crowd, letting myself drift with them across the cobbles, away from the bar. Surrounded by people, I couldn't see the ground. I tripped, stumbled. A big guy pushed into me, stomping his foot on to my left sandal, pinning me to the spot. As he twisted away, I felt a sharp pain, then the strap around my foot snapped. My ankle began to throb.

The crowd carried me with them, sliding along the uneven cobbles with one sandal flapping off my foot, useless. I needed to move quicker, or be able to stand my ground. I grabbed a lamppost, hung on with one hand as I tugged off my sandals with the other, dropped them right there in the street.

That's when I heard the shouting. Inside Thelma's, the cops were yelling at a suspect, telling them they were surrounded by armed police and to put up their hands. I turned towards the sound, listened harder.

There was a brief pause, then two shots. Fuck. JT? My heart banged against my chest. Had they gotten him cornered? Was he shot?

The rubberneckers closest to the bar started screaming. The crowd surged away from the building, pulling me with it once again. I tried to turn back, wanted to see what was happening. Couldn't. Felt crushed, my feet trampled. Jolted side-to-side, buffeted along, powerless to fight against the stampede.

I was held captive in the sweaty embrace of the crowd for a hundred yards, maybe two, until the street widened and the herd began to thin. Wrestling free, I headed for the steps up to street level then tore across the cobbles, the stone warm beneath my feet.

I felt my cell vibrate in my pocket. Couldn't answer it, not right then. Whoever it was, I needed to get gone, and fast.

So, I kept running, weaving through the streets of the historic district. The rules of this game had changed-up. Our plan was busted. The opposition had strengthened their hand with Scott and Dakota captive. And now they had JT too, maybe. At best he'd be lying low, waiting on a chance to get away unseen. At worse, he'd be dead. But I couldn't think on that scenario, had to keep moving, back to the Mustang and back to the motel. And so, with the sirens fading into the distance behind me, and the gunshots echoing in my mind, I ran.

I had to stay free to remain in the game.

28

I turned into the motel parking lot a little before midnight. Parked up at the far end of the car spaces, sandwiched between a yellow Jeep and the uncoupled cab of an eighteen-wheeler. Climbing out of the Mustang, I winced as my feet touched the ground. My soles were sore and blistered, and as I made my way across the lot each stride pressed dirt and grit further into my flesh. I clenched my jaw, and focused on reaching the building.

I took the concrete steps to the second floor. The sound of rock music played from somewhere up ahead. Despite the lateness of the hour the air was sweaty-warm-unpleasant, like a fur coat in LA.

Ahead of me, sat on the concrete floor, his naked back pressed up against the wall, was a big man with a small bottle of vodka. He held it out to me, slurring, 'Fancy some, darlin'?'

There wasn't much left. 'No, sweetie, you keep it.'

'Suit yourself, bitch,' he muttered, and slugged back the vodka neat.

As I'd guessed earlier, Motel 68 sure wasn't a family-friendly place. For a moment I felt relief Dakota wasn't with me, then straightaway came guilt. Wherever they had her captive, it would be a damn sight worse than here.

As I strode along the walkway the music grew louder. The door to the next room hung open. Two guys sat inside eating; a pizza box lay open on the floor. 'Evening pretty lady,' one called. 'Want to party?'

Guys from the paper mill I reckoned, looking for a little fun after their shift. I shook my head. 'Some other time.'

'Oh, momma, don't leave—'

The guy was still talking as I walked away, lengthening my stride to the end of the block. I glanced over my shoulder. Someone could have followed me from Thelma's. I had to be ready, alert. Perhaps JT was already back at the room, waiting. I hoped so.

I turned the corner. This block was furthest from the highway. Between the rooms and the start of the woods behind them was a large parking lot with bays way bigger than standard-sized spaces. Lines of massive rigs stood like gleaming metal dominoes beneath the floodlights.

Beyond the rigs, the trees stood dark and still. There was no moon. No wind. Somehow that made them more creepy, foreboding. Was anyone out there, watching? Cops, Emerson's men, the Miami Mob? I hugged my arms around me, walked faster.

I passed room thirty-nine. Mine was just a few doors down.

Outside room forty sat an older guy. He'd lifted a chair and side table from his room and placed it on the walkway like it was his own personal veranda. He watched me approach, dark eyes fixed on mine. His skin was deep tan and weathered, his black hair pulled back from his face in a long braid. In his right hand a cigarette burnt low against his fingers. From the scent I knew that it wasn't pure tobacco.

'Beautiful night,' he said.

I nodded, kept walking.

'You wish Sal was with you.'

My breath caught in my throat. I slowed my step. '*What* did you say?'

'You're afraid.'

I halted but didn't look back. My fear spiked; my mouth went dry. Who was this man? Did he work for Emerson? Focus, I told myself. I inhaled long and slow. Counted to three. Let the breath go.

I turned. The old guy squinted up at me. Pushing sixty, I reckoned, from the deep lines etched into his face and the grey peppering his temples. He didn't look like anyone's soldier. Not now, anyways. He flicked the ash from his smoke into a takeaway coffee cup. On the table, beside the cup, a small red candle burnt with a yellow flame. Beside it lay a gnarled piece of what looked like a tree root. Next to that, a knife.

He smiled, held the joint out to me. 'Fear has clouded your aura.'

I shook my head, started turning away again. 'Bullshit.'

The old man chuckled. He took a long drag on his roll-up, exhaled. The smell of weed grew stronger. 'No, I see it. Dark purple.'

Great. An all-seeing pothead, just what I needed. 'You know what, I've had a really long day. I don't need this shit.' Turning, I walked towards my room.

The old man sighed, deep and long. 'Why not let Sal help you?'

Despite the heat, a shiver ran up my spine. I spun back to face him. 'What?'

He smiled, the lines deepening around the corners of his mouth and eyes. 'You don't need to feel alone, just let Sal in.'

I frowned. I'd had way too much crazy for one day. 'She's dead.'

His smile grew broader. 'Just because someone has passed, it don't mean they can't guide us.'

I met his stare, held it for a long moment. Shook my head. 'You're wrong,' I said softly. 'Dead is dead.'

His expression changed to one of sadness. 'You believe that?'

'Yes.' Suddenly cold, I hugged my arms tighter around me and strode on.

'Just ask; Sal will help,' the old man called after me.

Closing the door to room forty-three I shut the world out. Told myself to ignore what the crazy old bastard had said. How could he know about Sal? For all I knew, *his* name was Sal. I couldn't let him get to me.

The room stayed gloomy even with the lights on. It made it seem more depressing than before. I made a quick sweep of the place, re-checking the layout and making sure I was alone. My carryall was still under the desk where I'd left it earlier. I checked the cupboard and behind the shower curtain, just to be certain. I don't like nasty surprises and there'd been way too many of them recently.

I locked the door and added the chain. It wouldn't do much to prevent someone getting in, but the noise of it breaking should at least give me some warning. JT could damn well knock.

I sank down on to the wooden chair beside the desk. It creaked, seemed a little wobbly, but held up okay. Seemed that was a pretty accurate assessment of how I felt. I stared in the mirror, noted the smudge of dirt above my right eyebrow, the rip in the shoulder of my dress, the guilty expression on my face. I glared at myself, snarled at my reflection, 'How the hell did you let this happen? What kind of a mother are you?'

No answer. The silence seemed claustrophobic.

Sixteen hours had passed since they'd taken Dakota. There'd been no further message after that first warning. We'd done as they asked. Told no one, waited for instructions. Still nothing.

Right then I felt real alone.

On the desk, beside the small kettle, was a bottle of water. I reached for it, tried to unscrew the cap. Couldn't. My hands shook, my fingers unable to grip. I cussed under my breath, threw the bottle on the floor and slammed my fist against the desk. I deserved the pain. But I also knew it wouldn't ever be enough.

What if I never got Dakota back?

Sobs heaved through my body. My breath came in gasps, as if a barbed-wire noose was tightening around my throat, constricting the oxygen. I struggled to breathe. Stumbling forward off the chair, I fell on to the bed, gasping.

I hugged my arms tight around my knees, shivering. Tears blurred my vision. Darkness closed in. I fought the images seeping into my mind. Couldn't let it happen again. Couldn't lose someone I loved.

Could not be responsible.

29

I didn't know how long I lay on the bed sobbing that way. May have been seconds, may have been hours. In the end it was the memory of a vibration in my purse as I'd raced back to the Mustang that brought me out of it.

Standing up, I reached for my cell and poked it awake. The battery symbol was red; almost no juice left. I grabbed the charger from my go-bag and plugged it into the power. As I did, I noticed the icon for a new email was showing at the bottom of the screen. My heart thumped harder as I opened it, then slowed again. The email I'd got was from Quinn. In the subject line were five words: *This might change your mind.* There was no other message, only an attachment – a thirteen-page file.

On the nightstand, the digital display of the ancient clock radio glowed 00:47. I made myself a strong coffee and started reading.

The file held four separate documents.

The first didn't spook me any. The Face Sheet, the court-certified document that listed a defendant's crimes, had changed. The first charge listed was assault, just as before. But a count of theft had been added to the tally. I'd done enough jobs to know that wasn't unusual; oftentimes charges get added to the Face Sheet after bail's been set and paid. Not usually this long after, sure. But perhaps Quinn hadn't kept his paperwork as tight as he'd ought to. I recalled our conversation in the office. I'd guessed the rub when I took the job. A high bounty on a simple assault, at an amusement park or no, was always likely to gather more charges.

The second part of the file seemed to be a chunk of the police file on JT's arrest: scanned handwritten notes from the arresting officer's scratchpad; typed file notes on progress from the police log. I wondered how Quinn had gotten a hold of it.

I paused, took a large mouthful of coffee, and continued reading. Three lines in I got my first surprise.

Quinn had said the 'minor incident' JT was charged with involved no guns.

Not true.

The file said JT had been carrying two Colts. Weird. I'd never seen him carry anything other than a Glock, and going tooled up into an amusement park, well that didn't sound like JT's style at all.

Had Quinn deliberately misled me? He was always minded to protect me from the more dangerous jobs, and given he knew I might be taking Dakota, I doubted he'd have sent me if he'd known. Mind you, Quinn would be in a whole heap of trouble if JT wasn't back for the summary judgement and CF Bonds forfeited the bond. A hundred thousand dollars was one hell of an incentive. Maybe he *had* lied.

I flicked through the details of the assault. Three men were involved: two security guards, and the amusement park owner, Randall Emerson. His name was already burnt into my brain. According to the police report, JT had broken Emerson's arm in three places and threatened to shoot him in the head. But was it true?

Given his cryptic email, I guessed that Quinn thought so. I scrolled through the document, searching for Emerson's statement. Short and economical on words, it stated that a man, later named as Robert James Tate, had been seen acting suspiciously in the Reindeer Street shopping area by one of Winter Wonderland's security advisors. When the security advisor had approached him, Tate had dropped a Percy Penguin premium Christmas bauble, hand-painted, with a retail value of a hundred and ninety-two dollars, and run. Suspecting Tate of attempted theft, the security advisor had pursued him, with the assistance of a second member of the security team.

Tate had taken a narrow passage between two of the park's attractions and trapped himself in a dead end. The file said that when they caught up with him he'd pulled two firearms. Emerson stated that he had witnessed the altercation while touring the park as part of his regular visit schedule, as owner of DreamWorld Inc. Tate had attacked Emerson and threatened to kill him if the security guards came closer. Emerson said he was terrified. Firearms were not permitted in the amusement park, and there were metal detectors on the arrival gates; he himself was unarmed. Tate hit him, and put a gun to his head.

That didn't work for me. JT threatening to shoot an unarmed man over a misdemeanour theft made no kind of sense. The file gave no evidence of any shots being fired, or that the Winter Wonderland staff carried weapons. A copy of the amusement park's operating policy confirmed what Emerson had said about firearms not being permitted onsite by anyone – employee or visitor.

Apart from that, JT's version of events suggested this whole police report was a crock of shit. He'd told me his reason for going to Winter Wonderland was to speak to Emerson. That he'd been looking into something personal. Whatever it was, Emerson didn't mention it in the witness statement. From what he'd said it seemed nothing had been said between them, that JT had attacked him unprovoked, and then been taken down when more security advisors arrived on the scene and shot him with a tranq dart. I noted that the employee who'd pulled the trigger had initially been taken into custody too, before being released a couple of hours later with no charge.

That's where things got even weirder.

When I'd first taken the case, Quinn told me the reason JT's bail was high was because the incident had occurred at an amusement park. Florida protects its major tourist attractions by coming down hard on the perpetrators, cleaning up the mess real quiet and keeping it out of the papers. That made sense; nothing bad can ever be reported as happening in the places where dreams come true. But in this case it seemed Randall Emerson *didn't* want JT to be charged. A file note detailed how Emerson had initially resisted giving a statement.

I stared at the screen of my cell. What was I missing here?

My mind felt sluggish. One question repeated in my mind: why would Emerson not want JT to face charges? I read back through the police file. I didn't believe the half of it. Someone had finessed the file after the fact, concocted a nice little story to explain away the incident at Winter Wonderland And it was completely plausible, just so long as you didn't know JT.

In spite of everything, or perhaps because of it, my money was on JT having truth on his side. Problem was, my beliefs didn't matter squat. All that would matter was how the jury saw things, and they didn't know him the way I did. They hadn't faced their fears with him. They weren't there the night JT had my back. If they had been, then my life would have played out real different.

That was when it hit me. The judge and jury, the reporters and the publicity, they were the real reason why Emerson didn't want to press charges. Had to be. He didn't want JT to have a platform to tell his version of events and for the truth to come out. JT might not have had proof, but him speaking out about the horrors going on in the parks was too much of a threat. Emerson had wanted JT released so they could eliminate the risk of him talking real fast. But things hadn't worked out that way.

Trying not to let myself wonder about this person who'd become so important to JT, I took another gulp of coffee. It'd gotten cold, but the caffeine hit was still good. I needed it. I'd lost track of the hours I'd been awake, but I reckoned I'd be near on my second lap of the clock. Didn't matter. Not until I had Dakota safe.

The third document I did not like, but I believed. It looked like a PDF copy of a police database search: a conviction record for Robert James Tate. I stared at the text. It seemed to jump around before my eyes. Shit. This wasn't JT's first time being arrested. He'd been up on a previous assault charge: a misdemeanour, for drunken fighting in a bar three years before.

He *had* changed. That was something I'd never have reckoned on him doing. I mean fighting, sure; but because he was drunk? Never. Still, it was the next line of detail that shocked me most.

I held the cell phone closer. Read the details again.

'You've gotta be shitting me,' I said out loud.

I'd read it right the first time. JT had been arrested at a bar in Winchester, West Virginia. The guy he'd battered was one Merv Dalton. The charge had stood. JT pleaded guilty.

His bounty-hunting licence had been pulled for twelve months, and he'd done thirty hours' community service at a children's home in Savannah. That'd been the end of it. But it didn't tell me why the fight had happened.

Still, the why of Quinn sending me the file was clear enough; he wanted me to give JT up and get the hell away from the case. Problem was, he didn't know the half of what was going on: not about Dakota, or Scott, or Emerson. There was no way that I could back away with my hands up now. I had to follow the trail to Dakota. Whatever it took.

It was the final document, a one-page lie that convinced me beyond doubt that JT had been set up. Quinn had highlighted the text in yellow. It detailed a new warrant, and four new charges, one aggravated assault and three counts of homicide: Merv Dalton, Gunner, and his two boys. All found at the ranch in Yellow Spring.

I scanned the details. Felt sicker and sicker. They'd gotten forensic evidence that put JT right there at the farmhouse with his fist in Gunner's face: plenty of DNA, and a whole marathon of fingerprints. Not one mention of me.

Instead there were three dead bodies and a fugitive's name in the frame. But, no matter what the file said had happened, *I* knew it wasn't right. I'd been there, I knew the truth, and besides, JT would never shoot an unarmed man. My mentor had always been real strict on his eighth rule: *Force only as necessity, never for punishment.* JT lived that shit. I was the one who failed to obey.

30

I woke with a jolt, stiff from falling asleep cramped-up in the chair and nauseous from too little rest. The grey light shining through the gap in the drapes told me it was morning. I scanned the room. The bed hadn't been slept in. The door was still locked, the security chain connected. JT hadn't come back. He hadn't knocked or banged on the door. We'd made a promise: if we got split up then we'd meet back at the motel. He had not kept his word. I didn't want to think on what that meant.

My cell was still in my hand. I stared at the cracked, blackened screen and remembered the final page of Quinn's file, the arrest warrant for multiple homicide. The file was wrong. JT had been set up, no doubt.

Gunner and his boys had been breathing when we'd left. Merv hadn't even shown. Whoever killed them did it after we'd gone and made it look like JT was responsible. It had to be Emerson's boys. Maybe they'd reckoned JT had escaped and framing him would help flush him out, make him easier to find. Maybe they'd not figured on him having been caught by a bounty hunter.

I stood and stretched, trying to ease the tension in my shoulders. Didn't help none. I felt weary deep to my bones: teeth aching, body feeble, mind scattered. In energy credits, I was broke. Beat.

If Emerson hadn't known there was a bounty hunter due to pick up JT from the ranch, he'd learnt about me pretty fast. By snatching my daughter and demanding the device as ransom, his men had gambled on the fact JT would help me. Last night, in Thelma's Bar, they'd threatened me in order to get him to come quiet. In ninety-nine percent of cases those tactics would never work: a fugitive wouldn't ever help out a bounty hunter. So how did they know it would work with JT?

Shit. Maybe they'd discovered our history.

I used my fear to force myself alert and assess the situation. First off, I had to be sure JT hadn't returned.

Padding across the room, I slid the chain back and opened the door. The air outside felt damp and thick, like you needed to grab it between your fingers and squeeze out the moisture. I reckoned the temperature was near on eighty and climbing.

I checked the walkway left and right. No one.

Promise my ass.

That's when I saw it. The carved figure, no more than two inches high, was sitting right in front of the doorway. I bent down and picked it up. Held it between thumb and forefinger. Studied it. It wasn't Sal, and it wasn't Dakota. It looked like me. I shook my head. That crazy old bastard really had been talking shit. I wasn't sure if I wanted to laugh or cry.

I didn't do either. Shoving the wooden figure into the back pocket of my jeans, I stepped over to the railing and stared out over the parking lot, past the huge rigs gleaming in the early-morning sun to the trees beyond. They stood dark and dense, blocking the light so the ground beneath them lived only in shadow.

What had happened to JT? If he'd gotten out of Thelma's, stayed in Savannah a while longer, hiding out or following the gunmen, then him not being back was still cause for hope. But what if the SUV guy had caught him, or the cops had taken him prisoner? I flinched, remembered the two gunshots, didn't want to consider the possibility of something worse.

Delayed, captive, or dead – I'd no way of knowing. Whichever it was, the end result was the same. Doing nothing was not an option. Getting Dakota back was up to me.

I needed the device to trade for my daughter. Scott had it, or at least knew where it was. Problem was, I had no clue where to find him. Last night JT had reasoned that Emerson's men had gotten to him. We didn't know for sure.

I strode back into the room, and, grabbing my cell, opened my call history and looked for the call JT had made to Scott the previous night.

I pressed the number. Waited as the call connected. In the silence, all I could hear was my pulse thumping.

Two rings, then the voicemail picked up. A nasal-sounding guy spoke on the recorded message, 'You've reached Scott. Leave a message, I'll call you right back.'

As the beep sounded, I hung up. Voicemail again, and JT had said Scott never turned his cell off. Damn. I guessed JT had been right. Somehow I doubted Scott would be calling back anytime soon. He was a dead end, for now at least, so that meant the device was too.

The knot in my stomach tightened. Without the device I'd nothing to trade. Worse, if they did have JT, and Scott knew his protector was captive, how long would it be before he gave up the location of the device? JT wouldn't cave, that was for sure. But Scott – JT had doubted that he'd last long. Once they'd gotten the device Dakota would become unnecessary.

I shuddered. Tried not to think about all the things JT had told me about Emerson and his sick sideline. I couldn't let that happen to my daughter.

I needed another plan. I had to find the men who had Dakota.

JT had told me Emerson travelled between amusement parks. Chances were that he'd not seen Dakota yet. I had to hope that, while she was still of value as an asset for blackmailing me, she would be safe from him. I just had to believe that. The alternative was too horrendous.

I strode to the basin at the far end of the room, ran the cold tap and splashed water on my face. My stomach rumbled. Moving back towards the desk, I grabbed the pack of cookies that'd been laid out beside the kettle and coffee sachets, and scoffed them down. Felt a little better. More alert. Good.

Now focus, I told myself. Treat it like a job. If Dakota was still with Emerson's goons, the men who'd snatched her at the gas station, then I had a chance. Track them, jump them, and take care of business. Think. What's the best way to track a moving target?

Find the constant. There's always one: a person, a location, an item. Find it, and you'll find the target. What was the constant here? The pieces of the puzzle circled in my brain: a bounty hunter and a security guard working together; a police report that didn't match JT's version of events; the men at the ranch getting killed; Emerson's men chasing us; Dakota kidnapped; the search for Scott.

I walked back to my carryall by the desk. Pulled my ruined dress off over my head and chucked it in the trash. Thought harder. The timeline of the last few days, it fitted together real neat, but it didn't help me none. Me, JT, Dakota, Scott, Emerson's men; the constant that linked us was the device. But the Miami Mob connection, JT had denied that had gotten anything to do with Scott and Emerson. So the device couldn't be the constant I needed. There had to be something else. I had to look further, past the obvious.

So, as I rummaged in my carryall for my spare pair of jeans, I made an effort to put aside my immediate concerns and thought about the file Quinn had sent me: the details of JT's previous conviction; the homicide charge; the rednecks who'd jumped me at the Yellow Spring ranch and the absence of Merv; the television news report linking the Miami Mob to the ranch shooting.

But the puzzle pieces just didn't fit.

I felt the nausea rising. Dropped the jeans on the floor, gripped the edge of the desk. The wood was cool beneath my fingers. I shut my eyes, concentrated on my breathing. Inhaled. Counted to seven. Exhaled. Counted to eleven.

That's when I remembered.

My mentor had always given me a tough time about my being so damn impatient. 'Trouble with you kiddo,' he'd say, 'is you assume that partial view you've got is all you need to know. You gotta be mindful of the bigger picture. You go making decisions based on one piece of evidence, acting like that one thing is the whole truth, and you're heading for trouble.'

Well, shit. Trouble couldn't have gotten much deeper than it was at this moment, now could it? I thought about rule number four: *Don't make assumptions.*

Maybe I wasn't looking at it right. What if I had all the puzzle pieces but I'd gotten them turned around the wrong way. What if the constant wasn't linked to the device? What if it was linked to JT?

I bent down, picked up my jeans and pulled them on. As I reached into the carryall for a tee, I thought that maybe Merv being the one to pick JT up hadn't been a part of JT's plan. Perhaps he'd reckoned on it being Bucky, hadn't known that Bucky had gotten himself all shot up on another job. And Bailey wouldn't have cared a damn about any bad history between Merv and JT. His eye would have been on the prize, not the practicalities.

Way I saw it, Merv was most likely still pissed about whatever happened between him and JT in that bar a few years back. He'd pressed charges against JT. Turned on one of his own, another bounty hunter. That was messed up. You had a problem, you got it straightened out between yourselves. Physical or verbal, whatever it took. But calling the heat? Never.

So the thing between them, I reckoned it had to be a big deal. Which meant that, whatever axe Merv had been grinding for JT back then, he was most likely still carrying. And with JT in his custody he'd have had the perfect opportunity to give it a swing.

Instinct told me Merv was balls-deep in this thing.

I thought back to the start of the job, two nights before at the Yellow Rock Ranch. Merv should've been there to meet me, but he wasn't. The three rednecks worked for the Miami Mob and, from what JT said, they'd been soldiers waiting for a higher-ranked gang member. We'd gotten out. Emerson's men must have pitched up a few hours later.

Both groups had been after JT.

Question was, how did they know where to look? Aside from me, and JT himself, only three other people had known his whereabouts: Quinn, Bailey and Merv.

I doubted that Quinn would have given me the job if he'd been planning to stage an ambush, and Bailey, bigoted son-of-a-bitch that he was, had no form at being a rat. So that left Merv. A man always after the fast buck, who'd hire himself out to the highest bidder, no questions asked.

Maybe this time, instead of his skills, he'd offered up JT's location. Sold him out. From the near-death whipping he'd gotten, I guessed he'd sold out twice – tried to take money from the Miami guys *and* from Emerson's men.

Well that move had been just as dumb as a stump.

From what I'd learnt so far about Emerson's guys it seemed they were out to neutralise any threat to their operation, purging all evidence and eliminating witnesses: the device, the rednecks, and, soon, most likely me. Merv had been real lucky to get out alive.

It was time I paid him a visit. If I was right, Merv would know how to contact Emerson's men, maybe even have a location. But to find out where Merv was, I'd have to go through Pops.

Like JT, Merv's biggest contracts were oftentimes with Victor 'Pops' Accorsi. Pops always had tabs on what his go-to boys were up to. Nothing happened without him knowing, a fact he'd always been real proud about. So I reckoned he'd be able to tell me exactly which hospital Merv was in. I just needed to persuade him. And I planned on being mighty persuasive.

I pulled on my boots and grabbed the keys to the Mustang from the nightstand. Getting information from Pops meant heading back downtown. This was a conversation I'd have to have face-to-face, eyeball-to-eyeball. Pops never would talk business over the phone.

It was time to spin my wheels.

31

Having ditched the Mustang in the lot behind the Marriott, I strode along Montgomery, past the palm trees lining the street outside the Savannah Springs Hotel, and along to Chatham County's concrete lump of a building. A couple of cops were leaning on the hood of their ride. I smiled real sweet as I carried on past, hung a right across the street and scooted around the back of a brown sedan parked up at the curb.

I'd caught the local radio news on my way across town, heard them talking about the shooting at Thelma's Bar the previous night. They said the cops had gotten two suspects in custody, but didn't give names. Gave me hope though. What with JT being a fugitive suspected of multiple homicide, I reckoned they'd have announced his capture real proud. So I figured that Emerson's man – SUV guy most likely – had taken him prisoner, or that JT was free and clear and, hopefully, on his way back to the motel.

But, as I hurried along the sidewalk, the other scenario nagged at me – that JT had gone, used us getting split up to take advantage and disappear into the wind. I hoped to hell I wasn't right.

Pops' place hadn't changed. Same big old red-brick, same blue-and-white striped awning, same cut-price, pink-neon-signed wedding chapel next door. Pops' sign was black on white, and real businesslike: *Bondsman – Open*.

I pushed open the door and entered. The office looked just like I remembered: a large desk and chair, two chairs for clients and a row of metal file cabinets.

'Hey, Deloris,' I said to the skinny woman behind the desk. 'Pops in?'

She leapt up, bangles jangling, and scurried round the desk towards me. 'Lori, my sweet child,' she said, wrapping her sparrow arms around me and giving a good squeeze. 'Where you been that you couldn't pick up a phone?'

'I'm sorry. I've got to see Pops, it's real important.'

Deloris sighed. 'First visit you pay us in years, and you still racing. It's like you got the devil himself chasing you, child.'

She was righter than she could possibly know. 'I'm sorry, Del.'

As she hugged me again I heard a chair scraping against the wooden floor in the back room, and Pops' deep growl said, 'What's with all the noise?'

'Lori's here,' Deloris called.

Pops shuffled through to the office. He was a little rounder and a whole lot balder than when I last saw him, but still looking good for his sixty-seven years. 'Thought you were dead,' he grunted.

I smiled. 'Missed you too.'

'Why wouldn't you call? Near gave Deloris an ulcer, all that worry when you skipped town.'

I shrugged, trying to make out me leaving had been no big deal. 'Felt my time here was done. Sometimes a clean break is best, y'know?'

Pops sighed. 'Heard you had a kid?'

I nodded. One thing I learnt real early on when working with Pops was never to tell him more than he knows.

'Real shame you left that way. Had a good thing going. I know he missed you.'

I gave Pops a warning look. It'd been years since I'd stepped foot in this place, and in under a minute he was riding me. 'Don't, okay?'

He didn't look too happy. 'Fine, if that's the way you want this to be.'

Deloris, as always, ignored the tension and handed me a mug of coffee. 'Strong and sweet,' she said.

Just as I used to like it.

'So you looking for work?' Pops asked. His smile was wide, but there was something a little forced about it. The warmth didn't quite reach his eyes. I wondered what was going on behind them.

He'd given me my first break: a skip trace on a college-kid drunk driver. 'Nah, I'm good. I'm looking for Merv.'

Pops raised an eyebrow. 'Is that right?'

'He knows something about the case I'm working.'

'Yep, heard about that.'

I shouldn't have been surprised. Pops is connected, if you know what I mean. Back in the day he had a piece of every racket going. Course, now he'd become almost as big a part of law enforcement as the cops, and was definitely more respected. Still had his connections though. Possibly more.

'I figured Merv might be able to help me out on something,' I said and took a sip of coffee.

He stared at me a moment. Ran his hand over his bald spot, smoothing an imaginary strand of hair back into place. Frowned. 'Bit of free advice: don't go asking him questions.'

Pops didn't give free advice. He never gave anything for nothing. This was a warning. But I held his eye. 'So where's he at? A local hospital?'

Pops shook his head, looked away, starting flicking through a stack of unopened mail at the side of Deloris' desk. 'Now why would *you* go and pick up JT? After everything that happened, shouldn't you have let him be?'

Damn. This was harder than I'd reckoned on. 'It was a job.'

'How could it ever be just a job, Lori? And to take him to Florida, surely you know what that means?'

Enough stalling. I needed an answer. 'Come on, Pops. Where's Merv?'

'Some things it's best to keep your pretty little snout away from.'

'Quit the drama. I'm asking because it's important. Tell me.'

Deloris scurried out of the back room, pressed a fresh mug of coffee into Pops' hand. She turned to look at me. Smiled a tight smile, her tombstone teeth gritted together like shields. 'If you're in trouble, sweetie, why not ask the Lord for help.'

I drummed my midnight-blue nails against my coffee mug, noticed the polish had started to chip. 'Me and the Lord don't see eye-to-eye much these days.'

Pops sighed. I guessed he knew I'd keep pushing until I'd gotten what I needed. 'Merv's been transferred to Good Hope. He ain't doing so well.'

I smiled. 'Appreciate it.'

Pops peered out of the window, towards the street. 'JT. You got him with you?'

I shook my head. 'Not here.'

He looked back at me. 'He's different, Lori. Ever since that whole thing went down, JT ain't been the same. Not even to Pops. Whatever you kids messed in...' He shook his head. 'You know the mob put a price on him, dead or alive, don't you?'

Shit. Now that I did not know. 'Why?'

'Don't play dumb with me, Lori. Old Man Bonchese was very unhappy. Tommy Ford – one of his best men – getting dropped? Well, that took a lot of smoothing out.'

He had to be shitting me. 'The Miami Mob thinks JT—'

'You didn't know?' Pops shook his head. 'Guess that figures. JT always was trying to protect you. After what went down they wanted blood. I managed to persuade them to be lenient.'

'How?'

Pops shrugged. 'I couldn't have them taking out my superstar bounty hunter, now could I? Me and the Old Man have good history. Some favours he owed me got called in.'

I stared at Pops. Tried to keep my expression neutral. Pretty sure I failed. How could JT not have told me? The Miami Mob put a hit on him because of Tommy. Which meant because of me. And he didn't think to damn well mention it? 'So what did you—'

'Real lucky JT was, that Pops was able to parlay for him.' Pops nodded as he spoke, looked real smug. 'They put a restriction on him, out of courtesy to me. So long as he stayed out of Florida he'd be fine. But if he stepped back across that state line even once, he'd be gone.'

I frowned. 'Even now?'

'Ten years ain't so long. Not in that business.' Pops sucked the air in through the gap in his front teeth. 'Real shame, but I can't do nothing. He's on his own.'

No he wasn't. He was with me. Still, now I knew why Pops couldn't believe I'd take JT back to Florida. More importantly, I knew why the mob was after him. When he'd crossed the state line into Florida, to find Emerson at Winter Wonderland, the hit must've become live again. He'd have known that would happen, and he'd still taken the risk. That told me whoever had been hurt at Winter Wonderland was real important to him, even more important than his own safety. Made me wonder again who they were, if there was someone waiting for him to come home. Whether he really had changed that much.

I pushed the thoughts away. Had to stay focused. I now knew taking JT back to Florida was like playing baseball with a grenade. Thing was, I didn't have a choice. I had to get Dakota safe and that meant getting her back, then taking JT to jail and collecting the bond money.

Pops looked real sorry about the whole situation, but that didn't mean that I could trust him any. I stepped towards him and planted a kiss on his cheek. Hugged Deloris, who looked like she might cry, then turned and strode to the door.

'Lori,' Pops said. 'Play it close, you hear. Listen to what people say. He *is* different. And he's wanted now. Not just by the law.'

'I hear you.' I kept walking, held up my hand and waved as I stepped out the door.

So what if JT was different now. Weren't we all?

32

Good Hope Hospital stood a few miles out of town. The well-maintained grounds and lush lawn around the building suggested it was the type of place where many good people's insurance dollars had been spent. Including Merv's, it seemed, because the briskly efficient woman on the enquiry desk checked her computer screen, told me Merv had gotten out of the ICU just that morning, and directed me to a private room in the surgical wing.

The room had glass walls on to the corridor, the kind that allow nursing staff to check in on a patient without waking them, but prevent any form of privacy. Sitting outside the door was a uniformed officer a cop, not hospital security. Damn. Guess they'd figured Merv might need protection – not so many witnesses to hits involving the mob tend to make it through alive.

The cop gave me a problem. To get past him into the room I'd have to show him ID, and, given what Quinn had told me about the cops and the Feds, as soon as he ran it, my connection to JT would flag. Not an option.

Still, the upside was that there was only one cop here, and he looked plenty bored. In his hand was a go-cup coffee, grande-sized. On the floor beside his chair, lying empty on its side, was another. After two grande coffees, my guess was he'd be needing the bathroom real soon.

I'd passed the restrooms on my way to Merv's room, back at the entrance to the wing, beside the elevators; a good ninety-second walk away. That meant, with the walk both ways and, say, a half minute to pee, once the cop left his post there'd be a window of three and a half minutes for me to talk to Merv. I'd have to move fast.

Until then it was a waiting game. I stepped into the seating area to the side of the corridor, chose a chair that gave me a good view of the cop but kept me partly hidden by a large display of artificial plants, and picked up a newspaper that'd been left on the chair beside mine. I opened it wide and pretended to read. Waiting.

⇓

The cop's bladder lasted another twenty-five minutes. It was still early and, as I'd hoped, no one came to take over his post. He stood, stretched, and set off in the direction of the restrooms. I checked my watch and, as soon as he was out of sight, dropped the newspaper and strode towards Merv's room.

As I got closer I had a good look at him through the glass wall. He lay still as a corpse, surrounded by machines that beeped and pumped God knows what drugs into his body. His usually tanned skin was so pale it almost matched the white sheets draped over him. He looked as good as dead.

I pressed the pad to the right of the door and it slid open. The smell of antiseptic and bodily fluids was just about detectable over the scent of the lilies sitting in a vase on the side table. I hate lilies. Lilies are for coffins and graves. I've never understood why you'd send them to a person in hospital. To me that just seems like a threat.

As I stepped into the room, Merv's eyelids flickered open. Not dead then. Good. I needed him alive.

He scowled. 'What the hell do you want?'

'Why, that's a real nice way to greet an old friend.'

'You ain't nothing to me.' He sounded drugged-up, his words slurred. 'You a vulture ... coming to pick my bones is all.'

I nodded. He wasn't wrong, no sense in pretending. Ever since I'd worked with JT all those years back, the battle lines had been drawn. JT and the Daltons had always been rivals. And Merv's younger brother, Bucky, hadn't liked it when I'd started getting jobs over him. I'd never had a specific beef with Merv, though. Still, I couldn't show weakness, and to those boys empathy was just a sign of it. 'How'd it happen, Merv? You Daltons aren't usually so careless.'

His fists tightened against the sheets. 'Goddamn...'

Good. I'd riled him, and, of course, he'd need to prove he'd not been caught out. 'Too much for you, were they?'

Merv growled.

I stepped closer to the bed. 'Does it hurt?'

He grimaced. 'Like the bastard child of a tank and an elephant used me for target practice.'

'Why'd you do it?'

He closed his eyes. 'You may as well get out. I got nothing to say.'

I glanced at my watch: just under a minute gone. I made like I was going to leave, turning and taking a couple of steps towards the door. Then I halted, twisting back to face him. Shook my head. 'I don't get it. Don't you want them caught? These guys whipped you, shot you in the head and left you for dead, yet you're happy to shrug it off?'

He ground his teeth.

The noise made my skin crawl. I tried to ignore it, to show no vulnerability, just as JT would have told me – *never show weakness unless it's part of your play*. 'Talk to me.'

Merv sighed. The machine beeping along with his heart rate quickened its rhythm. 'You know me and your boy, we had our differences, but he was good at the job. I could respect that but...' the beeping of the machine quickened again '... business is still business. Quinn offered good money, sweet. Thing was, I had another interested party ... willing to give more cash. Word was he'd gotten them pissed over some job ... they'd give big money to whoever handed him over...' He gasped, struggling to speak and breathe together. 'I called them ... Gunner and his people showed ... whole thing went to shit...'

I didn't need a bedtime story. 'So the mob guys shot you?'

Merv shook his head, winced at the pain. 'Not them ... others.'

'Others?' I needed the facts, the details: the what, the when and the who. That was the only way I could figure out where the sons-of-bitches that snatched Dakota could be hiding. I approached the bed. 'Tell me what you know about Emerson.'

'Don't know any ... Emerson.'

I glanced at my watch again. Two minutes gone. 'Sure you do. You just need to think a little harder.'

'Shit, girl, you shooting the wrong tree … don't even have the basics.'

Seemed Merv might be telling the truth. But that couldn't be right, not right at all. If he hadn't called Emerson's men, how the hell had they found the ranch? 'Tell me then, who'd you sell JT out to?'

'Can't say.'

I took another step forward. I stood over him, an inch from the edge of his bed. Wanted to scream at him, *They took my daughter, my child, she's only nine.* Didn't. The warning in the text had been explicit: Don't tell. I couldn't take the risk. 'Best you damn well do.'

Merv closed his eyes and turned away. I noticed the bruising across his ear was a deep purple. I'd never seen an ear bruised that bad close up. It looked like a piece of squashed eggplant.

I waited, watching the second hand of the clock on the wall above the bed tick round. Ten seconds, twenty. The smell of antiseptic and fresh, sickly-sweet sweat brought back the memories of Dakota's last hospital stay. She'd looked so tiny, so fragile, lying there helpless as the cancer and the drugs made her body a battlefield. The doctors feared the worst, said her only other hope would be a bone-marrow transplant. I got tested – but no damn match. They told me her father would be the next best chance.

I glanced at my watch: almost three minutes. I needed an answer, fast. Merv hadn't moved, his shutters were bolted down. I had to find a way to prise them open. I placed my palm on his shoulder, over the bandage covering one of his wounds, and pressed hard. 'Tell me.'

Merv's eyes snapped open. He cursed, a stream of slurred obscenity firing at me, at God and at the lying cocksuckers, double-crossing assholes, and at a good few similarly named unknowns.

I kept my hand where it was and leant closer to his face. 'How did they double-cross you?'

He ignored me. I saw movement in his hand; his fingers tightening around a small remote. The pump attached to his drip clicked twice. As the morphine hit his blood Merv smiled. 'Go to hell, bitch.'

Looking through the glass door I spotted two nurses charging towards us. Son-of-a-bitch hadn't just pressed for pain relief; he'd called for medical assistance. I didn't have long. 'Tell the cops Tate didn't do this.'

'Can't ... didn't see who did it.'

The nurses were almost at the door. I had less than half a minute before the cop would be back. I had to move. Leaning closer to Merv I whispered, 'You know he was long gone before they shot you, just tell the damn truth.'

'I do that, they'll do me way worse than this.'

I stepped back from the bed and shook my head. 'Shit, Merv. I thought you were tough. Why are you so afraid?'

He stared back at me and for a short moment I believed that he might tell me. But then he shook his head. I heard the glass door slide open behind me. We were out of time.

The nurses entered the room, shouting at me to leave. I stepped away from the bed, checked the corridor. My luck held good; there was still no sign of the cop.

I took the carved figure from my back pocket and placed it on Merv's tray-table – watching him. Threw my business card on to his bandaged chest. 'When you grow a pair, you call me.'

Then I turned, and I ran.

33

I got back to Motel 68 a couple of minutes shy of nine. I unlocked the room with a half-formed plan circling in my mind: collect my carryall, call Scott's cell again. After that I wasn't quite decided.

I'd opened the door two inches before I heard the water running. Someone was in the shower. Heart thumping outside of my chest, I stepped inside and closed the door with a soft click.

On the bed lay a heap of crumpled jeans and a blue shirt. A gun sat on the top of the pile. JT was back. As I had the only key, he must have picked the lock.

The first thing I felt was relief. He was alive, not captured. And he'd not abandoned me; he'd kept his word and come back to help find Dakota. The feeling lasted maybe two seconds.

I moved towards the bathroom. Beside the bed was a pair of brown work boots, scuffed and pulled off with the laces still done up and the socks inside. The bathroom door was half open.

I heard the running water stop, and saw the shape of a man reflected in the steamed-up mirror.

'You wanna quit sneaking around out there?' JT said.

I ignored the comment. 'What kept you?'

The bathroom door opened wider. JT emerged, the small, off-white towel around his waist the only thing shielding his nakedness. He shook his head, said nothing.

I clenched my fists, felt the anger building. My daughter was gone, taken, and he was pulling the strong-and-silent act. Mysterious, my ass, oftentimes him staying quiet was just damn frustrating.

I glared at him. 'Just tell me already.'

He avoided my gaze. 'I'm sorry.'

Sorry, again. I hated sorry. Sorry could not bring Dakota back. 'Shit.'

'I saw the guy from the SUV dive out through a window. I followed, tracked him as far as I could, but the trail went cold. Ended up hitching a ride back here. Took a while.'

'I was just leaving.'

He frowned. 'Why? I told you I'd be back.'

'You're way late, I didn't think you were coming.'

'Lori—'

'Quinn sent me a file last night, a load of information about you and the trouble you've gotten into these past few years. Got me to thinking that perhaps there's things you've not been entirely straight about. So I've been doing a little investigation of my own. Found out some stuff.'

He stepped closer, staring at me all intense with those old blues of his. 'What stuff?'

I could feel the heat coming off his skin. Avoiding his gaze, I watched a bead of water run down his chest, across his ribs, past the scar of an old gunshot wound and seep into the towel around his waist. I fought the urge to lean into him, to rest my head against his chest, just for a moment.

'Tell me, Lori.' His voice was husky, enticing.

I gazed up at him. He sure was pretty. Putting my hands on his chest, I felt the firmness of his skin beneath my palms. Remembered how things had been before. Knew they couldn't be that way again.

Going back with him now would most certainly be a mistake. I don't visit with a man more than once. Twice, and you start getting comfortable. And I had learnt my lesson about that the hard way. There's no comfort in a man. I married my first to escape my daddy's fists, and climbed into bed with my second – JT – to escape from the first. After JT, I wised up to the fact that I would always be better off on my own. The way I see it, sex is easy. Love's the thing that gets you hurt.

I pushed him away with everything I had. Fixed my expression to pissed, and raised my voice. 'You beat Merv in a bar a couple of years back. You were charged and did community service. What happened to force only as necessity?'

He didn't speak.

I shook my head. 'Pops said you'd changed. Guess I hadn't realised how much.'

He frowned, grabbed my arm. 'You spoke to Pops? Shit, Lori. When? Did you tell him I was—'

My cell began to ring. I pulled away, yanking the cell phone from my pocket. The caller's number showed on-screen.

JT was right behind me, looking over my shoulder. 'That's Scott.'

I put the cell on speaker and pressed answer. Waited.

No one spoke. I heard a rustling sound, like a butt dial.

I turned the volume to max. Aside from the rustling I heard two voices, both male. I held the cell closer to my ear, but still couldn't make out the words. All I could tell was that one sounded angry. The other didn't say much, just single words and the occasional grunt.

I glanced at JT. He was staring at the cell, concentrating hard.

There was something else: a tune; sleigh-bells and singing: '*... and we'll all have a jolly fun time. Happy holidays all year round. A joyful place to laugh and sing. Come along and we'll begin. Percy Penguin...*'

JT inhaled sharply. 'That's the Winter Wonderland theme song,' he whispered. 'They play it everywhere in the main park. Scott must be inside.'

One of the men's voices became clearer. 'No point you looking at the door, Scott, ain't nobody coming to rescue your sorry ass. I told you what happens next. Tell me where it is or I'll—'

'Please. Don't hurt him.' Dakota's voice; my baby was alive. My heart punched against my ribs so hard I thought it might bash its way clean out of my chest.

'I told you to shut up,' the angry man yelled.

I heard a crash. Dakota screamed. The call disconnected.

My pulse pounded against my temples. I hit the touchscreen, found my recent-calls list, and selected Scott's number.

JT put his hand over mine. 'Don't.'

I shoved him away. 'They've got my child. I have to know they've not—'

He didn't budge. Tightened his grip over my fingers. 'It's a set-up.'

I glared at JT. Jerked my hand and the cell from him. 'She was *screaming*. She—'

'Think about it, Lori. They've tried to get to us twice, and failed. Seems they've changed tact and are trying to draw us to them. That call was to get our attention.'

Shit. JT was right. That Scott had kept hold of his cell after he'd been captured; that he'd called my number even though he'd never met me; that Dakota had spoken while the line was open – it was all far too convenient. 'Well it sure as hell worked.'

'Exactly. Question is, what next? We go there, we're walking right into a trap.'

'But if we stay here, we've still got nothing. At least going to Winter Wonderland means we're getting closer. More chance of finding Dakota.'

JT frowned. 'Yep. I guess it does.'

It was a risk, sure. But I had to take it. 'So let's move.'

JT nodded, moved across to the bed. I turned away as he dressed, grabbed my carryall. Tried to block out the sound of Dakota's screams, still echoing in my mind.

Less than a minute and we were out of there. We ran to the Mustang. I threw my carryall into the back and slid into the driver's seat. Fired up the engine and sped out on to the highway. Moving into the outside lane, I accelerated, putting more room between us and the sedan riding tight on my ass; a brown sedan just like the one outside Pops'. Was it coincidence, or did we have a tail? I accelerated harder, watching in the mirror as the sedan stayed back, tucking itself behind another truck. Told myself it was nothing; brown sedans are pretty damn common.

'You were right about Scott,' I said after a spell. 'They already had him. At Thelma's, we were the target.'

JT stayed silent, his eyes fixed straight ahead.

'How close do you think he is to cracking?'

'Scott? He's held this long, at least.'

'And if he gives out?'

'I'd say that they'll want to catch us a whole lot more.'

Meaning, getting the device was no longer their only objective. While we were loose, we were a liability. And they needed Dakota to lure us in. 'Figures.'

'So drive,' he said, his voice low and tight.

I stepped on the gas, praying to a God I didn't believe in to keep my daughter safe. Winter Wonderland was in Fernandina Beach, Florida. It would take us the best part of two hours to get there. I hoped that Scott could hang on to his secrets a while longer.

34

The drive lasted an hour and forty-seven minutes. Neither of us spoke. We were past that, past trying to rationalise, past trying to convince each other that we would be in time. We didn't know. So we said nothing. It just seemed easier that way.

As I drove I tried not to think about all the times I'd not let Dakota to stay up late, or go with her friends to a place I thought too old for her, or watch a movie rated above her age. I'd done all those small things to protect her, yet when it really mattered, when the danger was real and present, I'd led her into it, smiling and telling her it would be an adventure. Now I knew for sure what I'd always feared deep down. I wasn't fit to be a mom.

But this wasn't about me. Those final moments as she'd been taken replayed on a loop in my mind. I leant forward as if doing so would get me there faster. Those sons-of-bitches were going to pay.

We passed the turn for Fernandina Beach and continued along the interstate. Up ahead, a blue sign with a picture of a grinning Percy Penguin – the signature character of DreamWorld Inc. – announced that there was one mile to go until the turn-off for Winter Wonderland. I felt sick, and then some.

'Take the next right.'

'Yeah, I got this.' I took the turn on to Dreamtime Boulevard. A hundred yards ahead, a twenty-foot-high archway, glistening with fake ice, straddled the blacktop. *Gateway to Wonderland* was painted across it in huge silver letters. Piloting us through the archway and into the grounds I slowed up. There was no sign of any actual park.

'Where the hell is it?'

'We're a way off yet. DreamWorld Inc. own hundreds of acres. They built the park right in the centre. Lets them get permits easy for late-night firework displays. And means they can control everything that goes in and out.'

'So how'd you get in before?'

'Through the front gate.'

'What about your guns?'

He shook his head. 'Didn't take any.'

I believed him. As I'd suspected, Emerson's police statement was false; and the two security guards had lied in their statements, too. I wondered how many people on the security team were corrupt. From the moment we entered the park, we'd have to assume they'd all be on the lookout for us.

Finally, JT nodded ahead. 'There's the outer perimeter.'

Up ahead, I saw a fifteen-foot wall of fake ice blocking our view.

Shit. The place was huge. A fast getaway would be impossible.

The gates were open. Beside them, a huge neon sign announced: *Two miles to Wonderland.* Following the line of cars in front, I took us through the gate.

Inside, the grass was dyed blue and the trees sparkled with glittered silver leaves. It felt like I'd entered an old episode of *The Twilight Zone* and become stuck inside a twisted cartoon world. Fear spread like real ice across my body. Somewhere nearby, Emerson's men were holding Dakota.

JT was sitting real still, his jaw clenched tight. He was psyching himself up, mentally preparing himself for whatever we discovered. I knew then that he expected it to be bad news. I pushed that thought away. It wasn't over until I knew for sure. Until then there was hope. After that, Emerson and his men would be as good as dead. I'd be sure to make that happen. 'Is this the only way in?'

'Yeah. Any other route and we'll trip the alarms.' He looked at me serious. 'Don't argue, I've tried before.'

'Okay.' I said, and wondered again about just who it was that'd driven him to confront Emerson. If Pops had been telling the truth, and JT had broken the terms of the deal made with Old Man Bonchese and crossed the state line, that person must be really damn special. JT would not have put himself back on the Miami Mob's target list on a whim.

Two miles into the park a white-toothed parking attendant, who looked like a college kid majoring in football, directed us into Chester Chipmunk Parking Lot Nine. The lot was immense. I'd never seen so many vehicles all in one place. There must have been four, maybe five thousand, and this was only one of the lots. I just hadn't anticipated the scale of the place. As we coasted along, following the line, a smaller, bearded guy, beckoned us across the lot and parked us in Zone C14.

I killed the engine and glanced at JT. 'You ready?'

He nodded.

We left most of our weapons in the Mustang, no sense trying to smuggle them in – the metal detectors would pick them up in an instant. All I took was the small plastic canister of pepper spray disguised as a perfume bottle that fit real snug in my pocket. From the glovebox, JT pulled out a faded navy cap, a red bandana and a pair of sunglasses. I twisted my hair into a braid and tied the bandana like a headscarf, the knot tight around the back of my head. JT put on the glasses and pulled the cap low over his face. Not much of a disguise, but better than nothing.

Slipping into the crowd, we followed the signs to the land-train – a line of six-person carriages pulled by a white tractor. The driver – a white-haired guy wearing a blue uniform, complete with hat and whistle – greeted each person with a smile and a theatrical, booming voice that bid *'Welcome to your Winter Wonderland adventure.'* He stopped a little longer in front of each child, telling them this would be the best day of their life, ever.

His words made me shudder, every time.

Still, I forced a smile as he passed us, and hoped that he drove the train faster than he walked. He didn't. The damn thing had a top speed of five miles an hour and stopped every few hundred yards to pick up more people from the Percy Penguin, Wally Walrus and Saskia Seal parking lots. By the time the driver announced that the land-train was now full and we would be proceeding direct to Winter Wonderland I thought I might burst with frustration.

At the entrance turnstiles, we waited in line, the only silent pair among the throng of tourists all jabbering on and trying to keep their overexcited kids under control. We paid almost ninety dollars for a pair of day tickets, and walked through metal detectors clad in more fake ice and signposted as the *Doorways to Wonderland*.

That's when I heard it.

'That's the music,' I whispered to JT.

He nodded. 'It only plays around Main Street.'

That meant the place we were looking for had to be nearby, right in the busiest area of the park. It didn't make sense. Why would they risk bringing Scott and Dakota here? Surely their cries would be heard by someone?

The area was packed. We picked our way through the crowd as fast as we could, skirting past an English family looking for the bathroom, a group of Chinese students having their photo taken outside the castle, and the hordes of parents trying to keep up with their children as they ran, laughed and cried with excitement. JT stooped a little, trying to disguise his height, I guessed. I tried not to think about the security cameras that would be watching us. There was nothing to be done about them. We just had to move. Fast. I had to find Dakota.

We hurried along Main Street and around the back of the Sparkle-Dust Castle, a huge pale-blue building designed like an ancient fort, covered in fake ice and glittering turrets.

The feeling of being stuck in the *Twilight Zone* cartoon remained. Although the park was designed to look like winter in New England – with artificial snow, plastic icicles hanging from the rooftops of the weatherboard-clad shops, and fake fires burning in the fireplaces – the colours all seemed too bright, too primary; like someone had techni-coloured an old black-and-white film.

The whole place felt out of whack. Incongruent. It made no sense to be walking down a faux-cobbled street, with fake powdered snow underfoot, when the temperature was pushing ninety in the shade. I hurried past Percy Penguin and his three penguin nephews wearing woollen hats and having their pictures taken with a never-ending line of kids, then paused, just for a moment, to gaze at the perfect, smiling faces of the SparkleDust Fairy Queen and King, posing in their carriage for a girl of about eleven to take a photo. As she took the picture on her cell, the child grinned, thanking the characters in a breathless voice.

'Lori, you listening?'

I turned away from the happy-ever-after bullshit, and got my head back in the game. 'Sorry, what?'

'Search this side of the street, I'll check out the other.'

I nodded. The ice caves, supposed homes of Percy Penguin's nephews, but in fact large, moulded-plastic huts, were too public to be what we were looking for. Still, I paced along the street, peering into each one, just to be sure.

The last one was different, though. Only the front half of the space was open, the rest was sectioned off. Hidden. The sign out front said: *No entry except for Ice Elves*. I was most certainly not an elf. But I ducked into the cave anyway.

Inside, I saw that a lime-green screen separated the back of the cave from the front. As I approached, I heard voices. Two people. Talking on the other side of the screen. I tried to peer through a join in the screen's panels. Saw nothing.

Where the screen and the wall met, I spied a gap, big enough to give a better view. Crouching down, I squeezed myself between the wall and a two-foot-high ice-cube seat. I kept quiet. Tried to breathe shallow, exhale lightly, not attract attention. I knew if I was caught I had no explanation for why I was there.

Wedged up against the fake ice cube, I peered through the half-inch gap between the screen and the wall and saw a large metal trapdoor swing up from the floor. Moments later a life-sized Saskia Seal character stepped up into the ice cave. The costumed characters travelled around the park beneath the ground.

Was that where Emerson's men were hiding Scott and Dakota?

Surely they couldn't be. I doubted it would be possible to hear the 'Happy Holidays' song so clearly, not unless they played it down there too.

I hurried from the cave fast, crossed the street and caught up with JT. 'There's an underground passageway. It comes out in the last ice cave.'

'I know.'

I'd not expected that. 'How?'

'I found out when I was studying the blueprints before. They're obsessed with keeping the fairy-tale illusion alive. No one playing a character can be seen in public without their full costume, or do anything inconsistent with their role. If they're above ground, they're in character.'

'So it's a no to Percy Penguin riding in a car or Bella Polar Bear smoking?'

'Something like that. There are miles of underground tunnels beneath the park. They connect to all the main areas and the resort hotels. The characters only appear above ground when they're ready to perform.'

'I don't think the call came from a tunnel.'

'No. I doubt there's a signal.'

So we'd got nothing. Again. I needed a sign, a clue, something that told me where to look. But all we'd gotten was the song, and every place it played was open to the public: souvenir shops, juice bars, restaurants. Nowhere was private enough to hide people from view.

I shuddered. 'Where the hell haven't we looked?'

JT pointed up ahead. 'Main Street ends at those gates. All the streets off this one lead around the park to the rollercoasters and other rides, but they don't play the 'Happy Holidays' song there; they each have their own music.'

I kept walking. Couldn't bear to stop the search. 'There has to be somewhere. They have to be close. How else would we have heard the song?'

'Maybe they were moving them through the park. It could—'

'No.' I felt my lower lip quiver, pursed my lips together, refused to admit defeat. Stay strong and be tough, I told myself. You have to make this right.

I turned away from JT, couldn't let him see me like this. Glanced back down Main Street.

That's when I spotted it; about thirty metres back the way we'd first come, near the SparkleDust Castle. I couldn't believe I'd not noticed before.

I hurried towards the short section of wooden panel fencing. It was ten feet high and painted bright green with huge pictures of ice-cream sundaes dotted over it like polka-dots. A big sign announced: *Coming soon: Percy Penguin's Gourmet Ice Cream Parlour.*

JT was beside me now. 'What about in there?' I asked.

He didn't say anything, but I could tell he was thinking on it.

The music was louder here, a speaker was attached to a lamppost right above the fenced-off area. I'd put good money on the song being audible in the construction area. And, although it was close to Main Street, the fence led away from the rest of the shops and attractions, so there were fewer visitors around.

JT nodded. 'We need to find a way in.'

35

A small gate was cut into the fence. It'd been almost invisible at first glance and was partly blocked by the snow-dusted conifers lining the perimeter of the nearest ice cave. The gate was locked – from the inside. We waited for a lull in the flow of tourists coming our way, and sneaked into the gap between the trees and the fence.

It was a tight squeeze. JT, cramped up with his shoulder against the wooden panels, interlinked his fingers to form a makeshift stirrup. 'I'll give you a bunk up.'

Putting my left foot into his hands, I hopped once and jumped, grabbing for the top of the fence. Swinging myself over, I landed, as catlike as I could, on the other side, wincing as the impact jarred my injured leg. Seconds later, the fence rattled and JT vaulted over to join me.

Well, shit. If Main Street and the rest of Winter Wonderland were like a technicolour cartoon, this place was its alternative-reality nightmare. Aged by weather and lack of attention, the single-storey building in front of us had long since lost its shine and glitter. Tall grass with blue tips had grown up in the front-yard area, fire nettles and other weeds twisted around the foot-high pink lollipops and twisted-liquorice railings lining the porch.

A faded sign, hanging from the railing, read 'The Gingerbread Grotto'. I guessed they'd planned on demolishing it and building the ice-cream parlour in its place. From the look of it, the grotto had been designed to look like it was made from candy: gingerbread bricks and roof tiles, marzipan window frames and cute little shutters. But cracks split the walls, and pieces of the faux candy cladding had fallen away, exposing the wooden skeleton beneath. One side of the porch had collapsed. Beneath the pile of splintered wooden joists I could just make out the smiling face of a small, plastic penguin. Its right eye was missing.

Despite the heat, I shivered. 'This has to be it.'

At the entrance, a battered '*If you're taller than this you can't come in'* sign pointed just below my shoulder. I ducked my head and strode through the three-quarter-height doorway into the grotto.

The place smelt musty and damp. It was claustrophobic in the gloom; I felt trapped, and fearful of what truth might await me. Even inside the grotto I could hear the 'Happy Holidays' song playing through the loudspeakers on Main Street. Such a saccharine-sweet song didn't fit with this place. It felt creepy, like something from an R-rated horror movie.

I glanced back. JT had taken his shades off and was following close behind me. He nodded. Aside from the small pepper spray canister I'd managed to conceal in my pocket, we had no weapons, no idea what we were up against, and no choice but to keep going. Dakota was depending on us.

I moved faster along the low-ceilinged passage. Chunks of the faux peanut-butter-rendered walls had crumbled away, exposing the plasterboard beneath. At our feet cockroaches scuttled for cover, unaccustomed to the company.

At the end of the passageway an archway led to the main room. Keeping my back flat to the wall, I peered through into the grotto.

Empty. Or so I thought.

I stepped into the room, and that's when I saw him. In the far corner, beside a fake-chocolate-panelled fireplace hung with long stockings filled with gifts, stood a throne sculpted from hundreds of plastic candy canes. Bound to it, his ankles and wrists duct-taped to the canes, was Santa.

Behind me in the passage, JT whispered, 'Lori, what is it?'

I stepped closer. Swallowed hard. Fought the nausea.

Santa's head had lolled back. His nose was shattered. Blood, red-brown, had congealed and crusted around its base and down his mouth, his chin. It had splattered his Santa suit, staining the white trim crimson.

The song seemed to get louder. *'Happy holidays all year round...'*

Purple bruising mottled his face. Eyes wide, bulging. Mouth open, as if still trying to scream.

'Lori?' JT's voice was louder. 'What the...'

He moved past me, hurrying across the room. Put his fingers to the man's neck, waited a couple of seconds, removed them. Cussing, he shook his head. 'He's dead.'

'... a joyful place to laugh and sing...'

'Is it—?'

'Scott. He must have used the suit as a disguise. He said in his message he was going to get the device. Well, damn. He must have hidden it here in the park.'

I felt panic rising in my chest. Stumbled across the crumbling mosaic floor to join JT. Scott's interrogators had ripped open his tunic. He was a big guy, hadn't needed padding to fill out the suit. From the dark bruising marbling his chest and ribs I saw he'd been worked over real hard. The breath caught in my throat. 'Where's Dakota?'

'... come along and we'll begin...'

JT looked around the grotto. He strode across to a child-sized wooden chair lying on its side by the boarded-up window. The dust on the floor around it had been disturbed. 'Not here, not now.'

'... and have a happy holiday...'

I fought the panic. Felt as if I was choking on the thick, mould-ridden air. 'She watched Scott die?'

'We don't know that for sure.'

'But the call, Scott was alive then, and Dakota was right there with him. She must've...'

JT didn't speak.

I looked away. Did they force her to watch them torture Scott? How could they do that to a child? I imagined her crying, pleading for them to stop, them ignoring her, beating Scott anyways. His cries of agony, the gurgling as blood from his shattered nose filled his throat. Dakota afraid. Alone.

Those images would never leave her. Whatever I did, they'd stay with her always. How would she ever get over it? Witnessing something like that changed you. That I knew, from bitter experience.

JT put his hand on my shoulder. 'We'll get her back.'

I shrugged him away. 'And if they've killed her, too?'

'They haven't. Emerson's men wouldn't want Scott dead, not without getting the device first. I don't think they planned for this to happen.'

I stared at Scott's corpse. Some accident. 'Why?'

'Look at this place. What does the scene tell you?'

I glared at JT. Didn't want to play this game. Wanted my daughter. Safe. And the last forty hours erased. But that wasn't going to happen.

Reluctantly, I scanned the room. Beside the candy-cane throne were piles of gifts, their faded wrapping paper splattered with blood. The two model reindeer by the fireplace looked like they'd gotten a bad case of measles. Even so, the wounds across Scott's face and body didn't look serious enough to be fatal. He hadn't bled out.

I turned to JT. Shook my head. 'What do you think happened?'

'My guess is his heart gave out. He was always popping pills. Kept going on at me about how he'd dreamt of joining the CIA but couldn't because of a heart condition. I'd pegged it as fantasy. Perhaps it was the truth.'

I peered at the face half-hidden beneath the blood-speckled Santa hat. Scott's sightless eyes were open, staring. I pressed my fingers over them, felt a slight resistance before they closed, letting him rest. Poor bastard. 'So why leave him here for us to find?'

'As a warning.' JT shook his head. 'If they didn't mean to kill him, I doubt he told them where to find the device.'

I realised what he was getting at. 'So we're their next best bet.'

'No, *I* am.'

I frowned. 'Then why didn't they try and grab you already?'

'It's too public in the main park. Too many witnesses.'

That made sense. 'And another dead body found while you're here, that'd be easy to pin on you I guess.'

'Except they want the device. I was working with Scott, and they know that. He must have told them it's here in the park. I reckon they're waiting to see where I go. They want me to lead them to it.'

Somewhere behind the grotto I heard the clanking of a rollercoaster climbing its rails to the summit. There was a brief pause. Then the screams began. I imagined the cars hurtling along their rails, plunging, corkscrewing, all in the name of fun. Emerson's men would have known about the rollercoaster. If they'd timed their punches right, not one of the tourists walking along Main Street would have realised Scott's screams were from real terror rather than manufactured thrills. He hadn't stood a chance. 'Or they'll grab you and torture it out of you.'

JT nodded. 'Yep. Or that.'

I glanced down at Scott's lifeless body. He looked so damn pitiful, still bound to the throne in that ridiculous outfit. What a wretched way to die. Leaning down, I tried to pull Scott's tunic over his rotund belly, give him a little dignity. 'Shit.'

'What?'

Tucked into the tunic pocket was a cell phone. Scott's, I guessed, the one Emerson's men had used to call us to lead us here. I removed it, flipped it open.

On-screen a video had been paused. My child. Freeze-framed. Her blonde braids fuzzy. Her azure-blue eyes staring into the lens. Terrified.

My hand trembled. The cell began to shake. I stared at Dakota's image. Tasted bile as it hit the back of my throat. Doubled over, retching.

'Lori, show me.'

Straightening up, I passed the cell to JT.

He turned real pale, despite his tan. He looked back at me, his big blues all earnest. 'You know we're gonna have to watch this.'

I swallowed hard. Couldn't trust myself to speak without breaking down. Knew that wouldn't help anybody or change anything. Tried to focus. Hugged my arms across my body. Nodded.

He pressed play.

36

The video had been filmed in close-up. Dakota's face – cheeks grubby, eyes pink and bloodshot, looking straight into the camera. Just as the man's voice commanded.

I stared at the screen. Blinked. Couldn't cry. Had to stay strong for my baby, even though I knew she couldn't see me.

'Momma, I'm so sorry. I tried to be good.' Her lower lip trembled as she spoke. She paused, looked to her right and glared at someone out of view. 'But they were hurting Santa. I had to help him, so I—'

The man's voice, off camera, growled, 'Say what I told you.'

She glared at whoever was to her right again. Flinched. Looked back into the lens. 'They didn't like me telling them off. Said Santa was a thief and I'm a naughty little girl.' She leant forward, whispering now. 'They said very bad things happen to naughty girls, and I'd find out what if I didn't stay real quiet.'

I heard laughter from the man off-camera. How I wanted to punch him. To rip his tongue from his mouth and stomp on it until all that was left was bloody pulp. I clenched my fists, dug my nails into my palms. Tried not to give in to the fear.

The man spoke again. 'Tell them what happened.'

'I wasn't quiet enough. That's why they made me wear it.' Dakota glanced down. Sniffed hard. 'Because I'm a naughty little smart-mouth.'

The camera started to pull back.

She jutted her chin out, like she always did when being stubborn. 'I don't like it, Momma. It's hot and it's heavy, and they said it has bad things stuffed in the pockets for punishing me if I'm naughty again.'

I watched. Numb. As the camera pulled back further.

Beside me, JT cussed. I felt his body go rigid, as if he'd stopped breathing. Half a second later he slammed his fist into the wall. A chunk of rendering crumbled under the impact, dropping in pieces to the floor. 'Son-of-a-bitch.'

I inhaled sharply.

The life preserver was navy blue, fitted tight over Dakota's purple t-shirt. I stared at the red, blue and white wires, at the two large blocks of explosive resting over my daughter's ribs, at her eyes, wide and afraid. I opened my mouth, tried to speak. No sound came out.

'Please, Momma. Bring them what Santa stole. If you don't, they say they'll have to use the magic button.'

37

The video ended. The screen faded to black, empty. JT was talking, pacing around Scott and the candy-cane throne, ranting. I paid him no mind. All I could hear was my own inner voice repeating over and again: *My fault, my fault, my fault*.

That was the only way this made sense. My child, my sweet girl, who'd kept up with her schoolwork, done her chores and, aside from being a little precocious on occasion, never given a moment's trouble. I should never have taken the job, never have believed anything involving JT would go smooth. I should have known I wouldn't ever be able to get that close to him and stay hidden from the past. No matter how deep down you think things have been buried, they always come right back to shoot you in the ass.

Well, I wasn't going to let Emerson beat us. We had to end this. Fight back. Hard, dirty, whatever it took.

I turned to JT. 'We need that device *now*.'

He stopped pacing. Gestured towards Scott. 'Maybe he's got it on him.'

I glanced at Scott's body. If the device was the size of my palm as JT had said, then I doubted there was anyplace Scott had been able to conceal it on or inside his body. '*They'd* have searched him.'

'They should have, but...'

Rule number four: *Don't make assumptions*. It was a valid point. 'Sure, do it then.'

JT leant over Scott. He patted down his body, trunk first, then each arm, followed by the legs. I looked away. I've never been squeamish, but there's something real intrusive about frisking a dead person.

JT stepped back from the body. Shook his head.

Shit. The whole set-up made no sense. If Emerson's men knew we were coming, why hadn't they grabbed us already? They could have picked us up at the front gate, or been waiting here with Scott's body. 'Why the hell did they make that video?'

JT exhaled. Shrugged. 'Trying to keep us focused. Messing with our heads. Just being sick fucks. Who knows?'

I felt another surge of adrenaline hit my bloodstream. I needed to get going. *Do* something. 'Whatever the reason, they know we're here. There's CCTV everywhere.'

'Yeah. So we have to be smart, figure out where it is and get out fast.'

JT was right. If Emerson's men found the device before us we'd have nothing. No bargaining power. 'And if they get to it first?'

'We won't let that happen.'

That was for damn sure. I stepped towards the exit.

JT stayed put. 'So what do we know?' he asked – he was talking to himself as much as me. 'Scott came back here to get the device. Seems he never made it to the place it was hidden.'

I shifted my weight from one foot to the other. Wanted to get going. Search the park. 'So where'd we start looking?'

'Scott was highly secretive. He'd have hidden it somewhere he could reach from the security office, but not exposed to other people. Someplace in plain sight but—'

I heard a floorboard creak in the passageway. Catching JT's eye, I put my finger to my lips. He nodded. He'd heard it too.

We weren't alone.

Question was, how many? Listening hard, I tried to work it out. But all I could hear was our breathing and the distant screams from the rollercoaster. Damn.

There was no easy way out. The grotto's boarded-up windows, solid walls, and single route in and out made our odds of a fast escape real slim. Seemed we were trapped.

I signalled to JT for us to split up. He nodded, stepped to his right and eased a large candy-cane-styled baton from the utensil stand beside the fireplace. Moving quietly, we slipped across the room to the archway, each flattening ourselves against the wall on either side of the entrance. JT held the candy cane as if it was a baseball bat and he was waiting for the pitch. Ready.

Sliding my right hand into my jeans pocket, I curled my fingers around the can of pepper spray and manoeuvred it free. Without any real weapons our best chance would be to get the jump on whoever was coming, take as many out as we could, then run.

So we waited.

Pulse thumping. Mouth dry. The muscles across my body tensed, ready to act.

'... *Lots of fun for you and me. Jolly times all filled with glee. Come and...*'

I cussed silently. Tried to block out the noise of the 'Happy Holidays' tune still jangling from the nearby speaker. Concentrated on my breathing, on the peanut-butter rendering scratching against my back. Listened for any sounds from the passageway. Focused on anything other than the damn song.

From the opposite side of the archway, JT watched me. I stared back.

His gaze flicked towards the passageway. I saw the flare of his nostrils as he inhaled, the rise of his chest, his shoulders. He raised the baton a little higher.

It was time.

The man came in fast with his gun raised. He took two steps into the grotto and had just enough time to register me, for our eyes to connect, before JT leapt forward. He whacked the guy hard with the candy-cane baton.

The man ducked right, firing his Beretta. The silenced shot zipped wide and embedded into the fireplace surround. JT hit him again: once to the head, twice to the back. The baton snapped. The guy went down.

I tensed, ready for others. Waited.

No one came.

JT grabbed the Beretta, then stepped into the passageway and walked down to the exit. Returned a few moments later. 'He's alone.'

I glanced at the man groaning on the floor. He looked like a regular guy, I guessed a little shorter than JT, and a few years younger. He wore a green polo shirt and cream cargo pants. Didn't look like park security. 'I don't get it. Why send only one man?'

JT frowned. 'He's not Emerson's man. His name's Ugo Nolfi. He's an enforcer with the Miami Mob; one of the top guys. He's who Gunner and his boys were waiting at the ranch for.'

Shit. Back outside Pops' bail shop I'd seen a man parked up outside in a brown sedan. I'd spotted a similar car later, out on the highway as we left the motel for Winter Wonderland. The brown sedan, I'd convinced myself it was coincidence. Now I knew I'd been wrong.

I remembered how freaked JT had sounded when I said I'd seen Pops. Maybe he'd assumed the mob would station someone there, waiting for him to show. 'They tracked us here. Must've tailed me from Pops' place.'

JT stared at the mob guy, this Ugo Nolfi. Didn't reply.

'Did you—?'

'Yep, I heard you.' He cussed under his breath. Looked back at me. 'And, just so as we're clear, it's me he's after, not us.'

I held his gaze. He didn't know Pops had told me the reason why the mob were after him. Didn't realise I knew the hit put out on him should have been for me. That I knew that, even after I'd left him, he'd been protecting me. And right now I didn't want to tell him I knew. If that was the way JT wanted to play it, fine. 'Well, whoever he is, and whatever he wants, we need to get moving.'

On the crumbling mosaic floor in front of us Ugo Nolfi pushed himself up to sitting. JT stepped closer to him, pointing the Beretta at his chest.

Ugo raised his hands. 'Wait. Let's talk. You know why I'm here...'

'Yep.'

Ugo nodded towards the gun. 'So you know even if you do this, we'll keep coming.'

JT frowned. 'And your point is?'

'You told Gunner you had information?'

JT nodded. 'I did.'

That was news to me. JT must've spoken to the boys at the ranch before I'd gotten there. I thought back to how things had gone down, remembered JT whispering something to Gunner about making a deal with his boss. I'd thought he'd meant Merv. Seemed he'd been talking about Old Man Bonchese.

'Your story checked out. There's a rival operation, taking trade from our Sweet-Sixteen business.'

JT kept the Beretta pointed at Ugo. 'So you're saying what?'

'The Old Man doesn't like people muscling in on our territory. You tell me what you know, who's in charge, how the operation works, and maybe there's a deal to be made.'

I heard a thud outside, like someone tripping over something solid. I pointed in the direction of the noise. 'Shush.'

JT nodded. Kept the gun trained on Ugo's chest. I hurried to a window where a section of the wooden cover had fallen away. Peered through the grimy plastic and spotted figures coming our way. I turned to JT, whispered, 'We've got company. Three of them.'

He looked at Ugo. Kept his voice low. 'These men coming for us, they work for Randall Emerson. He owns this park, and he's running the kiddie operation I told Gunner about. His men killed your boys out in West Virginia, not me.'

I squinted through the window again. The men were walking towards the entrance of the Gingerbread Grotto. They all had guns. 'They know we're in here.'

JT lowered the Beretta a fraction, kept staring at Ugo. 'So here's the thing, you back off me, and I can solve the Emerson problem for both of us, clear the way for you and the Old Man.'

Ugo shook his head. 'I don't know. The boys in WV, they were low-level muscle, but loyal. They died on my watch, waiting for me to show.' He paused for an agonising moment. 'Still, I guess we could swallow what happened there as collateral damage. But writing off payback for that other thing? That'll be harder to sell to the boss. He's held that grudge a hell of a long time.'

I looked through the window again. The men had reached the front porch. They were blocking the only door. Trapping us inside. 'We're out of time,' I hissed. 'Decide fast. We've got to get out of here.'

JT lowered the gun. 'I've got video evidence of Emerson's operation. I give that to the cops, he's screwed and you win. That doesn't work, I'll end him myself. Either way, there's no comeback for you, and the rival operation's gone.'

Ugo stared at JT a short moment, then nodded. 'All right. You make that happen, and I'll speak to the boss. That's the most I can promise.'

'I'll take that. So, we good?'

'Good enough.'

JT held out his hand, and helped Ugo to his feet.

Glancing back through the window, I saw the men step on to the porch. 'They're coming in. We need a diversion. They realise we're breaking out, they're going to be round back real fast.' I looked at Ugo. 'Can you do that?'

He nodded.

JT handed him the Beretta.

Ugo stepped towards the archway, flattened his back against the wall and blind-fired a volley of shots along the passage. The men returned fire. Ugo yelled something in Italian and fired again.

I grabbed the board still covering part of the window and yanked it hard. As the wood splintered free, JT shoved his fists against the window frame. Loosened by decay, it shifted away from the wall. JT pushed it clear.

I threw the wooden board on the floor. That's when I noticed the blue ball-cap, lying crumbled in the dust a little ways to my left. The gold lettering above a picture of Percy Penguin read: MAINTENANCE CREW. I grabbed it, before following JT out through the gap in the wall.

38

Back on Main Street, it seemed like another world. So many people enjoying themselves, oblivious that in the fenced-off construction area just a few hundred yards away, one man lay dead and another was under siege. Still, I couldn't think on what had happened. Had to push it from my mind. But the deal we'd struck with Ugo, it didn't sit right with me. I glanced at JT. 'When you told Ugo you'd help the Old Man did you mean—?'

'I said that to buy us some time.'

'But this Sweet-Sixteen business, is that—?'

'It's messed up. Seriously, it makes me sick. They sell a girl's – a sixteen-year-old's – virginity to the highest bidder. But I had to say something that'd get me clear of the ranch, and get us out of the Gingerbread Grotto.' He turned. 'Believe me, I'd *never* help Bonchese. I just had to make Ugo believe that I would, because right now my priority is getting to Emerson.'

I nodded. Felt guilty that I'd doubted him. What mattered now was finding the device, wherever the hell Scott had hidden it, before Emerson's men realised it was only Ugo Nolfi they'd got cornered.

We strode back past the ice caves. JT had his shades on. I'd dusted off the maintenance crew ball-cap and swapped it with my bandana. We moved with the flow of people on the street. The family in front of us, two parents and a small boy holding a balloon with 'Birthday at Wonderland' written on it, knew where they were heading: to the huge pale-blue SparkleDust Castle with its glittering turrets covered in fake ice. Me, I had no idea.

Anxiety tightened round my neck like a noose, pinching my skin. The place was too crowded, too vast. How could we ever hope to find the device? Ugo wouldn't be able to hold off Emerson's men for long. Then they'd be coming for us. Without a plan we were screwed, wasting time. Time we, and Dakota, didn't have.

'So how'd you want to play this?' said JT.

'We need to narrow the search.' That had to be our first move.

'Any idea how?'

That's when I remembered the map. I stepped to the side of the street and digging into my pocket, grabbed the crumbled page that the cashier had handed me with our entry tickets.

'We can plot the routes Scott would have taken each day,' I said, showing the map to JT. 'He's most likely to have hidden the device in a place he knew well, where he could be sure it'd be safe. You said he was into conspiracy theories, spy shit, so I reckon it won't be anywhere obvious. I reckon—'

'Sounds like a hell of a lot of assumptions.'

I frowned. 'You got anything better?'

'Perhaps. Scott told me the job got to him sometimes, even before the messed-up shit with Emerson. Said seeing what people did, especially when they thought no one was watching, could get mighty unpleasant. Grossed him out.'

I shrugged. 'And that's relevant how?'

'He told me he had a place that he'd go. To chill, clear his mind. A place the cameras couldn't see.'

I felt a surge of excitement. 'Where?'

'Didn't say exactly, just said he'd found it one time when he took a shortcut back to his car.' JT pointed to an unnamed brown building on the map. 'That's the security office where he worked. He arrived and left on foot each day, walking to and from his car in the staff parking lot.'

I scanned the map. It didn't have the staff parking lot marked. 'Which is where?'

He indicated a brown area on the outer edge of the park. 'Here.'

'So we search the route. That's our first move.'

JT studied the map then pointed to a narrow brown line. 'That's the path that connects the public area to the staff parking lot. It's the straightest route along the walkways from the security office. But a more direct route would be down here.' He pointed to the green space between the staff parking lot and the Big Freeze Zone. The route of the Frosty Looper rollercoaster snaked across it. 'If there's a way to get across that land, I'd say that's Scott's shortcut. The device will be hidden somewhere there.'

Still an assumption, but it sounded likely, and as good as anything else we'd got to go on. 'Okay. Let's head that way.'

I followed him back along Main Street. Long strides. Moving as fast as we could without running. In front of SparkleDust Castle we hung a right down Popsicle Drive. Scooting past the plastic stalactites that flashed blue, pink and green neon, we ducked between the groups of tourists, and pushed our way through the crowd.

I kept looking out for Emerson's men. Wished I'd gotten a better look at their faces. They had been dressed real casual, so they could be any number of folks around us, except they'd be acting different, like they were hunting. I'd surely be able to spot that. I had to find the device before they got to us. Couldn't fail. Just couldn't. Dakota was relying on me.

Twenty yards along we reached a corn-dog stand. JT pointed out a small pathway between the blue hedge and the side of the vendor's stand. 'Down there's the entrance to the security office. Scott would have come on to the main concourse here.'

It was a busy spot. Lots of folks in line for corn dogs, benches lining the walkway, a smokers' area off to one side, separated by a line of blue shrubs. 'Then where?'

He nodded towards the four-way crossing up ahead. A large silver signpost pointed to the different areas of the park. In the centre of the crossing a life-size Chester Chipmunk character was waving to the kids as they passed. I wondered if the staff had been warned to look out for two people acting suspiciously.

We hurried past Chester and his handler, an older guy sweating beneath his neon blue tabard, and took a right, following the directions to the Big Freeze Zone.

We loped along, dodging tourists and trying to avoid looking directly at the CCTV cameras. It was hard going. People were everywhere: teens dawdling, young children running, parents pushing strollers. The cameras were real regular, too. Disguised with glitter, peeping out from the fake ice that capped the streetlights. Watching.

⥥

Turned out that the Big Freeze Zone was the size of six football pitches and home to two rollercoasters – Big Chiller and Frosty Looper – as well as a whole bunch of other rides. It was also rammed with people.

So where to start? We needed to find the route Scott would have taken to the green space beyond the Zone. Searching the whole perimeter would take time we didn't have. I looked at JT. 'Any idea where he'd have gotten through?'

JT shook his head. 'No. I guess we search the fence line bordering the green space on the map. See if we can find a gate.'

The odds weren't great. We were basing our search on assumptions layered over other assumptions. But we had to do something. 'Sounds our best shot.'

We pushed through the crowds, following the signs to the Ice Wars ride on the far side of the Zone. My mouth felt dry, my throat ached. I could feel the sweat trickling between my shoulders and down my back. My jeans felt clammy against my skin. But we couldn't slow, couldn't rest.

In my mind's eye, I glimpsed Dakota in the freeze-frame image of the video left by Emerson's men: eyes wide and afraid. The navy-blue life preserver strapped tight around her. The wires. The explosives. And my daughter's words, the terror audible as she spoke, *'Bring them what Santa stole. If you don't, they say they'll have to use the magic button.'*

⥥

Past Ice Wars, which was like a supersized version of fairground dodgems, we split up and searched around the perimeter fence bordering the side of the zone adjacent to where the green space was on the map. The fence was solid white plastic, too high to see over, and no gaps to look or get through.

Ignoring the shrieks and laughter from the rides nearby, I stood back and scanned the area again. Over to the left, before the start of the line for the Big Chiller rollercoaster, was a SparkleDust Candyfloss stand. Beyond that stood the human driers – huge hot-air blowers that dried off visitors after they'd ridden Percy Penguin's Ice Rapids ride, a log flume that guaranteed a drenching. Beyond that, the path twisted away from the direction of the staff parking lot.

On my right, the path led past the line of people waiting to ride Ice Wars and back to Main Street. The thick blue hedge that lined the street left no way through to the space behind.

It didn't make sense. There had to be a way.

I tried to block out the dance music thumping from the speaker overhead and run through the few facts we had. We knew Emerson's men had engineered the phone call and lured us into a disused area of the park to trap us. Course, they'd not reckoned on Ugo Nolfi tailing us, and him holding them off as they tried to grab JT in the Gingerbread Grotto. But even if that'd been a surprise, they'd know by now that we'd gotten back into the park, and would be watching for us on the security cameras. Out on the open concourse they'd have spotted us quick enough. They'd know where we were and what we were doing. It wouldn't be long before they tried to grab us again.

JT joined me. Shook his head. 'Nothing that way, I must have gotten it wrong.'

'No. There's got to be a way. What else did Scott tell you about the place he went to chill?'

JT thought silently for a second.

'He did keep going on about that Ice Wars ride. He loved the thing, said he'd ridden it over a hundred times.'

I glanced over at the ride, watched the people in the dodgems laughing as they hurtled around the rink in their oversized cars. I could understand why Scott had liked it so much; it would have been one of the few rides that he could have ridden without feeling wedged in real tight. But it had to be more than that, him telling JT about it had to mean something. The more I thought about it, I reckoned that, with Scott's love of cracking conspiracy theories and reading about spy shit he would have given clues about the device's whereabouts without JT even realising. I just had to find out everything Scott had said and crack the code.

I stepped closer to JT. 'When Scott told you about his chill spot, what were his exact words?'

We stared at the people smashing their dodgems into one another. JT shook his head. 'Scott told me the view from this ride was the best in the park, but there's no view, just a fence.'

'That has to be a clue, doesn't it?'

'Meaning what?'

'I'm not sure.' I stared at the ride. On the far side of the dodgem rink the fence was about seven feet high. The plastic panels, decorated with huge pictures of the Winter Wonderland characters, obscured any kind of view.

The doubt crept back into my mind. Would we ever find the device? Would I ever get Dakota back safe? 'Maybe there's a way through further along the—'

A scream cut me off. On the far side of the rink a silver dodgem car was rebounding off the back of a pale-blue one. The girl who'd yelled was already laughing, steering back into the pale-blue car again. Getting revenge.

That's when I spotted it.

It was an emergency exit sign, white with small black lettering – not the usual white and green, not designed to catch the eye. But I'd seen it. Below it was a gate: a safety feature, mandatory for the emergency evacuation of the ride in the event of a fire or whatnot; a route to get through to the other side.

Dressed in a security uniform, Scott would have been able to get into any place in the park without being challenged. He could have gone through the safety exit and into the green space beyond. From there he'd have been able to look at the view. And hide the device.

I pointed towards the gate. 'We need to get through there.'

39

The digital display at the entrance to Ice Wars showed the waiting time to ride was one hour, twenty minutes. The line snaked around the barriers, corralling people together under the glare of the sun. Not good. We needed to get across the rink, through the gate, and search the area beyond. Fast.

Inside the dodgem rink a bell sounded, marking the end of the session. The cars began to slow. A shaggy-haired guy wearing a pale-blue jumpsuit and mirrored shades stepped in. He waved a chequered flag at each car in turn, directing them back to their start positions against the fence.

JT glanced at me. 'You got a plan for this?'

'We enter the rink with the next group. Say we're maintenance, checking something out.' It was the best I could think of, but still, I didn't much like it. We'd be exposed, vulnerable.

JT frowned. He nodded towards a couple of security guards patrolling over by the SparkleDust Candyfloss stand. Both were bulked-up, filling out their uniforms almost to bursting. 'We screw up, they'll be on us fast.'

'Then we best get it done right.'

The final bell sounded. The last dodgem car returned to its position and the riders climbed out. I straightened the Maintenance Crew ball-cap on my head, and strode with JT to the barrier at the front of the line. I tried to act casual, like I belonged. Wasn't real sure I pulled it off; it's tough looking calm when nerves are spinning in your belly like a Ferris wheel.

I glanced at JT. 'You ready?'

'Yep.'

We ducked under the safety rail and merged in with the next group of riders walking up the chute to the rink. Behind us, I heard a woman cuss, bitching that we'd skipped the line. I willed her to zip it. Hoped she'd not cause a scene.

Too late. A dude in baggy pants and an oversized tee jostled against JT. The woman was still cussing. People around us were staring, pointing.

JT pulled a white card from his pants pocket, flashed it at the dude, the cussing woman, and the others closest to us. 'Maintenance Crew, please step aside.'

I moved around JT. Waved to the guy with the chequered flag. 'Maintenance check.'

Chequered-flag guy looked pissed. He shook his head. 'But I got a full ride here, how about you—'

'Sorry, no can do,' I said. 'Boss told us to get it done. Only take a couple of minutes.'

Chequered-flag guy sighed. 'Well, okay, I guess. Come aboard.'

We stepped on to the rink. I could still hear the woman in the chute bitching. I ignored her, had to focus. The floor was more slippery than I'd expected. I couldn't run, instead I half walked, half slid towards the emergency exit. JT followed.

So far, all good.

I squeezed between a pink glittery dodgem car and the bumper of a shiny emerald-green one to get to the panelled fence at the spot beneath the exit sign. Pressed my hand along the join, looking for the gate release. Nothing. No handle, no button, no lever.

From across the rink, chequered-flag guy called, 'What'd you say you were checking?'

JT took a pace towards me. 'You got a problem with this emergency route. Faulty release mechanism, is all.'

'Didn't tell me,' the guy said, his tone doubtful. 'Who reported it?'

I heard the crackle of a radio and footsteps coming towards us.

'They're calling it in.' JT sounded tense. 'We need to move. Now.'

I twisted round, looked back across the rink. The operator, a chunky woman with pink cheeks and a pale-blue TEAM: ICE WARS polo shirt, had joined chequered-flag guy. She was talking into a handheld radio. Shaking her head.

Shit.

'Lori. Get it open.'

I turned back, scratched at the fence, dug my fingers into the gap between the panel and the gate. Pulled hard.

It wouldn't budge. I cussed under my breath. 'It won't. I can't—'

JT swore.

Turning, I saw the operator and chequered-flag guy were sliding their way towards us. Behind them, the two bulky security guards were approaching the rink at the run.

Launching myself at the fence, I climbed as best I could up the plastic panelling. The fence was slippery, unstable. My injured leg made me weaker, less agile. Just when I thought I might fall, I felt JT's hands on my thigh, boosting me higher. I scrambled over, tumbling on to the ground below.

Moments later, JT landed beside me.

On the other side of the fence I could hear shouting. The guards were coming for us.

'This way, come on.' JT sprinted forward through the bushes. I followed. Nine yards in, the bushes ended. Grass stretched out ahead of us for maybe eighteen yards. After that the ground fell sharply away. I paused on the top of the ridge. Looked out across the valley below. You could almost see the ocean from here. Scott had been right. The view was amazing.

I heard a yell behind me. Turned. Saw the guards. They'd come through the emergency exit, and were hurtling our way. They moved real quick for such big guys.

I scrambled down the slope, wincing from the pain in my ankle, skidding on loose dirt, stumbling, trying to catch up with JT.

He'd reached the bottom and stopped. Waiting for me.

I joined him, breathless. 'Where now?'

'Towards the staff parking lot.'

Made sense. That's the route Scott would have been taking when he found his chill-spot. Ahead of us the ground dropped away again. The slope led down to a second ridge, this one lined by large grey boulders. They'd block the guards' view of us. Perfect for cover.

We sprinted down the slope. Behind us the guards were shouting, telling us to stay where we were. I glanced back, saw tasers in their hands. We had to stay out of range. Too close, and it'd be game over. I wondered how long it'd be before Emerson's guys from the Gingerbread Grotto showed up, too.

I pushed myself harder. Faster. Blood pounded in my ears.

Reaching the ridge, we scrambled over the boulders, the rock scratching my palms. On the other side we ducked down, out of sight. Kept running.

Side by side, we ran along a set of narrow train-like tracks. Rails for Frosty Looper, I guessed. The device had to be close. We just had to find the specific spot Scott would go to chill, a place he'd have been shielded from the cameras. Everything so far had been too open, too vulnerable. Shit, I hoped that there *was* a place, that my assumption was right. That he hadn't just dug a hole and buried the damn thing.

I kept running, kept scanning the area for possible hiding places. Kept hoping. Saw nothing hopeful. There was no grass here. The hillside had been designed to look like the surface of the moon, with craters and boulders, only all in different shades of blue.

The guards were yelling, their voices getting closer. They'd followed us over the boulders and on to the rails.

Still we ran. JT looked like he could do this all day long. But the pain in my ankle was increasing, the limp returning. My lungs felt as if they could burst any moment. I focused on my breathing, in through my nose, out through my mouth. Pumped my arms harder. Kept pace with JT, just.

He gestured down the track. About twenty yards ahead the rails soared upwards into a huge double loop, then twisted right and plunged down the hillside out of sight. Below the loop, the ground dropped away into space. 'This way,' JT grunted out.

We followed the track, sprinting between the rails.

Fifteen yards to the edge. Ten.

I glanced over my shoulder. The guards were still gaining on us. Willed my legs faster.

Five yards.

JT stopped dead. I skidded to a halt beside him. Looked down, saw the problem: a sheer drop, at least eight feet on to sloping, uneven ground. In the distance, across maybe ten acres of grassland, was the staff parking lot.

He turned to me. 'Your call.'

There was a strange humming sound. The rails on either side of us were vibrating. I looked at JT. 'The rollercoaster. We can use it to—'

'Stop right there,' a man's voice yelled.

I whipped round. The security guards were closing in on us fast. Another few yards and they'd have us in taser range.

The humming grew louder. The rails vibrated faster. We were gonna have to jump. I raised an eyebrow at JT. He nodded.

Frosty Looper rounded the bend, hurtling towards us. For a second I didn't move, just stared at the front of the rollercoaster, at its brightly painted green-and-blue cars, at the kids screaming in the front seats. Watched the security guards leap off the track, their expressions angry, like dogs when the squirrel they're chasing darts up a tree. Next moment, they'd disappeared behind the rollercoaster as it shot along the rails in front of them, blocking their path. The rails on either side of me whined and pinged.

I jumped.

A brief moment of flight, then the ground met me. Stony and unforgiving. I bent my knees on impact, rolled to reduce the jarring. Scrambled up. Kept moving.

The rollercoaster looped the loop above us. The screams growing louder.

'Come on.' JT set off downhill towards the parking lot.

Before I began to follow, I glanced back at the ledge. No guards. They'd not followed us. Why? That's when I realised. The drop off was man-made; a chunk of the hillside had been cut away. Boulders, painted blue, had been used to reinforce the hillside, to stop landslides.

'Keep moving,' JT yelled back at me.

But I couldn't go. We'd missed something. Given his physical limitations Scott never would've made the jump. He'd have taken another route; a route that the security guards chasing us most likely knew. 'Wait. We need to—'

JT grabbed my arm, his fingers dug into my flesh. I tried to pull away. He wouldn't let go, squeezed my arm tighter, pulling me with him. 'There's no time.'

I smacked his hand away. 'Listen. The guards didn't try the jump. Scott wouldn't have either. He'd have used another route, gone around the drop, come out further along.' I pointed uphill to the spot where the drop-off tapered to merge into the natural incline. 'He'd have come around there. We need to check if there's a place he'd have hidden the device along his route.'

JT didn't reply. He didn't need to, I could guess what he was thinking: another assumption, his rule broken. Again.

I looked back up the hillside. 'I wasn't asking permission.'

'Lori, the guards will be on us any minute. It's a hell of a—'

Ignoring him, I set off up the slope at the run. There wasn't time to argue. He was right, the guards would be around the drop-off and on to us soon enough. I had to find the device before they were.

I stuck close to the drop-off. The buttress holding back the earth was made of hardened plastic laid vertically into the cut-out hillside. The blue boulders were just cladding, window dressing for riders of the rollercoaster who might glimpse them. Wild flowers and creepers had grown over the rocks, their roots wound tight into crevices. I scanned the gaps. None was big enough to fit the device. Kept searching.

I heard a noise, turned. JT was following a little ways behind me, watching for the guards.

We heard the static crackle of a radio at the same moment. I flinched. JT bounded towards me, grabbed my shoulder, forcing me to turn. 'We gotta go. You're no use to her caught.'

It was too late. I heard the guards' voices. Glanced at the end of the drop-off ten yards away. Couldn't see them, but knew they'd be on us in seconds.

There was no place to hide.

I heard another burst of static. Louder this time.

JT tightened his grip, tried to pull me back down the slope. 'Lori, come on.'

Out the corner of my eye, I noticed movement. A couple of yards further ahead the creeper trailing over the boulders was moving in the breeze. 'Wait, look.'

I shook JT's hand away, hurried towards the creeper. Its growth was thicker here, denser. It hung curtain-like from the top of the drop-off to the ground. Reaching out, I pressed my hand into the plant, then through it, into a gap in the rock cladding, an alcove maybe two feet wide and three feet deep. I yanked the plant aside. 'Quick, in here.'

JT leapt into the alcove beside me.

'Do you think this is where Scott came to—'

JT pressed his finger to my lips, and let the creeper drop back into place across the opening, shutting out the light. I flattened my back against the rocks. Froze.

I heard another burst of radio static and a set of footsteps, getting closer.

In the cramped space I could feel the warmth of JT's body just inches from mine. I heard him breathing, slow and shallow. I stayed real still, my palms pressed tight against the stones behind me. A bug crawled across my hand. I resisted the urge to flick it away.

Outside, the footsteps grew louder. Stopped. Waiting. A long moment later, I heard more footsteps; the second guard. They muttered to each other, comparing notes, getting their breath back.

I felt a trickle of sweat run along my spine and longed to wipe it off. I looked over at JT. He shook his head slowly, glanced towards the creeper.

One of the guards' radios beeped. He answered, then waited as the person on the other end spoke. I heard him grunt, and say yes. Then the guards muttered again to each other. Moments later I heard footsteps as they moved away.

Still we waited. Was it a ruse to lure us out? Were they searching nearby, so that, as soon as we stepped from the alcove, we'd be spotted? It was a hard call to make. Behind the creeper curtain we were virtually blind to the outside world. Whenever we broke our cover we'd be vulnerable.

And so we waited.

Minutes passed; hot, sweaty minutes. All the while I was acutely aware of how close JT was, of the small space we were in getting hotter, and our breathing getting louder. I hoped to hell the guards really had gone, and that we'd finally caught ourselves some luck.

I thought about Dakota, her image freeze-framed on the video. Her haunting eyes gazing terrified into the lens. I'd had enough of waiting. Had to find the device. Had to know if this was the place Scott had it hidden.

Twisting myself around to face the wall, I ran my hands along the rocks, looking for a big enough gap. The stone was rough beneath my fingers. JT moved a little further towards the entrance, giving me a fraction more space.

Without slowing my search, I whispered to him, 'What is this place?'

'A drainage shoot, I guess. Lets the water filter through in a storm. Stops water damage.'

Made sense. 'You think it's the place?'

'Only one way to know for sure.'

I searched as fast and as thoroughly as I could. It was too dark to see properly, and too risky to draw back the creeper that shielded us, so I explored the gaps between each rock by feel.

Low down in the left corner, my fingers touched fabric. 'I have something.'

Behind me, I felt JT shuffle closer. 'The device?'

I pulled at the fabric. It had been wedged tight into a crevice between two large rocks. Hooking my fingers into the gap on either side, I eased it out. Beneath the folds lay something solid, rectangular. My heartbeat accelerated.

I unfolded the material and stared at the object in my hand: a silver portable hard drive. 'I've got it.'

JT exhaled. 'Then we need to get out of here.'

I straightened up, twisted back around to face JT. 'Wait. Tell me why you broke the terms of the truce with Old Man Bonchese.'

'Emerson.'

'Yeah, I got that. But why? What happened that was so damn bad it made you cross the state line to get to him?'

He looked away. 'Her name is Kat. Katherine. She's eleven years old.'

Despite the heat, I shivered. Felt the hair on my arms stand on end.

JT's expression was sad in the dim light. 'She lives in a place in Martinez run by Child Services – Sunnyview Children's Home. I help them out every now and then: odd jobs, handyman stuff to keep the place nice.'

'Why?'

He sighed. 'That trouble between Merv and me, the fight that got me found guilty? – did six weeks' community service for it, assigned to Sunnyview. Kinda liked helping out. Those kids don't have shit, playing ball once a week made a big difference to them.' He looked down. 'To me as well.'

I nodded. What he said matched with the details in the police file Quinn had sent. Pops' words about JT came back to me: *He's changed*. Maybe he had. Maybe he didn't want to be the loner anymore.

'Kat was nine when she ended up at Sunnyview. Her father had never been around, her mom drank and then some. That last night she'd added oxy to her binge and wound up DOA at the emergency room. The kid found her after getting up in the middle of the night for a glass of water. Smart girl dialled 911 when she realised her momma wasn't breathing.'

'Shit.'

'Didn't do no good. Her mom was dead, and, without any close relatives, she ended up at Sunnyview. It was five weeks before Kat spoke.

She said her first words to me.' He paused. 'After that she did real good. Went to school, settled at the home. Every time I went she'd help me with whatever I was fixing. Asked me to go to father-and-daughter day at school.' He shook his head. 'Few months ago, Sunnyview Children's Home came here on a trip organised by some local roundtable. Kat got separated from the other kids. She was gone ninety minutes. They found her sitting in the smoking area off Main Street. She was dazed and crying, and had lost one of her shoes. No one knew how she'd gotten there. Kat wouldn't say; she stopped talking again.' He shook his head. 'The park brushed it off as nothing. We tried reporting it, but the cops didn't want to help, said it sounded like a lost kid who already got found, not a crime. Course, now I know they're in Emerson's pocket anyways.'

'Jesus.' What else could I say? Nothing seemed enough.

A muscle pulsed in his cheek. 'A week later, Kat still wasn't speaking. I asked her if someone had hurt her and she nodded. Emerson's people, they'd made a mistake. Kat's older than the kids they usually took, and tall for her age. They must have calculated the drug dosage wrong. She had memories of being taken. When I asked her to draw me a picture of who hurt her she drew two people. One wore a Felix the Arctic Fox costume, the other wore a suit and wire-framed glasses.'

It was starting to make sense. 'So you came here to find out who they were?'

He nodded. 'I had to know the truth, and I had to know who was responsible. Whatever it took.'

Shit, so much for violence never as punishment. 'So why didn't you?'

'Emerson's security guards took me down. I was going to ask him to have his security team search the CCTV recordings for the man Kat had drawn, but I didn't need to. I'd already found him.'

'How?'

'The man with the wire-framed glasses was Emerson.'

I stared at him. Didn't speak.

'Scott watched what really happened with Emerson and me that day on the CCTV feed. When Emerson told him to scrub the footage from any cameras that had recorded my movements, he saved it on to the device first.' JT looked at the hard drive in my hand. 'On there is all the evidence Scott collected. It includes the CCTV footage taken the day Kat visited the park. It also has the footage from the extra cameras Scott rigged in the place Emerson took the kids. It shows exactly what that man is responsible for.'

Despite the heat, I felt chills. I'd been kidding myself this whole time. A man like that, he wasn't ever going to trade my daughter for the device. He'd take it *and* Dakota; kill me and JT; then continue with his hateful business like nothing had happened.

I started to shake. I couldn't, wouldn't, let Emerson get away with this. The sick bastard had to pay, had to let my daughter go.

Unable to disguise the quivering in my voice, I hissed, 'We *have* to stop him.'

40

Guilt. Anger. Disgust. Those emotions can be real good motivators, especially if you need to override fear. Trick is, not to let them blind your focus. At that moment, I was having a little trouble on that count.

I felt conflicted. My priorities scattered.

I knew we couldn't hand over the device without copying the data. After everything, we could not allow the evidence to be lost. There must be justice, for all the victims: Dakota, Kat and the others. Emerson had to face his crimes, of that I was real determined. JT was, too. Thing was, I reckoned we might have different views on how that justice would get served.

But I'd have to worry about that dilemma later. First we needed to get ourselves to a place we could download the data. Sitting in the alcove, we figured out our closest option was one of the resort hotels that were located around the inner perimeter of the park. There was one less than a quarter mile from us, and from the map it seemed we could get there without having to go through the public area. In the hotel there'd be guest computers where we could copy the files and save them someplace safe, before handing over the device to Emerson's men.

We pulled back the creeper and emerged from the alcove, scanning the hillside for signs of the security guards. They'd gone. We decided to move.

I couldn't shake the guilt, though. Every moment we spent trying to copy the data, I was doing nothing to find Dakota. I'd always sworn to keep her safe. I'd failed her in that, and now I was failing again by choosing to delay her rescue.

JT frowned at me. 'We'll get her back. This won't take long. A quick diversion, is all.'

I said nothing. No words could help. This was on me. I jogged across the hillside in the direction of the hotel.

Trouble found us sixty yards later. Five security guards and three men in plain clothes, who must have been Emerson's goons, were heading up the hillside towards us. Fanned out, searching.

'Double back,' JT said. 'Keep low.'

We hung a sharp left, sprinted to the park. A few moments later I heard shouting behind us. We'd been spotted. Shit. I looked over my shoulder. All eight were coming after us.

I kept running. 'They're forcing us back to the park,' I said, my words coming in gasps.

JT didn't slow his pace. 'Head for the tunnels,' he said. 'Only way we'll make the hotel now.'

We reached the crest of the hill. The white perimeter fence stood thirty feet away. We hotfooted to it. Turned left, skirting the fence past the Ice Wars ride until we were almost level with the start of Popsicle Drive. It was a busy area, and there'd be plenty of folks for us to blend in with. From there it wasn't far to the access hatch in the ice caves.

Behind us, the men had reached the crest of the hill. They were shouting, yelling for us to surrender.

Never.

'You ready?' JT yelled.

I nodded.

Without breaking stride, we leapt for the fence, scrambled over and landed in the main walkway. We attracted some confused glances but we didn't stop. Just merged into the crowd and ran to Main Street.

We had to get to the tunnels.

⇓

Something was different. The 'Happy Holidays' song wasn't playing on Main Street anymore; instead thumping dance music pounded from the overhead speakers. We pushed through the mass of people, aiming for the ice caves. As we moved, I removed the maintenance ball-cap, unbraided my hair and handed the bandana to JT. He swapped his cap for the bandana, peeled off his shirt, revealing a grey tee underneath. We dumped the shirt and caps in the next trashcan we passed.

An athletic-looking woman, her tan chest squeezed into a pink neon waistcoat, brandished a handheld tannoy as she strode towards us. 'Stand back, please. Stay behind the blue line. Parade's coming.'

Around us, people moved on to the sidewalks. More neon waistcoated crew were roping off the parade route, keeping visitors behind the blue lines running along both sides of the street. Young, buff crew members with unfeasibly white smiles were stationed every fifteen feet, watching for people who might jaywalk. Any person stepping out of line was going to attract attention.

Shit. We'd not reckoned on there being a parade. I peered down the street towards the SparkleDust Castle. Glimpsed a troupe of penguin-costumed dancers waddling and wiggling to the music.

'Ideas?' I said over the approaching din.

'Best find ourselves another way.'

I shook my head. 'There's no time. The closest access to the tunnels is that hatch in the ice cave I saw earlier. We need to get across the street.'

'We'll need a security pass, too.'

True. At the top of Main Street the first floats were passing the SparkleDust Castle. The crowd clapped and whooped. If we were going to move, we needed to do it now.

On the opposite side of the street was an older, more spindly-looking crowd controller in a green neon vest. Attached to his belt I spied a plastic security keycard.

I leant closer to JT. 'Follow me.'

'What are—?'

Jumping over the rope barrier, I dashed across the street towards the willowy guy. He registered a brief moment of surprise, moved right, trying to block my path. Advantage me. I pretended to stumble, fell into him and, as he tried to help me up, unclipped the keycard from his belt and slipped it into my pocket.

Straightening up, I gave the guy an apologetic smile. 'Why, I am *so* sorry.'

He looked at me like I was some kind of whack-job. Spoke slow and clear. 'Off the street, ma'am. The floats are coming.'

JT took my arm and together we stepped over the rope barrier on the opposite side of the street. He leant in closer – so close I could feel his breath warm against my cheek. 'Nicely done.'

Walking fast, we moved around the edge of the crowd and headed towards the ice caves. It wasn't easy. The crowd was thirty deep, their attention on the parade. No one wanted to give an inch for fear of losing their view. Well, I had no time for that. Used my elbows to manoeuvre through. Ignored the dirty looks and muttered insults.

As we reached the ice caves, the dance music had gotten so loud, I thought my ears would bleed. The first float was painted silver, with pale-blue stars glittering across every surface and disco lights swirling in time with the music. On it danced people dressed as the characters from the recent *Frozen Moon* cartoon.

My breath caught in my throat. Dakota had loved that movie so much. As the characters waved at us, I thought again of my baby's tear-stained face. I clenched my fists. 'All set?' I whispered to JT.

Without taking his eyes off the parade, he nodded.

As the float drew level with us, we stepped back into the cave. Slow and steady, watching the crowd, waiting for someone to notice us.

They didn't. We reached the sectioned-off area, and stopped behind the screen, hidden from view. I exhaled. Knew that the bit we'd done had been easy compared to what was to come.

I pulled the keycard from my pocket. On the post beside the metal trapdoor was a card reader. The light above it glowed red. I held the keycard against the reader. Nothing happened. Shit. My heart beat faster. What if the crowd-control crew didn't get access to the tunnels?

'Try again,' said JT.

I pressed the keycard against the card reader again. Kept it there a little longer this time, held my breath.

The light turned green. I heard a metallic click.

JT turned the handle and pulled the hatch open. Beneath it was a short flight of steps down to a small, square platform. Some kind of elevator, I assumed.

I hurried down, my footsteps echoing in the small space. The platform wobbled as I stepped on to it.

JT bounded down the steps and joined me on the platform. 'All set?'

'Sure.'

He reached up and pulled the trapdoor shut. For a moment everything was pitch-dark, then the lights flickered on, light sensor-activated I guessed.

JT pressed the green button on the control panel. The platform started slowly to descend. I hoped to hell it wouldn't take long.

⇓

The tunnels were painted white, and better lit than I'd expected. Still, the clinical brightness didn't help the claustrophobic feeling of the place, and did nothing to disguise the stale taste in the air. Exiting the elevator, we hurried towards the main tunnel twenty yards ahead. I scanned the walls, noted the doors with signs to the break room and the dressing area. Couldn't spot any cameras. Didn't mean they weren't there though, concealed someplace. Watching.

Cameras weren't our only problem. We weren't alone. Up ahead in the main tunnel a steady stream of staff, some in costume, others in tabards and crew uniforms, scurried to wherever their work was scheduled. None paid us any mind. Yet. Still, I knew that as soon as we stepped on to the concourse our casual clothes would mark us out as different. We needed a better disguise.

I put my hand on JT's arm, nodding towards the dressing area. 'In here.'

Easing the door open, I checked the room was empty. It was. We hurried inside and bolted the door shut. Along the far wall, a row of character costumes were suspended like hog carcasses on hooks. Percy

Penguin, Chester Chipmunk, Saskia Seal, and a whole bunch of others that I didn't know the names for, stared sightlessly at us.

'We have to get through the tunnels without being spotted. These are our best option.' I stepped towards the costumes, glanced back at JT. 'Find one that fits.'

He smiled that crooked half-smile of his. 'Yes, ma'am.'

My fingers trembled as I sorted through the costumes and grabbed the first one that seemed it would fit – a white bunny ballerina, dressed in a blue leotard and tutu. The only one broad enough for JT was a walrus wearing some kind of German lederhosen.

We pulled the costumes on over our clothes. They were heavier than I'd figured and, despite the air-con, I felt myself start to sweat. Putting the bunny head on, I slotted the attachments into the clips on the shoulders of the costume and fixed it in place.

Squinting through the small peep-hole in the base of the neck, I looked round at JT. He'd gotten the walrus suit on, his body hidden by the chocolate-brown fur.

'You ready?' I said. My voice sounded real strange, kind of echoey.

JT finished pulling the long, plastic flippers over his hands and hooked them in position just above the elbow. He turned. The over-large, heavy-lidded eyes of the walrus stared right at me. He nodded. 'Yep.'

We exited the room and made for the main tunnel. It looked as busy as before, characters and staff moving in both directions. My heart rate accelerated as we got closer. Fifteen yards. Ten.

We waddled faster. I still felt uneasy, trapped. Even in costume we weren't safe. Maybe they'd seen us enter and exit the dressing room via the CCTV feed. Perhaps they knew to look for a walrus and a bunny.

Hustling towards the main tunnel, I ran over the plan again in my head: get to the resort hotel, copy the data, get the hell out and find Dakota. Not easy, but we couldn't fail. *I* could not fail.

We reached the main tunnel. From there, yellow signs told us to take a left for the Main Street and Frozen Moon Fantasia access points, go straight ahead for the SparkleDust Castle, or right for the Big Freeze Zone and resort hotels.

Parked up in a bay at the side of the tunnel were three blue golf carts. Numbers were painted in black on their bonnets: nineteen, thirty-six, eight. I figured there must have been a whole fleet of them. The resort hotels were all on the outskirts of the park. Given the distance we had to cover, and seeing as speed was a priority, the carts looked real attractive.

'What'd you think?'

The large head of the walrus nodded. 'Got to be easier than walking.'

We jumped into the nearest cart, number nineteen. Wriggling my fingers through the slits on the inside of the bunny's wrists, I freed my hands and pressed the start button.

I handed JT the crumpled park map I'd kept in the left paw of my costume, and pulled out of the parking spot. 'Which hotel?'

Having folded the plastic flippers back to his elbows, JT opened the map. 'The Ice Palace is closest.'

'Done.' I coaxed the cart to its maximum speed. It wasn't great. Twenty-five miles per hour, tops. Still, better than walking.

I drummed my nails against the steering wheel. Cussed as I had to brake before pulling wide around a group of park crew, waiting for them to stop us. They didn't. The whine of the electric motor echoed through the tunnel.

A few hundred yards later we reached the access points for the Big Freeze Zone. Elevator after elevator led up to the surface, signs giving their destinations: Ice Wars, Big Chiller, Frosty Looper.

The tunnel seemed to stretch into the distance for ever. Once we'd passed the access points to the Big Freeze Zone the traffic dropped to zero. I kept my foot pressed flat on the accelerator. Willed the damn cart faster.

Minutes passed: two, five, maybe ten. It was hard to keep track in the never-ending void of the tunnel.

'How much further?' I asked.

JT leant forward, the forehead of the walrus rested against the windshield as he checked the map. 'Must be close now.'

Good. I steered the cart through a sharp right-hand bend. Hoped JT was right.

Moments later I heard a low humming noise somewhere behind us. 'What's that?'

JT twisted in his seat, looked back along the tunnel. Cussed.

'What?'

'Company.'

I swung the cart around another turn. 'They could just be—'

'They've got guns.'

Shit. Emerson's men, they had to be. I pressed the cart faster. The steering wheel vibrated in my hands. The cart wasn't designed to travel at top speed for long. The whole chassis was juddering so hard it felt like it was going to shake apart beneath us.

JT released the clips on the shoulders of his costume and yanked the walrus head off. Dropping it on to the back seat, he leant forward and squinted ahead. 'There's a junction. The tunnel splits four ways. Get us there and I can throw them off the trail.'

I frowned. 'How?'

'Swap seats.' He pulled off the flippers, grabbed the top of the windshield and stood up. 'Give me the wheel.'

We flashed past a sign. It pointed right for The Ice Palace Resort Hotel. 'We're almost there. We can—'

'No. They'll be on us before we reach the elevator. You need to jump. I'll keep driving. Act as a decoy.'

My heartbeat raced faster, but I stayed right where I was. 'But they'll—'

'One of us needs to get to a computer. With all these bends they won't have had a clear line of sight to us yet. You best get gone before they do.'

Through the tiny peep-hole in my costume I looked deep into his big old blues. It sounded real like a suicide mission, but still, I knew he was right. Didn't make me like the odds on him getting free and clear any better.

The humming noise grew louder. Soon our pursuers would be too close to fool. 'All right.'

I slid forward in the seat, allowing JT to step across behind me. Felt the warmth of his thighs against my back as he reached around and took hold of the wheel. I scooted across to the other side, pressed my hand against the belly of the bunny suit, checking the device was still safely tucked inside my jacket.

I nodded.

JT slowed the cart, pulling it tight against the right-hand wall of the tunnel. The intersection drew closer. With one hand on the seat and the other on the front of side of the windshield, I braced myself, ready to jump. Glanced back at JT.

He smiled. 'Meet at the car.'

I nodded, the damn bunny head exaggerating my movement, probably making me look way more confident than I felt. 'Sure.'

He braked hard and I leapt from the cart, bending my knees as I landed to soften the impact. The concrete of the tunnel floor jarred through my bones, before the extra weight of the bunny head tipped me off balance, and the momentum pitched me forward. My knees hit the ground. I registered the pain, but couldn't stop, couldn't hesitate. I used the oversized paws to push myself up and started running.

In the main tunnel behind me I heard JT accelerate away. I sprinted as best I could to The Ice Palace elevator. Swiped the keycard against the card reader. Watched the door glide open, and stepped inside.

Turning around, I had a view down to the main tunnel. A cart whizzed straight past the junction, followed close by a second. I held my breath, listening for a sign that JT had gotten clear.

The first gunshot made me jump. It sounded so loud, so close. Echoing through the tunnel like a thousand separate shots.

I exhaled hard. Put my finger over the service-lobby button, but didn't press it, not yet. I heard shouting. Pictured JT. Surrounded. Trapped. Fought the urge to go back.

I pressed the button. Watched the door glide shut. Felt the elevator start to ascend. Tried to focus on the next stage of the plan.

Succeed or fail, *everything* now was on me.

41

I leant back against the cool metal of the elevator wall. Heart banging. Gunfire still echoing in my head. The sick feeling in my stomach was getting worse with every second; the guilt, too. What if JT was dead?

The elevator kept moving. I grasped the handrail. Squeezed it, tightening my grip until the metal was warm beneath my touch and my hands were numb. Didn't help. All the feelings I'd locked deep down ten years ago flooded back and mingled with the present: Sal, Dakota, JT. All lost.

Me left. Alone.

My breath came in gasps. I felt like I was drowning. I stared out through the peep-hole in my costume; the elevator walls seemed to warp and flex. Black spots floated across my eyes. I felt faint, light-headed from the exertion and the fear.

The elevator jolted to a halt. I reached out, pressed the door-close button. Wasn't ready. Needed to get a grip.

You can't fall apart, I told myself. JT would tell you to focus, to do what needs doing. Rescue Dakota. Bring Emerson to justice.

I exhaled hard. I could do this. I *had* to.

Deep breaths, long and slow. Be ready, I told myself. For our plan to work I needed to blend in with the hotel guests, but that was hardly going to happen with me dressed as a cartoon bunny.

I stripped off the costume. Glancing down, I saw dirt clinging to the knees of my jeans. I flicked it away. Looked at my face in the mirrored metal wall. My reflection was warped, distorted. I peered closer and wiped black mascara smudges from beneath my eyes, smoothed my hair back with my palm. Forced a smile. Not real convincing, but good enough.

I pressed the door-open button. And with Dakota's face in my mind, stepped out of the elevator.

The room I found myself in was narrow and, thankfully, empty. A waiting area for cast and crew, I guessed. Functional, with a cream-tiled floor and taupe walls. A large 'Crew Only' sign was fixed to the wall beside the exit door.

I dumped the bunny costume behind an orange couch, unlocked the door with the keycard and stepped on out.

The lobby atrium seemed like another world. The vaulted ceiling rose five stories above me. Hundreds of twinkling, star-shaped lights set in the plaster bathed the place in a pale-blue glow. Blocks of translucent bricks gave the illusion that it was carved from ice. Ahead of me, guests milled around. Kids climbed on leather couches, rolled and play-fought on faux-fur rugs, as adults lazed beside the huge marble fireplaces, taking afternoon tea.

They all looked so normal, so relaxed. In a different dimension from dead Santas, abducted children and open gunfire.

I didn't know if security were tracking the keycard I'd taken, but I had to work on the assumption they were, which meant I needed to move real fast.

My first step was to find a business centre. Any hotel as big as this would have one. Scanning the lobby, I spotted a hotel map a little further along the wall. I hurried over to it, checked my location, and soon found the business centre marked on the second floor. However, according to a note in italics, only hotel guests were allowed access. I needed a guest ID.

Over near the concierge, a large group of seniors had gathered around a perky-looking tour guide. She was welcoming them to the hotel.

Thinking fast, I moved closer to the group. The guide was saying she was going to hand out welcome packs, which contained everything they'd need for their stay. As the seniors pressed closer to their guide, I merged into the outer edges of the group. I figured inside the packs would be the ID I needed, but given I was near on thirty years younger than the rest of the group, my taking one was sure to raise a question. Still, I had to take the risk. What choice did I have? I moved forward, ready.

That's when I saw two of the seniors – a silver-haired lady in a pink flowery dress, and a bald guy with a large belly beneath his Hawaiian shirt – move away from the group. Deep in conversation, they were flicking through the hotel activities brochure, pointing out things that caught their eye. They'd left their packs on a table a few feet from them. The woman's was open. Her ID card was tucked just inside the flap.

Without hesitating, I strode out of the group and past the couple looking at the brochure. I stooped a little as I stepped around the table, grabbed the ID card without slowing and walked away.

No reaction, no shouting, nothing.

I kept moving. The stairwell was right across the other side of the lobby. I spotted a security guard standing nearby. I couldn't risk passing him. The crew elevator was closer, but if they were monitoring my keycard, using it would alert them to my exact location. So I hung a left around the atrium and headed towards the guest elevators.

They were way grander than the crew elevator, for sure. Styled like a 1920s cage lift, complete with uniformed attendant, these elevators had a metal mesh screen that pulled across before you rode, allowing those inside to see out, and those outside to see into the moving car.

Damn, so much for keeping out of sight. Every person in the lobby could see where I was heading. I couldn't help that none. It was still the least risky way of getting to the next floor.

As I stepped into the nearest cage, the attendant smiled. 'Good morning. Which floor can I take you to today?'

The risk of talking to people is that they'll remember you, be able to point you out in a crowd, blow your cover clean away. Help those hunting you make a kill. But in this situation saying nothing would have seemed plain odd, and that's all the more reason for being remembered. So I checked the name on her crew badge and forced a smile. 'Susan, hey. If you'd be kind enough to take me to second I'd surely appreciate it.'

'No problem.' Susan pulled the cage door tight shut, clicked the lock into place, and pressed the button for second.

As we rose upwards, I stayed alert, watching for trouble. I spotted it soon enough; three security guys stationed near the front entrance, and another two beside the gift store left their posts and hurried to the crew door I'd come through moments earlier.

Shit. Just as I'd reckoned, they knew I'd taken the keycard and had tracked me here. As soon as they realised I wasn't in the crew area or the lobby they'd search the whole hotel. I sure hoped they'd start on the ground floor.

As the elevator reached the second floor, I touched the outside of my jacket pocket and felt the device hard against my ribs. I couldn't let them take it. Not yet.

⇓

The business centre was not what I'd imagined. With its own private lobby, two uniformed receptionists and a leather-bound visitors' ledger, it looked more like a convention centre than an office. The signs said free Wi-Fi. Problem was, I didn't have a laptop.

I scanned the corridor for an alternative. Spotted a sign pointing to the Internet Café. Better.

The café only had four computers, three of them occupied. The two people on the right side of the room were older men; one was answering emails, the other reading CNN online. At the computer on the left, a teenage girl flicked between three social networking sites. No one looked to be going any place soon.

I strode to the free computer in the far corner. CNN guy looked up as I passed. I nodded hello, kept walking, not wanting to be getting into any kind of conversation.

I sat down in front of the keyboard and moved the mouse to wake the computer from hibernation mode. The thing was real slow. I glanced over my shoulder towards the archway into the corridor.

At the prompt, I typed in the guest ID code from the stolen card and pressed return. The screen opened at The Ice Palace homepage. Easing the device from my pocket, I plugged the cable into the USB port and heard the drive whir into life.

A folder opened on-screen. My first feeling was disappointment. There were only four files: three videos, saved with the date as their file name; and one spreadsheet. Immediately after, I felt guilt. I knew what each of the videos most likely contained. Children. How could I wish that there were more?

I didn't want to watch them, surely I did not, but I had to know the extent of Emerson's sick trade. Scott had known, and he was dead. JT had known, and he could be too. If I knew, even if somehow the data got lost, at least I could tell the cops. I tried not to think on whether I'd survive, and what happened if I never got Dakota safe.

Taking hold of the monitor, I twisted it towards the wall as far as the security cage around its base would allow. Gripping the mouse a little tighter, I double-clicked the first file. A video clip appeared in a small pop-up window at the bottom of my screen. I turned the audio to mute. Pressed play.

The date on the timestamp was early May. A girl of maybe ten or eleven, with short brown hair, wearing a cute, yellow flower-print dress was walking along a narrow pathway. Behind her I could just make out the sign for Percy Penguin's Ice-Skating Rink, and a couple of plastic penguins over by the entrance. It looked like the rink was empty. I guessed it'd been closed for maintenance.

The child seemed to be alone. As she disappeared around a bend in the path, the camera switched to another view. A middle-aged man in a security-guard uniform stepped into view. He approached the child, leant down to her and seemed to be asking her something. I gripped the mouse harder. Felt my pulse thumping against my temple.

Moments later, the girl nodded. The man smiled, held out his hand. She took it, skipping alongside him, away from the camera and out of view.

The next image was taken ninety-two minutes later. The child was slumped against a plastic penguin beside the still-empty ice rink. Head bowed, arms wrapped around her knees. A woman rushed into the shot, approached the girl, and shook her gently by the shoulder. The child tried to stand, looking real wobbly. A man joined the woman. He was pushing a stroller and had another two small children following alongside him. As he knelt to speak to the girl the video ended.

I stared at the screen, my mind spinning. Because I knew what Scott and JT had discovered I could imagine the horror that child had been through in the missing ninety minutes. But what Scott had captured on film, that wasn't proof. It was circumstantial for sure, but nothing more. Hating that I was hoping for something worse in the next video, I double clicked the second file.

I got my wish. Near made me sick. The second video was a mixture of CCTV footage from the public areas spliced with film taken by what I reckoned was Scott's hidden camera.

It showed a brightly lit room with heaps of toys lining the shelves along the walls. But it wasn't the toys I was looking at, it was the man wearing the head of a character costume: a grinning orange-and-black tiger face that jarred with the paleness of his naked body. On her knees in front of him, with a dazed expression on her face, was a blonde girl of twelve, maybe thirteen. She was touching him. The cartoon tiger head kept grinning, leering, and nodded, just slightly, as he coaxed the girl's mouth closer.

Sick son-of-a-bitch.

I gagged. Tasted bile, and coughed violently. Blinking away tears as I closed down the file.

CNN man, sitting over to my right, looked at me real strange.

I waved his concern away. 'Allergies,' I said, wiping my eyes. 'Get me every time.'

I stared at the monitor. Tried to get my breathing back to normal. Doubted I'd ever feel normal again.

That's when I noticed it. The filename of the last video wasn't just a date, it was a name too: KAT. I had to open it. Didn't want to, but I owed it to JT to check the evidence Scott found on what happened to Kat. So I hunched closer to the screen and pressed play.

Kat had been taken from a different area of the park. Dressed in jeans and a black tee, her long black hair pulled back into a pony, Kat was exploring the very place I'd been standing less than an hour ago: the ice cave.

I held my breath. Watched as the group of kids gathered around the cave's entrance moved away, leaving Kat alone. She moved to the back of the cave, investigating behind the faux-ice boulders, hidden from sight. I wanted to yell, to warn her. Tell her to get the hell out. Knew that it wouldn't make no difference. What was done was done.

She was taken real fast. A muscular guy strode out from behind the screened-off area at the rear of the cave. He wore cargo pants and a khaki shirt, a staff ID clipped to his pocket. Three strides and he was on her. She barely had time to turn around. He grabbed her shoulder in one hand and injected something into her neck with the other. She crumpled into his arms.

Picking her up, he carried her to the elevator, and in less than thirty seconds, start to finish, he and Kat had disappeared into the tunnels.

I stopped the video. Didn't want to watch what happened next. Couldn't bear it. There was enough on the device to make Emerson's sick business public. The data could bring down the whole Winter Wonderland operation, and surely open investigations into all Emerson's parks. No wonder he'd wanted to silence Scott Palmer so bad.

I clicked on the spreadsheet. Scrolled through the list of names, dates, and Scott's notes on how he thought they were connected. These were the people Scott was investigating, the ones he believed were involved in Emerson's business. There were more than thirty names, all men. Some I recognised: a sports personality, a junior congressman, the judge from that high-profile serial-killer trial in Miami a few months back. The local chief of police.

But no mention of Emerson. There was nothing on the device that would incriminate him personally. All we had was Kat's sketch. Emerson could plead innocence and, if a jury believed him, not a thing would stop him setting up another sick scheme just like this one as soon as the dust settled.

The horrific images I'd just witnessed kaleidoscoped in my mind. I wanted to howl with rage. Smash the monitor. Instead I gripped the table. Told myself to stay focused. But the louder voice, screaming in my head, repeated again and again: he's got Dakota, he's going to make her do that.

Whatever it took, Emerson had to be stopped.

I checked the time. Shit. Eight minutes had passed. I'd been sitting at the computer too long. I needed to transfer the files and move. I glanced towards the archway; still no guards. Good. But I knew my luck couldn't hold for ever.

The plan had been to email the files to my own account so we could recover them later, once Dakota was safe, and take them to the cops. But now, with JT gone, and security on to me, or as near as dammit, I needed a back-up plan. I wondered what JT would suggest. Thought about his rules, and about our situation. Realised I'd – we'd both – made a huge mistake.

Don't make assumptions.

Back in West Virginia, the text had said to give back the device or they'd kill Dakota. Here, in the Gingerbread Grotto, Dakota had pleaded for us to give it back or they'd press the magic button. Emerson's men wanted the device, for sure, but they'd never once said they'd give her back once they had it. That had been my assumption.

We'd been shot at multiple times. They'd killed Scott. Now we had the device, and had seen the evidence, we were as great a threat as him. Not one of their actions pointed to them having any intention of reuniting me with my child. Hell, Emerson's man at Thelma's told me he didn't know about any kid.

My fingers trembled against the keyboard. I had to do more than email the files to myself. If we didn't make it, if I didn't make it, I had to be sure someone would get Dakota safe. The video files were the way to get their attention, prove the threat was real. Question was, who should I send them to?

It had to be someone who would act. Not Quinn – I couldn't trust him with this. His eye was on JT's bond money, and until he had it nothing else would be his priority. He didn't even check his emails regular. I needed someone real thorough. I had to be sure.

Only one name came to mind: Alex Monroe – the Fed. I'd not met him, but something about his voice made me feel he was sincere. Could I trust him? Involving someone else was a risk, for sure. No cops, I'd been told. If Emerson and his men caught wind of it, they'd kill us all. But I had to take the risk. I needed to know that, whatever happened to me, Dakota had a chance.

I clicked on the internet browser and pulled up the FBI website. Quinn had told me the Fed hailed from Virginia, the Richmond office. I found the field office email address, copied it, then logged into my own account and pasted the Richmond FBI email into the *To* field.

The cursor flashed in the subject line. Decision time.

The clock at the bottom of the screen showed another minute had passed. I glanced over my shoulder towards the archway. Two women stood there, looking bored. The older one, who looked like she'd had a little more Botox than she could handle, looked pointedly at the sign on the wall. It told me there was a ten-minute limit for using the computers. All four of us were close to that, but the other three wouldn't worry if Botox woman caused a scene. For me, the stakes were a whole lot higher.

I nodded to the woman, forced a smile. Mouthed, 'One minute.'

She nodded, seemingly placated for now. That's when I noticed movement in the corridor behind her. There was a man just the other side of the archway. I didn't have a clear view of him, but as he turned I caught a glimpse of his blue shirt. There was a name badge clipped to the top pocket. Security.

Shit. If those women grew more tired of waiting, they'd ask the guy to move us on. I couldn't risk him getting a good look at my face; he could have been given my picture. I was all out of time.

I copied and pasted the files from the device to the email. Watched the progress bar as the data copied across. Twenty percent. Thirty percent. I glanced back to the archway. The man was still standing in the corridor. His body language looked relaxed, too relaxed to be part of the herd of guards looking for me.

I checked the progress bar: sixty percent, seventy. Cussed under my breath. Willed the computer to work faster.

As the files transferred I typed in the subject line: *'Urgent Attention of Special Agent Alex Monroe. From Lori Anderson. HELP ME'.*

I heard the crackle of a radio. Glanced back at the archway. A second man had joined the security guy. They'd turned to face the café. Botox woman was talking at them, flapping her scarlet talons towards the computers, towards me. I was out of time. I had to get out.

The files were still transferring. Ninety percent.

In the body of the email I typed: *'Daughter, DAKOTA, kidnapped. Randall Emerson owner DreamWorld responsible. Blackmailing me for these files. Paedophile gang in amusement parks. Scott Palmer got evidence – attached. Now dead. Body in Gingerbread Grotto – Winter Wonderland, near Fernandina Beach, FL. THEY ARE GOING TO KILL MY DAUGHTER. HELP ME.'*

The files finished transferring. I pressed send. Unplugged the device, and stood up.

As I walked to the archway I knew my shoulders were stiff, that I was moving too fast to look casual. I forced myself to slow down. Nodded to Botox woman and her younger sidekick. 'All yours, honey.'

Botox woman pushed past me. 'Took you long enough.'

Real charmed, I'm sure.

The security guys were chatting; they didn't even turn as I stepped out into the corridor. I kept moving, heading for the elevator.

Reaching it, I pressed the call button then peered through the gaps in the cage door, down on to the lobby. Well, damn. Six security guards were stationed along the exit. Another by the stairwell, more still by the elevator exit below. If I tried getting out that way, I knew I wasn't gonna make it. I needed a different route.

I turned away, followed the corridor and tried to figure out my next move. I took a right at the end. Stepped up my pace. Ignored the pain in my leg. If I couldn't escape above ground I'd only one other option: get back to the tunnels.

Up ahead I spotted a 'Crew Only' door. From there I hoped I'd be able to get to the crew elevator. I pulled the crew keycard from my pants pocket. If I used it, I'd alert security to my position. Without it, I had no chance of getting back to the tunnels.

I swiped the keycard over the card reader. Got a red light, no beep. Shit, what if they'd deactivated the card? I pressed it against the reader again. Red light.

There was movement at the other end of the corridor. The two security guards from the Internet Café were heading my way fast. Their shoe leather squeaked against the cream floor tiles as they ran. The one in front had his taser out of its holster, ready.

My pulse jabbed at my temple. I fought the urge to flee, touched the keycard against the reader, kept it in place a little longer than before. 'Come on you fucker, come on...'

Green light. I heard a clunk as the lock released. Tugging the door open, I leapt through. As it swung shut behind me, I heard the guards shout for me to stop.

I started running.

42

The crew corridor stretched ahead of me, long and narrow. No windows, no doors, just yards of grey utility carpet and taupe walls. I was trapped, like a goldfish in a barrel of uniform-wearing piranhas. I had to find a way out.

I sprinted along the corridor, searching for an elevator or stairs, anything that would take me back underground. My lungs were heaving. I pushed on. Took longer strides.

Twenty yards ahead I reached an elevator. Pressing the call button, I bent over and tried to catch my breath. I closed my eyes a moment. One stage of the plan was complete. But I had to stay strong, stay free. Next I would find Dakota.

I heard footsteps. Pressed the call button again and again. Looked back along the corridor in the direction I'd come. Heard male voices shouting.

The elevator doors opened. I ducked inside, pressed the button labelled LB. Hoped to hell that was where I'd find the tunnels. Out in the corridor, the footsteps thundered closer, the angry voices grew louder.

I jammed my finger against the door-close button, held it down, cussing under my breath. Real slow, the doors began to close.

With nine inches to go I saw him, one of the security guys who'd been chatting in the corridor. He wasn't chatting anymore. Now his face was red from exertion, mouth open, breathing heavy. He stormed towards me, drew his taser.

I stepped back as far as I could. Kept my finger on the door-close button.

Five inches.

He lunged at the doors. His face contorted with effort, like the worst sex face ever. He thrust the taser into the gap, pulled the trigger. I threw myself to the right; the taser probes missed. Jumping forward, I shoved my thumb and index finger in the guy's face. Jabbed them hard into his eyes. Kept my other hand wedged against the door-close button.

Security guy yowled from pain and anger. Recoiled.

The doors shut tight. I could still hear security guy's whimpering as the elevator started to descend. I leant back against the cold wall and tried to figure out my next move.

Meet at the car, JT had said. I owed him that.

My cell buzzed in my pocket. I yanked it out. A number I didn't know was flashing on the screen. Was it Emerson's men ready to arrange a meet? There was only one way to know for sure. I pressed answer. 'This is Lori.'

'Thought about what you said,' a male voice wheezed. 'You know, it's mighty rich, all that self-righteous bullshit you yakked on about.'

I could hear the bleeping of a machine. That, and the wheezing, helped me figure out who I was speaking with. 'Merv? I'm a little busy.' I glanced at the floor counter, wondering how long the cell-phone signal would hold out.

'That price on his head. It's all 'cos of you, and you let him carry it. So you don't have no right to come to me and start preaching some shit about what I done.'

'What *did* you do?'

He didn't speak. Still, I heard him. His breathing, quick and shallow, rattling in his chest with each inhalation.

I used my stern-momma voice. 'Merv?'

'So what if I wanted me some extra? He was going down anyways. Didn't matter who did what.'

It sure as hell mattered to me, but I held my tongue, couldn't risk spooking Merv, not when he'd called me special. 'Who knew about the ranch? Who did you call aside from Quinn and the mob?'

'Shit, girl. Listen. This ain't no man you want to be messing with.

He wicked bad, real nasty. I doing you a favour not saying, you best believe.'

'Just tell me.'

'Something JT done messed bad with this man's game. His boy said they wanted to talk but, after all the shit at Yellow Rock, I'm thinking they want JT gone. Some questions, for sure, but then...'

I felt sick. Merv was right. Fucked-up, weird-assed, bat-shit crazy right. But still right. If they'd gotten rid of Scott and JT before I'd arrived, it wouldn't have mattered where the device was hidden, the only two people on to Emerson would have been dead and his nasty little secret safe. Now I knew things were different. I said nothing about that to Merv though, wouldn't do no good. This situation was too many twisted layers of wrong to start explaining. 'Give me a name.'

Merv gasped. 'Well, shit, woman. That man didn't never stop protecting your sorry ass, even when you split. Beat me good, just for saying so. You all kinds of ungrateful.'

I glanced at the floor counter. The display changed to *Basement*. I didn't have long. The signal could cut out any moment. 'Tell me.'

A brief hesitation, a louder wheeze that might have been a sigh, then he spoke, 'Boyd. No family name. Just Boyd.'

'Merv, I need a number, a location. Give me—'

The cell phone cut out. I checked the screen: no signal. Son-of-a-bitch.

The elevator stopped. The display showed *Lower Basement*. The doors opened. Shoving my cell into my pocket, I stepped out into the passageway. It seemed quiet, empty. I jumped as the elevator doors slid shut behind me. Heard the elevator start to rise. Shit. Things might be quiet now, but security would be heading this way. I had to keep ahead of them. Get back to the Mustang. Figure out who the hell Boyd was, and where he was holding my daughter.

The only weapon I had was the small canister of pepper spray. It was false comfort though, only good for a couple of sprays.

I sprinted down the passageway to the main tunnel. Merv's words still echoed in my mind: *Ungrateful bitch, self-righteous bullshit*. He was righter than he knew. If the mob had learnt the truth about Tommy, they'd be after me, not JT.

The guilt made it harder to focus.

⥥

I reached the intersection where the passageway connected with the main tunnel. Directly ahead, the narrowest tunnel was empty. Couldn't bet on the main tunnel being the same. I had to be real close to where the shots had been fired. Could be Emerson's men were lying in wait for me.

I stopped, pressed my back against the smooth concrete of the wall and edged closer to the corner. Peered into the main tunnel. To my left it was clear, just yards of white walls and strip lights. I checked the right. Inhaled sharply. Twenty yards away stood an abandoned cart. Black tyre-tracks burnt into the concrete showed the path the cart had taken as it swerved across the tunnel and stopped, its front end crushed against the wall.

I ran to it.

Three yards out, I stopped. Stared at the number on the bonnet: nineteen. The cart JT and I had taken earlier. No sign of the other two.

The black rubber marks showed the driver had been braking at the time it'd crashed. I imagined the two security carts bearing down on JT, him trying to outmanoeuvre them, zigzagging across the tunnel, trying to block them from overtaking. I guessed the guns had changed an even match into a dogfight. They'd shot at JT, forced him to pull over. Taken him prisoner.

Stepping closer to the cart, I peered inside. My breath caught in my throat. A smear of crimson stained the white plastic seat. I spotted more, in the footwell, a pool of it, red-brown and congealing. Blood.

Behind me, I heard voices and footsteps, getting louder. I turned, and saw a bunch of security guards from The Ice Palace round the corner into the main tunnel.

'Stay right there,' a squat guy with a shaved head yelled.

Yeah, like there'd ever be a rat's ass chance of that.

I leapt into the cart, coaxed the engine awake and, pushing it to the limit, fled through the tunnel, following the signs to the parking lots.

I tried not to think on the blood, on what it could mean. Gripping the steering wheel, I wrestled to keep the cart straight, its battered front end pulling hard to the right, druthering like a fresh-broke mustang. The friction jarred through my hands, up my arms to my shoulders. I fought the urge to cry.

The electric motor screamed. A shrill, constant screeching that set my teeth on edge. The same two words repeated over and over in my mind: *Your fault, your fault.*

I reached the park boundary, beyond that point the only access was to the parking lots. I kept the accelerator pressed to the floor. Passed the elevator for Lot One. Hoped the battered cart would function long enough to get me to nine.

But as I rounded the next bend at top speed, I found the tunnel blocked. Two carts were parked across my path, three of Emerson's men behind them guns drawn. All pointed at me.

I skidded the cart to a halt. I was trapped. The security guys from The Ice Palace weren't far off. Forward or back, whichever way I went now, I was done.

One guy stepped out from behind the carts. He gestured with his gun for me to move. 'Get out. Hands high, where we can see them.'

I recognised him as the SUV guy from Thelma's. I stared back, didn't move, tried to figure a way out.

He stepped closer. Kept the gun pointed at my chest, nodded upwards. 'I got your little girl.'

'You bastard, what have you—?'

'You come nice, you'll get to see her. Don't and, well...' He shrugged.

My playbook was empty. I was outnumbered and outgunned, and the son-of-a-bitch knew it. Didn't have no kind of choice.

I climbed slowly out of the cart. Kept my hands held high, and waited for him to come get me.

43

We rode to the surface in the elevator for Parking Lot Two. It was the same kind as the one to the hotel, only smaller: a metal box, little bigger than a vertical coffin. As we travelled upwards, I hoped to hell that wasn't an omen.

The elevator stopped and the doors slid open.

SUV guy pushed me forward. 'Walk.'

I felt the gun barrel press against my ribs, and was reminded that this time I didn't have JT at my back. This time I was alone. I stepped out into a kind of fake log cabin, with walls of wood-effect plastic, and those neat New England-style shutters folded back at the sides of the windows. From the land-train operator instructions and timetables pinned around the walls, I figured it was the crew booth for the Parking Lot Two pick-up spot. Through the window I could see new arrivals to the park waiting in line for the land-train: kids laughing and playing, parents chatting. None aware that there were armed men just a few yards away.

I turned to SUV guy. 'Kind of public isn't it?'

He ignored me. Had his gaze fixed on the outer door and the two guys entering through it. One was the muscle – a heavy guy with vacant-looking eyes and a deep tan. The second was a whole other deal: dark jeans, sport coat, gold watch, nice shades. Real expensive looking, like he worked on Wall Street. I guessed that he was top dog. He nodded to SUV guy and drew a suppressed Glock 17 from a concealed holster. The way he held it, sure looked like he knew how it worked.

Top Dog took a couple of steps towards me. He moved easy. Athletic, like he hadn't a goddamn care. The gun was pointed at the ground, not me. That told me he was real sure of himself and the speed of his draw.

'I'd like you to come outside and get into my jeep.' His tone was conversational, friendly even. Was this Emerson? I'd always pictured him as older; Top Dog looked nearer my age.

I frowned. 'And if I refuse?'

He took off his shades and squinted at me, like he was considering the question real hard. Shook his head. 'Yeah. See, I don't think that's going to happen.'

'How so?'

'I got your kid and your man. Y'all want to get reunited, you do as I say.'

Son-of-a-bitch. 'They're here?'

'Outside.'

I felt dizzy, the breath spiky in my chest. My baby was here. 'Okay.'

Vacant Eyes strode over to the crew lockers on the far side of the booth. He opened the end one and pulled out three sets of crew tabards and ball-caps. Putting his on, he handed the others to Top Dog, then walked to the outer door.

Top Dog handed me a tabard and cap. 'Wear these. Look happy.'

I did as he said. And quickly. Anything to get me to Dakota.

As we moved to the door, Top Dog stayed close. He'd holstered his gun, but with him at my side and SUV guy and his chum right behind me, they weren't taking any risks on my getting lose. They directed me out of the booth.

A little ways to our right, one of the parking-lot crew – a young, blonde cheerleader-type – was trying to get the crowd gathered around a white-and-silver jeep to move back. The vehicle had been outfitted to look like a snowmobile: faux sled-skis over the wheels, a plastic snow plough on the front, and big old spotlights rigged on the roof-rack.

The cheerleader kept jabbering away. 'Keep back folks. Winston Walrus and Polly Penguin aren't stopping here, but you'll get to catch up with them soon enough. Over in the park there's a whole bunch of characters just bursting to meet you.'

Top Dog leant a little closer to me. 'Neat idea, you wearing the character costumes as a disguise. Thought we'd borrow it to get y'all out the park.'

I felt adrenaline surge through my limbs. Rushed towards the jeep. On the back seat sat two characters, a small penguin and a large walrus. Dakota and JT.

I jumped on to the back seat. Blinking back tears, I reached out to the small penguin, took its flippers in my hands. 'Dakota? Oh thank God...'

She didn't move, didn't speak.

Confused, I turned to JT. Registered the dark stain and matted fur stretched across the thigh of the walrus costume, saw that the sleeves were loose and the chest oddly puffed out: they'd bound JT's wrists inside the suit. I put my hand on his shoulder. 'JT, shit. Is it bad?'

He didn't speak either.

I leant across him to Dakota, tried to pull her to me in a hug. Felt the joy, and the fear, pulsing through my body. Thought I heard muffled noises from inside the cartoon head, like she was trying to speak. I held her tighter, never wanted to let her go. 'Dakota? Sweetie, I'm here now. It's going to be—'

'Quiet,' Top Dog said from his seat in the front. He smiled, forced and false. The look in his eyes told me he'd make good on every one of his threats. 'Sit down, smile, and don't try anything.'

Like hell was that going to happen. My baby was right there, how could I just sit still and smile? Heart thumping in my mouth, I clawed at the fastenings on the side of the grinning penguin's head. 'It's okay, baby. Momma's here now. I'm going to get you—'

Vacant Eyes yanked me from my baby. I felt the hard outline of a gun barrel press against my ribs. I turned to look at him. Beneath his dead-looking eyes, his faked smile was chilling.

Top Dog leant close, whispering, 'She's still wearing that special vest. Any trouble now, and you're only going to make things a whole lot uglier later. Are we clear?'

I glared at him. Nodded.

Vacant Eyes released me. Climbing into the driver's seat, he started the jeep's engine and eased the vehicle past the crowd and along the land-train path.

Top Dog looked at Dakota. 'Wave, kid, like I told you. Wave to the people, or I'll have to press that button.'

The penguin nodded. She lifted her flipper and waved at the gathered crowd. The little kids waved back, smiling, laughing and calling hello to Polly Penguin.

Beneath the oversized penguin head, I could hear my daughter crying.

⇓

They drove along the land-train route to Parking Lot Nine. Each lot we passed, numbers three through eight, were busy with new arrivals. Top Dog made Dakota wave every time. I heard her cry again. Made me defy Top Dog's instructions and speak to my baby, tell her it'd be okay, that I was with her now, that I'd make things right. She didn't answer. JT stayed real silent too.

Up ahead, a model of Chester Chipmunk pointed to Parking Lot Nine. Vacant Eyes took the turn, swinging the jeep through the entrance and into the lot. The whole place looked deserted. Lane upon lane of vehicles, their paintwork glinting in the sun, but not a human in sight. He steered the jeep along the rows until we reached C14 and pulled up in front of the Mustang.

Top Dog smiled. 'Now, don't think about calling for help. We've directed arrivals away from this area, and delayed the return land-train until we're done.'

Dakota's crying grew louder. The sound damn near shredded my heart.

I tried not to think on what she'd seen, what they could have already done to her. Had to focus. Needed to get us through this. After – that would be the time to think. Right now, I had to act.

Vacant Eyes climbed down from the driver's seat. Looked at Dakota, then JT. 'Get out and take off those costumes.'

Dakota did as he said. Standing on the black-top beside the jeep, she unzipped the penguin suit, and lifted off the head.

I gasped, jumped out of the jeep and rushed to her. 'Baby, oh no, sweetie, I—'

Top Dog stepped into my path. Gun raised, pointed right at my chest. 'That's far enough.'

I stopped. Stared past him towards my daughter, my poor baby. Her eyes red-rimmed, face dirty, duct tape across her mouth. The life preserver, with explosives instead of floats, was bound around her body and covered by a blue plastic rain jacket. I fought back tears, couldn't show this bastard any weakness. Knew I had to play this real cute. Live or die, what happened next was down to me.

Vacant Eyes pulled JT from the jeep. As JT held on to the bonnet for balance, Vacant Eyes unclipped the walrus head from his shoulders, and yanked it off. JT's mouth was taped shut, just like Dakota's. Still, his eyes burnt with a fury that told me he was far from done.

Top Dog nodded at the Mustang. 'Get in the car. You're driving.'

'Why?'

'We're going to see the boss.'

Emerson? I couldn't let that happen. Somehow I needed to get us out of here, away from these people. I stayed right where I was.

Top Dog sighed. Glanced at Vacant Eyes. 'Persuade her.'

Like an obedient hound, Vacant Eyes lumbered towards me. I moved fast. Planted a jab to his nose. He bobbed, ducked back. My fist barely connected. I moved with him, stepped in closer, and slammed the heel of my fist into his throat. He didn't seem to feel a thing.

Too close to punch, I hooked my right leg around his left, and pulled hard to bring him down. He was too quick. One solid punch to my ribs pushed the breath right out of me. I gasped, doubled over, gulping for air. I clawed at my pocket for the pepper spray. Got a hold of it and pulled it out. The can felt cold, slippery. I couldn't grip it. Heard it hit the ground. Failed.

He hit me again.

I staggered sideways, black spots dancing across my vision. I fought the urge to vomit. Dropped to my knees.

Dakota squealed. Ran to me.

I opened my arms, pulled her close, kissed her matted hair. Never wanted to let go. Whispered, 'It's okay, baby. Momma's here, it'll be all right. I'll make everything all right. Promise.'

I could feel her trembling. Felt the fury inside me rising. 'Baby, it's okay, he won't—'

'Shut it, bitch.' Vacant Eyes dragged me to my feet, turned me to face Top Dog. I kept hold of Dakota's hand, pulling her close.

Top Dog had his Glock trained on JT. 'You should stop. The first bullet will kill him. The second is for your daughter.'

Bastard. I looked at JT. His face was flushed, the muscles in his neck taut and strained. The walrus suit was off. As I'd guessed, his hands were bound with duct tape. The left thigh of his jeans was stained dark red. Fresh, crimson blood oozed through a tear in the denim. 'JT? Stay strong, okay.'

Top Dog raised his voice, 'You hear me?'

I heard him all right, and I did not doubt the man's word. I held Dakota tighter. 'Yeah.'

'Good.' Top Dog glanced at his watch, frowned. 'We need to go. The boss is waiting.'

I had to stall. Had to figure us a way out. 'So is that what you are, Emerson's bitch?'

Top Dog shook his head. 'Who I am doesn't matter. Play nice, or I shoot.'

I looked at JT. The stain had spread wider across his jeans, his breathing was laboured, his eyes half closed. 'He needs help.'

Top Dog shook his head. 'Not gonna happen. We're on a schedule and you've already made us late.' He looked at the Mustang. 'Nice ride. Fast, I'm guessing.'

Schedule or not, I had to stop JT losing more blood. I looked into the jeep. Spotted a roll of duct tape in the passenger foot-well. 'You want him alive for your boss, don't you? So let me stem the bleeding.'

Top Dog shrugged.

Grabbing the roll and keeping Dakota at my side, I hurried to JT. I wound the tape tight around his thigh, layering it twice, three times, keeping the tension strong to form a makeshift tourniquet. I hoped it would work.

'That's good enough,' Top Dog said. 'Now put him in the trunk.'

I looked at Dakota. 'I'm going to help JT, okay, honey? I'll be back real quick.'

She stared back at me, her eyes wide, unblinking. Gave me a tight smile.

I turned to JT. The duct tape tourniquet seemed to be holding. He met my gaze. Despite the pain, he still didn't look defeated. I wanted to tell him I'd copied the data, that his diversion had worked. That I felt so grateful he'd taken the blame for what I did all those years ago. I wanted to say that I was sorry. Instead I touched the duct tape covering his mouth, ran my fingers along the stubble on his jaw, and said, 'Lean on me, okay.'

He nodded. Gripping my shoulder, he took a step towards the Mustang. The pain showed on his face. His body went rigid. I put my arm around his waist, supported his weight as best I could.

'Come on, bitch.' Vacant Eyes glared at me. He grabbed JT's free arm, and dragged him to the car, where he popped the trunk and nodded to JT. 'In.'

It wasn't a large space; no way big enough for a guy like JT to be comfortable. I turned to Top Dog. 'You can't make him travel in there. He'll suffocate.'

'He'll be fine. And so long as *you* do as I say,' Top Dog pointed his gun at Dakota, 'so will your kid.'

JT gripped my wrist, squeezed it. I looked into his eyes. Felt sick. Couldn't figure out a way to stop this. Couldn't choose between Dakota and JT. Had to save them both, but I didn't know how.

JT nodded. I let go.

He rolled backwards into the trunk. The heel of his boot caught one of the taillights, cracking the glass. Vacant Eyes didn't seem to notice;

he grabbed JT's injured leg and forced him to bend it. JT groaned, but as he did, his sharp blue eyes held my gaze.

Vacant Eyes slammed the lid shut.

I hurried back to Dakota. She was staring up at Top Dog, fear in her eyes.

'Get in the car,' he said. 'You're driving. Put her in the back seat.'

I led Dakota to the Mustang, folded the driver's seat forward and helped her climb into the jump seat beside my battered leather carryall.

As she belted herself in, I leant closer and whispered, 'Sweetie, I'm going to pull the tape off your mouth. It's gonna sting, but I need you to be real brave. Can you do that for me?'

She nodded.

I peeled back a corner of the tape. Figured whichever way I did it it'd hurt. A fast pull would get it done quicker. I yanked it off. Dakota cried out and I pulled her to me, muffling her cry against my shoulder. When she was silent, I released her. 'Good job.'

She looked up at me. Put her hand on mine, curling her fingers around my thumb like she used to as a baby. 'Can we go home, Momma?'

I forced a smile. 'Real soon, sweetie.'

Top Dog opened the passenger door and slid the seat forward, ready to climb in the back. He looked at me. 'Enough of the family reunion, just get in the car already.'

Vacant Eyes hurried around to join him. 'You want me riding shotgun?'

Top Dog shook his head. 'I got this.'

Vacant Eyes frowned, a puzzled expression on his face. 'But I thought the boss said—'

'Plan's changed.' Top Dog glared at him. 'Get the jeep out of here, and tell the boss we're en route.'

Vacant Eyes paused a long moment then nodded. 'Sure, Boyd.'

I stared at Top Dog: Boyd. *He* was Merv's contact – the man who'd had those three rednecks killed in West Virginia, who'd ordered the attack on us at the gas station, snatched my daughter and tried to take us in Savannah.

He waved at me. 'Get in, you've got driving to do.'

But I kept staring at Boyd. My mind felt scattered; I couldn't think straight; the thumping in my head was so loud I could hear little else. The pain in my leg and ribs had intensified. The exhaustion, the hopelessness, added to the blazing sun and the fact I'd not eaten or drunk anything for hours, threatened to overwhelm me.

I thought of JT, blood-soaked and cramped in the trunk; of Dakota, terrified and strapped into the explosive life preserver. It was all my fault. I should never have taken the job.

Still, for all my regret, I couldn't think of a plan. So I did as Boyd said. Slid the driver's seat into place. Held on real tight as my legs turned to jello.

'Now get in.' Boyd raised the gun, nodded towards the back, where Dakota was sitting. 'Don't make me use this.'

For a brief moment I thought I might vomit, or pass out, or both. Boyd got into the back, next to Dakota. He peeled off his sport coat and laid it over his lap, concealing the Glock. I took a long breath then climbed into the driver's seat and fired up the engine.

As we exited down the long private road back to the highway we passed by a bunch of new arrivals.

Not one person gave us a second glance.

44

As I drove, Boyd searched my carryall. Leaning across Dakota, he opened the zippers and felt inside. Pulled out my Wesson Commander Classic Bobtail and the ammo.

'Well, lookie lookie,' he said, loading my gun, and sticking it into his waistband. 'You got anything else?'

I shook my head. Didn't tell him about the taser hidden beneath my clothes in the main body of the carryall.

He gestured to the ramp a little ways ahead. 'Take I-95 towards Miami.'

I did as he said and kept driving. The freeway stretched ahead of us. Miami was near on three hundred miles. Factoring in a gas stop, it'd take us four hours, minimum; time enough to work on my game plan.

Behind me, Dakota sighed. I felt her fidgeting, her feet digging into the back of my seat. 'You okay, sweetie?'

'I'm hot, Momma.'

No surprises there. It was damn hot, the temperature pushing ninety at least, and for Dakota, trussed up in Boyd's homemade suicide vest and the rain jacket that covered it, the heat had to be even worse. I peered in the rear-view mirror. Her cheeks were flushed, sweat beaded across her forehead.

'I know it's warm, sweetie. I'm sorry.' I felt the sweat forming on the back of my own neck. It ran down my back, between my shoulder blades and along my spine. We needed air. I reached for the lever to wind the window down.

Boyd leant forward. 'Windows stay up.'

Damn. The Mustang was too old for air-conditioning, and the fan had little effect on the sauna-like heat. I could only imagine how much worse it would be for JT in the trunk. 'But it's—'

'Enough talking, I've got the gun.' He turned to Dakota. 'And, kid, that button is still good to go.'

She whimpered.

I glanced in the mirror again. Her face was turned towards the window, like she was watching traffic, but her eyes looked vacant, unfocused. I hoped the fear hadn't sent her catatonic. 'Baby, are—'

'I told you to be quiet,' Boyd said, his tone real serious.

I nodded, no sense in making him pissed. Kept the Mustang at a steady sixty and moved into the right lane. When I glanced at Dakota next, I saw she was blinking. Hoped it was a good sign.

Boyd had his cell out. He dialled a number, and spoke real quiet. 'I have Tate ... gotta do something first ... six hours, seven max ... I'll call when I'm close ... yeah, I get that.'

Who was he calling? Boyd had told Vacant Eyes to tell Emerson we were en route, so why the need for a second call? Also, if we were heading to Miami, it'd take us nearer four hours, not six or seven. I thought back to the parking lot. Vacant Eyes had seemed real surprised that he'd not be riding with us – like Boyd had changed the plan last minute. Didn't make no sense, unless taking us to Emerson wasn't Boyd's endgame.

I glanced in the mirror at Boyd. He'd ended the call and was sprawled out, his left arm resting real casual along the back of the seat, his fingers inches from Dakota's head. It sickened me how close he was to her.

He noticed me looking. 'What?'

'Why'd you do it – work for Emerson?'

He shrugged. 'Money, why else?'

'And it doesn't bother you, what he does?'

'It's business.'

'It's children.'

'It's a service plenty of people want to pay for.'

Emerson's man, definitely. 'It's sick. You're no ’

'Enough talk.' He shifted in his seat and pulled back the sport coat lying across his lap, uncovering the Glock beneath. He raised the gun a fraction. 'Just drive.'

So I drove on in silence, very aware that Boyd, with his black baseball cap pulled low over his eyes, was watching my every move.

⥥

As the miles passed, it seemed we had ourselves an uneasy truce, at least for a little while. But I couldn't let it fool me. There was still more than enough danger. Boyd had my gun in the back of his pants, his own Glock concealed beneath the sport coat on his lap and the button, the trigger for Dakota's vest, somewhere. JT was still bleeding in the trunk. Getting safe was never going to be easy.

We'd taken a gas stop a few miles back, but it had offered no chance for escape. Boyd had picked an old-style place, where the attendant pumped the gas for you. Asked the guy to bring us water and corn dogs. Had me pay cash. It meant we got to eat, but none of us left the car. Still, I devoured the corn dog, and Dakota wolfed hers down too. I slugged the water fast, almost vomiting from the liquid hitting the back of my parched throat. I worried about JT in the trunk with no water or food, and said as much to Boyd. He just laughed. There was nothing I could do to help JT right then.

So I kept driving. Glanced back at my baby every few minutes, checking she was doing okay. I was her Momma; it was my job to protect her. I'd found her, now I had to get us free.

I focused on the freeway, kept a few car lengths from the Dodge Grand Caravan up ahead. Tried not to get distracted by the two little dogs, the yappy kind, peering out of the back window at me. I couldn't shake the feeling I was missing something real important.

I counted the miles as Miami got closer. With the noise of the wheels on the blacktop and the ever-oppressive heat, I just couldn't seem to focus. The adrenaline hit I'd gotten from the fight in the parking lot was long gone. In its place came exhaustion.

The situation was simple: I needed a plan. Before long we would get to wherever the hell Boyd was taking us, and I would have to be ready. But my mulish brain refused to work. The facts seemed scattered and disjointed, just out of reach.

Look at the wider view, JT had always said. I knew I'd stopped doing that the moment he was taken. I'd gotten myself drawn into Boyd's trap, not worked on the long game, as I should have done. I'd made that mistake before.

I thought about what the crazy old bastard at Motel 68 had said about Sal. He'd been talking shit. Dead *is* dead, and Sal had died because I'd focused only on Tommy, because I'd not made the call when I should have done. JT had been drawn into the sights of the Miami Mob because I'd been so damn tunnel-visioned about finding Tommy – about getting justice, even though it was too late because Sal was already dead and nothing would ever bring her back.

I wondered what Sal would have said about the situation I'd gotten into. I could almost picture her sitting in the passenger seat, those long legs of hers stretched out, pink-glitter pumps kicked off in the footwell. She'd have been shaking her head, for sure. Telling me to focus. Wanting me to remember the thing that was missing, the thing Boyd didn't say.

Why hasn't he asked for the device?

Son-of-a-bitch. I replayed the whole parking-lot conversation again. Shit. That whole exchange, Boyd never mentioned the device. Not once.

I looked in the rear-view mirror. Caught his eye. 'Why haven't you asked me for the device?'

He smiled, real smug. 'I know you're good for it.'

'How?'

He nodded towards my ribs. 'Inner jacket pocket, left side. I got your friend, Tate, to tell me all about it while you were off having your little adventure. Had my associate back at the park check it was on you when you had your little tango.'

'JT would never have told you—'

Boyd laughed. 'You sure about that? It's amazing what a good bit of pain can do. A bullet in the leg – well, you apply enough pressure to the wound, I find a man will tell you pretty much whatever you want.'

Bastard tortured JT. 'You son-of-a—'

Dakota's scream jerked me back to reality. 'Momma, the red car!'

My heart pounded like I'd been scared awake by a nightmare. The Dodge's bumper was just inches ahead. I braked hard, put some distance between us. Glanced at the speedometer, and realised I'd been more than twenty over the limit.

'It's okay, honey,' I said, glancing in the mirror at Dakota. But it wasn't okay. It really wasn't.

Boyd cussed. 'Keep your shit together. We don't wanna get dead before Miami.'

His meaning was real clear. The killing would start once we reached our destination. 'And is Emerson waiting for us in Miami?'

'He is.'

Sal had died because of me. I would not, could not, let Dakota and JT join her. We needed to shake ourselves loose. I had to do something that'd flip the odds in our favour.

Whatever Emerson had planned, it wasn't going to be good. I had to be ready, and one of the first rules of preparation was know your environment. 'So this place we're heading got a name?'

Boyd chuckled. 'Sure it does, but it'll be way more fun if it's a surprise.'

I did not like the sound of that.

The minutes passed in silence. Boyd was studying me closer; Dakota was alert and watching the road. No doubt both were worried I might mess up the driving again. But that wasn't going to happen. I was thinking about escape.

We passed a sign for Coral Springs. It was barely forty miles to Miami.

Boyd leant forward, nudged me in the ribs with the Glock. 'Take the next ramp.'

A flash of blue caught my eye. I glanced in the rear-view mirror. Inhaled real quick and clutched the wheel a whole lot tighter.

Next moment, I heard the siren.

45

The State Trooper was right up my ass, and not in a good way, lights all flashy and shit. Ahead, the freeway stretched straight and clear. Real inviting. The Mustang was purring nice, I had plenty of gas and way more horsepower than the Trooper. But the blue lights had dazed me. Black spots danced across my eyes, the blacktop seemed to blur and warp. Made me pause, made me think.

The way I saw it, we'd got ourselves two choices: stop or run.

I glanced in the rear-view mirror. Boyd had slouched a little lower on the back seat, his sport coat still covering the Glock. Sure, the gun might have been hidden, but I knew he'd got it pointed at a sweet spot between my ribs. A bullet at this close range would be game over and we both knew it. 'What do you want me to do?'

He tugged down his ball-cap, shielding more of his eyes. 'Pull over.'

I indicated right, and steered on to the dirt at the side of the freeway.

Boyd leant forward. Stuck the Glock against my ribs, just firm enough that I could feel the outline of the barrel. 'Act natural, the both of you. Don't make me do something you'll regret.'

The State Trooper had gotten out of his ride and was stomping towards ours like he was the king of the friggin' road. 'Dakota. Stay calm, sweetie, okay?'

'Will we tell him, Momma?' she whispered, panic in her voice.

Not this, not now. Who knew what Boyd would do if the Trooper got him spooked? I twisted around to look at her proper. Used my serious Momma voice. 'Sit still, baby. I'll talk.'

Beside her, Boyd reached over and did up the top button on her rain jacket, making sure the life preserver was totally hidden. He looked at me, held my gaze till it got real uncomfortable. 'Don't screw up.'

The State Trooper, all mirrored aviator shades and overly fitted shirt, leant in through my open window. 'Hands on the wheel, ma'am.'

'Why sure, officer,' I said, trying a broader southern accent for size. I placed my palms against the centre of the wheel and rested each of my midnight-blue nails on the rim. 'Is there a problem?'

Up close the officer looked younger – much younger – and a whole lot greener. Just a babe. Wasn't any wonder that he didn't realise what was really going down. 'You know why I pulled you over ma'am?'

I shook my head, batted my lashes just a little. 'I'm sorry, sir. I do not.'

'You got a tail-light out.' He leant in a little closer, no doubt checking out my legs under the cover of those mirrored lenses. 'I'll need sight of your licence and registration.'

Yeah, like that'll happen. Damn that tail-light.

I gazed into the officer's eyes. Calculated the risk. Could I tell him? Whisper it real quiet. *Hostage*, I'd say, or maybe *kidnap*. Or *help*.

I wanted to, real bad. But I didn't. Wouldn't do no good, not even if I mouthed the words. Boyd would have a bullet in my side and one in the officer's brain before the poor boy had reached for his radio. No, that play just wouldn't do.

That was the moment I heard the first thump.

My first feeling was relief. Despite everything, JT was still alive. Then the officer stepped away, turned his head towards the rear of the Mustang, listened real hard.

A second feeling kicked in: gut-punching, breath-stopping fear. I glanced over my shoulder. Boyd's gun hand had gotten real tense. Shit. I needed to divert the Trooper's attention, find a way to get us all out of this alive.

'What was that, my licence and registration?' I said, all sing-song. 'Well I know they're around here someplace.'

But my jibber-jabber couldn't disguise the third thump, quickly followed by a fourth. I didn't need to look at Boyd to know what he was thinking. What with him being a man of little patience and no compassion, he'd be waiting on the right moment to end the good officer.

But with the traffic moving pretty constant along the stretch of freeway beside us, it seemed that, just maybe, luck was taking my side. Multiple witnesses would be real undesirable. I hoped to hell it'd buy me enough time.

Still looking towards the rear of the Mustang, the Trooper said, 'Ma'am, I need you to pop the trunk.'

I played real dumb. Frowned a little, looked vacant. 'Officer?'

He leant back in through the window, his elbows resting on the walnut trim. I pressed myself closer to the door, got the angle just nice so he'd get a look-see down my top. I glanced in the mirror, caught Dakota's eye. Flicked my gaze to the carryall on the back seat beside her, my go-bag. She knew I always packed my taser, and she also knew how to use it. Learning how had been another of our self-defence games. Right then, I needed her to use it to save the Trooper.

She gave a little nod.

I gazed up at the officer. 'Why I thought you wanted my licence? I'll have it for you in just a moment.'

As I made a show of flipping through the papers in the side pocket of the door, I hoped to hell that Dakota had gotten my meaning. If she had, she'd be easing her hand into the pocket of my carryall and finding the taser. I hoped that she'd have the courage to use it.

'Got it,' I said, smiling up at the young, green, clueless officer's face. 'And then would you like for me to pop the trunk?'

He nodded. Reached in to take the licence.

I handed him JT's library card, hoping the bluff would buy Dakota enough time to act. Forced a smile.

I felt Dakota's feet press hard against the back of my seat. I imagined her fist curled tight around the taser, her finger on the trigger. I smiled at the Trooper. Felt tension radiating from Boyd like shockwaves. Told myself this was right, justified.

Behind me, I heard a crackle as the taser volts discharged.

The Trooper's mouth dropped open. Boyd fired the gun. Dakota screamed.

Everything went to shit.

46

Dakota wasn't fast enough. One thousand four hundred volts pack one hell of a mule-kick when fired directly into your jugular, disrupting the signals from your brain to your muscles and stopping you right where you are. Real effective. But fired at the cream leather seat of the Mustang, not so much.

Boyd had seen her pull it from my carryall. In the mirror I saw his hand, and the Glock, moving beneath the sport coat. Swinging upwards.

Twisting in my seat, I tried to stop him, but I wasn't fast enough. Time seemed to slow. I saw the rage on his face, watched his fist slam into Dakota's chest and connect with the life-preserver, flinging her back against the seat. Heard the zip of the silencer as he fired the gun.

Dakota screamed.

The Trooper spun and fell.

Boyd pointed the gun at me, yelled, 'Drive, bitch.'

I leant out through my window. The State Trooper stayed down, panting, his blood leaking out on to the sun-bleached blacktop. He stared up at me, his expression changing, registering surprise first, then confusion, then pain. A whole lot of pain.

Stay still. It'll be okay, I thought.

His lips moved. I couldn't make out the words. With his good arm, he reached for his radio. Every inch of movement was a battle. His breath grew more laboured, but he kept trying, clawing at the radio. Got it in his grasp, and slid his index finger on to the red button at the side: a way to call for backup, to alert control to an officer down.

'Fucking drive,' Boyd yelled.

I felt the hot barrel of the Glock press against my skin. Dakota was crying. JT thumped in the trunk. I ignored them all. Watched the

Trooper press the red button, and hold it down. I hoped help would come real fast. They had to have a GPS tracker on his ride.

Boyd shoved the gun into my shoulder, yelled and cussed some more.

I'm sorry, I thought.

The Trooper closed his eyes, lost consciousness.

I accelerated away in a cloud of dust, the back end of the Mustang swinging like a steer on a rope. But that was the least of my problems. Boyd lunged at Dakota, yanked the taser from her, pulling the discharged pins from the backseat beside his head. 'You little bitch. You thought you'd play me?'

'Leave her the hell alone.'

He grabbed Dakota by the throat. Shook her. 'You were gonna tase me, is that right? Is it?'

Her arms flailed, her scream was snuffed into a gurgling, strangled sound.

'Boyd, shit!' I slammed on the brakes, skidded the Mustang to a halt. Turned in my seat, lunged for him. 'Get the fuck off her.'

He let her go, flung my baby across the seat like a ragdoll. 'Little bitch. Fucking bitches the pair of you.'

Dakota cried louder, cowering against the door, her knees hugged into her body, her arms wrapped around her legs.

I touched her shoulder. 'Sweetie, it's okay now. He won't hurt you again.'

She looked up a fraction. Met my eyes. Her look told me she didn't believe me. I'd failed her. Again.

Boyd cussed under his breath and jabbed me again with the Glock. 'Drive, will you. Before the cops get here.'

I put the Mustang back into gear, and accelerated down the freeway. In the rear-view mirror, I could see my baby sobbing. The guilt stabbed at my belly. If only JT'd stayed quiet, maybe none of this would have happened.

'Hey, little bitch.' Boyd was looking at Dakota. He gestured to the carryall. 'Hand me the bag.'

Lower lip still quivering, Dakota pushed the carryall across to him. He shoved the taser into the open pocket and dumped the bag on to the floor beneath his feet.

'No more surprises, bitch,' he told me in the mirror. ''Cos the next time I get surprised, one of you is gonna get dead.'

'Sure. No surprises.'

'Good.' He slumped against the seat. Pulled the cap lower over his eyes, and rearranged the sport coat over the Glock. 'Keep driving. It's not far.'

47

Driving those last few miles felt like the pause between pulling the trigger and the bullet hitting its target. Everything was in play; nothing was guaranteed. It would be only a short moment until I knew: escape or capture. Live or die. Three days ago I'd not known that, in taking this job, I'd signed on for a game of Russian roulette in which the gun rotated between the child I adored and the man I'd always loved. How could I hope to save them both?

Boyd told me to take a ramp off the freeway, heading towards the start of the Everglades. Swamp territory. Not a terrain that I'd ever been comfortable with. You never can tell what lurks beneath the murky water, or in the dense undergrowth that surrounds it. I have always preferred my predators in clear sight and on solid ground. Fights seem fairer that way, no matter the odds. This was a whole bunch of different.

'We're here,' Boyd said. 'Slow down. I'll tell you when to turn.'

Ahead I spotted two thick poles with a slab of timber slung between them high above the road. On the wooden slab, the word GATORWORLD was spelt out in two-foot high lettering made from tree branches.

At that moment, I thought we were dead for sure.

A little ways further along, another sign, fashioned like a Wild West sheriff's 'wanted' board, gave the opening times: ten until four-thirty. I wondered what time it was. The clock on the dashboard was bust, permanently set at ten after two. As the sun was sinking lower in the sky, I figured it was past six at least, maybe near on seven. So the park would be empty. Good. Whatever it took to end this, I'd do it. Things would be a whole lot less complicated without tourists.

Boyd shifted forward in his seat. 'Take the next right.'

I made the turn into a narrow road flanked by high trees that served well as a shield. I couldn't get a proper look-see at the layout.

A few hundred yards later we reached a gate: rustic construction, spike-topped. Beside the gate was a square cabin.

'Stop here,' said Boyd.

The door to the cabin swung open and a heavy-set guy in khaki pants and a white beater emerged. From inside the cabin, I heard the roar of a crowd cheering, and a sports commentator talking animatedly over them.

The guy gestured for me to roll down the window. 'Y'all set?'

Boyd nodded. 'The boss is expecting us.'

Without a word the guy returned to the cabin, keen to get back to watching the game, no doubt. There was a brief pause, then the gate swung open. Electronically operated. Interesting – the place looked like a two-bit joint, all tacked together with nails and timber, but that was just a façade. I figured there'd be plenty of tech: security, computers. Cameras too. Right then, I wasn't real sure if that was good or bad.

I drove through the gateway slow and steady. The gate swung shut behind us. The twist of tension in my belly tightened.

The park seemed deserted. Perhaps it was the contrast with the busy freeway, or that the high trees lining the road blocked out most of the light. Either way, the effect was the same, I felt corralled. Trapped.

'Keep going,' Boyd said, like he could sense my hesitation.

I inched the Mustang forward. Swallowed down the panic. Glanced in the mirror at Dakota. 'You okay, honey?'

She nodded, didn't speak.

I got that. The time for talk had gone. What happened next would be all about action.

I kept the Mustang crawling along the road – past a bunch of one-storey cabins ringed by chest-height post-and-rail fencing clad with wire mesh. Gator-proof, I guessed. The track curved around a bend and opened out into a parking lot.

'Park up,' said Boyd with a nudge of the Glock.

'Here?' There was nothing. All four parking slots were vacant. No one was waiting. I pulled into the nearest slot.

'Get out. We go on foot from here.'

In the mirror, my baby's expression was exhausted, terrified. The light was beginning to fade. She must have known that in another hour or so it'd be dark.

'All of us?'

Again, Boyd shoved me with the gun. 'Yeah. All. So move.'

Opening my door, I climbed out and folded the seat forward to free Dakota. 'Come on, sweetie. Time to stretch our legs.'

She scrambled from the car. Stood close to me. 'Momma, I'm real hot.'

She looked it. Her cheeks were flushed, her eyes bloodshot.

I knelt beside her, started unbuttoning the rain jacket. 'I know, honey. Let's get this off you.'

Boyd leapt out of the car. Pointed the Glock at me. 'The jacket stays.'

I glared at him. 'My daughter's sick from the heat. Unless you want her to pass out, it's coming off.'

He kept the gun trained right at my chest and shrugged. 'Just the rain jacket.'

I pulled it off, and saw, beneath the bulk of the life preserver, Dakota's purple t-shirt was dark with sweat. I smiled at her, stroked her face. 'It's going to be just fine, sweetie.'

She didn't smile back. 'Okay, Momma.'

Only I wasn't sure it would be fine. Boyd had given in too easy. He'd let me ride roughshod over his instruction to keep the jacket on, pushing on his authority. I had a bad feeling that the change was not a good thing.

'Over here, kid.' With the gun still trained on me, Boyd beckoned Dakota closer. I followed them both around to the rear of the car.

He nodded towards the trunk. 'Open it.'

I popped the lid. Inside, JT lay motionless. More blood had crusted across the thigh of his jeans, turning them dark red, almost brown. Beneath the tan, his face was pale.

Shit. Don't be dead.

Holding my breath, I put my hand on his forearm. 'JT?'

His eyelids flickered open.

I exhaled in relief. Smiled. 'Hey.'

'Get him out,' ordered Boyd.

It didn't go well. JT was six foot three and a whole lot of muscle. He'd been cramped in the trunk for near over four hours, and weakened by blood loss. He tried to push himself up to sitting, failed twice, dropping back on to his side, unable to break his fall with his hands bound. The second time he banged his head, groaned.

I leant into the trunk, wrapped my arms around his shoulders and supported him as he tried a third time. Wasn't easy, but it helped.

Boyd cussed under his breath. 'Hurry it up.'

I glared at him. 'Things'd be a damn sight quicker if you helped.'

He checked his watch. 'Just get it done.'

I wanted to argue. To tell that son-of-a-bitch to go hang, but it wouldn't do no good. Pick your moment real careful, my mentor had always told me. So I fought my instincts, kept quiet, and did as Boyd said.

Somehow we managed. As JT's left foot hit the ground he inhaled real sharp, and pitched forward. I grabbed his arm, stopped him from falling. The pain must have been a real bitch. He twisted to face me, his breathing laboured, his nostrils flared. He needed more air.

I ripped the duct tape from his mouth.

He took great rasping breaths until he got the pain under control, then straightened up as best he could. Beneath the bruises and the blood, his expression was unbeaten, determined.

'Let's go.' Boyd nodded across the parking lot to a narrow path between the trees. 'Kid, you're walking with me.'

Dakota shook her head. 'No.'

The bug chorus seemed to grow louder.

Boyd pointed the gun at Dakota. 'Didn't your momma teach you how it's rude to answer back?'

She stared at him. Silent.

'Look, kid. You remember what I told you about that jacket you're wearing?'

Her lower lip trembled.

Boyd raised his voice. 'Remember, kid? Yes or no.'

JT stumbled towards Boyd. 'Leave her be.'

Boyd swung the gun, pointed it at JT's head. 'You're in no position to tell me to do anything.' He looked back at Dakota. 'Answer, or I'll shoot him again.'

'Yes,' she whispered.

'Good. So you walk with me. If you try to run off – boom. You start crying or whining – boom. You dawdle. Boom.'

She glanced at me. 'Momma?'

I could see the gun pointed at her had gotten her freaked. And Boyd's original calmness had gone; now he was acting real twitchy. Not good. We'd seen what happened when he got spooked with the State Trooper. I didn't want him shooting one of us. The more agitated he got, the more likely that was. I couldn't let Dakota do anything to force his hand.

So I forced a smile. 'It's okay, honey. You go on ahead, I'll be right behind. It'll be fine. All the gators are sleeping.'

'You promise?'

Boyd's finger was rubbing against the trigger of the gun. We should do as he said. Just for a little while longer.

I nodded. 'Sure.'

She approached Boyd. Flinched as he put his hand on her back, and pushed her ahead of him. I told myself we'd be out of this soon, that I'd get us free. Wasn't sure if I truly believed it.

'Haul ass,' said Boyd over his shoulder.

I put my arm around JT. 'Put your weight on me. We have to stay close to her.'

He took a step. Grunted as he forced weight on to his injured leg. Tried again, fighting through the pain. 'Tell me you've got a plan.'

'I'm working on it.'

We followed Boyd and Dakota out of the parking lot and along a dirt path that took us deeper into the swamp. We made slow progress. JT limped, every step torture. I struggled to help him stay upright. The evening air was thick and chewy, making the yards seem longer and the effort greater. Sweat glistened on our skin, and I felt the nip of bugs biting.

From up ahead, Boyd yelled, 'Move it. We're on a schedule here, people.'

He pushed Dakota around a turn in the path, the pair of them disappearing from view. Shit. 'We need to stay close. I told Dakota I'd be right behind her.'

JT nodded. 'Loosen off the tape. If I can lean on you better, I'll be able to go faster.'

I peeled away the duct tape binding JT's arms. Left one strand slack but intact, for show. 'Okay, put your arm around me.'

He did as I said. From there things went a little easier, but he was getting weaker. The blood loss, the heat and the bullet lodged in his thigh were starting to beat him. He looked like he'd aged more in the last few hours than he had in all the years we'd been apart. I guessed being together wasn't so great for either of us.

Up ahead, Boyd and Dakota had reached a wooden walkway. The dirt track ended as the ground underfoot changed from dry to damp. The walkway led out across the water.

'How much longer?' I heard Dakota ask.

Boyd ignored the question.

The sun had gotten lower still. By my reckoning it must be way past seven o'clock. Another half-hour and the sun would be gone. The last light shone between the tree branches, casting twisted patterns on the water either side of us. The shapes seemed to move and warp, like the flow of the water changed them. Except the water shouldn't have been moving. Swamps are stagnant, static things. Movement meant one thing: gators.

The sudden noise of Boyd's cell phone ringing made me jump. As he answered, he clutched a fistful of Dakota's t-shirt sleeve, holding her still.

'We need to get closer,' I whispered to JT.

He nodded.

We sped up, JT labouring with the effort, dragging his foot more than before, taking shorter strides.

Boyd was talking, half turned away from us. He didn't seem to notice I'd relaxed JT's bonds. '... It's done. You got my money?'

With him distracted, this could be our chance. I glanced at JT, nodded towards Boyd and raised an eyebrow. JT shook his head. *Not yet.*

Boyd was still talking, 'Dead or alive, yeah? ... Good, good. I'm thinking it'll be dead.' He listened, checked his watch and said, 'I'll be there by nine, maybe before.'

Shit. Boyd sure as hell was playing something. Was taking us to Emerson just the start? Had he made some kind of deal with the mob? If he had, that meant Ugo Nolfi hadn't managed to call in the truce, or that Boyd had made him a better offer. Either way, things were going to get a whole lot worse.

Ten yards later the walkway ended. We were back on firm ground. An island of sorts: dirt, some patchy scrub, and a small, doorless wooden shack, with heaps of crates piled high outside it.

I shivered. We should have acted when we had the chance.

As we followed Boyd across the island I noticed the algae was thicker around the water's edge, an uneven green crust lying on the surface. I peered closer. Shit. It wasn't just algae. Below the crust I could just make out the outlines of motionless gators.

Up ahead, I heard Dakota cry out. She thrashed against Boyd's grasp, trying to break free. 'Let me go ... stop ... Momma?'

'Sweetie, what is it?'

We rushed forward. JT cussed.

I followed his gaze and read the sign: *Gator Feeding Station 6.*

48

A man emerged from the shack. He didn't look much of a threat. He was in his early fifties, wiry in build, with neatly cropped hair and wire-framed glasses. He looked like a businessman on vacation. But, from the sudden change I felt in JT's energy, I knew it had to be Emerson.

I hurried to reach Dakota, half dragging JT along with me. I put my hand on her shoulder. 'Stay close, sweetie.'

Boyd gestured at me with his gun. 'Stay there.'

The man from the shack smiled. 'Tate, it's good to see you again. Ms Anderson, welcome, I'm so glad we finally meet.'

His face wasn't unattractive, but his smile still creeped the hell out of me. I wondered what I'd expected him to look like – a monster? I'd seen those video clips, knew the sick trade he dealt in. Whatever he looked like on the surface, inside he was twisted and rotten for sure. I stared at him, didn't smile back.

'Nothing to say? Shame. I expected you'd be kinda chatty.' He glanced at his watch, the smile faded. Looked at Boyd. 'You're late. Light's almost gone.'

Boyd took a step forward. 'We had a few problems I had to—'

Emerson held up his hand. 'Don't need details, bring them here.'

Boyd pointed the Glock at me. 'You heard Mr Emerson. Move.'

We walked forward, slow and steady. I kept one hand on Dakota, my other arm still wrapped around JT. As we moved, I scanned the layout. Noticed the short wooden jetty to the right of the shack and the white speedboat moored there. Guessed it was Emerson's ride.

Four yards short of Emerson, Boyd stopped us. 'That's far enough.'

Emerson looked at JT, then me. He had a hard, unblinking stare that made my skin crawl. 'You and your friend Scott have caused a hell of a lot of trouble. You've messed with my business. Lost me money.'

I said nothing. Felt JT's body tense beneath my grip and knew he was doing all he could to contain his rage. In my peripheral vision I noted the steep slope into the water to our left, checked the routes between us, the water, the jetty and the boat. Calculated the distances.

Emerson took off his glasses and inspected the lenses. He took a tissue from his pocket and polished them in a smooth, circular motion. 'I don't like to lose money.'

'You're fucking sick,' JT said.

Emerson shook his head. 'Who's to say what is sick and what isn't?'

JT hobbled forward. 'That's a bullshit question and you—'

'Don't.' Boyd raised his gun.

Emerson laughed. 'He's right. It *is* bullshit.' The smile vanished, his expression got real serious. 'You know how long I've owned Dream-World Inc.? Thirty-two years. I built it from nothing save the land my daddy's crop farm stood on. It was a joyful time, the day I concreted right over the soil that old bastard had loved so much.' He gave a bitter laugh. 'You know, he told me I'd never amount to anything. I proved him wrong.'

I stayed silent, kept my own expression neutral. Wondered if I could take him down before Boyd got a shot off. Figured I couldn't, not yet. So I held Emerson's gaze and said, 'Doesn't make what you do anything close to right.'

He put his glasses back on. 'Maybe not, but it makes me powerful friends and a lot of money.'

The implication of his words hit me. He really didn't give a damn about those he hurt. 'It's disgusting. How can you—?'

'Because he's one of them,' JT said, his voice raspy with anger. 'He's been careful, real careful, but if you dig deep enough there's stuff to be found. He likes teenagers. Sweet sixteens, and younger. He regularly uses aliases to bid in the online virginity auctions.'

Emerson put his hands up. 'Very good, Mr Tate, you got me. But really all I'm doing here is meeting a need, providing a product. My clients come to me because I have a reputation for being discreet; they trust me, and I offer them a unique service in a unique location, with unmatchable choice. Demand is high. But trust is a fragile thing; the slightest hint that my security's been compromised, and it's over. I can't let that happen.' He looked almost sad. 'That's why I had Boyd bring you here. I have to eliminate the risk. You understand.'

Sure, I understood just fine. We were too great a threat; he'd got no choice but to end us. And what better place to disappear a few bodies than a gator feeding station.

That's when he turned his attention to Dakota. He smiled at her. 'Well, hello sweetheart, what's your name?'

She shrunk closer to me. 'Momma says I can't talk to strangers.'

'Why, I'm no stranger, I'm a friend of your momma's.' Emerson beckoned her to him. 'You come over here, let me get a proper look at you.'

I felt my adrenaline spike. I couldn't let that vile man touch my baby. I gripped her shoulder tighter. 'No, sweetie, he can't tell you—'

Boyd swung his gun towards me, but not fast enough. I dodged sideways, out of reach, shielding Dakota with my body. JT tried to follow, stumbled.

I reached out. 'JT...'

Boyd lunged for him. JT tried to duck away, too slow. Boyd slammed the gun into the side of his skull, metal on bone. JT's knees buckled. He was out cold before he hit the floor.

I stared at him: slumped on the ground, blood oozing from a wound above his temple, dripping down his jaw and on to the dirt.

Dakota hadn't moved. She was crying. 'Is he...'

I shook my head. 'No, sweetie, really, the cut's not so bad.' Told myself he was still breathing at least.

She looked at me. 'Will he be okay?'

I nodded. Sure hoped so.

With his gun trained on the centre of my chest, Boyd grabbed Dakota and pushed her towards Emerson. As I watched her step across the baked earth I felt my heartbeat pounding harder in my chest. I swallowed hard, trying to rid my mouth of the taste of bile.

Emerson smiled as he knelt beside Dakota. 'Nice to meet you, sweetheart. What's your name?'

She looked up at him, frowning uncertainly. 'Dakota. I'm nine.'

'Nine. Is that so?' He took hold of her arm, coaxing her closer.

Dakota writhed against him, trying to pull away. 'I want to go home.'

Boyd kept the Glock pointed right at me.

I imagined my fist slamming into the side of Emerson's face, knocking those round glasses from his nose and feeling his cheekbone crack beneath my hand. 'Get the hell off her. She's nothing to do with this. It's me and JT you wanted. Not her.'

Emerson didn't look at me. Kept his attention on Dakota. 'Sweetheart, you must be mighty hot in that jacket?'

She eyed him warily. Nodded.

'It's all right.' He let go of her arm. 'You go ahead and take it off.'

'Okay.' Dakota wriggled out of the life preserver and gave it to Emerson. 'Thank you.'

'You're very welcome.' He turned, gestured to Boyd. 'We have business to attend to; it's not right for the child to bear witness.'

Maybe I should have felt relief, but I didn't. I wanted Dakota to stay right where I could see her.

Boyd nodded. 'Where do you want her?'

'Put her on the boat.'

The boat was small, but it looked fast. If Emerson took Dakota away in that, I'd have no way to give chase. I'd have failed her, again.

I stepped towards Boyd. 'Don't, please.'

But he walked away, pulling Dakota to the jetty.

Emerson reached behind his back and pulled a silver Sig Sauer 1911 from his waistband. Light from the fading sun glinted off the barrel. He aimed it at me.

I could hear Dakota crying, pleading with Boyd to let her stay with me. It felt like my heart might snap clear in two. I took a pace towards Emerson. 'Let her go.'

'I don't think so, Ms Anderson. She's coming with me.'

Glancing across to the jetty, I saw that Boyd had lifted Dakota on to the boat. She was crying, struggling to get free.

Emerson called to Boyd. 'Put her in the front. Use the padlock.'

Boyd nodded. Dakota turned one last time to look at me. I held her gaze, blinking as my vision blurred with tears. A moment later Boyd pushed her below deck and she disappeared.

Boyd climbed off the boat alone.

I glanced back at JT. He was still out cold. I thought about what he'd said before about how my emotional attachments affected my ability. He was right, all I could think about was Dakota, her fear and her courage. But as I stood there, waiting for whatever fresh hell Emerson had planned, I felt another emotion surging through my body: rage.

I assessed the distances: thirteen strides would take me to Emerson, eight more and I'd reach Dakota. Emerson didn't look physically strong. I was pretty sure I could disarm him: a fast jab to the kidneys, one to the stomach, then hook a leg and he'd be down. Problem was, Boyd would shoot me before I got the chance.

I needed a better plan.

Boyd was loitering over by the jetty, checking his watch. He'd gotten that twitchy look about him again. He shouted to Emerson, 'So we done? You wanted them, I got them. But if you want me to end Tate here, there's some negotiating to be done.'

Emerson shook his head. 'I don't think so.'

Boyd walked back towards us. His expression was smug, his tone real cocksure. 'I've got a better offer for him, a seriously higher offer, so I figured we could have a chat, work out a better deal. You raise your—'

'You've worked for me a while, haven't you?' Emerson's voice was calm, his tone soft. But his body language didn't match.

Boyd spotted it too. He stopped, frowned. 'Near on four years. I know *everything* about your business.'

'True.' Emerson's expression was neutral, impossible to read. He kept the Sig Sauer pointed at me, but it was Boyd he was watching. 'And haven't I done good by you?'

'Sure.'

Their attention was on each other, not me. On the ground behind Emerson, I saw JT open his eyes, conscious again. I held his gaze a moment, and started to inch towards the jetty, real slow.

'So why play me?' said Emerson. 'Why get into bed with those boys from Miami, making deals that aren't yours to make?'

Boyd backed away. 'The price on Tate's head, it's—'

'I value loyalty, you know that.' Emerson shook his head, disappointed.

Boyd raised his gun. Too slow. Emerson swung his from me to Boyd. Fired two shots to the heart, one to the head. Boyd's finger snatched at the Glock's trigger, but his shots went wide and low, ripping holes along the jetty and taking huge chunks out of the hull of Emerson's boat. Boyd was dead before his body hit the dirt.

I heard Dakota scream. The boat was taking on water fast.

Emerson was staring at Boyd's body. Distracted, just for a moment. It was the only chance I might get.

I sprinted towards the boat.

'Lori!' JT shouted.

Glancing over my shoulder, I saw the Sig Sauer aimed at me, and JT lunging for Emerson. The gun fired. I heard the zip of the suppressed gunshot. I hit the ground face down; tasted dirt, grainy on my tongue. Looked back. Saw Emerson kick JT hard in the belly – once, twice, again.

I crawled forward, scrabbling to get to the jetty. Twelve paces and I'd have gotten to the boat. I didn't make one.

A weight in the centre of my back pinned me down. Square and hard, like the heel of a boot. Wasn't no point in moving, Emerson still had the Sig Sauer; at that range he could blow a hole right through me before I took another breath.

I glanced at the boat. The nearside of the craft had sunk a foot or so lower in the water. Dakota was banging, yelling for me. If I didn't get there soon my baby would drown.

The pressure lifted from my back. 'Roll over. Slowly.'

I did as Emerson said. Kept my eyes low, saw his dark-tan cowboy boots: hand-tooled scrollwork, blue stitching and silver toecaps. Far too clean to be a real man's boots.

'Give me the device.'

I ignored him. I needed him to lose the gun and get a whole lot closer if I was going to have any chance of getting us out of this.

He leant down. Flicked up my singlet with the barrel of the gun then traced it along my belly and between my breasts. The metal was hot against my skin. I forced myself not to flinch away. Stared up into his eyes, unblinking.

Emerson looked me up and down like a filly in a sale. 'If you don't give it up, I'm going to take it. Trust me, you won't like it if I do.'

I said nothing. Needed him just a little closer. Tensed my right leg, ready to knee him.

But I'd revealed my hand too soon.

He shook his head. Slid the gun an inch to the right and jabbed it hard between my third and fourth rib. 'Too slow, darlin'.'

I felt pain, real intense. Twisting on to my side I retched, spitting up on to the dirt. I aimed for his boots, got the gleaming toecap of the left.

'Bitch.' He launched himself on to me.

As his weight hit me I rolled, taking him with me towards the water. Four more yards and we'd be at the edge. Briefly on top of him, I managed a soft punch, knocking his glasses sideways.

That was all I got.

I'd underestimated him. Wiry frame or no, he had some skills. He jabbed me in the ribs, right in the spot where the gun barrel had done its damage. Winding me. As I gasped for air, we rolled again, over a bunch of rocks, closer to the water.

We stopped, Emerson on top.

He grabbed my wrists, yanking them high above my head with one hand. 'I told you not to make me take it.'

I tried to twist away. Over to my left something in the water, something gnarled and long. There was more than one, a lot more.

We were two feet from the water. I spied rocks all around. Across the jetty, Dakota was still banging on the side of the boat. Time was running out.

'Inner jacket pocket, left side,' I spat.

Emerson shoved the Sig Sauer into its holster and thrust his hand into my pocket, ripping at the lining to yank the device free. I let him. Lay there, passive. Waiting. He didn't seem to notice. All his attention was on getting the hard drive.

He looked at the silver device and grinned. 'Is this it? Did you make copies?'

I shook my head.

He relaxed his grip around my wrists. 'You sure, I—'

Wrenching my right hand free, I grabbed a large rock and swung it at his head. He shied away. Not fast enough. I smashed the rock into the bridge of his nose. He pitched sideways, snorting blood.

Let go of the device.

It flew towards the water. Dropped beneath the glassy surface with a splash.

Across the water, just visible a fraction above the surface, the gnarled old shapes began to move.

49

I didn't pause, didn't weigh up the pros and cons, didn't think on the consequences. Every piece of me ached, but there wasn't time to worry about that. Dakota had stopped banging inside the boat. That could not be good.

Mustering the energy I had left, I scrambled to my feet. Feeling wobbly and lightheaded I lurched towards the boat.

'Where you going?' Emerson's voice sounded thicker, more nasal.

I turned. He was facing me, blood still pouring from his nose. Gun in hand.

A yard away lay Boyd's body. Tucked in his belt was my Wesson Commander Classic Bobtail. I knew what I had to do.

As Emerson fired the Sig Sauer I threw myself down beside Boyd. Bullets zipped into the dirt wide of me.

I grabbed my gun. Slid my hand around the familiar wooden grip. Told myself this time was different; I'd be shooting to *save* a life.

Swinging back around, I pulled the trigger. The kick of the gun felt just as I remembered. The bullets hit him in the shoulder. Emerson fell backwards, disappearing into the water.

Moments later he spluttered to the surface, arms flailing, drenched in swamp water and green algae.

He coughed, fighting the water and the weight of his own clothing. A little ways past him, maybe six shapes – four-footers and bigger – were all heading for him.

Panicked, he clawed wildly towards the bank, those bony fingers of his scraping at the sludgy earth, failing to get a firm grip. He dipped below the surface, bobbed back up, spitting water. 'Pull me out. Please.'

I heard, but I didn't answer. Instead I turned and sprinted towards the boat.

Emerson screamed as that first gator bit down on him. When I glanced back he was gone, pulled beneath the surface, thrashing against the gator. But fighting wouldn't do no good, once a gator has you in its jaws the chance of you breaking away from the death roll are slim to zero. I caught sight of an arm, a tail, then both creatures disappeared. The water lay still; an uneasy calm.

Seconds later, the water coloured crimson. I didn't feel sorry.

I raced up the jetty. The nearside of Emerson's boat had sunk further into the water and the back end seemed to be rising higher every second. It was going down, nose first.

Legs weak, uncoordinated, I stumbled twice as I sprinted the last few yards and leapt on board. Holding tight to the handrail, I waded through the water flooding the cockpit. Up front, there was no cabin to speak of, just a cupboard to the left of the controls. The door was padlocked.

The boat was tipping at a crazy angle. Muddy water swirled around my calves. I grabbed the lock, tugged hard. No luck.

I scanned the cockpit, looking for a key. Banged on the door. 'Dakota?'

Nothing.

The water kept rising. Among the algae that surrounded the boat, pairs of yellow eyes were watching. If the boat listed another foot lower to the right, the water would rise over the side and the gators could crawl on board.

My foot slipped, I fell back, grabbed the wheel, just stayed upright. 'Dakota, can you hear me?'

I heard a bang against the other side of the door. Dakota's voice: 'Momma?'

'Baby. I'm gonna get you out. Get as far to the left as you can.'

I aimed the Wesson at the padlock, hands shaking. Couldn't keep the gun steady. Felt the panic. What if I shot wide, hit Dakota? Remembered my mentor's words: *Breathe in, fire as you breathe out.*

Pulled the trigger.

Direct hit. The padlock was gone, the wood of the door splintered open. I dropped the gun. Yanked the door open.

At first, all I could see was water. The cupboard was dark, just a foot of breathing space above the waterline. A splash to my left. 'Dakota?'

'Momma?' She was huddled against the far side of the hull, fingers curled tight around a rope hanging from the ceiling. Her face inches above the water.

I reached into the small space, pulled her to me. 'I'm here, you're safe.'

She clung tight, arms and legs wrapped around me like a limpet, sobbing. I waded back through the cockpit.

But as I made to haul us out of the boat, I halted. Two massive gators had crawled out of the water on to the jetty, blocking our path. Beneath us, the boat creaked and groaned, tipping further to the right. Another inch and the water would pour in over the side.

On the island, JT was crawling towards Boyd's body. He reached it, grabbed the Glock from Boyd's hand, and fired into the dirt on the edge of the jetty. The gators slithered back into the water.

Carrying Dakota, I hurried off the boat and along the jetty. 'It's okay, baby. It's all okay.'

JT lay propped up in the dirt beside Boyd's body. He smiled, more a grimace really, I knew he must be hurting bad. 'Good job,' he said.

'And you.'

Behind me, the boat creaked and groaned. I turned and watched as it sank beneath the water until the only clue it had ever been there was a trail of bubbles breaking the surface. Within moments the water lay calm. The boat, like Emerson, was gone.

But Boyd still lay where he'd dropped. Not good. A body meant an investigation, and an investigation meant questions. I couldn't have that. It'd be too hard to explain. Knew we couldn't leave any trace.

I stroked Dakota's hair. 'Sweetie, can you sit with JT for just a moment.'

She looked up at me, still crying. Her eyes were pink-rimmed, her skin goose-bumped, even though she felt hot to my touch. I needed to get her dry and get her safe. But first I had to get rid of the evidence. 'It'll only be for a minute.'

She sniffed, gulping back the sobs, and said in a quiet voice, 'Okay.'

I set her down beside JT. Wasn't sure how to react when she snuggled up into him. He put his arm around her, and used his body to block her view of what I was about to do.

Boyd wasn't far from the water's edge, but he was heavy. I tried to roll him at first, but it was too slow, too awkward. So I grabbed his legs and dragged him to the jetty, leaving a thin trail of blood behind us; there was nothing to be done about that. His eyes were open, staring off into the middle distance. I left them open and shoved him into the water.

The gators got to him fast. Battled over his carcass. An arm, instantly severed at the shoulder, floated to the water's edge.

I turned away and walked back to Dakota and JT.

Dakota looked round. Stared at the blood.

Kneeling down beside my baby, I pulled her to me. 'It's over. You're safe now.'

She looked at me, tears streaming down her face. 'Promise?'

'I promise,' I said, wiping away her tears with my fingers. I looked at JT. 'Can you move?'

'With help.'

Dakota trembled against me. I hugged her tight like I'd never let go.

I nodded at JT. 'Let's get out of here.'

50

It wasn't easy. Dakota clung to me, soaked through and trembling. JT had gotten weaker. I supported them both as best I could, and we stumbled back through the swamp to the parking lot where we'd left the car.

Had Emerson told anyone else of our meet? I didn't know. What I did know was that the guy on the gate knew Boyd had entered the park with a woman and a child. If no one left, he'd get real suspicious.

JT knew it too. 'Put me in the trunk.'

On one level that made sense. The guard on the gate hadn't seen JT. But he had seen that Boyd had me at gunpoint. To have any chance of getting clear we needed to recreate that look. Three people in the Mustang: a man, a woman, and a child. Without Boyd, we were gonna have to bluff.

I shook my head. 'No, get in the back, behind the passenger seat.

JT frowned. 'Why?'

'It's dark. If you hunch down a little, you can pass for Boyd.'

He nodded, smiled a fraction. 'Bold.'

'Yeah.'

Opening the door, I folded the seat forward and helped him ease through to the back seat. His leg was bleeding again, blood oozing through the duct tape.

I carried Dakota around to the other side of the Mustang. Despite the muggy heat of the evening and the hot, clammy feel to her skin, she was shivering from shock. I set her down. She kept her arms around my hips, clung tighter.

'Dakota, honey, you need to get out of those wet clothes.' I picked up the rain jacket that was lying on the back seat of the car where I had left it earlier. 'Take off your pants and t-shirt, and put this on.'

She recoiled, pushing the rain jacket away. 'Don't make me, Momma. I don't want to—'

I knelt beside her, put my hands on her shoulders. 'Sweetie, I wouldn't ask if it wasn't real important. We need the guard to believe we're still Boyd's prisoners.'

She stared at me a long moment, her eyes flitting from me to the rain jacket and back.

I forced a smile. 'You don't need to keep it on a minute longer once we're out of the gate, but until then, I really need you to wear it. So we can go home.'

She nodded. 'Okay, Momma.'

I stroked her cheek. 'Good girl.'

As Dakota stripped out of her wet clothes, I reached into the Mustang for my carryall. I noticed JT's breathing was laboured even at rest. He needed medical help, and soon.

I unzipped the main pocket of the carryall and found my Bail Runner baseball cap. Dark navy, not an exact match for the black cap Boyd had worn, but good enough to give the illusion of Boyd's silhouette. I handed it to JT. 'Put this on.'

He took the cap and pulled it on. I nodded, good enough.

Dakota climbed on to the back seat. She looked petrified. I wished I could tell her everything would work out.

JT must have seen my fear. He leant closer to Dakota, said, 'When we draw up to that gate, keep close to me, kiddo. We'll be out of here fast, and when we're clear I'll fix you up with one of my famous hot-chocolate drinks, how about that?'

Dakota looked at him. 'Will it have marshmallows?'

'Sure, whatever you like.'

'And whipped cream? I'm not allowed whipped cream from a can.'

JT smiled. 'I'm sure your Momma will say it's all right this one time.'

Dakota looked at me.

I nodded. 'Whatever you like, honey.'

She gave a weak smile. 'Okay.'

I climbed into the driver's seat, fired up the engine, and crept the Mustang towards the gate.

⥥

A light was on in the gatehouse. I crawled the Mustang up to the barrier and stopped. Kept looking straight ahead, hands at ten and two on the wheel, just like I had before. Out the corner of my eye I saw the cabin door open and the security guard, the same guy as earlier, step out. Through my open window I heard the noise from the televised game. Hoped it'd been loud enough to stop him hearing the suppressed gunshots.

I glanced in the rear-view mirror, caught JT's eye. 'He's watching for a signal.'

JT looked blank. 'Like what?'

'I don't know.'

'What did Boyd do?' His voice sounded weak, his words almost slurred.

The security guy stopped on the porch, peering at us through the gloom. I needed for him to stay right where he was. Any closer and he'd realise that JT was not Boyd.

JT had to do something. He was supposed to be Boyd, in charge. 'Wave at him or something.'

He did neither. Slumped a little more against the back seat, his head bowed, one hand gripping his injured leg. Shit. He was losing consciousness. He'd lost too much blood. That, and the effort to hike back from the feeding station, had dulled his instincts.

The guard stepped off the porch. Took a stride towards us, then another. Ducked down a little, squinting past me into the Mustang. 'You good?'

I looked in the mirror. JT's head was down. The cap pulled low so I couldn't see his face.

'He's talking to you.' I hissed.

Nothing.

I glanced at the security guy. He was still seven yards from us, and didn't look too concerned. Not yet. I figured, with the distance and the darkness, he'd not gotten a good look at JT yet. We needed to keep it that way.

Dakota wriggled closer to JT. Whispered, 'Give him a thumbs-up.'

At her touch, JT seemed to come round. He leant forward, wincing from the effort, and stuck his hand out of my open window. Gave the guard the thumbs-up.

The guy stopped a couple of yards from the car. 'The boss say if he's coming back to the office tonight or heading straight out?'

JT shrugged.

The guard ducked down, peering into the back. 'You hear me? Did the...' He paused and glanced towards the cabin as a huge cheer sounded from the television.

'Didn't say.' JT said, his tone an octave or two higher, his accent less like his own and more like Boyd's.

I barely dared breathe. Dug my nails into the leather trim of the steering wheel.

The guard peered once more into the car. Nodded. Then turned and hurried back to the cabin.

Moments later the gate swung open. I fought the urge to step on the gas and gun it out of there at maximum speed. Instead I eased the Mustang through the exit and on to the highway at five miles an hour below the speed limit.

What had seemed impossible an hour, hell, even a half hour ago, had happened. We'd gotten free. Dakota was safe. We all were.

Now we needed to stay that way.

51

I took the turnpike back towards Clermont. Drove us within a half hour of CF Bonds. Couldn't go home. Not yet. Emerson was gone, but JT was still wanted – by the Miami Mob, the cops. The Fed.

So I pulled into the Home-from-Home, a small motel a little ways outside Williamsburg. Parked up in an unlit spot just past the reception, I decided my next move.

JT and Dakota had been asleep for the past two hours. Dakota had snuggled up against him, curled into the crook of his arm like a cat. He'd not moved away. Seeing the pair of them so close made me feel less uneasy now. Not happy, exactly, but heading closer to it than not. I figured after the past few days they both needed the comfort. We all did.

Grabbing my purse, I slipped out of the Mustang, locked the door and pocketed the keys. I didn't think I'd been tailed. I'd checked the cars around us real regular, and not seen any of them twice. Still, I wasn't going to take any chances.

The bottle-blonde on reception listened to my requirements, nodding and smiling in the right places: two rooms with a connecting door, ground floor, opposite side of the motel from the road.

She took my last sixty bucks, handed me the keys to rooms twelve and eleven and asked if I wanted the key to the mini bar. I said that I did.

I returned to the car. JT and Dakota were still sleeping. No sign of trouble. I got back into the driver's seat and pulled round back. As I'd planned, the motel building shielded the Mustang from the view of the highway. I hoped that would be enough for us to stay hidden.

Putting my hand on Dakota's leg, I gently nudged her awake. 'We're at the motel, honey.'

She blinked her eyes open, smiled. Almost immediately her eyelids began to droop. 'Can't I just stay here, Momma?'

'No, sweetie.' I reached across between her and JT. Undid her seatbelt. 'It's time you slept in a proper bed.'

I got out of the car and folded the seat forward.

Detaching herself from JT, Dakota shuffled across to the door and climbed out. She looked real sleepy, swaying as she stood. I lifted her into my arms, balanced her above my hip like I used to when she was a little kid, and grabbed the carryall with my spare hand. Took them both to room twelve.

Pushing open the door, the smell of max-strength air freshener was the first thing I noticed. The second was the shabbiness of the room and the dated furnishings, like the before picture on some makeover show: pink-and-green-striped wallpaper, overwashed linens, a threadbare pink carpet. Didn't bother me none. Not even the artificial scent of lilies, not that time. The room was clean, dry and, hopefully, safe. All things we needed right about then.

I carried Dakota inside. Put the carryall on the bed, opened the connecting door and took my baby through to room eleven. It had the same fake lily scent and washed-out linens, but lavender walls rather than the stripes.

Setting Dakota down on the bed, I wrapped the duvet around her. Kissed her forehead. 'Goodnight, sweetie. I'll be right in the next room if you need me.'

She turned on to her side, pulling the duvet right up to her chin. 'But, Momma, I didn't brush my teeth.'

'Don't worry, honey. They'll wait until morning.' I stroked her hair. Switched on the nightstand lamp, so she'd not be in darkness if she woke in the night. 'I'm going to be right next door. I'll leave the door ajar, okay? You need me, you call.'

She yawned. 'Yes, Momma.'

'Good girl.' I kissed her cheek. Smiled. 'Sleep tight, baby.'

I walked back to the connecting door. Listened to the soft inhale and exhale of her breath as she fell asleep. Knew another night without brushing her teeth didn't matter a damn. She was alive. That was all that mattered.

⥥

JT was awake when I got back to the car. He'd folded the passenger seat forward and gotten himself propped on the edge of the back seat, ready to exit. Ready, but not able.

He didn't look good – his face was even paler and blood crusted across his jeans. When I touched his arm, his skin felt clammy. Bad signs, all three. Most likely meant the bullet was still inside his leg. Not clean, not a through-and-through. I'd need to do something about that, but first I had to get him to the room.

I scanned the parking lot. Empty. A few doors down I spotted a chink of light visible through a gap in the drapes. All the other windows were dark. Good. I didn't want to draw any attention. Needed to get JT out of sight, at least until I'd figured out my next move, maybe longer. 'You ready?'

He nodded, gripped the seat and the doorframe, and levered himself out. As the foot of his injured leg hit the ground he cussed, leant against the side of the Mustang, hands on the roof, breathing hard.

I waited for him to get his shit together.

He exhaled hard. 'Well, damn.'

Following his gaze, I spotted the hand-sized patch on the back seat where the leather had been stained red-brown by his blood.

He shook his head. 'Never could keep a car nice, now could you?'

'Never could.' I smiled. 'Want some help?'

Without the adrenaline of earlier, his six foot three of muscle was harder to support. JT tried as best he could, but his leg was a dead weight. With my arm around his waist, and his arm resting over my shoulders, we struggled to the room in a blood-splattered imitation of the three-legged race.

Inside, I locked the door, put the security chain across and closed the drapes. JT flopped on to the bed.

'I need to get a look at that leg.'

He nodded.

Opening the carryall, I pulled out my washbag and found my nail scissors. Reached for the seam of his jeans. 'Hold still.'

'Don't. These are the only pants I've got. Can't leave tomorrow with none.'

True. I looked at the bloodstain. It stretched from mid-thigh to knee, along the outside of his leg. Just above the wound, a thick layer of duct tape, my emergency tourniquet, had begun to peel away from the denim. 'If I pull them off, it'll hurt like a bitch.'

'Yeah.' He unbuckled his belt and leant back on the bed. 'Do it.'

I snapped the duct tape, then gripped the waistband of his jeans, and eased them across his hips. Wasn't the first time, but this sure was different. No pleasure, only pain. I tried to be gentle, but there is no nice way to peel a pair of blood-drenched jeans from a man. Give him his dues, JT clenched his jaw, and for the most part stayed silent. Cussed only once, as the denim pulled away from his wound, yanking off the crusted scab that'd formed between the material and his skin.

The leg didn't look good. The bullet had gone in clean enough, but it'd lodged low in his thigh muscle. What with all the hiking and travelling we'd done, it'd gouged out a deep well of pulpy flesh. 'I should get you to the emergency room.'

He propped himself up on his elbows. Glanced at his leg. 'How bad?'

'Bad.'

'You'll have to do it.'

'That right?' Getting a bullet out of muscle ain't so easy, especially without proper equipment. If I took him in, the cops would get him a medic. They'd fix him up right; less than an hour from booking and he'd be done.

But we'd be done too, and I wasn't real sure that was something I wanted. Didn't feel ready to hand him over, not after all that had happened, all that I'd learnt these past three days.

Still, something had to be done. The bullet had stayed bedded in his thigh since Boyd shot him more than eight hours before. JT was lucky it hadn't already gotten infected. The longer it stayed in his flesh, the higher the risk. So if I wasn't taking him in right then, and he was refusing a hospital, there was only one thing to be done; I'd have to get the bullet out.

JT nodded at my carryall. 'You got your kit?'

'It was in the truck.'

We both knew what that meant. No proper kit always led to two things: mess and pain. Both were real undesirable. Neither could be avoided.

'What else you got?'

Not a whole lot was the short and honest answer. But that wasn't what he wanted to hear. He'd trained me to improvise when necessary. Right then, it was our only option. 'Give me a minute.'

First step: Assemble your kit.

I tipped the contents of the carryall on to the bed. Sifted the useless from the possible, looking for anything that might help me dig out the bullet. I had the nail scissors, sure. To them I added a wodge of cotton pads, a single stocking and a travel sewing kit. As far as improv went, all could be put to a purpose. Thing was, we still needed something to extract the bullet.

'Problem?' JT said.

'Are there any tools in the Mustang?'

'In the trunk there's a jack, maybe a wrench or something.'

Stepping across to the window, I lifted a corner of the drapes and peered outside. Clear. The Mustang was the only parked car nearby. I moved to the door, glanced at JT over my shoulder. 'Don't move.'

He shrugged. 'Wasn't planning to.'

I loped to the car, popped the trunk. The carpet covering the spare was stained with JT's blood. I thought about how Boyd had been planning to hand JT over to the Miami Mob, and how our deal with Ugo Nolfi didn't seem to have been relayed to Old Man Bonchese. Wondered what he'd do when Boyd didn't show with JT.

I knew this wasn't over.

I rolled the carpet back. The spare was pristine. Sliding my fingers around one side of the tyre, I heaved it out of the recess. A jack rested in the curve of the wheel, and wedged alongside it was a canvas tool roll. Jackpot. Grabbing the roll, I dropped the spare back into the recess, pressed the trunk shut and hurried back to our room.

JT was lying on the bed, eyes closed. Not asleep. Resting, almost peaceful. I knew that wasn't going to last.

I re-bolted the door. When I turned back, JT was watching me.

'You found it?'

'Yeah.'

I untied the roll and unfurled it on the bed, counted one pair of metal handcuffs and ten tools: spanners, screwdrivers and a pair of long-nosed pliers. Perfect. Pliers would do the job just fine. I set them on the bed with the rest of my improvised kit.

Second step: Sterilise.

On the desk in the corner a coffee-making set was laid out nice on a plastic tray. The water-boiler was empty. I picked it up, filled it from the basin tap and switched it on.

JT raised an eyebrow. 'You making coffee?'

I smiled. 'Maybe later.'

As the water boiled, I found the mini bar and unlocked it. On the top shelf stood a half-dozen miniatures: bottles of rum, whiskey and gin. Great. My methods of sterilisation, pain control and courage were right there.

I carried them across to the bed and added them to my kit. I took a closer look at JT's leg, the crusted blood, the jean fibres stuck into the wound. Picked up the pliers. Even cleansed with alcohol and the boiled water they were still a crude piece of equipment.

'You sure about this?' I asked JT.

He nodded. 'The mob's still after me – Emerson's guys too if they've figured out what happened back at GatorWorld. Boyd's guys at Winter Wonderland saw me get shot. They find out we escaped, they'll know I'd need medical.' He glanced towards the door to the room where Dakota was asleep. 'Can't let you risk it.'

I got it. Appreciated his sacrifice. 'It'll hurt like hell.'

He forced a smile. 'Yeah, figured that.'

The kettle reached boiling.

I carried it, the pliers and a bottle of gin across to the basin. Poured the boiled water over every inch of the metal. When the kettle was empty, I twisted the cap off the gin, and poured it over the business end of the pliers.

Taking care to hold the pliers by their handle, I grabbed a couple of fresh towels from the bathroom and took them over to the bed.

'You ready?'

JT nodded.

'Okay then.' Folding one towel double, I threaded it under his thigh.

Third step: Pain control.

I took a bottle of whiskey from the bed and handed it to JT. 'For the pain.'

He twisted off the cap and gulped two-thirds, then held it out to me. 'For your nerves.'

He always could read me, no matter how hard I tried to cover my emotions. I took the bottle and finished it. The whiskey tasted spicy-sour.

I knelt beside JT. Opened a bottle of vodka and tipped some on to a cotton pad. I swabbed the area around the wound, then poured a little of the alcohol into the hole.

JT cussed. Punched the duvet.

It must have hurt like a bitch. But I couldn't let that stop me.

Fourth step: Get it the hell done.

Taking the pliers, I opened them about a half-inch wide, and eased them into the wound.

JT inhaled sharply, gripped the duvet in both fists. His eyes were closed, his face pale, jaw rigid.

I couldn't stop now. Knew he wouldn't want me to. I rotated the pliers inside the wound, searching blind. Blood oozed out, dribbling down his leg. I ignored it, focused on hunting out the bullet. Went deeper, glad the pliers were long-nosed. I had to be getting close.

JT's whole body went rigid. 'Jesus fuck.'

Millimetre by millimetre, I eased the pliers further in. Then hit something solid. 'Found it.'

He kept his strangle-hold on the duvet. 'Well don't take it out for dinner. Get it done.'

I widened the mouth of the pliers a fraction, then pulled them closed. Felt the bullet between their jaws. Squeezed tighter, just to be sure, then withdrew the pliers real slow. The suction of the wound held the bullet in place a moment longer.

JT gasped. Cussed, louder this time. Started to twist away.

'Come on, you son-of-a-bitch.' I'd gotten the thing, and I'd be damned if I was letting it beat me. I held the pressure. Put my other hand on JT's calf. 'Hold still.'

He kept cussing, but stopped moving. After a short moment the flesh yielded, and the bullet came free. 'Got it.'

JT didn't speak. His face had flushed red; his breath came in gasps.

I stayed focused. Put the pliers, and the bullet, on the nightstand, and grabbed the closest bottle of alcohol. Gin. Tipped it into the wound, using the whole thing. Hoped it would do the job.

Frothy blood coursed down his thigh and on to the white towel beneath. Blood mixed with gin. It smelt fruity yet metallic. A real strange combination, and not one I ever wanted to smell again.

His breathing sounded laboured.

I glanced at his face. 'You okay for me to keep going?'

'Yep.'

Opening the sewing kit, I threaded a fine needle with a length of black cotton, and got to work. I'd never been a needlepoint kind of girl, but this I could do. Keeping an even pressure, I brought the skin together.

Done.

Grabbing the remaining cotton pads, I pressed them tight against the wound, binding them in place with the stocking. It wasn't pretty, but the bullet was out and the bandage seemed functional.

I glanced at JT. 'You okay?'

Stupid question, I knew. His leg would be hurting real bad.

He nodded, but still gripped the duvet.

'There's a couple of whiskeys left.'

'Sounds good.'

I twisted off the caps, and handed him a whiskey. Propping himself up on an elbow, he took the bottle. 'Thanks.'

'Sure.'

He held my gaze. 'I mean it.'

'I know.'

He kept staring. 'I've missed the hell out of you.'

I took a gulp of whiskey. Looked away. Counted to three. Looked back.

He was still staring.

I frowned. 'I don't want to talk about the past.'

'Neither do I.'

I kissed him. Wasn't planned, not wise either. I knew that, but did it anyways. Could've blamed it on the liquor, or the shit that'd gone down those past three days, or some nostalgic bullshit. But it wasn't none of that. He was just something I wanted.

He tasted as I'd always remembered: bourbon, smoke. Him.

I pulled away, glancing at the door that connected our room to Dakota's. It was pulled to but not shut, so I'd hear if she woke in the night and called for me. Inside she'd be sleeping, unaware how close her parents were getting next door.

Her parents.

I looked back at JT, into his blue eyes. The eyes he'd passed on to my baby. Hell, Dakota reminded me of him every time she looked at me.

'Hey.' JT brushed a strand of hair from my face, tucking it behind my ear. 'She'll be okay.'

I forced a smile. Nodded. He'd misread my thoughts. I knew Dakota was safe That wasn't what was bothering me in that moment.

Things had always been complicated between me and JT. The secret I'd kept from him all these years would only make it worse. Still, as I gazed into his eyes I knew I couldn't hide the truth any longer. 'There's something you should—'

JT pressed a finger to my lips, stopping me mid-sentence. I let him, allowed myself to pretend it was a sign for me not to tell him. I said to myself that I'd tell him later. I traced my fingers across his jaw, over his throat, down his chest. Wanted to blot out the past, and not think about the future.

Wanted him.

JT whispered, 'Thought you said the old times weren't so great?'

I held his gaze. Thought of all the things I could say, should say, then told the truth. 'I lied.'

He pulled me to him, his lips on mine. My heartbeat accelerated.

I knew, again, that I was ruined.

52

The vibration of my cell woke me. The room was dark, like a Florida sky in hurricane season, just a thin shaft of daylight visible around the edge of the drapes. I knew it was early. Even so, I reached for the cell on the nightstand and checked the caller ID: Quinn.

I didn't want to speak to him. He'd ask too many questions, force me to think about facts I did not want to face. Not yet. I dropped the vibrating cell on to the duvet and snuggled closer against JT.

He looked down at me. 'Who is it?'

'The office.'

He raised an eyebrow. 'You not answering?'

'Not right now.'

'Good.' He caressed my cheek with his thumb, kissed the tip of my nose.

I tilted my head so my lips met his. Reached beneath the duvet, felt the contours of his chest beneath my hand. Traced my fingers lower, across his stomach. Felt his abdominals tighten beneath my touch. He pulled me closer, pressed his mouth on mine.

The cell began to vibrate again.

I ignored it.

Moved my hand lower still, felt him harden. Moved astride him. Kissed him, felt his stubble rough against my face, his tongue strong against mine. I'd missed this, craved him all this time, but never let myself acknowledge it. Instead I'd denied the memory, changed it into something else. Anger.

I felt him hard beneath me. Bit my lip as he slid inside.

He exhaled fast. Held my gaze.

We moved, slow at first, then faster. JT grabbed my hips, thrust deeper.

I didn't want him to stop. Ever.

How had I kidded myself to believe I didn't miss this? Miss him. The way he felt, the way he made me feel. I moved with him, quickening the pace. He bucked harder beneath me.

I came with him, his name on my lips. Kissed him, and collapsed against his chest, breathless.

It was never like that with the others. Never had been. The raw, real, urgent need I'd always had for JT was something different. No act: just me and him.

I felt him run his hand up my back, stroking the nape of my neck where my hair lay against my skin. He kissed my forehead. 'You okay?'

'Yeah,' I said, but I wasn't. No matter how hard I tried to ignore it, reality was creeping into view: Quinn, the Miami Mob, Emerson. The eight o'clock deadline to collect the bounty on JT's head, and the final demand for Dakota's medical treatment.

I glanced at my watch. Ten minutes before six. Soon I'd have to make a decision.

JT smoothed the hair from my face. 'You ever think about what might have been if—'

This time I put *my* finger to *his* lips. 'Don't. What's done is done.'

He pulled me closer, kissed me again. 'I guess it is.'

⇓

We lay there a long while. Neither of us wanted to end the moment, both of us knew what happened next wouldn't be real easy. As it was, I got up first. I needed some time to think, to decide my next move.

So at a quarter after six I rolled out of bed and moved across to the connecting door. Easing it open, I peered through the gap to check on Dakota. She was still asleep, cocooned in the duvet. Safe. Leaving her be, I walked to the bathroom and locked the door behind me.

I stood in the shower, hot water pouring down my aching body, and tried to think of a way we could all be together. I stayed in there far too long, until my skin wrinkled prune-like, and the water ran cold.

Still, however long it'd been, it wasn't long enough. I hadn't found an answer.

Shutting off the water, I grabbed a towel from the rail and dried myself off. I caught a glimpse of my reflection in the mirror – not a great sight: a black eye, dark red bruising across the left side of my jaw and a split lip. I looked away. It didn't matter what I looked like, my three days would be up in less than two hours. I had to make a decision. Whichever choice I made I'd lose one of the two people I loved. If I was unlucky, I'd lose both.

I walked back into the bedroom. JT was still in bed. His tanned skin dark against the white linens, his dirty-blond hair mussed up and flopping over one eye, the few days' old stubble making him look sexy as hell.

He threw off the duvet and pushed himself to sitting. He didn't say anything, but from the tightness in his jaw as he moved his injured leg, I could tell the wound must have hurt like hell. He picked my cell off the nightstand and held it out to me. 'Thing's been buzzing again.'

I checked the display: one new message, CF Bonds' number. It was no good; however much I wanted to stay in the protective bubble of this motel room, I'd soon be forced to make a choice about the reality of our situation. I guessed I may as well start now. I looked at JT.

'It's Quinn.'

He nodded. 'I figured.'

I played the message. Quinn sounded real nervous. 'The cops are crawling all over us here. There's a warrant out on you, Lori. They're saying you've been helping Tate, that you'll do time for it. I'm so sorry.'

I hung up. Stared at the cell. Felt dizzy, sick. With a criminal record I couldn't work as a bail runner in Florida. Without the bond money from JT's skip trace I couldn't pay for Dakota's treatment. From a jail cell I couldn't be her momma.

'What'd he say?'

I met his gaze. 'Seems there's a warrant out on me.'

He said nothing, just blinked slowly and breathed.

I heard movement in the adjoining room. Dakota's voice. 'Momma?'

I pulled on my jeans and searched for my bra. Found it on the floor beside my improvised medical kit. Put on a clean singlet from my carryall 'She can't know about us,' I told JT.

He didn't argue. A part of me wished that he would.

Easing open the connecting door, I gazed at Dakota. She looked so tiny, lying in the queen-sized bed alone. She looked worried. 'What is it, honey?'

'Is JT okay? He was bleeding. In my dream he—'

I sat on the edge of the bed beside her. 'I fixed him up. He's just fine.'

She looked relieved. 'He's not a bad man is he?'

I smiled. 'No, he isn't.'

She gazed at me a long moment, then smiled. 'Can I take a shower?'

I took her hand in mine, stroked her palm with my fingers. 'Sure you can.'

'And can we go home after?'

It couldn't be possible that the things she'd seen hadn't affected her. She'd been abducted at gunpoint, had a bomb strapped to her, seen a man shot, and nearly been drowned. She had to be in shock. I wondered how long the delay would last, and what would happen when the events of these few days finally hit her. Hugging her to me, I kissed the top of her head. 'Soon, honey. I promise.'

With a heavy heart and a deep sense of dread I knew what I had to do.

53

At five after seven I called Quinn's number. It rang only twice before he picked up.

'I'm coming in now. I've got Tate.'

'Lori?' The relief in Quinn's voice was clear. 'Thank God. I thought—'

'Yeah. Things got tough for a while, but I have him. I'll be at the precinct before eight.'

'Good job. I'll tell the boss.'

'Yeah, you do that.'

'Look, I never doubted you. I want you to know that.'

'Quit the bullshit.'

'It was—'

'Whatever, okay, Quinn? I've had a hell of a few days.'

Quinn cleared his throat. 'I'll call the precinct, let them know you're en route.'

I ended the call before he could say anything else. Looked at JT. 'It's done.'

He nodded. 'You should cuff me.'

I knew that I should. Our plan was for JT to stay silent, and for me to talk. I'd tell a story about how my pick-up turned bad. We needed the cops to believe JT had forced me to act with him rather than me having been a willing partner. They had to think I'd feared for my life, for my daughter's life, and that had only changed when I'd managed to wound him. The fact I'd emailed Special Agent Monroe the CCTV evidence played into the story. I'd tell them I'd managed to do it in a brief moment when JT wasn't watching me, but that he'd grabbed me again before I could escape the park. The story we'd concocted would be a stretch for sure, but ultimately believable, or so I hoped.

JT held out his wrists. 'Go ahead.'

I slipped the steel over each of his wrists in turn, snapping the cuffs closed. His skin felt warm beneath my fingers and I didn't want to let go.

I looked to the door where Dakota was waiting fresh from the shower, her skin scrubbed clean of the dirt of the past few days, her damp hair hanging long and untangled down her back. I smiled at her. Knew I'd made the right choice, the only choice: Dakota.

JT had chosen her, too. That didn't make it any easier; in fact, it made it worse. Not for the first time I wondered if I should tell him the truth.

He leant closer. 'She's tougher than you think.'

'But after what they did?' I shook my head. 'I just can't imagine what she—'

He looked at me real serious. 'Not your fault.'

I shook my head. 'She was in that situation because of me.'

'No. She was there, you both were, because of me.'

I remembered that night after Sal had died. How he'd held me as I cried. How he'd said those very same words. I looked up into his big old blues, knew he remembered too. 'It's time.'

54

As we turned into the precinct parking lot, I saw that three police cruisers were parked out front. The clock on the welcome board showed seven fifty-three. Our time would be up in seven minutes.

I parked the Mustang in the space furthest from the building and turned to look at JT. 'You ready?'

'Yeah.'

'Okay then.' I opened my door and stepped out into the morning heat. It didn't seem right that the sun was bright and perky when I felt numb, like something deep down inside me was withering and dying.

Opening the passenger door, I leant inside and undid his seatbelt. I felt his breath warm against my neck. Fought the urge to kiss him and pulled away fast, conscious that Dakota was watching me. Couldn't let her see how what we were doing really made me feel. Couldn't let her know the truth, not now.

JT swung his legs out of the vehicle. He was dressed in his blood-stained clothes. Looked real dishevelled, like a fugitive who'd been in the wind a long while should. Ready to play his part.

I took his arm, helped him stand.

He leant against the Mustang. 'How about a last smoke?'

I studied him, taking a mental picture of how he looked. The way the skin around his eyes crinkled into laughter lines, the smooth line of his jaw, and the intensity of his gaze. 'Sure.'

He glanced down. 'Top pocket, if you'd do me the kindness.'

I slipped my fingers into the pocket of his plaid shirt. Found the pack: Marlboros, battered but serviceable. I opened it and saw the Zippo I'd given him all those years back tucked inside. There was one cigarette left.

I felt my stomach clench. I knew that, after we stepped inside the precinct, I wouldn't be able to control the outcome. I also knew that I wanted to try.

Placing the cigarette between my lips, I used the Zippo to light it, then handed it to JT. Went to put the lighter back in his pocket.

He shook his head. 'You keep it.'

'I'll hold it for you, till you're out.'

He gave me that crooked half-smile of his. 'Could be a while.'

I held his gaze. 'Yeah.'

From the back seat of the car, Dakota said, 'Momma?'

I leant down, looked through the open door. 'Yes, honey.'

'It's two minutes before eight.'

I glanced at JT. 'You ready?'

He nodded. 'You?'

I held his gaze. Said nothing, just couldn't find the words. Instead I turned back to the car, and peered inside. 'Dakota, sweetie, you need to come with us.'

She climbed out of the car, and looked up at me, her eyes tearful. 'Momma, if JT's not a bad man, why do we have to take him to jail?'

I knelt beside her. 'It's real complicated, sweetie. He's not a bad man, but because of the things that happened he still has to go talk to the cops.'

She looked hopeful. 'So they won't put him in jail?'

JT looked down at her. 'They will, for a little while.'

She frowned. Didn't understand. Started to cry.

With one hand supporting JT under his elbow, and the other holding Dakota's hand, I walked across the parking lot towards the booking office. As we drew closer, I spotted two cops waiting inside.

Stopping a few yards short of the doorway, I called out, 'I'm Lori Anderson, Bounty Hunter. I have Robert James Tate in my custody. We have no firearms.'

A voice from inside said, 'Keep your hands where we can see them, and no fast moves.'

We did as instructed. The cops, with their guns and tasers pointed right at us, filed through the door.

Dakota gasped and shrunk closer against my side.

I gripped her hand tighter. 'It's okay, honey. It's okay.'

As the cops approached, JT leant closer to me and whispered, 'Whatever happens, take good care of our daughter, you hear?'

Then they took him.

⇓

Four hours later they told me.

JT had been charged. I was free to go, to take Dakota. No charges, no Child Services, just a mumbled apology for the confusion and a dig about never knowing whether to trust a bounty hunter. They had to be sure I'd not broken the law, I could understand that, right? Sure, I'd said. I understood just fine.

What I didn't understand was why JT talked. He was meant to stay silent, not give them anything. Instead he'd confessed to every crime they threw at him: skipping bail, kidnapping, assault. Homicide.

The cop that told me sounded real smug. He said the prosecutor would push for the death penalty. Might just get it, too. This was a proper career case, and the prosecutor was real ambitious.

The death penalty; what the hell was worth that? I suppose, deep down, I knew. Maybe he'd worried they'd not swallow the lie; or perhaps a false confession had been his plan the whole time and he'd not told me he was going to take the blame so I couldn't protest none. Either way, he was protecting me, just like he'd done ten years before. Only this time, he was also making sure his daughter stayed with her momma. By taking the fall for everything, he thought he was keeping us safe.

He didn't know about Dakota's illness. About how, if the cancer returned, she'd need a bone-marrow transplant, and that the ideal match was most likely a relative, a parent. He couldn't know that I'd been tested, and I'd failed to be a compatible match, or that he, her father, might be her best chance.

Right then, I vowed I'd do whatever it took to keep JT safe and alive, for Dakota's sake, and maybe, also, for mine. So I swallowed down my fear, and made the call. Knew it was the right thing to do.

Even if I had to tell the truth.

55

I take a sip of the raspberry-flavoured water. Look up, and meet the gaze of the man sitting opposite me. It's the first time I've looked at him since I began to tell my story. 'That's it. You know the rest. I called you, you came here, we're talking.'

Special Agent Monroe nods. 'I believe you. Sounds a hell of a three days.'

'Sure was. Do we have a deal?'

'Thing is, I could've cut a deal for you. Got you out, charges dropped, no problem. That data you sent from Winter Wonderland, it's good. My people are on it. We'll shut down anything continuing without Emerson. But Tate's already confessed.' He shakes his head. 'Making that go away? That's a bigger ask.'

'So what happens next?'

'I need to make a call.' He pulls out his cell and starts dialling.

'And then?'

He holds up his hand. An order: *Be quiet*. I watch him turn away, pace across the windowless room to the corner. Speak real hushed into his cell. He glances back at me once, twice. Keeps talking.

While I wait, I stare at the docket on the table. JT's booking ticket, proving I've brought my fugitive in before the deadline. It's all I need to claim my percentage of the bond from Quinn: fifteen thousand dollars. I'll be able to pay the final demand for Dakota's medical treatment and put a little aside for a few months' rent.

Sure, I knew I had to do it. Collect on the bounty, use the cash, but still, it doesn't feel right. Feels like blood money.

Monroe crosses the room. Catches my eye. 'Gibson Fletcher – you caught him?'

I nod. Two years ago. He was my biggest bounty, more even than JT. Without Gibson 'The Fish' Fletcher, I'd never have paid for Dakota's initial treatment. I'd have lost her. Been lost. My eyes start to well up, but I blink the tears away. This isn't the time for emotion.

Monroe doesn't notice. 'Think you can do it again?'

I shrug. 'If I caught him once, I could find him again for sure. But there's no need; he's serving triple life in super max.'

'Not as of two days ago he isn't. His appendix busted; got transferred to hospital for urgent medical attention. The op was successful. Few hours later he killed three guards and shook off the marshals. Could be anywhere.'

'There's plenty of other people who'd like a shot at him. Why ask me?'

'Like you said, you caught him once. Plenty had tried then, no one else got close.'

'And if I do?'

'We'll ensure leniency for Tate. Make sure he doesn't get the death penalty, and have him moved somewhere comfortable to do his time.'

I shake my head. 'Get him free and I'll do whatever you want.'

'Isn't that simple. He's confessed to murder, assault, kidnapping. There's a State Trooper fighting for his life in—'

'That State Trooper saw Boyd. He knows JT wasn't the one who shot him.'

'Which he'll be able to tell us, if he lives.' Monroe's expression implies that isn't so likely. He shakes his head. 'Look, these aren't misdemeanours, they're—'

'I *know* what they are. What I need for you to do is tell me whether you can get him cleared.'

He makes another call. It's shorter this time, less than a minute. He goes back to the corner, turns away, voice too quiet for me to hear.

When he's done there's something new in his expression. Triumph? Satisfaction perhaps? He comes back to the table. Sits down opposite me. 'Reduced sentence, ten years tops. With good behaviour he'll be out in eight. It's a good deal.'

Monroe doesn't need to tell me the deal is sweet. I know it, but I still feel uneasy. There's a knot of tension tightening in my belly. Something's not quite right. To deal down that fast from the death penalty to ten years, Monroe must have the ear of someone very high up. That, or he's playing me.

I look him straight in the eye. 'How do I know I can trust you?'

He smiles. It's a nice smile, looks genuine, and stretches all the way to his eyes. I notice that they match his hair – dark brown. His voice is rich, confident as he says, 'You've got my word.'

As I stare into his eyes, I think of Dakota sitting outside with a female agent. Remember how it felt when she was lying in that hospital bed, face as white as the sheets around her. Of how it felt every time I couldn't make the pain go away. If this deal will let me stay with her, pay for her treatment, and keep her father alive, then I've no choice but to take it.

So I nod, get us to fourth base, and the game ends win-win.

I hope to hell it's enough.

Acknowledgements

I fear that this may turn into one of those rambling, overlong Oscar-acceptance speech kind of monologues but, in truth, there are many people who have helped me on my journey to publication, and it's only right to acknowledge how much the support of these fabulous folks has meant to me. So here goes...

Thank you Mum and Richard, Dad and Donna (my technical adviser on Americanisms!), and Will and Rachael – for being there, no matter what. Special thanks to Mum for making me believe anything is possible with enough determination, and to Pod for showing me that it's true (and made easier with gin!).

Thanks to my friends – Jitse for encouraging me, Caroline for bringing the awesomeness, and Baz for being fabulous and providing much tea. And to the NOMAD writers – Jock, Tors, Steph R, Flick, Tony, Ro, Iti and Davina – for the laughs and encouragement along the way.

To my crime-writing sisters – Alexandra, Helen and Susi – who have kept me sane with a heady mix of advice, hugs and wine – I love you and owe you muchly. And to Jock, Steph R, Susi, Rod and Andy, for reading *Deep Down Dead* in draft (sometimes multiple drafts) and giving your critique. Your insights are appreciated, always.

To Rex – a real bounty-hunting legend, and as generous and gentlemanly a guy as you could ever hope to have train you – thank you doesn't seem enough. You are a guru. For any inaccuracies about bounty hunting in this book, I apologise; they are entirely my fault.

To my tutors and mentors at City University, London – Laura Wilson, Claire McGowan, and Zoe Sharp – your advice and feedback has been invaluable, and your own writing an inspiration. To the City Writing crew – Rod, David, Laura, Rob, James, Seun, Jody, Emma,

Philip and Kylie, plus 'original band member' Mark – it's been one hell of a journey, and all the better for making it with you guys.

The crime-writing community is a warm and welcoming place and big thanks has to be given to the special group of crime writers who have made me laugh, gasp (usually with shock at their smuttiness) and have shown me the ropes. You guys rock!

To the amazing Karen Sullivan, the mastermind behind Orenda Books and the most energetic and passionate book person I have ever met, I cannot thank you enough; it is a thrill and a delight to be part of the fabulous Team Orenda. Thank you to editor West Camel for teaching me about grammar (I'm trying, honest). A big pom-pom shake to the effervescent blogger Liz Barnsley for being the best bookish cheerleader you could wish for. And a big thank you to my brilliant agent, Oli Munson, from A. M. Heath.

And finally, thank you (I think) to the US car-hire company that gave me a car with a broken tail-light. I got halfway from West Virginia to Florida before I realised, but without the fear of getting pulled over by a State Trooper for the rest of the trip, Lori and her story might never have been conceived!

Exclusive Extract

DEEP BLUE TROUBLE

STEPH BROADRIBB

Coming soon from Orenda Books

It wasn't the most romantic of settings, but then I've never been a candles and roses kind of a girl. Armed guards, metal doors and security cameras do create a certain type of ambience, but it was nothing that I hadn't handled before. As a bail runner, you get familiar with the county's law enforcement facilities. Still, going to that place to visit with JT made it feel real different. Personal. This time, I felt afraid.

Monroe had pulled some strings and gotten me a visit at the Lake County Detention Facility without the usual seven-day wait. He'd made sure we were given a private room too, and for that I was grateful. Me and JT, we had a whole bunch of things to talk about, and I knew some of that conversation wouldn't come easy.

Take good care of our daughter, you hear. They'd been the last words JT spoke to me before the cops took him into custody. Eight words that told me he'd guessed the truth about Dakota, spoken in a moment that gave me no chance to explain. That'd been six days ago, and six days was a long time to think on the things I should have said.

But even after all that time, I still hadn't managed to wrestle the words I'd rehearsed so they fitted together right. Yes, he had a daughter. *We* had a nine-year-old daughter; and I'd not told him. Wouldn't have ever told him. And, if it hadn't been for my last job bringing us back into contact after ten years apart, he'd have never known.

The sound of the door unlocking behind me jolted me from my thoughts. I turned and saw the guard – a younger guy, as tall as JT but maybe twenty pounds heavier – step into the room. He nodded towards the table and the two chairs bolted to the floor in the centre of the space. 'Take a seat, Ma'am.'

I did as he asked. The guard pushed the door open wider and nodded. JT limped into the room.

He wore a grey sweater and jogging pants. Fresh bruises, in dark, eggplant shades of purple, were layered over the yellowing ones he'd gotten as we fought off Emerson and his men six days ago, determined to get Dakota safe from them, whatever the cost. 'What happened to your—'

'It's nothing,' he said, sitting down heavy.

I reached out to touch JT's face. 'Looks like a damn hard dose of nothing.'

The guard cleared his throat. 'No contact, Ma'am.'

I put my hand back on the table.

As JT eased himself back in the chair his gaze didn't quite meet mine. Trouble had found him again, for sure. I thought about Emerson's man, Boyd, and how he'd planned to hand JT over to the Miami Mob – the crime family who'd put a price on JT's head after thinking it was him who killed my ex-husband, Thomas Ford, who'd been one of Old Man Bonchese's best enforcers; something I'd only found out at the end of our marriage. Emerson and Boyd had fallen out over it, and Old Man Bonchese hadn't gotten his hands on JT. But the price on his head remained, so even if he wasn't speaking about it, I knew the situation with the Miami Mob and Old Man Bonchese was far from over. And as long as JT was in jail, he would be an easy mark.

'Why'd you come here, Lori?'

JT's tone sounded defeated rather than angry. I hadn't expected that.

'I needed to see you.'

'I'm fine.'

'Yeah,' I said, gesturing to his face, and the arm he was holding across his ribs. 'Sure looks that way.'

He stared at me. Stayed silent. I couldn't read his expression, but he didn't seem real pleased to see me. I hadn't figured on that either. I felt tension tightening at the base of my throat. Thought we'd gotten close again on those three days chasing Dakota's abductors across the South. We'd gotten physical, and at the time it'd felt like it'd meant something to the both of us. I wondered if I'd made a mistake.

'I've made a deal.'

He frowned. 'Tell me.'

So, I told him what Monroe wanted me to do – about catching Gibson Fletcher – and why I'd agreed to do it, for the most part anyways. All the while JT stared at me, his expression unreadable.

'So that's the deal. I find Fletcher. Monroe gets you free – or gets your sentence reduced, at least.'

JT raked his hands through his dirty-blond hair, pushing it back from his face before letting it fall shaggy across his forehead again. 'Walk away from this, Lori.'

I shook my head. 'I'm not going anywhere.'

'You've got Dakota. You can't take the risk; not now. Not for me.'

'I can, and I will.'

'I don't want you to.'

'It's not up to—'

'You only just got her safe.' His tone was no-nonsense tough. 'She had a hell of a shake-up – getting snatched by Emerson's men; being held prisoner and watching a man die; almost drowning when Emerson's boat sank into that swamp.' He held my gaze. 'Meeting me.'

I looked down at the table. Traced the cracks in the plastic laminate with my gaze. A hell of a shake-up, that was one way to describe getting abducted by a paedophile ring pedalling made-to-order porn from amusement parks.

'I know. But the DA's talking about going for the death penalty; making this his career case. I can't let that happen. So I talked to Monroe and—'

'I didn't ask for you to do that.'

'No, you'd didn't have to. But the thing I don't get is why'd you take the fall? We had a plan, so why'd you go and confess to a bunch of things that weren't your fault? The men killed in that farmhouse – the Miami Mob did that. Why are you lying?'

JT flicked his gaze towards the guard and gave a tiny shake of his head.

Never trust no one. That was JT's first rule. Either he didn't want to speak on it, or the Old Man Bonchese had men inside that were loyal to him, some of the guards among them. From the way JT was acting, I figured what we had going on was most likely half and half of both.

Frustration, and the fear of what would happen next, fireworked in my stomach. I slammed my hands down on the table. Watched the plastic top vibrate from the blow. Wanted more than a one-liner-style conversation, and needed JT to answer me straight. The stakes were top-dollar high; there wasn't room for ambiguity.

'Enough of the silent act already,' I said.

He slid his hands across the table towards mine, stopping them so our fingertips were a couple inches apart.

'How's Dakota?' he asked, his tone softer.

I exhaled hard. Shook my head. 'Honestly? Not so great. She won't talk about what happened.'

'I get that. Those three days, they were a whole lot for anyone to deal with, and she's just a kid.' He looked real thoughtful. 'But she's strong, like her momma. You give her time. She'll talk when she's ready.'

I nodded. I knew he was right, I'd been telling myself the same thing, but it didn't make it any easier.

I looked into his eyes. 'What you said before, about Dakota being your—'

'Don't, Lori, okay. Not here, not now.'

I stared at him. Thought about telling him why I'd never told him about his daughter; that it was easier to rely on myself because, in my experience, men always let you down; better to never depend on them in the first place. I knew I should tell him about her illness; about how, although she was in remission, there was the ever-present threat that the cancer could return. That if she needed a bone-marrow donor, he would be her best shot at a match, because I wasn't viable. But I didn't want that conversation to be this way: him with his barriers up; me all angry and confused. So I said nothing.

He exhaled. 'You should go.'

'I only just got—'

'You coming here, it ain't right.' He sounded real determined. 'Go, Lori. Please.'

His rejection stung like a bitch, but I gritted my teeth, refusing to show the hurt. 'I'm doing this to get you out faster. To stop them—'

He shook his head. 'I don't want you to take the deal.'

'Yeah, I hear that.' I felt the anger building inside me. Pushed my hands against the table and stood up real fast. 'But it doesn't mean I'm going to listen none.'

I strode away from JT. Left him sitting in that dreary box of a room with the plastic table and chair bolted to the floor. As I passed the guard he nodded.

I tried real hard to ignore the pity in his eyes.

*